**Praise for the co...
of...**

"Those who think the specter of nuclear apocalypse has receded forever need to read this extraordinary, thoughtful, eloquent book. Mitchell is able to ask the hard questions, squarely face the horrifying answers, and still find reason (and need) to hope. And she understands the heart as thoroughly as the hardware; her characters are as real, as commonplace and fascinating, as my own family and neighbors."
—Spider Robinson

"Syne Mitchell has done it again. *End in Fire* is great space suspense. I was on the edge of my seat—I could barely put the book down. *End in Fire* is a believable cautionary tale, a warning much like Orwell or Huxley. Syne has done an excellent job of showing both the worst and best of humanity, of setting duty and love and brilliance and loss against both the huge black backdrop of space and a single small family in everyday America."
—Brenda Cooper, coauthor with Larry Niven of *Building Harlequin's Moon*

The Changeling Plague
A #1 *Locus* bestseller

"Explores the fascinating ground where cyberpunk meets medical thriller. . . . An atmospheric blending of William Gibson and Michael Crichton—a creepy and engaging story that will keep readers on the edge of their seats until the last page is turned."
—Lyda Morehouse, author of *Apocalypse Array*

"A very intriguing read!"
—Vernor Verge

"An exciting look at a realistic danger."
—*The Denver Post*

continued . . .

"An engrossing hard sci-fi novel . . . will not fail to hook readers. [Mitchell's] books are always suspenseful and engaging, with core ideas that are too tantalizing to ignore."
—*Locus*

"A breathless bullet-train of suspense. . . . Enthralling stories, tangible characters, and a chance to examine our own views on the world that is changing at light-speed around us. What more could you ask of an author?"   —*SF Site*

"Further solidifies [Mitchell's] reputation as one of the best new science fiction writers."—SciFiDimensions.com

"A compelling and frightening picture of human nature. . . . A fast-paced, suspenseful read."   —*The Davis Enterprise*

"Impossible to put down. Compelling, with many unexpected twists and turns of plot."   —*Library Bookwatch*

"Interesting speculation and a satisfyingly exciting plot."
—*Chronicle*

Technogenesis

"Perhaps the most captivating science fiction read of recent months . . . [a] terse thriller that holds many unexpected twists and turns. An exceptional story."
—*Library Bookwatch*

"Hard SF with romantic spice . . . satisfyingly rich . . . a taut and suspenseful read . . . great for fans of writers like Catherine Asaro—the romance structure and high technology setting work well together." —Science Fiction Weekly

"Imaginative and pleasing . . . a fresh and entertaining tour . . . a suspenseful read which creates some tough problems and then deals with them in some realistically messy ways."   —*Locus*

ALSO BY SYNE MITCHELL

END IN FIRE

Syne Mitchell

A ROC BOOK

ROC
Published by New American Library, a division of
Penguin Group (USA) Inc., 375 Hudson Street,
New York, New York 10014, USA
Penguin Group (Canada), 10 Alcorn Avenue, Toronto,
Ontario M4V 3B2, Canada (a division of Pearson Penguin Canada Inc.)
Penguin Books Ltd., 80 Strand, London WC2R 0RL, England
Penguin Ireland, 25 St. Stephen's Green, Dublin 2,
Ireland (a division of Penguin Books Ltd.)
Penguin Group (Australia), 250 Camberwell Road, Camberwell, Victoria 3124,
Australia (a division of Pearson Australia Group Pty. Ltd.)
Penguin Books India Pvt. Ltd., 11 Community Centre, Panchsheel Park,
New Delhi - 110 017, India
Penguin Group (NZ), cnr Airborne and Rosedale Roads, Albany,
Auckland 1310, New Zealand (a division of Pearson New Zealand Ltd.)
Penguin Books (South Africa) (Pty.) Ltd., 24 Sturdee Avenue,
Rosebank, Johannesburg 2196, South Africa

Penguin Books Ltd., Registered Offices:
80 Strand, London WC2R 0RL, England

First published by Roc, an imprint of New American Library,
a division of Penguin Group (USA) Inc.

First Printing, June 2005
10 9 8 7 6 5 4 3 2 1

PUBLISHER'S NOTE
This is a work of fiction. Names, characters, places, and incidents either are the
product of the author's imagination or are used fictitiously, and any resemblance
to actual persons, living or dead, business establishments, events, or locales is
entirely coincidental.

For Kai, who taught me how much a mother can love her son; and for Eric, my partner in love, life, writing, and now . . . parenthood

ACKNOWLEDGMENTS

When I sat down to write *End in Fire*, I was daunted by the task in front of me. There was so much to learn about orbital mechanics, nuclear physics, NASA procedures, and space habitation. Fortunately, several very talented people were generous with their time and helped this poor writer out. Any scientific errors in the book are due to my misunderstanding their sage advice, or were necessary to tell the story. Many thanks to my science advisors: Astronaut K. Megan McArthur, Ph.D., Donna Shirley M.S. (who for several years managed the Mars Explorer Program for JPL), Geoffrey Landis, Ph.D., Richard Kline, Ph.D., Brian Tillotson, Ph.D., John Anderson, Ph.D., and Robert Mitchell, Ph.D.

In addition to getting the science right, I also needed to tell a compelling tale. My intrepid first readers gamely read early versions of the book and steered me towards a better story. The book is stronger for their efforts. A debt of gratitude to: Astrid Bear, Steve Husak, Melissa Shaw, Carol Pinchefsky, Rob Wojtasiewicz, Michael Belfiore, Renee Stern, Trissa Barney.

Thanks as well to my agent, Jennifer Jackson, for handling the business details so I could focus on writing, and for her judicious feedback.

This book owes much to my editor, Liz Scheier, whose analysis of the book was as insightful as it was encouraging. Thank you for helping me deepen the story.

As any working mother of a toddler will tell you, no work gets done without great childcare. The following people made the writing of this book possible: Jo Thorsness, Audrey and Dana Christenson, Amber Smith, and Kristen Herstrom. Thank you for taking such good care of Kai and enabling me to be a writer *and* a mom.

Most of all, I must thank my family: endless gratitude to my husband, Eric, for all the support, love, laughs, baby care, unstinting encouragement, pep talks when the writing was hard, and celebrations when it was good. This book could not have been written without you. And thank you Kai, for sleeping so much when you were tiny, for putting up with Mommy going upstairs to write now that you're older, and for showing me just how much a mother can love her son.

Prologue

"Tensions between India and China continue to escalate over ownership of the Digboi oil field, which borders the Himalayan Mountains. Producing seven million barrels a day, Digboi is one of the few remaining sources of oil to fuel the billions of vehicles and generators not yet converted to renewable energy sources."
CNN World News Report—Monday, July 11th, 2022

Tuesday, July 12, 2022, GMT: 16:34:01

Grant Williamson, the Undersecretary of Defense for Intelligence, thumped his knuckle against the printout, stamped TOP SECRET in multiple places. "Has this been verified? I can't give news this incendiary to the President and National Security Advisor unless it's hard-core solid."

The lights in the walnut-paneled conference room were dim, obscuring the face of the man at the far end of the table. A CIA field agent called back to Washington to confirm his report. He shifted uneasily in his seat, as if wishing to fade completely into the shadows.

When he spoke, it was through a voice-altering microphone, lending his words the low scratchy tones of a horror-movie serial killer. "We lost three agents getting that. Yeah, it's good."

Grant felt the sushi he'd eaten that afternoon form a cold lump in his stomach.

The Director of the CIA spoke quietly. "You see why we informed you immediately."

Grant pulled out his encrypted cell phone, no bigger than a pack of gum, and unfolded it. He peered into the shadows at the far end of the table at the agent, but could see nothing. He paused, his finger on the call button. "You're sure these numbers you intercepted were launch codes? They couldn't be . . . anything else?"

The CIA operative jumped to his feet and slammed the voice modifier against the table. The black plastic shattered against mahogany. He leaned into the light. It was an oval face, brown hair, brown eyes, unremarkable except for the utter stillness of his expression and cheeks pockmarked by fresh cigarette burns.

"I promise you," the agent said in a low rumble. "Unless we stop them, China plans to launch a nuclear attack sometime in the next seventy-two hours."

CHAPTER 1

Tuesday, July 12, 2022, GMT: 18:56:19

Claire Logan orbited Earth at 28,000 kilometers per hour, protected from killing vacuum by only the hull of Space Station *Reliance*: aluminum seven millimeters thick.

Lab four was a claustrophobe's nightmare, the walls cluttered with handholds and elastic straps, coils of tied-down cabling, photographs of the crew's family, mission patches, white nylon cargo bags. There was no empty space to rest her eyes.

Claire hunched her slender shoulders over a laptop mounted on a maneuverable ball-and-socket arm. Her foot was tucked under a handrail to keep her position in weightlessness. To her right was a joystick, to her left a slider to control the pincher hand; before her were flat-screen monitors displaying three different views from cameras mounted on the Canadarm16.

Behind her, so close she could feel their breath on the back of her neck, hovered the rest of the crew of *Reliance* station.

Commander John Cole was closest. She glanced over her shoulder, holding onto a handrail mounted on the wall. In his fifties, he was athletically lean, with narrow, squinting eyes that looked like they'd seen everything and been surprised by none of it. He gave Claire an encouraging nod.

Above him, clinging to the light grid, was Josephine Jones. Her ponytail streamed from the back of her head in waves of blond, red, and brown. A newly minted Ph.D. on her first flight, she'd been dubbed "Jo-Jo" by the crew. Her eyes were wide with wonder and anticipation.

Rob Anderson floated free over Claire's right shoulder, occasionally tapping the wall to position himself. She could see him mentally checking her every move and calculation. He was twenty years younger than Cole, with a deceptively boyish face tempered by the test-pilot hardness in his eyes.

Farthest away was Hyun-Jin, an astrobiologist from Indiana. He looked nervous, his olive-skinned fingers erratically tapping the handhold he clung to.

They watched her every move . . . waiting for her to make history.

Claire wiped her sweating palms on the knees of her pants. She glanced at the picture of her husband, Matt, and their four-year-old son, Owen, tucked under an elastic strap on the wall above her. It had been taken three months ago, shortly before she launched, Matt and Owen wrestling on the patch of lawn behind their house. Matt was flat on his back and Owen reared over him, ready to plunge down. They were both laughing. It was the last picture she'd taken where Matt looked happy.

Claire inhaled deeply, clearing her head, and unlocked the joystick.

This moment, the deployment of the Equatorial Solar Reflector, was the culmination of two years of hard work.

If she did everything perfectly and didn't damage the fragile ESR during extraction, it would boost itself to geosynchronous orbit, where it would unfurl over twenty kilometers of 400-micron-thin solar collectors. Energy collected by the solar station would be transmitted to the collection station in White Sands, New Mexico, in a continuous beam. It was the prototype for a network of satellites that would replace on-Earth nuclear power plants and the dirty coalburning facilities—and in doing so, end the war between India and China.

Claire rubbed her hands together, then took hold of the

joystick with her right hand, the pincher control with her left.

Watching the video feedback on the monitors, she used the joystick to drive the robotic arm along its rails into place over *Reliance*'s cargo bay. All systems reported nominal functioning.

She pushed the joystick forward to cause the arm to bend down and retrieve the Equatorial Solar Reflector payload.

The arm didn't move.

On the laptop's screen was the vague diagnosis: GEAR MOTILITY ERROR.

Claire cleared the error and reran the procedure. The same three words blinked back at her on the screen: GEAR MOTILITY ERROR.

Jo-Jo craned her neck to peer at the laptop. "What's going on? Is something wrong?"

Claire felt her face go hot.

She'd spent three months in space constructing and preparing to launch the ESR. This was supposed to be the highlight of her mission. Plastic pouches of sparkling apple cider were already chilled and stowed in a nylon mesh pouch near the bank of laptops, waiting for the post-launch celebration.

"Hold on," Claire said through gritted teeth. She typed in commands to reinitialize the arm and re-sent the move operation: GEAR MOTILITY ERROR.

Anderson snorted. "Anyone see Corley sneak onto the station?"

Claire scowled at the screen. She didn't find Anderson's joke funny.

Lucius Corley, Ph.D., led a group of scientists who protested the ESR project on the basis that it was unknown what a microwave signal of that strength would do to the upper atmosphere. The controversy had raged in the United Nations for years, but the recent energy crash had raised oil prices to the point where alternate energy sources had to be found.

Sweat beaded on Claire's brow as she hurriedly ran through the Canadarm's diagnostics.

"Enough," said Commander Cole. He waved a hand through the air, directing the crew towards the hatch that led from lab four to the rest of the station. "Back to your scheduled tasks. Claire will tell us when she's got this bug worked out." He gave Claire a significant look as he followed the others out. "And you *will* solve it."

Four hours later and a full reinitialization and system analysis of the Canadarm, including external camera scans, had turned up nothing more definitive than GEAR MOTILITY ERROR.

Cole popped his head in through the hatch. "How's it going?"

Claire skimmed her chin-length hair back from her forehead with her palms, flattening the golden afro it formed in weightlessness. She blew out a frustrated sigh.

She was exhausted and wrung dry by frustration. Claire wanted to scream, to pound her fists against the keyboard of the laptop controlling the recalcitrant Canadarm. She was this close to a perfect mission, to making a real difference in the world. *This close.* "I need to EVA," she said. "Check out the problem firsthand."

Cole's right eyebrow rose. "There isn't another EVA scheduled. The crew's due to rotate home in two days. That's barely enough time for the prebreathing protocol. You'd better leave any EVAs to the replacement crew."

"No!" Claire's voice came out sharper than she'd intended. "Sorry, sir, I mean—I can do this. I *need* to do this. If Hyun-Jin and I camp out overnight, we won't lose much time off the work schedule. Most of the work we've got left is data analysis and can be done remotely from the crew lock. Please. I've been working on the ESR release for the past two years. I can't go home with it unfinished." Claire was damned if she was going to leave with the deployment of the solar reflector incomplete. Failure wasn't the way to earn a place on future missions.

Cole pursed his lips and contemplated Claire for a long moment. Then he clipped his palmtop computer back into place on his thigh clip. "Let me check with Mission Control." At Claire's grin he warned her, "No promises. They aren't going to like an unscheduled EVA any better than I do."

Wednesday, July 13, 2022, GMT: 03:27:01

Risaldar-Major Bisnu Rabha scanned the Himalayan Mountains that bordered Assam to the east. On this moonless night, they were present only as the absence of stars, a serrated edge of blackness rising halfway to the sky. It was another absence, however, that worried him.

The winking lights of the Chinese encampment were gone. Reconnaissance reported that the Chinese Army tanks and ground troops had pulled back into the foothills of Nepal. After nearly three months of entrenched ground fighting, with the Indian army doggedly clinging to the Digboi oil fields despite heavy losses—the Chinese had backed off. The mood in the camp was equal parts relief and bravado. Assam's troops had beaten back the invaders, shown them that though the Chinese Army was larger and better armed, India was a tiger to be reckoned with.

Bisnu didn't trust it. Not one bit.

"Why the long face?" asked Lieutenant Rasmussen. He held an open canteen in his right hand, a yeasty smell wafting from it. Rasmussen offered the canteen of illegally brewed beer to Bisnu. "This is a time for celebrating." He gestured at the United States troops camped to the north. They had arrived earlier in the day. Six battalions of marines, led by Colonel Trent Garrett. "The dragon has realized he cannot fight both the tiger and the eagle."

Bisnu frowned and pushed away the canteen. Another time he would have chided his subordinate for drinking, but the Lieutenant-Colonel—an insipidly foolish man—had tacitly permitted the festivities by hosting a celebration of his own among his top officers.

Bisnu was already late for the event, but he couldn't stop himself from looking at the darkened hulks of mountains in the east. There were rumors the Chinese hid weapons of mass destruction in Himalayan caves after their recent invasion of Nepal. "I do not trust an enemy who backs away in the night."

Wednesday, July 13, 2022, GMT: 04:46:27

Claire Logan climbed out of the air lock into the merciless vacuum of space, her protection now even thinner, just a multilayered space suit between her and the endless universe. Her breath rasped inside her helmet as she fought to maneuver her pressurized suit.

Cole had won the argument with Mission Control; Claire got her EVA.

Before her was a view that—even after three months in space—took her breath away. They were over Europe, and the nighttime Earth glittered with a lattice of man-made lights illuminating cities and roadways, outlining the paths of rivers. A blue-green aurora danced around the North Pole. Beyond was the black infinity of space.

The juxtaposition of planet and universe always gave her a melancholy sense of wonder, a feeling of being at once endless and insignificant. She was struck once again by the tiny muddy miracle that was Earth.

The radio in her helmet crackled. "Everything all right?" Hyun-Jin asked from where he hovered, still inside the open air lock, his slender form bulky in a white space suit identical to her own: NASA and mission patches on the upper arm, controls mounted on a rigid chest plate, and a pair of headlamps rising up beside his helmet.

"Yes." Claire fought to keep from sounding sheepish. "Just distracted by the view." With her left hand she clipped in a second, longer tether and released the first.

Hyun-Jin was her backup for this space walk. With her, he had camped out last night in the air lock, prebreathing an oxygen mixture to prepare their bodies for the lower pressure used during extravehicular activity. If something went wrong, he was the only person on the station able to come to her rescue. It didn't comfort Claire that he was an astrobiologist from Indiana, with only six months of preflight training, and had never EVA'd before.

Ahead of her the crippled Canadarm16 was frozen in place, its elbow gear unresponsive to commands from the station. Claire pulled along the row of handholds to the malfunctioning arm, conserving the fuel in her EVA jet pack.

She crawled to the arm's base and clipped her tether to a handhold. The Canadarm16 loomed above her, fifteen meters of white-painted titanium that ended in a two-prong pincer.

Claire's breath reverberated in the closed sphere of her helmet. It was harsh from her exertions manipulating the inflated space suit. She tasted the brine of sweat in the recycled air and her pulse pounded in her throat.

"I'm in place," she called back to Hyun-Jin. "Beginning visual inspection."

Claire clung to a handhold at the base of the Canadarm 16. The robotic arm shouldn't have failed. Each of its six joints had an electronic monitor. If any of the electronics driving the gear-motors had malfunctioned, the controller should have been able to reroute the commands through redundant systems.

A white outline against the star-studded blackness, the pitch and yaw shoulder joints at the base of the Canadarm16 looked normal. Claire attached a computerized multimeter to the electronics. Everything checked.

She sighed and fogged her faceplate. The solar reflector had already been delayed by the catastrophic decompression and subsequent decommission of the aging *International Space Station* six months ago. If she couldn't repair the arm, the Space Program would be further discredited and the solar reflector's schedule would slip until new parts for the arm could be sent up on the next supply ship, three months hence.

Worse would be the look of disappointment from her son, Owen. She'd promised him pictures of the solar panels unfurling, and four-year-olds were not known for their patience. Astronaut mommies were supposed to come back heroes, not failures.

And Earth needed a hero. Since the oil crash, the global economy had been in a tailspin, blackouts were more common than reliable power, and the skies were dark with soot as energy companies turned back to mining coal.

By launching the solar reflector, Claire could be part of the energy solution and create a better future for Owen. It would justify all the hours she'd spent away from him in astronaut training . . . and the late-night studying that had made her a stranger to her husband.

She crawled farther along the arm. Leaning close, she saw a tear in the housing of the elbow pitch joint.

"Found something. Looks like a micrometeor strike or a collision with space junk. There any record of previous damage to the housing of the elbow joint?"

"Let me check," Hyun-Jin said. A moment later, his voice returned over the radio. "Nothing listed in the maintenance logs."

Claire unhooked the top flap of a pocket on her thigh and pulled out a socket wrench. She braced herself and loosened six bolts, removed the housing, then pointed her flashlight inside.

There. A gash cut across the disk of the interior gear where a fragment or rock had punctured the housing.

She ran the beam of light along the damage. "Looks like a—"

A flash dazzled her peripheral vision.

Startled, Claire jerked her head up, throwing her off-balance. A green afterglow imprinted on her retinas. In weightlessness, her sudden movement caused her to tumble backwards. Claire scrabbled blindly for a handhold.

The brilliant white light had come from the horizon of Earth, on the Asian subcontinent. In its aftermath, an elongated fireball rose, surrounded by a luminous red sphere hundreds of miles in diameter. Below it, for just an instant, was a flat, glowing disk.

The fireball expanded and faded out. That region of the globe looked strange. It took Claire a moment to recognize the difference: The ground under the explosion was dark, city lights had been snuffed out.

"What the hell was *that*?" Claire shouted over the radio. Her heart pounded in her chest. It was unthinkable, but it had looked like a nuclear explosion.

Cole, the station commander, spoke over the ship-to-suit frequency. "Yi, Logan, get in here."

Claire protested, "But the space walk—"

"We just lost satellite communications with Houston. Attitude control and guidance subsystems report circuit failures. I want you back inside, ASAP."

Claire activated her tether's winch at full speed and reeled back to the air lock. She drew her arms and legs into fetal position, forming a ball against the pull of inertia.

Hyun-Jin was already inside. His pockmarked face was pale and there were beads of sweat on his upper lip. When Claire was in, he sealed the air lock behind her and started the pressurization cycle.

Claire touched her helmet to Hyun-Jin's so they could speak without the radio. "What *was* that?"

His eyes slid to the small air lock window. "An accident at the Digboi oil refinery?" His voice held more hope than confidence.

Claire shook her head. "That wasn't a ground explosion.

I saw a pancake luminescence, charged particles bouncing off the atmosphere. That was a high-altitude burst. At least a hundred kilometers up." Her voice quavered. "An explosion with that much power . . . it had to be nuclear."

Risaldar-Major Bisnu was crossing the encampment to the Lieutenant-Colonel's tent when the sky above the Himalayan Mountains exploded. Bisnu threw his hands over his face and dove to the ground. His training kicked in, too late. When he opened his eyes, he saw nothing but a green retinal afterimage. He heard shouts and curses. A hot wind blew across him, stinging sand and gravel across the back of his neck.

Then the face of Shiva, the destroyer, appeared to him through the haze. Red and growing overhead. Feeding off the air around him.

Scrabbling across the packed earth of the encampment, Bisnu half-ran, half-stumbled back to his tent. He fumbled the gas mask from his footlocker and jammed it over his head. He inhaled deeply, sucking hard to pull air through the filters.

Through the amber-tinted glass of the faceplate, Bisnu was nearly blind, but he saw the rising fireball he had mistaken for the face of a god. Only one kind of bomb could create such destruction: nuclear. High-altitude, or they'd already be dead.

A junior lieutenant backed into him, spun off his feet, and fell. It was Rasmussen.

Bisnu picked him up by his collar. The young man cried out in fear. He struggled and kicked.

"Courage," shouted Bisnu, over the din of half-drunk and frightened soldiers. To the man he held, and all others in earshot, Bisnu shouted: "Put on your gas masks. They may follow with a chemical assault. Assemble troop formations in the central commons."

The camp had gone dark, save for intermittent fires around which the men had warmed themselves and drunk to the Chinese retreat. The electric power was out.

"Assemble the squadron," Bisnu ordered Rasmussen. "I'll meet you in the commons."

Bisnu raced unseeing through the darkness towards the radio tent. The glow of the fading fireball lit his passage.

A satellite dish was mounted on the central pole of the tent. Bisnu lifted the flap and ducked inside.

Two men huddled around the radio. One held up a cigarette lighter while the other worked the dials in its feeble glow. Static poured from the speaker.

"The main radio is blown," said the light-skinned Farsi holding the lighter. His deep-set eyes were wide with fear. "This is the battery-operated backup, radiation-hardened. But there's no signal. We cannot contact the satellite network."

"High-altitude . . . nuclear . . . explosion," Bisnu panted. "Satellites . . . destroyed."

With the nuclear bomb, the Chinese had cut off long-range communications without destroying the precious oil field. But why? The conflict was months old. What point was there in secrecy now?

Incoming missiles whistled overhead.

Bisnu stuck his head out and saw one hit the mess tent. Billowing yellow smoke roiled out of it. Men inside the spreading cloud crumpled to the ground screaming and twitching.

He checked the seals on his gas mask and lowered the flap. "Nerve gas. Or something like it."

The radio technicians scrambled for the gas masks hanging on hooks near the door.

In the distance the rumble of Chinese tanks and cannon fire grew louder.

"What about the ground-based repeater towers?" Bisnu asked, his voice muffled by his gas mask.

The darker of the two radio men twiddled a few knobs, then shook his head.

"Keep trying," shouted Bisnu. "We have to let headquarters know about the attack."

Bisnu ran outside. Men milled around in panic and confusion. Only a quarter of them wore gas masks.

Greenish sheets of flame lit the sky to the north and the south.

"It is the end of the world," Bisnu breathed.

Lieutenant Rasmussen had fifty men assembled in the commons, all in gas masks. They were half-dressed, some sagging as if drunk. All snapped to attention when Bisnu entered the clearing.

Bisnu grabbed a bullhorn from the general's review table to amplify his muted voice. "The Chinese are attacking the Digboi oil field. It is up to us to save India's most precious natural resource. Are you ready to fight?" He was grateful his sweating face was hidden by the mask. His bellow sounded more confident than he felt.

"Sir, yes, sir!" shouted fifty masked faces.

Bisnu waved at the tanks parked a hundred yards away. "Tank battalion. Let's show the Chinese this tiger has claws."

Pajama-clad Owen Logan hopped onto his bed. There were cartoon rocket ships and spacemen on his PJs. He scrunched up his face at Matt and pouted. "I wish Mommy was here."

Matt distractedly rummaged through a toy box for a goodnight book. He pulled out *James and the Giant Peach* and *Wiggo and Wanky Go to Space*. He put the book about puppy-dog astronauts back and selected *The Wind in the Willows* before Owen could see the other book. "You'll see Mommy soon," Matt told his son for the hundredth time that day. "Tomorrow we fly to Florida—"

"Disney World! Disney World!" Owen chanted, bouncing in a kneeling position on the bed.

"—and visit your Grandma Logan," Matt continued as if there had been no interruption. "Then two days later Mommy lands. And *then* we'll all go to Disney World together." He held out the two books. "Which one do you want?"

"Wiggo and Wanky." Owen leaped out of bed and snatched up the picture book from deep in the toy box where Matt had buried it. He held it out with glee. "Wiggo and Wanky!"

Matt sighed and sat down on the bed, drawing Owen into his lap. Owen had requested this book every night for the past three months while Claire was in space. After dozens of readings, Matt could recite from memory every line of dialogue the two space-faring puppies yipped to each other.

While his colleagues at the University of Houston taught English Literature, debated the descriptive prowess of Flaubert, and attended colloquiums on the symbolism of Shakespeare, Matt Logan barked and growled his way through the story of two cocker spaniels' adventures on the spaceship *Bone*.

In two days Claire'll be back, Matt promised himself. Two days until I have help with Owen. Two days until I get my life back.

Claire's mind raced while she and Hyun-Jin waited for the air lock to finish cycling them back into *Reliance*'s atmosphere. She couldn't have just seen a nuclear explosion. That wasn't possible. Countries built nukes and threatened to use them—but no one actually did. The repercussions—both political and environmental—were too great. It must have been something else. Once they made contact with Houston, they'd know what had really happened and have a good laugh.

As soon as the air lock finished cycling, Claire popped her helmet seal and Hyun-Jin pushed open the round hatch. They kicked through into the rectangular crew lock and desuited in record time, bumping into each other and the cluttered walls as they helped each other crawl out of their space suits' hard torso units and pull off leggings.

Claire hastily jammed her suit's components onto the storage frame, uneasy about neglecting its post-EVA maintenance.

Hyun-Jin followed Claire as she grabbed one of twenty metal handrails that lined the walls and exited the docking-and-stowage module. Claire yanked herself up the connecting passages: rectangular hallways with equipment and drawer pulls covering all six surfaces. It was like traveling through someone's cluttered walk-in closet. Two levels above, they reached the cramped command module.

Twenty feet long and five feet wide, the walls of the command module were paneled with storage drawers and a bewildering number of handrails and smaller handholds. Over the drawers were elastic straps that held equipment to the walls: binoculars for the portholes, a cordless screwdriver, battery charger for handheld computers.

The walls were painted different shades of neutral grays and greens to provide orientation, but that only added to the industrially cluttered feel of the place.

At the far end, three laptops were mounted on ball-and-socket arms, the nerve center of the station. Commander John Cole and the other two crew members hovered around the radio, clinging to the walls from various angles.

The meter-wide round cover had been removed from the forward viewing window and the twinkling lights of night-time Earth filled its view.

Commander Cole wore a sage-green clamshell radio headset that positioned a boom mike near his lips. He floated in front of a laptop, gripping his own knee to hold himself in a seated position.

Despite the headset, the speakerphone was on. Static hissed from its grid, punctuated occasionally by a garbled word. "I don't copy," Cole spoke into the microphone in slow, distinct syllables. "Please repeat. *Reliance* over." Sweat beaded his forehead, dewing the white hairs of his crew cut. "Houston, this is *Reliance*. Do you copy?"

Anderson hovered shoulder-to-shoulder next to him, in the cramped space in front of the laptops. His round face twisted into a frown of concentration as he typed, toggling through frequencies. "I'm not getting a signal on any of the ship-to-ground channels. The satellite network isn't responding." Anderson's lips tightened into a white line. Claire recognized the expression from training simulations . . . when everything had gone wrong.

Josephine Jones hovered above Cole and Anderson, lying prone in the space above their heads. She held a pair of Zeiss 20x60 stabilized binoculars and peered through the meter-wide window. She steadied herself by grabbing the window's cover, which was flipped back on its hinge. Jo-Jo tilted the field glasses against the window for a better angle. "There's a dark patch near the Himalayan Mountains. Looks like power is out in one of the major cities."

Cole turned at Claire's approach. He passed the headset to Anderson and pivoted to the rear of the comand module. "Keep trying." He waved Claire and Hyun-Jin forward. "Tell me everything."

Claire grabbed a handhold, then closed her eyes and summoned the image from her memory. "There was a flash. Then a growing red pinpoint of light. It looked like the fireball elongated vertically. There was an instant where the fireball seemed to rest on a glowing disk, but the disk wasn't completely flat, more of a low-sloped cone." She opened her eyes and met Cole's blue gaze. "There was also a red glowing sphere around the fireball." She shaped the sphere with her hands. "It must have been hundreds of miles in diameter."

"Holy shit, look at that," Jo-Jo shouted, pointing out the window.

They all pressed towards the porthole, clinging together to hold their position. Claire smelled the garlic Hyun-Jin had had for lunch and felt Anderson's breath on her cheek.

In the window, twin blue-green auroras danced on the horizon, lighting up the Himalayan Mountains and the Bay of Bengal.

"What is that?" Jo-Jo asked. She squirmed upwards so the others could move in closer. "Turn off the cabin lights."

Claire reached above their heads and hit the touchplate that controlled the overhead lights. The only illumination left in the cabin was the glowing screens of the laptops and the backlit touchpads of the instrument panel. It took a moment for everyone's eyes to adjust.

"It looks like the northern lights back home," said Anderson.

Claire watched blue-green fingers of luminescence elongate and flicker. The eerie light made the hairs on the back of her neck prickle. "But that isn't the North Pole."

"I've got a bad feeling about this." Cole ran his fingers over his scalp.

"I've seen this before," said Claire. *"Starfish Prime."* All eyes turned to her, and she swallowed. "A film I watched as an undergraduate." She licked her lips, "Of tests the U.S. performed in 1962 of high-altitude nuclear bombs."

The command module went silent. The only noise was the background hum of the station's computers and air-filtration units and the groaning and flexing of the hull.

"It has to be an accident," sputtered Hyun-Jin. "No one would deliberately—"

"Don't be stupid," Anderson interrupted. "It's the war between India and China, over that oil field in northeast India. It's gone nuclear."

"Let's not jump to conclusions," Cole boomed, pushing away from the window and back to his station in front of the command module's controls. "One explosion is not a war. We need to contact someone on the ground and find out what's happened." His expression was relaxed and confident, but Claire saw that the muscles in his neck were corded with tension. "In the meantime, we'll record this event. The data may be useful groundside." Cole checked his wristwatch. "I'm marking GMT of the explosion as 04:52." Cole pointed at Jo-Jo. "Keep watch out the window and let us know if anything else happens." He turned his head. "Hyun-Jin?"

The astrobiologist startled at the sound of his name. "Yes?"

"Pull up a map; try to figure out which cities have gone dark." Cole pointed at Claire. "Claire, take over the radio. Anderson . . ." Cole swallowed. "Anderson, I want you to go run preflight on the lifeboat."

The crew stared at Cole.

He ran his hand over his scalp. "We don't want to jump to any conclusions, but we don't want to be caught with our pants down, either."

"Yes, sir." Anderson slipped the headset off and handed it to Claire. She slid into the place he had occupied next to Cole and tucked her foot under a handhold.

The station was a civilian post, but Anderson still snapped a salute to Cole before he left. It worried Claire that Anderson's military reflexes had clicked into place. It meant that on some level he expected a battle. And a battle was one thing for which *Reliance* was not equipped.

Claire clamped the headset over her ears and adjusted the microphone in front of her lips. She typed in command codes to open channel-S communications. "Houston, this is *Reliance*. Do you copy? Over. Houston, *Reliance*. Do you copy?"

"Holy shit," breathed Jo-Jo. "Half of India's gone dark."

Claire pulled her foot from under the handhold and kicked off it towards the window. Hyun-Jin and Cole were behind her. Cole stretched his arm over her head for a handhold and Hyun-Jin lightly grasped her shoulder for position.

The space station, orbiting at twenty-eight thousand kilometers per hour, had overtaken the horizon, and the site of the eruption was now in view beneath them.

Three months of Earth-watching had made Claire familiar with the brilliant diamond webs that covered the nighttime globe. City lights spread out from centers of commerce, trailed along rivers. The pixie dust of electricity highlighted industrialized nations. Usually India burned like a white tiger's tooth in the center of the Indian Ocean. Tonight, however, over a third of the tooth on India's eastern border was missing, chipped away by the explosion that had taken place ten minutes ago.

A light went red on Hank Rubin's command board. He put down the cup of black coffee he'd been about to drink from and looked over the rows of computer stations to Communications.

Amanda Jackson was CAPCOM for this shift. Thirty-something, black, and holding a Ph.D. in electrical engineering from Georgia Tech, she had washed out of the astronaut program when she'd developed adult-onset diabetes. She dressed more sharply than any other engineer on his team, and always looked in control—except now. "Sir, we've lost contact with *Reliance*."

Hank lumbered over to her station and squinted at the green monochrome screen. The eye doctor had prescribed reading glasses, but Hank didn't wear them. He wasn't ready to be that old. "Can you route it through another satellite?"

Amanda typed rapidly on her keyboard, her red-lacquered nails clicking. "Sir, the entire eastern network is down. I can't raise anything east of Europe or west of Australia." She brought up a log of NASA's communication satellites. "There was a spike ninety seconds ago. Then—nothing."

"Solar flare?" Hank asked. Heartburn flared in his gut. This was a mystery, and Hank didn't like mysteries—not on his shift.

"I don't know, sir. Nothing was predicted. The sun's in a quiet period, but I'll call NOAA, see if they picked up anything." There was a note of panic in her voice. "Be a hell of a solar flare to take out the entire East Asian network."

The phone at Hank's workstation rang. He pointed his finger like a gun at Amanda. "Find out. We've got a launch scheduled in two days, and five astronauts in the air. We can't afford to lose contact."

Hank picked up the phone and jammed it against his ear. "Hank Rubin, Houston Command Center."

"Grant Williamson, Pentagon. The bhangmeters registered an event."

Cold sweat trickled down Hank's back. The bhangmeters were instruments mounted on radiation-hardened military satellites, able to detect the characteristic light of a nuclear explosion. Hank licked his suddenly dry lips. "Where?"

"Assam, India. High-altitude burst. We've lost satellite coverage of that area. We need your astronauts to visually monitor the situation."

Claire, Cole, Jo-Jo, and Hyun-Jin clustered in a ring around the observation window, transfixed by what they saw, or rather didn't see—the missing city lights over eastern India.

"If it was a nuclear explosion," Hyun-Jin said, "where are the fires?"

Only half the usual bank of lights in the command module were on, to facilitate Earth observations. Amber and red warning lights cast the small chamber in a hellish glow, reporting the failure of half a dozen nonessential systems that had gone down since the blast.

Squeezed in next to him at the window, Claire shook a negative. "Not if it was a high-altitude burst." She hadn't had time to clean up after her EVA, and stank with the musk of fear and stale sweat.

Claire pushed Jo-Jo's foot out of her face.

"Sorry," the younger woman murmured, pulling a handhold to pivot position. She was dressed in navy shorts sewn with six blue stripes of Velcro across her thighs, a white tank top with the JPL logo printed on the front, and slate-blue hiking socks. Jo-Jo drifted above Claire, using binoculars to look out the large viewing window.

"Why not use a conventional groundburst ICBM?" asked Hyun-Jin. He clung to the rim of the window with a white-knuckled grip. "It would do more damage."

"If Anderson's right and this is about the Digboi oil field"—Cole pushed off from the frame and folded his body in front of the bank of laptops in the middle of the module—"China might have used a high-altitude burst as a warning shot, or to knock out India's satellites and power grid without damaging the oil fields." He nodded at Claire to take the com.

Claire pushed off from the wall and caught a handhold on the wall, sliding her knees under the pull-out workshelf near the communications laptop. She pulled a clamshell headset off the wall with a Velcro rip and settled it around her head. Once she was in place, she used the laptop to activate a radio transmission: "Houston, this is *Reliance*, do you read me? Over." She pulled the boom microphone of her headset away from her mouth. "I'm not getting anything. I can't even reach the radiation-hardened military satellites. I don't know if there's too much radiation interference, or the digital tuner got fried." She looked over at Cole. "I can try a line-of-sight radio signal to Moscow, use the old analog tuner, and bypass the satellite network completely."

Cole sucked his upper teeth, considering. "Do it. But let me talk to them if you get through."

Claire moved the microphone back into position, changed radio protocols, and tried again: "Moscow Mission Control, this is *Reliance* space station. Do you read me? Moscow, this is *Reliance*. Do you copy?"

Static. But there was a rhythm in the hiss, the cadence of a distorted voice.

Claire pressed the earpiece into her ear and turned on the speaker. Hyun-Jin and Jo-Jo were still at the window. They turned to look.

Cole put on a second headset and spoke into the microphone. "Moscow Mission Control. This is *Reliance* Space Station. Do you copy?"

". . . nity, this . . . Mos . . . control."

"Moscow, *Reliance*, come again. I missed that last."

A Russian-accented voice said, "*Reliance*, Moscow. We read you."

Claire blessed Wilbur and Orville for being American. At any airport in the world, you could address the control tower in English. This had carried over to space flight.

Jo-Jo whooped and blew a kiss to Hyun-Jin, who blushed.

Cole's grin was tempered. He took the headset from Claire. "Moscow, *Reliance*. We're having trouble contacting the satellite network. Can you patch us through to Houston?"

A pause. Then the same heavily accented male voice, "We, too, experience difficulty. The eastern network is non-responsive. Do you have information of this malfunction?"

Cole turned off the radio's VOX so his next words wouldn't be transmitted. "If that was a nuclear explosion, there's going to be a lot of political tension that I don't want any part of. And if it wasn't, I don't want to start a panic." He keyed the microphone manually. "Moscow, this is *Reliance*. We've seen an event we need to report to Houston, but we don't have any conclusive evidence. Can you patch us through?"

Sweat beaded on Cole's head as seconds ticked by.

While they waited for Mission Control Moscow to respond, Claire said, "They'll listen in on any communications we have over their network."

"Probably they know already." Cole blew on his hands. "They've got at least as many nuclear-blast detectors as the U.S. This,"—he gestured at the still-silent speaker—"is just politicking."

"I can see more of India," said Jo-Jo from overhead. She panned the stabilized binoculars across the window. "It's still blacked out. The power outages are spreading."

"*Reliance*, Moscow. We have made contact with Mission Control Houston, patching you through, now—"

A metallic thunderclap reverberated through the station. *Reliance* lurched forward. Claire's ankles cracked against the handrail. Her body flung forward, slapping her chest against the laptop in front of her. Its telescoping arm folded forward, crumpling beneath her body.

A loud clanging, then a hollow grinding that sounded like a trash can rolling along *Reliance*'s hull.

Jo-Jo's head thwacked against the metal rim of the window. "Shit!"

Cole's ribs slammed into a wall of drawers. His body bounced off and tumbled like an out-of-control skydiver.

Tiny pings chimed from all over the station. Under Claire's stomach the laptop arm shimmied. Carabiners clipped to a handhold near her face rattled.

Hyun-Jin clung to a handhold on the side of the control panel. "What the hell was that?"

A high-pitched emergency alarm keened in alternating tones.

Cole pressed a hand to his side. "Pressure readings!"

Claire checked the gauge on the instrument panel. "It's 14.0 psi and falling." Her heart flip-flopped in her chest.

Cole jerked the emergency procedures manual off the wall. The flip-top book ripped free. He opened the tab for decompression. "Open Channels 1 and 2, and transmit."

"But Mission Control can't hear—"

"—Do it. Then get Anderson on the radio."

Claire jabbed the channel 1 and 2 radio buttons and the button marked XMIT. She reported her actions as she worked: "Channels one and two open. Transmitting." There was comfort in the routine that she had practiced a thousand times. All three membrane buttons illuminated. Then she changed to the ship-to-ship frequency. "*Exodus*, this is *Reliance*. Anderson, you there?"

There was no answer.

"Damn. Where is he? We've got to evacuate," said Cole. "Claire, disconnect the air duct between the service module and the crew escape vehicle."

Claire typed commands. "Disconnected."

Cole waved Jo-Jo and Hyun-Jin through the hatch.

Claire kicked off from the command center. Cole caught her hand and pulled her through the circular hatch, then slammed it shut behind them.

They hurried along the gray-paneled access tunnel leading to the lifeboat, kicking off of drawers and the white nylon cargo bags strapped to the walls, grabbing and yanking the long handrails.

Hyun-Jin's foot caught Claire in the face. He looked back. "Sorry, oh, God—sorry."

Cheek throbbing from the impact, Claire shouted: "Go! Just go!"

They turned the corner to the lifeboat. Anderson hung in the middle of the passage, one hand on the closed and locked hatch. Blood trailed in oscillating bubbles from a cut above his left temple and drifted towards the ventilation filter. His eyes fluttered open.

Cole grabbed Anderson's shoulders. "What the hell happened? We've got decompression. Why aren't you in the lifeboat?"

The pressurization alarm cut off in mid-warble.

Hyun-Jin and Jo-Jo looked around at the cargo-cluttered walls in amazement and tentative relief.

Anderson breathed hard. Between gulps of air, he said. "I've got. Good news. And bad news." He panted until his breathing slowed. "Good news: I isolated and contained the leak. Bad news: We were hit. The lifeboat won't hold pressure.

CHAPTER 2

In the Houston Command Center, Amanda's head popped up. "We've reestablished contact through Moscow Mission Control. They've got *Reliance* on line-of-sight. I'm getting telemetry data."

Hank blew out a sigh of relief that tousled his graying, too-long hair. He braced his hand against the desk and bowed his head, grateful that *Reliance* had survived. "Give it to me."

Amanda's quick dark eyes scanned the incoming file. An alarm sounded on the emergency board. "Decompression in the Crew Evacuation Vehicle. Station's pressure is down to 13.5 psi."

Hank popped a Tums from an open candy dish on his desk and crunched it between his molars. He pointed at Lou Johnson. "Medical: What's the status of the crew?"

Lou's face was dominated by fleshy red lips that gave him the appearance of a basset hound. Those lips now quivered. "I'm not getting any readings."

A nuclear bomb goes off in orbit, explosive decompression, and no readings from the crew's wireless biosensors. Not good. Hank clipped a phone headset around his head.

His forefinger punched the button to autodial the Secretary of Astronaut Affairs.

"Yes?" Clarissa Henly answered with a Texan drawl that drew the interrogative into two syllables.

Usually the sweet twang of her voice made Hank smile. Not today. "Clarissa, we've got a situation on *Reliance*. I need you to contact the astronauts' families."

He heard Clarissa suck in a sharp breath. "Has there been an accident?"

"We don't know anything yet. I just need you to locate the families. In case . . . just in case."

"What happened?" asked Cole. His face looked ashen under the banks of short-tube fluorescents in the access tunnel. He rubbed his shoulder as if he'd pulled a muscle in his hurry to reach the lifeboat's hatchway. "Tell me everything."

Anderson pressed his palm against the cut on his temple to stem the bleeding.

Jo-Jo caught Anderson in a half nelson to put them in the same frame of reference, then braced her shoulders against one wall, feet against the other, and inspected his wound. They all had first-aid training, but Jo-Jo had cross-trained for the mission as an EMT. Drifting bubbles of blood impacted her tank top as she probed the wound, dotting the white fabric red. "It's shallow, but needs bandaging." She looked at the sealed hatch door. The main medical kit—and all their other emergency gear—was stowed in the most logical place: the lifeboat. Now completely inaccessible.

Hyun-Jin stripped off his gold-colored NASA T-shirt. "Use this." He passed it to Jo-Jo.

She pulled a small Phillips-head screwdriver out of a nylon sleeve on her thigh-board and started a hole near the shirt's hem. Then used her teeth to tear a strip free. She folded the rest of the shirt into a compress and began tying the makeshift bandage in place.

"I came down and began preflight on the lifeboat." Anderson's eyes unfocused as he relived the event. "Everything was nominal. I heard a loud clang—for a second the whole room fogged over. There was a weird sensation as air rushed out of my lungs, but I wasn't exhaling. It was like our decompression training in the altitude chamber at Wright-Patterson Air Force Base.

"I heard a hissing. Loose objects flew towards the rear of the crew evacuation vehicle: my flight checklist, a lost pencil, two loose screws—ow!" Anderson pushed Jo-Jo away, tightening the bandage himself. The tail ends trailed from his scalp like golden seaweed. "Whatever hit the CEV punctured its hull. Figured I didn't have long before the rupture expanded, so I got out of there and sealed the hatch."

"What about the emergency medical kit?" Jo-Jo's voice rose. "Our *space suits*?" She tapped the locked hatch. "Are you telling me that you didn't grab anything on your way out?"

Anderson caught the free end of the bandage and tucked it under the compress. "There wasn't time. The lifeboat was sucking atmosphere out of the station."

"We need that gear," Jo-Jo complained. In her blood-stained tank top and navy shorts, she looked childlike and vulnerable; her bare arms and legs too exposed.

"Uh, we've got a bigger problem." Hyun-Jin clung to a handrail. The skin on his chest prickled with gooseflesh. "Has anyone else noticed we're tumbling?"

Claire looked at the tunnel walls. She hadn't noticed the motion during Anderson's story, but now that she held her eyes on the hinge of the hatchway door she saw it revolve around her. "The venting," she said. "It's pushing us off course and adding rotation."

"Twelve cubic meters pressurized at one atmosphere," said Cole, "plus whatever vented from the station before Anderson closed the hatch. That's not trivial. Shit. We'd better get back to command."

The tunnel corkscrewed around them as they kicked and climbed back to the command module.

Claire scraped her elbow across the corner of a lashed-down multimeter that moved unexpectedly with the station's new rotation. Stifling a curse, she cupped her hand over the pain.

They burst into the command module.

The radio was still on VOX and static poured from the speaker.

Cole caught the wireless headset out of the air and held

the microphone. "Moscow, this is *Reliance*. Do you copy? Moscow, *Reliance*, do you read me?"

Only more static.

"Damn," said Cole. "We lost our line-of-sight to Moscow." He caught the drifting Emergency Ops book. It was still open to the depressurization tab. "What're our pressure readings?"

Claire slipped her foot under a handrail and checked the pressure readout. "Pressure in *Reliance* is 13.5 psi and holding. We lost .58 psi during the decomp. The CEV is reporting zero pressure." She pulled forward the laptop she had crushed during the decompression. It was still running. Claire silently blessed the engineers that had hardened the onboard computers against radiation and vibration. She adjusted its multiarticulated arm to position the laptop in front of her and began a systems check of the station.

Hovering over her shoulder, Hyun-Jin read: "Solar panel reports a puncture in panel two. Fuel reserves in the lifeboat are holding steady." He tried a smile, but it was tissue-thin. "At least the tanks weren't damaged."

Anderson settled into the station next to Claire, brushing her shoulder as he tucked his foot under a handrail. He typed rapidly on the laptop dedicated to navigation. "We're tumbling at a rate of six degrees per second. With the solar panels off-target, we're chewing through our battery reserves. In a couple of hours, we'll be out of power." He looked over his shoulder at Cole.

Cole's normally ruddy complexion had gone pale. His lips compressed into a thin line as he weighed the options.

Course corrections were usually handled by Mission Control in Houston, sent up as commands that directly fired the station's positioning jets. But there wasn't time. The station was designed to run off battery power only for the forty-six minutes the station was behind the Earth. When the batteries ran out, *Reliance*'s life support and temperature control would fail. The station would become a deadly tin can.

"Do a burn to stop the rotation and try to reacquire the solar positioning," Cole decided. He rubbed his chest as if it pained him.

"And the course correction? Anderson asked.

"Leave it. Cold-gas venting won't affect our orbit significantly. When Houston comes back online, have them verify the course correction. We should conserve fuel until we know . . ." He looked out the window. They had traveled eastward over the globe. India's ragged profile was almost beneath them. "Until we know what we're up against."

Anderson typed in coordinates. "Prepare for burn."

Claire grabbed the metal shelf in front of her. Jo-Jo, Hyun-Jin, and Cole grabbed handholds and straps on the walls.

"Initiating burn," said Anderson. He pushed an oversized white button. The station's hull groaned as it rotated in reaction to the jets.

Claire felt the station arc around her. Her hip drifted sideways into a nest of cables strapped to the wall with Velcro self-ties. The white cords pressed uncomfortably into her flesh. As quickly as it had come, the sensation of acceleration lifted.

"Burn complete," Anderson reported.

"What we need to know now," said Cole, releasing his grip on the handrail floating above the laptop station, "is what hit us, and whether there's more out there."

Reluctantly, Claire looked up and offered, "I could go EVA. Check out the damage on the CEV, see if it's repairable."

Cole pinched the bridge of his nose, considering. "No. Too risky. There might be more debris and"—he pointed at the dosimeter—"radiation outside the station is elevated. I don't want us to take any unnecessary chances."

"We could get a visual read on the damage," Anderson suggested, "using the external cameras."

"Good idea," Cole said. "Anderson, reposition them to check out the lifeboat. Hyun-Jin, Jo-Jo, go through the station and close the hatches between modules. I don't want a rupture in one section to vent all of *Reliance*."

Jo-Jo and Hyun-Jin scrambled out of the hatchway, intent on their mission.

Cole rubbed his shoulder absentmindedly. "Claire, try Houston again."

Claire slid on a headset and positioned the boom microphone. The channel was still open from their previous attempts to make contact. "Houston, this is *Reliance*. Do you read me? Moscow, *Reliance*. Do you read?"

"Got visual on the lifeboat!" Anderson said excitedly.

Cole and Claire leaned towards the flat-screen display from their relative positions above and beside Anderson. The stubby-nosed crew-return vehicle was docked to *Reliance* by a side port. Anderson manipulated the camera to pan down the CEV's length. A long furrow of twisted metal and broken tiles ran along the side opposite the docking port. Whatever had hit had struck a glancing blow, but had been going fast enough to gouge the side of the lifeboat. The furrow ended in a cone-shaped explosion of metal where the hull had been punctured and had explosively decompressed.

"Goddamn," said Cole. He looked over at Anderson. "You're lucky to be alive.

Anderson's face was gray. "That's not the worst of it." He moved the camera, swinging past the stubby wings, set at a jaunty angle, to focus on the rear of the CEV. Normally, the main engine of the CEV ended in four rocket nozzles, stacked tightly together and surrounded by a nest of pipes. A ball of shrapnel had burst through them like a bowling ball, tearing the engine assembly loose from the CEV. The engine was tethered to the CEV by only the delicate fuel and cooling pipes. The precision-machined cones of the bottom and right nozzles were crushed.

Claire found it hard to breathe. Whatever had hit them was big enough that if it had slammed into the station instead of the lifeboat, there'd have been no time to close the hatches . . . they'd all be dead. And now their only escape vehicle was completely disabled. She swallowed hard. "Any idea what hit us?"

Anderson zoomed in on the crumpled ball wedged between the destroyed rocket engines. "It was small, and must have been moving at an orbital velocity close to our own, or it would have vaporized. Satellite, maybe?"

Claire thumped the heel of her palm against her forehead. "Of course. If what we saw was a high-altitude nuke, soft X-rays generated by the blast would blow apart any LEO satellites in the area. It would also disturb the orbiting space junk, throwing some of it into our path."

Hyun-Jin popped in headfirst through the tunnel. Jo-Jo was close on his heels. She did a somersault to reverse direction, caught the handle of the circular hatch that joined the command module to the rest of the station, and screwed it closed behind them.

"Hatches secure," Hyun-Jin said. His right hand held a polo shirt from the crew quarters, light blue, with the mission patch on the front pocket. He slipped it over his head, then stopped in the act of pulling it down his chest. He stared at the display of the lifeboat's wreckage.

Jo-Jo turned at his reaction and saw the monitor. Her eyes widened. "Holy shit. What's that?" She climbed up behind Claire, clinging to her shoulder to get a better view of the monitor.

"Satellite strike," said Cole.

"I don't understand," Jo-Jo said, shaking her head. "The United States Space Command in Colorado plots our orbit to avoid satellites and space debris."

"A high-altitude blast," said Hyun-Jin, "If that's what we saw—would have blown space debris outward from its epicenter. The USSC debris mapping is no longer accurate."

Jo-Jo's pale face whitened. "There's more than ten thousand trackable objects in low-Earth orbit. That's a lot to miss."

Cole wiped bubbles of perspiration from his brow. "We can't contact USSC. We're flying blind up here with potentially scattershot debris. What are our options?"

"Space is big, hope for the best?" offered Hyun-Jin bleakly.

Cole glared at him. "*Constructive* ideas."

"We could suit up," muttered Jo-Jo. She shot a pointed glance at Anderson. "If we *had* suits."

"It's not his fault," Claire said in Anderson's defense. "If he hadn't acted quickly, the whole station would have depressurized."

"What about EVA suits?" asked Hyun-Jin.

Cole shook his head. "We only have two. They're too bulky to use inside the station, and I don't want crew in the docking and stowage module. It's not as shielded as the command module. Until we know what we're dealing with, everyone stays here."

"Radiation levels are still climbing," Anderson said. "We've received thirty millisieverts in the last hour."

"Almost the maximum yearly dose allowed by NASA in

an *hour*?" Jo-Jo looked stricken. "How much more are we going to be exposed to?" asked Jo-Jo. Her arms wrapped protectively around her abdomen.

Claire sympathized. The younger woman had questioned Claire about motherhood over coffee. Jo-Jo and her fiancé planned to have children . . . someday.

It was comforting to know that Owen was safe on Earth. She put an arm around Jo-Jo's shoulders. "We're only seeing elevated levels because we were over the blast zone. As we move away, it will lessen, and NASA will evacuate us as soon as they know what's happened."

Jo-Jo nodded without looking up. "What I don't understand is: why? Why would any country risk starting a nuclear war?"

"Oil," said Cole. "The last oil on Earth." He looked out the window at the darkness. "We're witnessing the end of the petroleum age."

Bisnu's battalion crawled towards the mountains, eighty-five Russian-built T-90 tanks in tight formation. Bisnu rode behind them in a Humvee. He stopped when they passed the American encampment.

Soldiers in desert-khaki loaded crates into covered trucks.

Colonel Trent Garrett came out to meet Bisnu's Humvee.

"What are your men doing?" Bisnu asked by way of greeting. He pointed to his column of tanks. "The enemy is that way."

Garrett pulled off his cap and scratched the top of his head. "We signed up for ground combat, not nukes. I've got standing orders to protect my men from biological or nuclear warfare. We're pulling back to Guwahati."

Bisnu's face flushed. "What manner of men are you? You promised us aid. To stand by us and protect the oil fields."

Pulling his cap back on, Garrett pursed his lips. "I don't like it any better than you, but the politicians back home don't like sending our boys home in body bags. I've got my orders." He turned and walked back towards the men loading the Humvees, shouting, "Pick up the pace. We're out of here in two minutes."

Bisnu spat on the ground. He should have known better than to trust the Americans. They'd grown soft on McDonald's hamburgers and big cars. No matter. Though the odds were against them, his men were resolved. He climbed back into his Humvee and ordered the driver to catch up with the tanks.

"We need information, people, and we need it now." Hank Rubin addressed the assembled engineers in Mission Control. They were scattered behind their stations, craning to look back at him. "We've got reports of a high-altitude nuclear burst—"

A ripple of murmured conversation passed through the room at that news.

"—over India," Hank continued. "We don't know its origin or magnitude. It seems to be affecting communications, and that may explain why Lou isn't getting any readings from the crew."

Lou wiped sweat from his forehead with a damp handkerchief and checked his terminal again.

The fax machine built into Hank's desk hummed and spewed forth a cover page. Hank jerked it up and checked the sender: Grant Williamson at the Pentagon. The title of the document was "The Argus Effect and Other Risks to the Telecommunications Infrastructure." What the hell? Hank dropped the paper back into the fax machine's out tray.

Hank pointed at Amanda: "I want you to use every means to make contact. Route through other space agencies: Moscow, Japan, Brazil. Use every transmitter you can find. I want to hear Cole's voice before I go home tonight."

Amanda's lips compressed into a determined line. "Yes, sir."

"Lou, look up all the biological effects of radiation. Assuming they survived decompression and that our current lack of sensor readings is a communications glitch, I want to know what health risks they're facing."

Lou dabbed at his balding head and nodded.

Hank gave out assignments to the rest of his team: use telemetry to locate the source of the decompression, calculate the potential radiation dose to the crew, determine the threat that secondary electrostatic discharge would disable *Reliance*'s electronics, and plan an emergency evacuation using the lifeboat.

When everyone else was busy with a task, Hank picked up the fax again and began reading. What the Pentagon had sent made the hairs on his arms prickle. "Mother of God," Hank whispered.

Claire stared at Earth through the window where Jo-Jo held vigil. The station, circling the globe every ninety minutes, had caught up with the horizon.

A thin crescent of rainbow blossomed on the planet's horizon as the station crossed the transition between night and day. It faded into the brilliant blue of the daytime Pacific Ocean. In the upper atmosphere, a storm was brewing, dark thunderheads massed inside a swirl of white cloud.

Claire couldn't stop thinking of the people in Asia. Even a high-altitude burst would kill thousands. Thousands more would die from lack of infrastructure and emergency services. She felt sick inside.

There were three other stations in orbit: a Brazilian biomedical research facility, a Chinese nanomachine manufacturing plant, and a Japanese weather station. Maybe twenty people in all currently orbited the Earth. She wondered if they too were feeling isolated and powerless. It must be worst for the Chinese, knowing their relatives were down there—in a nuclear war zone.

There was nothing she could do for them. With a sigh, Claire pushed off and settled in front of the radio. Claire continued to try Mission Control in Houston or Moscow. Neither answered. While they waited for contact, Cole had them perform diagnostics on *Reliance*'s systems. It took thirty minutes and kept them too busy to brood about what had happened. Aside from a slight degradation in solar power and the loss of thirty millimeters of pressure, the station was nominal.

Claire slipped on the headset and said, "Houston, this is *Reliance*. Do you read me? Houston, this is—"

The communication center's central screen lit up.

"*Reliance*, we copy. This is Houston." Hank Rubin's craggy face broke into a grin. "I can't tell you how glad we are to hear from you."

Claire exhaled and pressed her clasped hands against her chin. They had established—however tentatively—satellite communications. Her voice was lost among Anderson's triumphant whoop and Jo-Jo's shout of "Hello, Houston!" bouncing off the aluminum walls. Jo-Jo and Hyun-Jin hugged each other in glee. Anderson grinned like his face might split apart.

Only Cole's happiness was tempered. He leaned forward and slipped the headset off Claire. Adjusting it on, he said, "Houston, *Reliance*. As you heard, the feeling's mutual. Are you aware of the event that occurred at GMT 19:12?"

There was a pause, then Hank's expression sobered. "*Reliance*, that's affirmative. Initiate encryption protocol alpha."

Claire pulled her foot from under the handrail and gave Cole the com. He braced his thigh under a slide-out tray near the workstation and typed in the commands to switch to add additional security to the channel-S communications. "Houston, *Reliance*. Alpha encryption confirmed. Do you read me?"

"*Reliance*, Houston." The humor was gone from Hank's face. "We copy. Give us your report."

"Houston, *Reliance*. At 19:12 GMT, we observed a flash of light over the Indian subcontinent. Claire Logan and Hyun-Jin Yi, who were on EVA at the time, describe a fireball rising over a glowing pancake luminescence. Power is out over northeastern India, and we experienced elevated radiation levels over that area. Can you confirm a nuclear strike?"

Hank sucked his lips. A retired astronaut, he'd been leader of the Eagle ground command team in Houston for the past decade. Even with his years of training and experience, his wide face was as open and expressive as a toddler's. "*Reliance*, that's affirmative. Washington has put the nation on orange alert. The blast took out half the communication satellites over Asia. And the Argus effect will take out all of the unshielded satellites over the next few weeks. Even if no more bombs fall, it's going to be economic chaos."

"The Argus effect?" whispered Jo-Jo.

Claire was uneasy. She'd heard the term before. Had it been in a *Scientific American* Webcast? One of NASA's technical memos?

"*Reliance*, Houston. The Argus effect is caused by free electrons from a nuclear blast. The buildup of electrons in the Earth's magnetic field will affect *Reliance*, too. In a couple of days to weeks, anything in low-Earth orbit that isn't radiation-hardened to withstand a nuclear blast will fail. You need to evacuate immediately."

Cole exchanged a look with Anderson. He rubbed the side of his neck. "Houston, we can't comply. One of the satellites destroyed in the blast hit our CEV."

There was a long moment of silence. Then Hank said, "*Reliance*, describe the damage."

Cole described what they'd seen out the window, the deep rent, loss of hull integrity, and the destroyed engines. While he spoke, Claire floated over one of the three laptops in the command station, clinging to the case with one hand as she typed to upload the images they'd taken.

On the other end of the connection, Hank sucked in a breath. "*Reliance*. Let me check with our engineers and see how they want to proceed."

Claire grabbed Cole's shoulder and whispered, "I don't know about you, but while the Ku band is available, I'd like to call home." If they were in danger of losing satellite communications, Claire wanted to talk to Matt. Now.

Cole patted her hand. "Houston, *Reliance*. While we're waiting for your feedback, we're going to place family calls."

"*Reliance*. Negative. We can't authorize—"

"Hank, my people won't talk about the bomb. They know better. But we've got a situation up here, and they could use a distraction while your boys on the ground figure out a plan."

A moment of radio silence while Hank conferred with the NASA publicity officer. When he came back online, his expression was guardedly sympathetic. "*Reliance*, I'm going to allow it. But no mention of the nuclear explosion or hull breach. They can only say their return to Earth may be delayed due to routine maintenance. Any mention of unauthorized subjects and we cut the line. Understood?"

"Houston, *Reliance*. That's a copy."

"*Reliance*, don't worry. The best minds in North America are working on this. We'll get you down."

"Thank you, Houston. *Reliance* out." Cole disconnected the radio and pulled his headset off. "You heard the man, anyone who wants to make a phone call, take five minutes, then I want you back on task. Alphabetical order."

Hyun-Jin Yi groaned.

With a ripping sound, Anderson pulled his wireless palm-top off the Velcro straps on his thigh and powered it up. Anderson retreated to a position near the hatch, farthest away from the laptop station.

"Hi, Dad, it's me . . . no, Rob." Anderson's voice sounded strange: hesitant, deferential. Claire had noticed the change in timbre before when he called his father. "Yeah, I know it's game night—hey listen . . ."

With the station sealed off, there was no chance of privacy, but everyone in the crew pretended he was elsewhere and tried not to listen in on the conversation.

While Claire waited, she squeezed in next to Cole and used a laptop to look up the Argus effect. Piggybacking packets onto Anderson's conversation, she found a Department of Defense Web site. As Hank had said, the Argus effect was triggered by a high-altitude nuclear blast. Electrons trapped by the Earth's magnetic field would oscillate between its magnetic poles, causing radio interference and the aurora Jo-Jo had spotted. The effect took a few days to build up. Electrons would impact the dielectrics in all space craft—thermal blankets, cable shielding, circuit boards—building up charge until the dielectrics broke down and released that charge in tiny lightning strikes. In weeks, the increased radiation would damage the communication satellites until all nonhardened circuitry failed. The effect was like the worst solar storm ever. What Hank hadn't told them was that the effect would take years to dissipate.

If the crew of *Reliance* and the other three space stations in orbit didn't evacuate in the next seventy-two hours, systems on board the station would crash. Eventually, she and the rest of *Reliance*'s crew would be floating in a dead tin can, without protection from the temperature extremes of -170 to 300 degrees Fahrenheit, and without life support.

"Cole." She nudged him with her elbow. "You need to

read this." She positioned the arm holding the laptop so he could read it.

Cole scanned the text. His face drained of color. "Good thing the crew rotation was scheduled for Friday. Space shuttle *Defiant* is already prepped for launch."

Claire pointed at a graphical representation of accumulating electrons on the screen. "You think they'll send a manned vessel through this?"

Hyun-Jin pushed off the viewing port in the floor to hover over Claire's shoulder and examine the display. Jo-Jo, already above them at the main viewing window, rotated her head down to see it. Her eyes widened in dismay.

"Don't worry," Cole assured them. "They'll get us down."

But Claire knew it wouldn't be easy. NASA took months to prepare for a launch. She didn't believe ground control would authorize a rescue mission that put more astronauts at risk. Could they scramble an unmanned launch with only a few days' warning?

Anderson finished his call, snapping his palmtop closed.

Cole waved Jo-Jo to go next with a halfhearted smile. "Commander's prerogative; I'll go last."

Jo-Jo undocked a nonessential laptop and carried it to the rear of the room, plugging a headset into its microphone and speaker ports. Bringing up the communications program, she dialed, then said, "Katie. This is Aunt Josephine. Yeah, in space. Can you get Grandma for me?"

Cole pulled Anderson and Hyun-Jin into a huddle. "I want you to go through the station and shut down the experiments and all nonessential systems. We need to lock this station down for evacuation." He glanced at Claire. "It may be some time before we get back."

"But my xenobacteria," Hyun-Jin said, forehead wrinkling in dismay. "The run's only got eighteen hours left." He looked earnestly at Cole. "I need that data. I have to publish my results so I can extend my NSF grant—"

"Flush it," Cole said. "Getting home just became our top priority." He handed Anderson Claire's palmtop with the information about the Argus effect.

They read it together, Hyun-Jin floating over Anderson's shoulder.

Anderson whistled. "Years to dissipate? These days *ev-*

erything runs on wireless. What's going to happen to the economy?"

Cole pinched the bridge of his nose. "Nothing good."

Jo-Jo finished her call, pulled off the headset, and dabbed at her eyes.

Anderson and Hyun-Jin exited the command module. At the hatch, Hyun-Jin called back to Claire. "Page me when you're done."

Claire took the headset from Jo-Jo. She was struck with a terror of not knowing what to say. She dialed Matt's cell phone number and prayed it would work.

The cell phone rang in clipped, digital, tones. Then a warm, deep voice answered: "Claire, is that you?"

"Matt." Tears born of stress and relief prickled her eyes. "How's Owen?"

"Good. He can't wait to go to Disney World when you land. We're at the volcano pool of the Polynesian Resort." Matt took the phone away from his mouth to yell, "Owen, get over here. Mom's on the line."

There were sounds of squealing and splashing.

"Matt, there's been a change of plans." Claire felt Cole's gaze on the back of her neck. "Nothing I can go into now, but my return might be delayed."

"What? Again?" His voice held an all-too-familiar edge.

Claire rubbed the spot between her eyes that always tensed up when Matt went on one of his "you always put work ahead of your family" tirades. She reminded herself that he had no idea what had happened or how petty his complaint sounded right now. Claire forced herself to chuckle, but even to her ears it was hollow. "You know how it is with NASA, plans change."

In the background, Owen chanted, "Mommy. Mommy. Mommy."

Claire wiped her eyes and tried to keep her voice calm. "Can you put Owen on the phone?"

Matt's voice dropped to a lower pitch, concern replacing irritation. "Claire, what's wrong?"

"Nothing. Please. Let me talk to Owen."

There were fumbling sounds as the phone was passed.

"Mommy!" squealed Matt. "Daddy let me go down the water slide—all by myself—and I wasn't even scared! Then I did a cannaball!"

"That's great, sweetie. Do you know how much Mommy loves you?"

"Thiiiis—" His voice faded. Claire could picture him, his arms flung wide, still holding the phone. The last word was faint—"much."

"That's right, sweetie. Put Daddy back on."

The phone rattled and Matt said, "Claire?"

"Matt, I've got to go. There's a lot to do up here. I just wanted to tell you how much I love you, and—whatever happens—take care of Owen for me."

"Whatever happens?" Matt's voice was tense. "What the hell does that mean? What's going on up there?"

"Nothing. Everything's all right, I just wanted to tell you I love you."

"Bullshit. There's something. I can hear it in your voice. I took a leave of absence from the college so you could go into space. Don't treat me like a goddamned housewife. Tell me what's wrong!"

Cole gave her a sharp look and sliced his hand across his throat.

"I've got to go, really. Love you."

"Claire, don't—"

She cut the connection. Her stomach hurt. She'd only made things worse by worrying Matt. Hearing Owen's enthusiastic piping had only brought home how far away they were. Three hundred miles of altitude and the deadly vacuum of space lay between her and those she loved.

"I told ground control we wouldn't raise any alarms," Cole growled. "You cut it close, Logan."

"Sorry, sir." Claire suppressed the tears prickling in her eyes. Astronauts didn't cry. Not even mommy astronauts. She pulled the headset off and Velcroed it to the wall.

Cole used the station intercom to let Hyun-Jin know he could place his call.

Claire was scared. If NASA couldn't scramble a rescue ship before the Argus effect made space travel impossible, she'd never see Matt and Owen again. Claire didn't want her last words to Matt to be an argument.

"*Reliance*, this is Houston. Do you copy?"

The hiss and pop of the ship-to-ground radio shook Claire out of her misery. The good thing about working in space was it left little time to feel sorry for yourself. She grabbed up the radio headset. "Houston, *Reliance*. What's going on down there?"

"*Reliance*, Houston. We're going to initiate a burn for course correction. Prepare in: five, four, three, two, one."

Over the uplink channel, Houston sent commands to *Reliance*'s attitudinal jets. They fired so softly, Claire barely felt the acceleration.

Cole slipped a headset on and adjusted the microphone. "Houston, *Reliance*. Should we prepare for a docking maneuver?"

"*Reliance*, Houston. That's still under discussion. Until a decision is made, we want you to shut down all nonessential systems and prep the station for decommission."

The words sent a pang through Claire. For the past four years, the station had been her obsession, the reward waiting for her at the end of a grueling regimen of training and simulations. In the past three months, it had become her home.

Cole winced, apparently sharing her sentiment. "Houston. That's a copy. When will we have a decision about our evacuation procedure?"

Hank's voice was tense. "*Reliance*, as soon as we know, you'll know. That's a promise."

Cole's face was ashen.

The crew was so silent, you could hear the droning hum of the air purifiers and the whine of the overhead lights.

Hyun-Jin stared into the distance, his expression bleak. Jo-Jo rubbed her hands along her bare shoulders. Anderson's jaw set with grim acceptance: What would come, would come.

Cole clapped his hands, purposefully breaking the mood. "You heard the man. We need to shut down this station."

"Sir," said Jo-Jo in a trembling voice, holding out her palmtop. "You should look at this."

Cole took the computer and Claire read over his shoulder. CNN had found out about the nuclear blast. There was a video clip from a press conference with President Tucker.

"Damn. He didn't waste any time. It's only been two hours since the attack." Cole pushed PLAY.

On the screen, the florid face of Ellis Q. Tucker, President of the United States, was a rigid mask of barely suppressed anger. "China has done the unthinkable. The use of

nuclear arms against a civilian populace is unconscionable."
Tucker's jowls wobbled as he pounded his fist against the
podium. "The United States demands the immediate with-
drawal of China from eastern India and that they surrender
their mountain-based ICBMs to U.N. weapons inspectors.
If these conditions are not met within forty-eight hours, the
United States will respond with overwhelming might."

CHAPTER 3

Flight Director Hank Rubin chewed on the edge of an already-bloody cuticle. How the hell were they going to get *Reliance*'s crew down with no lifeboat and a shrinking window of opportunity for a shuttle launch? He'd have to pull the launch in to take off two days early, and that required approval from on high.

"She's on the floor," Amanda whispered.

Hank didn't ask who 'she' was. There was only one person at NASA who got that tone of subdued awe from Amanda.

Cas Walker was the Mission Operations Directorate Manager, liaison from the Flight Control Room to top NASA and Johnson Space Center Missions Operations Directorate management. She was a tall woman, six-foot-two in heels—and she always wore heels. Her face was long, thin lips surrounded by what could only be grimace lines, because Hank had never seen her smile. A second web of fine lines creased her eyes—they were a startling pale blue that looked almost white under fluorescent bulbs. Her gray-blond hair was styled in a short severe cut.

"Who the hell wants to launch early, and why?" she demanded.

Hank took a swig of tepid coffee. "Good afternoon, Cas. I take it you read my summary email on the Argus effect."

Cas crossed the to Hank's station and leaned against his monitor. "I did. It's the perfect argument for why we shouldn't launch at all. The only thing worse than five dead astronauts is nine." Cas jabbed a finger towards the floor. "Mike's team stays on the ground."

A dull pain in Hank's stomach radiated up into his chest. He forced himself to stay calm. "The Argus effect may last for years. Even if they had enough food to last that long, the increasing radiation will kill *Reliance*'s electronics in months. If we don't get them out of there now, they'll die."

"And if we launch Mike's team in a shuttle that's not ready, into a radioactive hell that causes a deadly malfunction, *Reliance*'s crew still dies. It's the first rule of any rescue operation—you don't put more lives in danger. You'll have to figure out another way to bring them back."

Hank rubbed his neck. "The shuttle is our best shot. The ground crew says the *Defiant* can be ready in thirty-six hours. They'll have to work around the clock, but the supervisors say they're up for it. We've got a window of opportunity before the Argus effect closes in—if we act fast."

Cas put her hand down on his work surface and loomed over him. She spoke in a low undertone. "NASA can't afford another black eye. Not after the explosion on the ISS. We act irresponsibly and rush a crew into space and they don't make it back—Congress is just looking for an excuse to pull our budget."

Hank licked beads of sweat from his upper lip. "You're not listening. There isn't going to *be* a manned space program. The Argus effect will shut everything down for years. Our people aren't safe up there. We have to bring them back."

Cas shook her head, "You can't send the shuttle, it's not—"

Hank grabbed her arm, felt hard bone under flesh.

She looked up, her blue-white eyes registering surprise and outrage.

"I'm telling you," Hank ground out over the throbbing

in his chest. "We're bringing *Reliance*'s crew back—or you'll have to find yourself a new Flight Director."

Matt sat on the edge of his hotel bed, eyes riveted to CNN, where President Tucker addressed the nation. In a split screen was video footage from Greece of the aurora effect generated by the nuclear explosion.

"My fellow Americans. China has attacked U.S. forces on the ground with nuclear weapons, against international law. They have invaded our ally nation, India. These are actions we cannot ignore—"

Owen dropped his dump truck, climbed into his father's lap, and cocked his head at the screen. "Why is that man angry?"

Matt hugged his son, taking in the scent of chlorine that a bath hadn't been able to wash off.

Wriggling free, Owen placed both hands on the television screen, covering the aurora. "Pretty!"

Matt dragged Owen back to the bed. His chest burned. The world was on the brink of World War III, and Owen had no idea. While they were safe in Orlando, his wife was in danger. Every ninety minutes Claire passed over a war zone. He felt scared and helpless. As an astronaut's spouse, he should have been used to the emotion—but he wasn't. No matter how many times Claire went into space, each one was like the first time. Months of jumping each time the phone rang, trying not to think what he would do if anything happened to her, trying not to think of all the other astronauts who'd died in the line of duty. They took great risks and were awarded glory, while their spouses stayed home, invisible—and worried.

One of Owen's chubby hands reached up to pat Matt's cheek. His face screwed up with sympathetic sorrow. "Why do you look so sad?"

Matt forced a smile. "How would you like to see Grandma?"

Owen flipped his hands over in a shrug. "But why? Mommy's coming home in . . ." He counted on his fingers. "Two days! Then we're going to Disney World." He couldn't contain his excitement, and danced an impromptu jig on the carpet.

Owen saw echoes of his wife in the color of Owen's eyes, the shape of his hands, his passionate enthusiasm. "Mommy's going to be late. While we're waiting we'll go see Grandma. She can't wait to see how big you've grown."

Owen cocked his head, considering. "And *then* we go to Disney World?"

Matt hugged his son close, wishing he could protect him from all the dangers and unhappiness in the world. "Yes. I promise."

A note in Matt's voice made Owen turn. His blue-green eyes bored into Matt's. With a child's unnerving perception, he asked, "Is Mommy going to be all right?"

Matt bent his head over his son and kissed the top of his head. "Yes, of course." He whispered into Owen's golden-brown curls. "I hope so."

Reliance's crew scrambled through the station: hurrying through access tunnels and cargo-packed corridors, shutting down experiments and workstations in a rush to conserve power, packing up and securing equipment, and closing bulkheads before they were hit by more debris.

Claire braced her shoulders and feet against opposite walls of lab one. The room was a pack rat's closet of equipment and old experiments. The elastic straps on the wall held Velcro cable ties, Sharpie pens, a screwdriver, scissors, hemostats, a multimeter, and a collection of empty plastic bags with Velcro pads on them.

Reaching past a laptop on a positionable arm, Claire shut down a liquid-adhesion experiment. She turned off power to the computer monitoring it, and flipped a switch to pump the fluid back into a metal-walled dewar. When the pump finished cycling, she tucked the thermos-sized dewar under a set of elastic straps on the wall.

Josephine vacuumed up seedlings in the lab further down the access tunnel. She called across. "Claire, you think there's going to be a nuclear war?"

It was the question on everyone's mind. But, until now, no one had voiced it.

Claire bit her lip. Before today she would have bet money that no nuclear weapon would be used after the horror of Hiroshima and Nagasaki. They were too dangerous to be anything other than a deterrent, the environmental impacts too severe. But now bombs had exploded over India, and remade the world. Anything could happen.

"Of course not," Cole responded from lab two. He was across the hall from labs one and three, turning off the heaters and O2 flow across a high-temperature superconducting sample. "China's had a lot of questionable leaders, but even President Mao Du Feng would retreat from full-on nuclear conflict. The high-altitude bombs were just a way to soften up communications so the Chinese ground troops could move into Digboi."

Cole had military experience. He sounded confident. Claire wanted to believe him. But the tightness in her chest warned her that worse things might yet come.

Every seat in the conference room was taken, and another dozen people stood against the wall. Cas was there, and the top NASA and JSC Missions Operations Directorate management. She spoke to them in a huddle as Hank walked in with his nineteen flight-room engineers. George Byers was already there, setting up his laptop to display on the wall screen. The four astronauts that comprised the *Defiant*'s crew leaned against the wall. Mike Marshant nodded to Hank. Alice Depuy, at his side, looked grave.

"We have to cancel the shuttle flight," Cas said as Hank sat down. "In the current political environment, it's too dangerous to risk a launch. We can send an automated recovery—"

"Come on, Cas," replied Hank, knowing that she hated his use of her first name. "China and India are at war, not the U.S."

The wall screen flashed blue, then displayed the opening slides of Byers's presentation on the Argus effect and the risk analysis of mounting a rescue attempt that Hank's team had put together. They needed to move fast to save Cole and his crew. It made Hank's teeth ache to have to sit in a meeting while precious minutes ticked away.

The NASA bureaucrats listened to Byers's presentation. Johnstone, a thin man in his late fifties, interrupted Byers when he displayed a chart of the expanding belt of charged particles circling the Earth. "This Argus effect—*all* satellites will be destroyed?"

Byers blew a strand of limp brown hair out from behind his glasses and pushed them higher up his face. The thick bottle lenses made his temples appear indented. "Radiation-hardened military satellites may survive. It depends on the intensity of the effect, which is directly proportional to the number of high-altitude missiles fired. Satellites in high orbits, like geosynchronous, will be fine. But the low-Earth satellites we use for communications—" He pushed his glasses up again. "Yeah, they're hosed."

"What I don't understand," said Wilton, a grizzled black man on the directorate, "is why we don't send an unmanned vessel that can bring them back down?" He spread his hands. "*Reliance*'s crew is saved, and no further lives are endangered."

Three engineers started to speak at once. "But—that would—won't—"

Hank rapped on the table to get their attention. "The ATVs are designed to burn up on reentry. They have no passenger or landing capability."

"What about using one of the old Russian Soyuz?"

Hank pinched the bridge of his nose. The man was asking for months of work. "The Argus effect is already affecting equipment up there. We've got days—maybe hours—before *Reliance* is nonfunctional. The Russians don't have anything they can launch that quickly, and there's no way the ground crew could turn an ATV into a lifeboat before the Argus effect closes in."

Cas jumped on the suggestion, her pale eyes gleaming. "Then why not send up an unmanned vessel with a replacement thruster and a patch for the hull so they can repair the lifeboat on *Reliance*?"

"There's no way they could effect repairs before the radiation in orbit got too hot for a safe EVA," Hank shot back. "It'd be crazy to even ask them when we have a safer alternative already on the launchpad: space shuttle *Defiant*."

"Not to mention," Byers interjected, "the extreme unlikelihood that a patch will adhere well enough to survive reentry."

"And I say it's madness to throw more people at the problem." Cas half-rose from her seat. "We've already got five astronauts in jeopardy; adding four more is foolhardy."

The tightness in Hank's chest made it hard for him to draw a deep breath. "What if it were you, Cas? Wouldn't you want us to do *everything* we could to bring you back?"

"Astronauts know the risks." Cas jabbed her finger at Hank's chest. "They accept that every time they launch—they might die."

Hank flipped a sweaty lock of hair off his forehead. "Astronauts know the risks, yeah. But they also know their ground crew supports them one hundred percent. They don't give up. We don't give up." He pushed his chair away from the table and stood, pounding it with his fist. "We don't cut them loose because it makes good politics." He pointed at Cas. "Which you'd know if you didn't have a calculator for a soul."

"Hey, now," Wilton said. "Let's take it down a notch. Making this personal won't help us make the best decision."

Leaning against the wall, Mike Marshant put the front two feet of his chair down and raised his hand. "As one of the people whose butts are going to be on the line if this goes through, may I speak?"

Wilton gestured for the astronaut to speak.

"Alice and I discussed the mission on the walk over here. We could fly *Defiant* with a skeleton crew: just her and me. We've read the reports about the Argus effect. The longer we take to make this decision, the worse it gets. We heard the science, we know the political realities." He nodded at Cas. "Can we take a vote and get on with this? All in favor of saving the lives of the five finest astronauts I've ever trained with?"

Mike Marshant and Alice Depuy each raised their right hands.

Reliance flew over the Rocky Mountains. White-capped peaks protruded through swirls of cumulus clouds. They had line-of-sight communications to White Sands and all the palmtops were transmitting. Everyone was taking advantage of the clear channel: browsing the Web for news about the conflict, transmitting email, and downloading technical information about the station. Of their ninety-minute orbit, only twenty minutes was within line-of-sight of U.S. relay stations.

Underlying the silent hum of transmission, the station stank of sweat and fear.

"*Reliance*, this is Houston," the radio speaker announced to the cabin.

Cole tapped the button to answer the call, but left the radio on speakerphone. "*Reliance*. We read you, Houston. Go ahead." Anderson and Claire were seated on either side of him. Claire ran diagnostics over the oxygen-filtration unit and Anderson downloaded video of President Tucker's press conference. Floating near the window, Hyun-Jin uploaded data from his aborted xenobacteria experiment. Jo-Jo hovered near the hatch, tapping furiously on her palmtop with a stylus.

Hank's voice was tired. Claire wished she could see his expression, but they'd elected not to use video. The bandwidth was needed for other transmissions. No one knew how long the connection would hold; every passing moment distributed electrons further around the globe.

"*Reliance*, we've got a plan. It's in two stages, and the timing is close."

Anderson closed the lid of his palmtop, and Claire tapped hers to save the place in the checklist. Hyun-Jin and Jo-Jo also paused their projects to listen.

Cole piped the radio over the intercom to lab two, so Hyun-Jin could hear. "Houston, we're all ears."

Hank continued: "There are two goals. First: the safety and evacuation of the crew. We've moved the shuttle launch up from Friday to Wednesday. It'll have a skeleton crew: just a pilot and copilot: Mike Marshant and Alice Depuy."

Two of the best astronauts in NASA. Claire breathed a sigh of relief. If anyone could bring a rescue ship through that hell of radiation and safely back to earth, it was Mike and Alice.

Claire imagined the flurry of politics Earth-side. Hidden behind the media furor over China's attack would be NASA's scramble to avoid the death of more astronauts. The failure of the International Space Station last week had left many questioning NASA's value now that other countries had stations in orbit. There were other venues to perform weightless experiments; NASA couldn't afford more bad publicity.

Hank continued: "But the shuttle isn't going to rendez-vous with *Reliance*—"

Claire's breath caught in her throat.

"—Houston, can you repeat that last?" Cole asked, inter-rupting. A frown creased his forehead. "I'm not sure we copy."

Hank's voice was weary. "*Reliance*, I assure you, bringing the crew back safely is our main concern. But our second-ary goal is to raise *Reliance* into a high enough orbit to safely deploy the solar reflector and to survive the Argus period. Then we can bring her back into service once the effect subsides. *Reliance*'s a twenty-five-billion-dollar in-vestment, and the ESR will be crucial to the U.S.'s eco-nomic future as the oil crash intensifies. There's going to be economic chaos while the satellite network is being re-built. This directive comes from the highest levels." Hank cleared his throat. "The shuttle will rendezvous with *Reli-ance* at the Mars-Mission fueling depot. Then it'll use the depot's engine to boost into mid-Earth orbit."

Anderson and Cole exchanged uneasy looks. "Houston, the Mars platform is more than one hundred kilometers higher than us. Even if we're incredibly lucky enough to be in the same orbital plane, we don't have enough fuel on board to get there."

"Not to worry, we're sending one of the European Auto-mated Transfer Vehicles up loaded with fuel—"

"An ATV only carries 4,500 kg of re-boost propellant. That's not enough to—"

"Relax, Cole. The engineers are in the hangar now, weld-ing fuel tanks into the dry-cargo area. You'll have 7,600 kg of fuel available."

Cole didn't look mollified. "How, exactly, will the fuel tanks in the cargo hold feed into the engines?"

"That's the tricky part. We need to get this bird in the air now—before the Argus effect makes sending an automated vehicle impossible. There's no time to redesign the main pressurized fuel tanks. We're slapping four additional off-the-shelf tanks into the dry-cargo area. In eighteen hours, when the ATV arrives, one of your people will need to EVA and manually route a fuel hose from the cargo area, through the exterior hatch, to the ATV's engine intake."

Cole's white eyebrows bunched together like warring caterpillars. "Houston. Did you say eighteen hours? The ATV can't get here that fast. It takes two days to launch and synchronize speed."

There was a pause. "*Reliance*, we're using a steeper orbital path."

Cole exchanged a glance with Anderson. Neither pilot looked happy.

The standard forty-eight hours allowed incoming vessels to gradually match speed and position with *Reliance*. It permitted a gentle docking procedure. The thought of an ATV ship coming in at a steep trajectory and a mismatched speed made Claire's neck clench.

"Houston, I don't like the sound of that," said Cole. His watery-blue eyes were hooded with anxiety.

Hank sighed audibly. "*Reliance*, I don't like it either. But it's the best we can do with the time constraints."

Claire tapped Cole on the shoulder and pointed at the dosimeter. On the far side of the planet from where the blast had exploded, the radiation was lower, but still above NASA guidelines for a spacewalk.

Cole nodded his acknowledgment. "Houston, are you receiving our radiation telemetry data?"

"*Reliance*, we know it's hot out there." Another sigh. "There's no other way. If the station is going to be saved, someone's going to have to go outside. We've timed the procedure to minimize exposure—"

"Houston, I won't order my crew—"

"I'll do it," Anderson interjected.

Cole, Claire, and Jo-Jo stared at him.

"You're not qualified for EVA," said Claire. "You've only got ten hours of pool training."

Anderson's round face was set in a stoic mask. "I'm a fast learner. Talk me through it."

Cole made a slashing gesture across his throat to cut off their conversation. "Houston, can you send up details of the work involved?"

"*Reliance*, we are transmitting now. Have you received the file?"

Claire checked the incoming email. There was a message from Mission Control. She opened it and diagrams of *Reliance* and checklists displayed. "Got it."

"Houston, that's affirmative."

The three of them downloaded copies of the plan to their palmtops. The EVA was tricky, involving a tight crawl to connect the hose to the four tanks in the dry-cargo area, controlling eight meters of fuel hose in weightlessness, and another tight crawl to pressurize the hose once the connection to the ATV's fuel intake had been checked for leaks.

If all went well, it shouldn't take more than two hours. *Reliance*, however, circled the globe every ninety minutes. Even if the astronaut returned to the air lock during the worst radiation, they'd receive more than the lifetime dose allowed by NASA. In addition to an increased risk of cancer, whoever did the EVA would forfeit any future space missions.

It went against every NASA directive to ask them to take that risk; Hank must be desperate.

Claire pointed to a simulation of the four tanks installed in the dry-cargo area. There would be only three inches of clearance for the EVA suit when she checked that the tanks had survived launch and connected the fuel hose. "There's no way I could *talk* you through this," she said. "It's a matter of practice, being familiar with the suit. Snag it on one of the angle brackets they're using to attach the fuel tanks, or knock too hard against a wall, and you could get trapped—or worse, rupture your seals."

Anderson's hazel eyes were challenging. "You got a better idea?"

Claire exchanged a glance with Hyun-Jin. She and Hyun-Jin had trained for three months for the EVA to assemble the solar collector. Claire had also EVA'd on two previous construction missions. Of all the people on the station, she was the best trained, with the most experience. She felt the weight of their expectations.

Balanced against that was the thought that going outside would cut short her life, steal years she should have with Matt and Owen. Was a twenty-five-billion-dollar station worth that?

Hyun-Jin looked down at his hands. "My daughter. She's only eighteen months old."

"It's a dangerous mission," Cole agreed. "There will be health effects, there's no getting around that. The medical charts indicate a significantly increased cancer risk. If something goes wrong and the EVA is extended, perhaps even mild radiation sickness." He met each astronaut's eyes, one by one. "No one goes outside unless they volunteer." Cole's gaze fixed on Claire.

Her pulse pounded in her ears. She'd known being an astronaut was dangerous, but NASA had strict health protocols, took great pains with the safety of station crews. Trusting that a shuttle would launch safely, that the station would hold together, was one thing. To deliberately go out into high radiation levels was another. The nuclear detonation had changed the rules, raised the stakes.

Claire's face went red. She should be volunteering. It was expected, it was the loyal thing to do, the heroic thing. But . . . "I-I can't."

"There. No one else wants it. Let me go," Anderson urged.

Cole ran his fingers through his gray crew cut. "No. You've never EVA'd before. I'll go."

"But your training," said Hyun-Jin. "It's years out of date."

"Just let the station die," Jo-Jo said. "It's not like it's going to survive anyway. What if this kludged-together procedure fails? You'll have given yourself cancer for nothing."

Cole's eyes narrowed. "*Reliance* is my command. If there's any chance she can be saved, I'm taking it."

Guilt weighed like a stone in Claire's stomach. She wanted to do the right thing, finish the mission, deploy the collector, save *Reliance*—but Cole didn't understand how hard this EVA would be. "Space walks," Claire said, "are physically taxing. This isn't a simple procedure—"

Cole looked back and forth between Claire and Hyun-Jin. Neither met his eyes.

"Sir," Anderson said. "Let me. I can—"

"No. You're our best pilot. I need you monitoring the docking of the ATV. God knows we can't afford to let anything else go wrong."

"You should at least have backup."

"No. Risking one life is enough. If I can't get the job done, then we'll do as Jo-Jo said, let *Reliance* and the solar collector die. The shuttle will come back for us." Cole clenched his hand into a fist. "But that's not going to be necessary. I won't let it."

Claire, Cole, and Hyun-Jin went over the plan, discussing what could be done from inside the station. When they ran out of ideas, they took a break to eat power bars.

Hyun-Jin looked out the window as he chewed. "I wonder what they're thinking down there."

Claire pivoted at the waist. It had been hours since the blast, and they were back over Asia. Their path was different, due to the way their orbit spiraled around the globe, but India was still visible, the lights out and red fires aglow.

"One word," said Anderson. "Revenge."

The Indian army tanks rumbled into Brahmaputra pass, hot on the trail of the retreating Chinese. The top of the gorge was heavily forested and the steep cliff walls on either side of the pass cast dark shadows despite the cloudless morning.

Missiles streaked in from overhead. The sound of their passing pierced Bisnu's ears, even two miles behind the tank column.

He watched in horror as the missiles from unseen aircraft collided with the front row of tanks. They flipped like overturned turtles, their treads spinning them in circles. Flames erupted from ruptured fuel tanks.

Chinese tanks appeared around the corner of the canyon, crawling towards the broken phalanx, cannons blazing, punishing the downed tanks and driving the others back through unrelenting artillery blasts.

There were more enemy tanks than in the previous attacks. The Chinese had pulled back into a false retreat, meeting up with reinforcements from the east.

Bisnu shouted into the short-range radio. "Pull back! Ambush! Fall back!"

It was too late. More Chinese tanks roared out of camouflaged pits dug along the canyon walls. They closed ranks behind Rasmussen's forces, cutting off escape. Tanks overturned as they were forced against the canyon walls. Another erupted in flames from an artillery strike. Shrieking men tried to climb out of the hatch, only to erupt into flames, dancing in agony, their hands raised skyward in supplication.

Fear tightened Bisnu's chest. He'd brought a harrying force to a full-on assault. He repeated his order to retreat.

The driver kicked the Humvee into full reverse, spunout, and drove away from the conflict.

Of the eighty-five tanks that rolled into Brahmaputra, only four returned.

The short-range radio crackled. "Risaldar-Major." Bisnu recognized the voice of the man he'd met in the radio tent. "I have word from Assam command. They order us to pull back. We are needed in Guwahati, to quell citizen riots."

Jostling and bumping along the rough canyon floor, Bisnu could barely hold the radio to his mouth. "Repeat? We are to abandon the oil field?" His voice rose with incredulity.

"Guwahati has gone mad. The people think Shiva walks among us. The city has no power, and criminals are looting shops. They order you to retreat." There was a pause. Then the radio technician spoke the code words that Bisnu had memorized. "It is time for Rabha to respond."

Assam command would respond to China's nuclear attack with bombs of their own.

Bisnu closed his eyes, nauseated. Did their leaders not realize that reprisal would damage their land for years to come? That wind and water would carry the poisonous radiation miles from the bombed site?

"Did you receive the message?" the radio technician asked.

"I did," Bisnu replied. "Vishnu preserve us all."

"Look." Claire pointed to the terminator, the line between light and dark on the Earth.

Launching from the Baikonur Cosmodrome in Kazakhstan, the ATV supply ship broke through the clouds, tearing them into streamers behind it. It crossed over Lake Balkhash and the Altai Mountains of Mongolia.

From their vantage point on *Reliance*, it was nothing more than a speck. But that speck carried nearly three tons of fuel and rocketry, enough to see *Reliance* through the next three years of solo travel.

Claire felt a pang as it soared into orbit. If it had failed to launch, the space walk would have been canceled and the shuttle sent to rendezvous with *Reliance* instead of the orbital electrolysis platform that broke water into liquid oxygen and liquid hydrogen, stockpiling fuel for the Mars mission. With a sigh, she turned back to the schematics to figure out ways to shorten the procedure.

Cole tried to contact the other stations in orbit. All he got back was static. "High-energy betas are interfering with our transmissions."

No one contradicted him.

Claire tried not to imagine all the things that could have gone wrong on an orbiting space station since the nuclear explosion. She pushed away thoughts of debris fields and EMP effects. Tried not to contemplate how lucky *Reliance* was to have survived . . . thus far.

Three orbits later was the beginning of another sleep cycle, but no one could rest. Adrenaline hummed through them like an electrical current. Through sporadic channels of communication they received the latest news from Earth—no further developments, just the political posturing of world leaders.

Everyone huddled in the command module. It was like hiding in the bathroom of a three-thousand-square-foot house during an earthquake: suffocatingly close. Floating in the confined space, they kept bumping into one another. All nonessential areas of the station were powered down. The silence from the missing hums and clangs was disconcerting.

Below them, the Pacific Ocean gleamed in sunlight: a hundred shades of sapphire frosted by clouds. One white spiral hinted at the beginnings of a tropical storm, but from orbit, all was peaceful. Looking at the Earth from this angle, it was hard to believe the planet was on the brink of war.

Static blared from the radio speaker, startling them all.

"*Reliance*, this . . . Oahu Repeater . . . receive?" The connection was bad; static pounded like an electronic surf in the background.

Cole jolted out of a slumber and caught the headset. He fumbled it on. "Oahu, this is *Reliance*. What's going on?"

"*Reliance*—have . . . reports of another . . . detonation . . . China, please confirm."

Everyone but Cole flew to the meter-wide window and craned to look back over the western edge of the Pacific Rim.

"I don't see anything," Claire said. "It's too far away."

Jo-Jo pointed. "There's a weird glow on the horizon. See it?"

Claire squinted and thought Jo-Jo might be right. Green ghosts writhed along Earth's curved edge. The dancing curtains of light were a man-made aurora, created by electrons stripped during a nuclear explosion. Her heart seized. Not again.

Cole's forehead creased with worry. "Oahu, we have possible visual sightings of auroral aftereffects, but we're too far away to be certain. What's been reported?"

A pause. "*Reliance* . . . losing . . ."

Cole's voice rose, as if volume could overcome the faulty signal. "Oahu, this is *Reliance*. Oahu! Oahu!" He pulled off the headset and breathed heavily, clutching his chest. "Shit. Not now."

Claire took the headset from him. "John, are you all right?"

Cole nodded. "Just need to catch my breath. Try to reestablish contact with Oahu, Moscow, or Houston. We need to know what's going on down there."

Anderson caught Cole when he drifted away from the workstation, snatched a hydration pack from a mesh bag on the wall, and handed it to him. The commander took small sips.

Jo-Jo and Hyun-Jin exchanged worried glances.

Claire looked at the dosimeter. The radiation on the station's surface showed a total received dose of 112 mSv, and was still accumulating. If this kept up, an EVA would be suicide. Then she looked at the reading of the total received dose inside the shielded command module: 85 mSv. Claire wrapped the headset around her head. Who was she fooling? If this kept up, they'd all be dead and the EVA would be moot.

"Oahu, this is *Reliance*. Please come in. Oahu, this is *Reliance*. Please come in."

The California coast was visible on the horizon. Claire transferred to the U.S. Continental frequency. "Houston, this is *Reliance*. Come in." She chanted the words until they were directly over New Mexico and her throat was hoarse.

"It's no use," Anderson said. "The satellite tuner is dead and now there's too much radiation in orbit to get a signal through using the line-of-sight transmitters."

"You mean," Jo-Jo said, her eyes wide, "we won't be able to contact ground control?"

"Not until we're back on Earth," Cole said. He smiled, but his face looked gaunt and pale. "Don't worry."

The unasked question hung in the air: given the current environment, could NASA, *would* NASA still launch a rescue shuttle?

Claire bit her lip and wished she'd said more to Matt when she had the chance, had told him how much she loved him, even after twelve years of marriage. They'd ended on an argument. She prayed their last words to each other wouldn't be that tense exchange.

The thought of Owen growing up without a mother made her eyes prickle, and she caught onto a drawer pull to steady herself. She clung to the hard metal until it bruised the pads of her fingers, and that pain drove away thoughts of her family.

Jo-Jo hugged her knees to her chest, a small ball precessing in the center of the cabin. "I was so thrilled to be going into space." Her eyes were bright. "I don't want my first trip to be my last."

Cole grabbed her elbow and pulled the young woman into an awkward hug. "It won't be. We're in a tough spot, but we'll get through it." He looked over Jo-Jo's shoulder at the rest of his crew. "Right?"

"Absolutely," Anderson said, his stony face at odds with his statement.

"Of course we will," Hyun-Jin echoed.

"I'm sure as hell going home," Claire blurted. "This morning I put on my last clean pair of underwear."

A stunned pause. Then everyone laughed. Chuckles burst into guffaws. Laughter all out of proportion rocked the station. It was a release everyone needed.

Dabbing at her eyes, Claire pointed to the window. "Look, there's the ATV."

Sunlight glinted off the pinpoint supply ship. It had survived the latest detonation. Hope flared in Claire's chest. If the ATV, flying automated by an online guidance system, could reach them, surely a manned vessel could too.

* * *

Mission Control was a flurry of activity: planning the shuttle's trajectory, maximum gee the crew could be exposed to, the burn times to boost *Reliance* and the Mars fueling platform into mid-Earth orbit. Every calculation, every simulation, was triple-and quadruple-checked.

Hank Rubin's phone rang. He scooped it up and cradled it in his shoulder. "Yeah."

"Hank, we've got a problem." It was Lou Benson, the launch integration manager. The man in charge of prepping the shuttle for launch. "One of the actuator gears on the shuttle's rudder speed brake is below tolerance."

Hank rubbed his forehead. Not another damn problem. "Well, *fix* it. You've got twenty-two hours before launch."

"I can't sign off on the launch if the shuttle's not ready." Lou's voice rose in pitch. "I've got a safety checklist of more than *five hundred* pages. We can't blow that off. Do you want another *Columbia*? Another *Challenger*?"

Hank wanted to pound the phone against his desk. He took two deep breaths. "No, of course not. But we've got five astronauts whose *lives* depend on us launching before the Argus effect hits full-force. I know you're doing two weeks' worth of work in two days. But if there's anyone who can do this, it's you."

Lou blew out a breath. "Have you seen what the President's been saying? He's talking about war. Full-on nuclear war."

Amanda came back from the cafeteria and dropped a Philly cheese steak with extra onions on Hank's desk.

Hank peeled back the wax paper. Savory steam rose from the sandwich.

"No one's going to start a nuclear exchange," he assured Lou. "Not even President Tucker. Focus on the shuttle prep." What the hell was he doing watching television anyway?

"I'm not signing off on the launch if the shuttle's not ready," Lou repeated.

"Well then, make damn sure it *is* ready." Hank slammed the phone into the cradle. His chest was tight and his heart fluttered. He shook his head and muttered, "Am I the only one who wants to bring Cole's team back alive?"

* * *

With all nonessential modules of *Reliance* shut down and fifteen hours before the ATV arrived, there was nothing to do but wait. That was worse than if they'd had an impossibly full schedule. Too much time to think . . . to worry.

Reliance's crew read the articles about the conflict they'd downloaded before communications were lost, and listened to news clips.

"Listen to this." Anderson pulled the bud out of his ear and turned up the volume on his palmtop.

Two voices spoke, layered one over the other, one speaking Chinese, the other translating the words into English.

". . . deeply concerned about the U.S.'s involvement in the Indian conflict. I urge President Tucker to refrain from becoming involved in a situation that does not concern him."

Hyun-Jin's brow furrowed. "That's not what he said." He cocked his head and listened closely to the broadcast.

The translator's voice droned on, ". . . to take action would be regrettable."

Hyun-Jin's eyes widened. "The translation is literal, but misses the meaning. President Mao Du Feng implies that if the U.S. tries to stop their conquest of Assam, India, they will react with overwhelming force. It can only mean he's threatening nuclear strikes against the U.S."

"That's a state department translator," Anderson said. "They don't make mistakes."

Hyun-Jin snatched the palmtop from Anderson and pressed PLAY again. The tinny voice repeated the press conference speech. "The translation is wrong."

They sat in stunned silence.

"Does the President know?" asked Jo-Jo.

"Of course he knows," Anderson snapped. "Hyun-Jin isn't the only American who speaks Mandarin."

Hyun-Jin's hands trembled as he handed the palmtop back.

"Perhaps you heard the Chinese leader out of context." Claire said. "Perhaps if you heard the whole speech the translation would make sense."

"It was just political bluffing," Cole said. "No one wants a full-scale nuclear war." Cole squeezed Hyun-Jin's shoulder.

"Maybe you're right," said Hyun-Jin. But he didn't look convinced.

"It's time for dinner," Cole said. "We're packing out of here in two days. Any food we leave behind will be wasted. Let's have a feast to send *Reliance* off."

More like a wake, Claire thought. But she didn't say the words aloud. Everyone was already on edge.

Claire and Hyun-Jin went to the galley to grab food.

Claire crawled through the hatchway, noting as she always did that the room looked more like a medical lab than a kitchen. Along one wall were the gleaming silver tanks of the potable water heater and slide-out racks of food. Pinned to the opposing wall by elastic straps were place settings for each crew member: fork, spoon, and napkin. The spoons had the overly long handles of Russian design.

Below, striking an incongruously homey note, was a nylon mesh sack containing a plastic bottle of Heinz ketchup and individual packets of strawberry jam of the type served in diners.

The frozen prefab meals didn't offer much in the way of festive foods. White microwaveable trays were stacked behind Plexiglas doors. Labels on the end identified each meal and who had requested it. Claire pulled out trays of comfort food. Cole: turkey and dressing, with apple crumble. Anderson: Pad Thai with shrimp. Jo-Jo: Peanut butter and jelly with banana. Hyun-Jin: Hamburger and baked potato with A-1 Steak Sauce.

From her own menu she chose spaghetti with Italian sausage and garlic bread.

She completed the meal with foil drink pouches of cranberry, apple, and grape juice, each with a valved straw.

One by one, Hyun-Jin attached the water hose to the tray's intake valve. Then Claire loaded each tray into the microwave. While they cooked, she took care of incidentals, unpacking cutlery for each of them, grabbing a plastic garbage bag for the command module.

Her meal was the last to go in. The sausage popped as it cooked, spreading the smell of savory meat throughout the galley.

The greasy smell took Claire back to her own kitchen,

the lazy Sunday morning in October that had started it all. She and Matt had been cooking waffles and grilling sausage patties. Owen was still asleep upstairs, only eleven months old.

The wall phone rang and Claire picked it up. "Logan residence."

Hank Rubin's gruff voice answered. "Ms. Logan, I'm pleased to offer you a position as one of this year's astronaut candidates. Are you interested?" he asked.

Her "Hell, yes!" was so loud it woke the baby. Owen began to wail.

Claire nodded for Matt to go upstairs and take care of Owen. Flustered, she said, "I mean, yes. I accept."

Over the phone Hank chuckled. "Not many people turn me down." An information packet will arrive by courier. See you in Houston in six weeks."

Claire hung up the phone, already weightless. She ran up the stairs, nearly knocking into Matt and Owen on their way down. She grabbed Matt's arms to steady him, and bounced up and down. "That was NASA! They picked me! I'll be training to be an astronaut!"

Matt grabbed the banister with his free hand. "That's great, Honey. But can we have the rest of this conversation on the ground?"

Claire hoisted Owen from Matt. His thin golden hair was matted from sleep and stuck up on one side. She carried him down the stairs, then kissed his chubby cheek and bounced him high. "Mama's going to be an astronaut. What do you think about that?"

Owen rewarded her with a snaggletoothed grin. "'Stronaut!"

The sausage patties were smoking. Claire had forgotten them in her excitement.

Matt took the pan off the burner and turned off the heat. When he turned back to Claire, his expression was pensive. "Are you sure you want to accept? It's an intensive program."

Owen made vroom-vroom sounds as Claire flew him through the air.

Claire settled Owen on her hip, frowning. "We talked about this. It's what I've been working towards my whole career."

Matt's eyes flicked to Owen. "But that was three years ago, when you sent in your application. Now we have Owen. . . ."

Claire looked down at her son. He clung to her like a limpet. The grin had faded from his face, and he looked back and forth between his parents, unsure if he should worry, too.

Guilt tore at Claire. The training was intense. If she followed through, she'd miss a lot of Owen's childhood. But . . . if she refused, she'd be giving up her lifelong dream. Each year only a handful of people were chosen. Fewer than a thousand humans had ever been into space. To turn away from this opportunity would be to deny her purpose in life.

"Owen, Mommy's going to be an astronaut," she said quietly.

His blue eyes lit up. "'Stro-naut," he repeated, as if it was a joke between them.

"It's a dangerous profession," Matt continued. "What if you're not around to see Owen grow up?"

"Don't worry." She had wrapped her free arm around Matt and kissed him. He'd tasted of grease and maple syrup. "Space flight is routine these days. Nothing's going to happen."

How naive those words seemed now.

The microwave timer chimed, startling Claire. She jerked the tray out, burning her fingers on the superheated steam under the plastic. "Damn." Claire dropped it and the tray tumbled in midair, mixing its contents together.

Hyun-Jin pulled his sleeve down over his hand, and with the extra insulation, captured the tray. "Are you all right?"

Claire sucked on her finger. She took it out of her mouth to say, "Yes. It's just a little burn."

His dark eyes stayed on her, demanding truth.

She blew out an exasperated sigh. "No. I'm not all right. I'm so scared I can hardly breathe. You?"

The left side of Hyun-Jin's mouth crooked up in a wry smile. "That about covers it." He helped her gather up the heated trays and herd them towards the command module.

Dr. Ronald Hadley of the British Atmospheric Data Centre mopped his forehead with a linen handkerchief.

Seated at a centuries-old oak table were two representatives from the Met Office, the Prime Minister, the Deputy Prime Minister, and five members of parliament.

An automated screen expanded from a concealed opening in the walnut paneling and displayed the wind chart drawn by Hadley's laptop. His hand trembled as he hit the key to advance to the next slide. He'd been asked to report on the implications for the United Kingdom of the recent nuclear detonations above India—and the news was not good.

"The data from our atmospheric satellites has been spotty since the event. We believe this is due to interference in the ionosphere. But as you can see here," he ran a shaky laser pointer over the wind lines, "the prevailing weather pattern in the summer is tropical-continental." Tiny arrows indicated that the wind blew from the south. "If the blast had occurred during any other time of year—"

"This is all quite fascinating, I'm sure," said the Deputy Prime Minister. "But what we need to know, what the people need to know, is whether they are in danger from radioactive fallout."

Hadley dabbed his forehead again and returned the handkerchief to his pocket. "Given the current estimates that three ten-megaton blasts were detonated at high altitudes over eastern India, with the prevailing winds from the southeast—the cloud could reach England in the next week."

The Prime Minister tapped her fingers together. A thick-waisted woman in a tweed suit, she looked like a younger and darker Margaret Thatcher. "Will there be a significant health hazard?"

Hadley had spent the previous four hours in consultation with nuclear physicists and health experts. He'd looked at pictures of the victims of Nagasaki and Hiroshima, enough to fuel his nightmares for weeks to come: burns, tumors, cancers, birth deformities.

He rubbed his throbbing temples. "Yes. There is significant danger, even this far from the conflict. We must act immediately to protect the water supply and food sources, and advise people to remain indoors."

* * *

After the meal, *Reliance* passed over Asia again. China was pockmarked with outages. Chengdu and Beijing were dark. Green auroras danced over the glowing embers of cities.

"It's the end of the world," Hyun-Jin breathed. His hands gripped the rim of the window, knuckles tight with more strain than was needed to hold his position. His face was so close to the window that his breath created puffs of fog in front of his mouth.

"Not yet," Anderson said. "The conflict could still be contained."

Hyun-Jin whirled on him, his normally congenial face twisted in fury. "People are *dead*. It was the end of the world for *them*. Would you be so calm if the bombs fell over Houston—over your father in Washington State?"

Anderson raised his hands palm out, in a placating gesture. "Take it easy, I just meant—"

Hyun-Jin muttered something inaudible, wiping his nose across his sleeve.

Claire floated up behind him and put her hand on his shoulder. "You've got family in Beijing, don't you?"

He nodded, eyes red, and continued to stare out the window for a long, long time.

Cole turned the lights in the command module down. "We've been up for thirty-six hours, we're all exhausted. Let's get some rest. The transfer vehicle will be here in eight hours and we'll need to be at our best to deal with it. Claire, you've got first watch." He pointed around the room. "Then Jo-Jo, me, Anderson, and Hyun-Jin."

Hyun-Jin unrolled his sleep sack and Velcroed it to the wall near the window. He zipped himself all the way in, closing it over his head. When he was done, it looked like he was sealed in a body bag.

Claire worked at a laptop, calculating the possible damage Earth-Side. All around her, the sleeping forms of the rest of the crew drifted and bobbed. She tried not to look at them. In weightlessness, their arms floated above their bodies in neutral position. They looked like corpses. Only the soft susurrations of their breathing let her know that she wasn't the only person aboard *Reliance* who was still alive.

The view of Earth through the window was no comfort.

Red smudges of fire glowed among the darkened cities. And the auroras of nuclear electrons, though pretty, were the harbingers of the bands of radiation threatening *Reliance* and all her crew.

Two uneasy hours later, Claire woke Jo-Jo to take over the watch. When the younger woman had crawled out of her sleep sack, rubbing her eyes, Claire started her preparations for sleep.

Claire didn't want to float around the module, and risk bumping into anything during the night, so she slipped her sleep sack under two of the elastic bands clipped to the wall near the hatch and settled in between a white nylon cargo bag filled with computer cables and a mesh sack that contained a cordless screwdriver and a multimeter.

Sleep was a long time coming. Adrenaline and worry about the spreading conflict kept her heart racing. Claire listened to the sounds in the module: Hyun-Jin's nose whistled, Anderson snorted and turned fitfully in his sack, Cole took deep regular breaths as he slumbered. Jo-Jo's fingers tapped lightly on the keys of a laptop. The sounds blended together into a background hum that lulled Claire to sleep.

Claire jerked awake, and thrashed against the restraints of the sleep sack before struggling free. She looked around, unsure of what had woken her. Jo-Jo drifted in a sleep sack near the ceiling, Anderson hunched in fetal position over the laptop station, and Hyun-Jin was still swaddled next to the port window.

It was 09:42 GMT, the middle of Cole's shift, but he was gone.

Claire jostled Jo-Jo awake. "Where's Cole?" she whispered.

Rubbing sleep from her eyes, Jo-Jo mumbled, "Don' know. Here a min' ago." She turned away from Claire. "Prob'ly in the head. No big."

Likely, Jo-Jo was right . . . but enough had gone wrong. And Cole had seemed off today, rubbing his shoulder and looking pale. What if something had happened to him?

Feeling foolish, Claire eased out of the hatch, careful not to wake Hyun-Jin as she floated past him, and into the tunnel that linked the command module to the rest of the station. Four tunnels branched off from the hub. Claire turned right, towards the living quarters. If Cole was indeed relieving himself, she'd feel foolish. But better that than miss an emergency.

The station was dark save for visibility strips along the access tunnels. That combined with the silence from inactive systems made Claire feel as if she were crawling through a tomb. They were on the dark side of Earth. When she passed by the window in the central hub of the living quarters, she saw white pinpoints of stars, thousands more than she'd ever seen back home. They looked like diamonds scattered carelessly across black velvet. Normally the sight filled her with hope and wonder; now their brilliance chilled her. She'd worked all her life for this view, and she'd trade it forever for the commonplace sight of her husband and child, streaked with mud from working in the garden.

She passed through the galley. Lights indicated that the freezer still maintained their meals and a timer glowed 00:00 on the microwave. But no Cole. Kicking off a wall, she propelled herself through the galley into the living quarters.

The toilet was empty. Claire pulled back the accordion privacy screen to be sure. Stainless steel fixtures gleamed at her. Empty.

A sound from one of the personal chambers. Claire pulled herself down a level, crawling over the ergometer and rowing machines.

Reliance had eight personal chambers. Each was the outside wedge of a cylinder and approximately the size of a walk-in closet. There were drawers for personal gear, hooks for sleep sacks, and a fold-down computer station.

Claire hovered outside Cole's chamber. The lights were off inside, but she heard a gurgling sound. Was he choking? She jerked back the privacy screen.

Cole convulsed in surprise. "What the—" He lost his orientation, and flailed wildly.

A bottle of Kristall vodka drifted across his small room, trailing a silver path of liquid through the air.

Claire watched it pass in horrified wonderment. Alcoholic beverages were prohibited on the station.

Cole snatched a plastic waste bag from a dispenser and lassoed most of the errant liquid. He used a shirt to absorb random drops. When this cleanup was done, he stowed the bag in a drawer with the now-empty bottle. He looked at Claire, then back at his hands. "It was left by a visiting cosmonaut. A good-luck gift."

Claire didn't know what to say. Cole's drinking brought to mind her Uncle Charlie, who drank himself to death before he was forty, stumbling around the house in his underwear, speaking in slurred non-sequitors. Emotions warred inside Claire: anger at Cole's weakness; fear that his decision-making abilities would be compromised; pity.

"It isn't easy for me," Cole said, without looking up, "keeping things together while everything's going to hell. I should have retired two years ago, when my pension vested. Marcy asked me to get out. I'm getting too old for this shit." Cole flexed his fingers. He looked up at Claire through hooded eyes. "Everyone's looking to me for the answers. And I don't have them." He pinned her with his stare. "I'm just as scared as the rest of you."

"I'm sure you are," Claire said quietly.

He covered his face in shame. "Are you going to tell the rest of the crew?" Cole asked.

Claire's eyes followed him to the drawer. "No." She looked up. "Not unless it becomes necessary."

"Cole!" Jo-Jo's voice was panicked. Dull clangs resounded down the corridor as she bounced off the tunnel walls in her haste.

"In here," Cole answered in a loud, steady voice. He latched the drawer that held the vodka and kicked off to intercept Jo-Jo.

Claire followed.

Hyun-Jin's eyes were white-rimmed with panic. "Come quick! The ATV is here."

Cole checked his watch. "Four hours early? Impossible."

"The proximity alarm went off. We've got visual confirmation."

"Shit." Cole kicked off towards the command module. Jo-Jo and Claire close on his heels.

All the lights were on in the command module. Anderson was at the laptop station, checking trajectories. Hyun-Jin hung above him, upside down and monitoring the ATV's approach on a screen that displayed input from external camera eight.

Cole slipped next to Anderson and tuned to the video

signal emanating from the ATV supply ship. An onboard camera should have been transmitting the view of the station's docking port.

On screen: fitful gray static.

"Damn." Cole rubbed his chest.

Claire looked out the window at the approaching ATV. It was a tiny dot, swelling swiftly into a cylindrical pebble with four solar-panel wings. It wobbled as it came at them, listing first to one side, then to the other, like a drunken water beetle.

Twelve tons of metal aimed at the station.

"It can't get a lock," Claire said, working hard to keep panic out of her voice. "Its automated docking system isn't working."

CHAPTER 4

Cole tapped the video monitor: still only fuzz. Breathing heavily, he said, "Anderson, you'll have to bring it in on manual."

"Sir, yes, sir." Anderson rotated sideways fifteen degrees, positioning himself in front of the laptop that controlled communications to the ATV. "Claire, video's out and I can't see out the window from here." Anderson unlocked the joystick that could control the ATV from *Reliance*. "You'll have to tell me what the ATV is doing."

The ship expanded in the window, like the ground rushing up to meet a skydiver whose chute had failed to open.

"It's coming in fast. Too fast." Claire fought to keep her voice calm.

Anderson pushed the thumb button that fired the braking thrusters.

The ATV did not slow.

"It's not responding," Claire said, her voice rising in volume. "There's too much radiation; it's interfering with the control signal."

The ATV filled the window now, blotting out the view of Earth.

Anderson jabbed the button repeatedly. "Come on. Come on."

Claire could see the rivets on the ATV. She hovered frozen, expecting to die, unable to look away. The braking thrusters sputtered, then came on full force, white-hot and blinding. Claire squinted to see through the glare. Miraculously, the supply ship slowed. Then paused. Then began to dwindle. "You got it!" she shouted. "It's reversed course."

"Hoo-yah!" Anderson crowed.

Claire murmured course corrections, "Port three degrees. Gently forward."

The ATV bobbed sideways then eased forward.

"Too much, reverse," Claire said in a rush, her pulse racing. "Okay. Down ten degrees. Good. Ease it forward."

His hands flew like a teenager playing a video game. Using the thrusters he rocked the ATV back and forth, inching it towards the docking port.

"Acquire," urged Claire.

Anderson pushed the button that would capture the progress. The clamp sounded throughout the station. "Got the bastard." He grinned, bringing out a devilish dimple in his cheek. "Can I fly, or can I fly?"

Claire sagged in midair.

"Good work." Cole gripped Anderson's shoulder, panting as if he'd run a race. "Nice teamwork."

The adrenaline faded from Claire's body. She was exhausted. But it had been worth it. The ship that, only seconds ago, had threatened *Reliance* was now its only hope of survival.

Cole pushed off from the pilot's leg restraints, and caught the rim of the hatch to slow his motion. "I'll be in the air lock, prebreathing. See you outside in half an hour."

Claire whipped around. "That's not long enough, even for the accelerated protocol. You're risking the bends."

Cole nodded towards the dosimeter. "We're at 213 mSv total dose and it's only going to get hotter out there. The sooner I get the job over with, the better."

Claire chewed her bottom lip. She should be doing the EVA. Everyone on *Reliance* knew it. Cole was older and less qualified. Hating herself for her cowardice—and for making the offer—she asked quietly, "John, do you want me to do the EVA?"

Cole met her eyes and held them for a long moment. "No. But . . ." He swallowed. "If anything . . . I've left a message on my palmtop for Marcy."

"You should have someone out there with you as backup," Hyun-Jin said, exchanging a glance with Claire.

Another long pause. "No. Better to only risk one of us."

"Nothing's going to go wrong," Anderson said in a false-hearty tone. "Cole won't let it."

Claire wondered how much of the vodka Cole had imbibed before she found him. She pushed off from the window, did a somersault in midair to change course, and grabbed Cole's elbow.

He was sweating.

"You sure you're up to this?" Maintaining her grip, she looked deep into his eyes. Was he drunk? "If you don't feel well . . ." Her heart pounded, afraid he would take her up on the offer she was about to make—

Cole pulled free of her grasp and pushed his legs through the hatch. "I'm fine. Don't put me out to pasture yet." He rotated to face her. "Just stay on the com and walk me through the procedure. I've been an astronaut for eighteen years, I know how to get the job done."

Claire felt the reproof in his last words. She, Hyun-Jin, and Jo-Jo were new-generation astronauts, the ones who were fast-tracked through training using the latest VR simulators. She knew the old-timers considered them "virtual" astronauts, without a full appreciation for the hard work and dangers involved in space travel. Claire grabbed the rim of the hatch. "You'll need help with the equipment."

"All right." Cole kicked off down the access tunnel towards the service module that housed the equipment and crew locks.

In the equipment lock, Cole removed an oxygen mask from a drawer and began the prebreathing protocol to drive nitrogen out of his blood. He pumped his arms and legs against the resistance of a fold-out ergometer to hasten the process.

While he exercised, Claire reconfigured Hyun-Jin's suit to fit Cole. She dismembered it at the seals and stored the shorter arms and legs. Then she pulled out a longer set and attached them to a frame mounted on the wall of the air lock. It would hold the pieces of the EVA suit until Cole was ready to suit up. Then Claire refilled the oxygen tanks, replaced the half-eaten fruit bar in the helmet, and topped off the water. Claire grabbed the other EVA equipment Cole would need for the walk: a TIG welder, reaction wrenches, and round clamps.

While she waited for Cole to finish, she ran through the maintenance procedures on her suit that she'd neglected during her rapid entry from the last EVA.

Cole climbed off the ergometer, his skin beaded with sweat. He panted into the oxygen mask.

He pulled out a fresh maximum absorption garment from a supply drawer.

Claire turned her back and busied herself rubbing the inside of his helmet with anti-fog compound. When she turned back, he was naked except for the oversized diaper. His gray chest hair and skinny legs made it doubly ridiculous: an old man dressed as Baby Time for a New Year's party. Under other circumstances, she might have laughed; now it just made her sad.

Cole pushed past her into the air lock. There he pulled on the tight-fitting liquid cooling and ventilation garment. The white spandex and nylon suit fit like long underwear and was ribbed with thin tubes that circulated water over the astronaut's body during the space walk, venting off excess heat.

While Cole squirmed into the LCVG, Claire attached the electrical harness to the hard upper torso of the EVA suit. The harness would monitor Cole's vital signs during the space walk, as well as provide radio communications to the station. It lined the inside of the torso, a vest-shaped fiberglass shell that reminded Claire of a medieval steel breastplate. Whenever Claire EVA'd, she felt as if she were preparing to do battle with the vacuum of space.

Cole zipped up the front of the cooling garment. Floating near his hip were the silicone tube ports that attached to the inside of the manned maneuvering unit.

Claire grabbed the display and control module, intending to attach it to the MMU jet pack for him.

Cole grabbed her wrist. "That's enough. I need to close off the crew lock to continue depressurization."

She looked at the array of gear, felt a knot in her stomach. "Are you sure . . . we both know it should be me—"

Cole rotated the neck seal to lock it. "Times like this teach a person what's important. You want to go home healthy. I want to save *Reliance* and the solar reflector."

Her throat choked with guilt and grief. "I just . . ."

"Logan"—Cole's tone was authoritative—"You made your decision, live with it. I've got work to do." He crawled through the hatch connecting the equipment lock to the crew lock, and sealed it behind him.

Angry at her cowardice, Claire kicked hard against the handholds of the access tunnel and shot through them at breakneck speed. She reached the command module in time to hear Cole announce over the ship's intercom: "I'm in position."

"Lowering pressure to 10.2 psi," replied Anderson as he typed in the command.

No one met Claire's eyes as she settled behind the work-station next to Anderson. Claire Velcroed her palmtop containing the EVA plan next to the laptop's display of Cole's vital signs.

"I've got the suit on," Cole called from the air lock. "Testing for leaks." A minute later. "Looks good. Go ahead and finish depressurization."

Anderson typed in the command to evacuate the air lock. "Depressurization, check."

When the pressure had dropped, Cole reported: "All systems go, I'm heading out."

Claire looked at the bioinstrumentation readouts. Cole's heart rate was already at ninety beats per minute, up from his usual sixty-two, and he hadn't yet started the hard work of manipulating an inflated space suit.

The external camera picked up Cole's white figure and displayed it on a monitor halfway between Claire and Anderson.

"Pressure steady," Cole reported. "I'm heading over to the ATV."

Hank was back in Mission Control. The ground crew was prepping the shuttle for flight in twelve hours. Finally things were starting to come together. Hank popped two TUMS in his mouth to quell the heartburn that had been plaguing him all day.

Amanda sipped a cup of steaming liquid only a few

shades darker than her skin. She grimaced. "Decaf. I had to pick this week to give up caffeine."

Hank's phone rang. He scooped the headset up and settled it over his ears. "Hank Rubin."

"This is Grant Williamson's office, at the Pentagon. The president has initiated protocol Hailstorm. Your call-up code is Echo-Bravo-Niner-Four-Two. A car will pick you up in half an hour to take you to the airport."

A chill crawled up Hank's spine. Protocol Hailstorm was evacuation to an underground emergency operations center. "Is this for real?"

"The Pentagon doesn't make jokes," said Williamson's secretary. "Be ready to leave when the car arrives."

Hank swallowed. He'd been given the call-up code six years ago, shortly after he became ground controls head manager. In the event of a nuclear war, the President and a cadre of handpicked scientists and advisors would relocate to the underground bunker in the mountains of Virginia. The implications made his blood run cold.

Amanda looked at him, her brow furrowed. "Who was that? What's happened?"

Hank shook his head. "Just more Pentagon stupidity." Silently, he thought: The kind that can get us all killed.

Hovering above the laptop station in the command module, Claire's skin itched thinking about how vulnerable Cole was, spacewalking without a partner. It was a massive breach of NASA protocol. Any of a thousand things could go wrong: His suit could rupture, he could be trapped under a massive fuel tank, the tether holding him to the station could break. If anything went wrong, they were helpless; help was more than a half hour away. She looked over at Hyun-Jin. The skin between his eyes puckered with worry. Claire guessed his gut burned with the same guilt.

Cole narrated his movements as he worked, giving them audio as well as visual confirmation of his actions. "Opening the external hatch."

The ground technicians' plan was straightforward. The ATV supply ship was filled with fuel, both in its fueling tanks and in the modified dry-cargo area. There had been no time to design an internal feed from the dry-cargo bay into the main fuel tanks. Any changes to the pressurized tanks would need extensive testing, to make sure there were no leaks that would cause the vehicle to explode on the launching pad.

Because the fuel tanks in the dry-cargo area were not piped into the main tanks, when the ship docked to the station, Cole would route a fuel line from the tanks in the dry cargo, along the outside of the ATV's hull, to its main engine fuel intake.

Then a radiation-hardened controller NASA had hastily installed would automatically fire the engine for the first burn of the Hohmann transfer—the least-energy path to transfer *Reliance* to a higher orbit. Later a second burn would settle *Reliance* into an orbit matching the Mars fuel platform. What had Claire holding her breath was the crawl through the dry-cargo area. Cole would have only three inches of clearance for his EVA suit and could easily get trapped.

"Open . . . for . . . hatch . . ." Cole's voice broke up over the suit-to-ship radio.

Anderson, at the radio workstation below Claire, pressed the earpiece into his ear. "Cole, *Reliance.* Can you repeat that last, you're breaking up."

". . . Cole. Can't . . . copy . . . peat?"

Claire looked out the window. They were over Africa and pockmarked China loomed on the horizon. "The radiation levels are climbing. It's affecting his EVA suit's electronics."

Anderson brushed his palm across his brow. "That's not good." He pressed the com. "*Reliance,* Cole. Do you copy?"

"Cole . . . ty . . . repeat?"

He pulled the headset off. "Shit. He can't hear me."

On the bioinstrumentation readouts, Cole's heart rate had climbed to 110. On the video monitor, Cole tapped his helmet over the radio receiver and shook his head. He pointed towards the ATV where fuel hoses billowed half out of the round external hatch.

"He's continuing the mission," Claire said.

"Why not?" said Anderson, cradling his forehead in his palms. "There's nothing we can do to help him from inside the station."

"Someone should be out there with him," Hyun-Jin said.

Claire's head throbbed with tension. She turned on Hyun-Jin. "You volunteering?"

Hyun-Jin's mouth closed with a snap and his eyes wrinkled in pain.

"Don't give him shit," Jo-Jo shouted, pointing her finger at Claire's chest. "I didn't see you pushing to the front of the line."

Claire opened her mouth to respond—

"Something's wrong," Anderson said, his voice tense. He hunched over the monitor.

Claire checked Cole's stats. Heart rate was one-eighty and climbing.

On the monitor, Cole pounded at the manned maneuvering unit on his back. His left hand clung to the fuel hose he'd taken out of the hatch. The jets on his manned-maneuvering unit fired, and Cole drifted farther away from the ATV supply ship.

"What's he doing?" Anderson asked.

Over the com came a garbled shouting. ". . . fire . . . won't . . . de . . . tivate."

Claire's breath caught as she translated: "The jets on his MMU won't shut down."

Cole hit the end of his tether and bounced with a bone-jarring jerk. It sent him into a tumble. With one hand still clutching the fuel line, it looked like he wrestled with a white anaconda. Its coils spilled out of the hatchway and sprawled across space, writhing and springing in response to Cole's movements.

Cole's heart rate was 220, and his blood pressure was 140/90 mmHg. Respiration was thirty breaths a minute.

"Tell him to disconnect the MMU!" Claire shouted at Anderson. It was a new safety feature on the MMUs. Not available on the older suits that Cole had trained on.

"Cole. You're going to be okay," Anderson transmitted. "There's a procedure to disconnect the MMU in-flight."

On screen, Cole gave no response that he had received the transmission. At the end of his tether, he whipped back and forth like a rat in a terrier's mouth.

"Damn. That tether can't take much more." Claire kicked off from the wall towards the hatch. "Hyun-Jin, keep transmitting the step-by-step protocol for emergency removal of the MMU."

Anderson's head whipped around to follow her. "What are you going to do?"

"What I should have done in the first place. I'm going out there."

"But you can't—"

Claire didn't wait for him to finish the sentence. She thrashed her way down the access tunnel, kicking and grabbing at handholds, cargo bags, anything she could use for leverage. There wasn't time to be terrified. If she was going to save Cole, she had to act now. In the equipment lock, she scooped up the oxygen mask Cole had used and hyperventilated into it while she dressed. There was no time to stow the pieces of the suit in the wall-mounted harness, so they floated in midair, a three-dimensional puzzle that she assembled on the fly.

Over the station's intercom, Anderson said, "Stop. There isn't time for the prebreathing protocol."

Claire couldn't waste precious seconds answering him. She tugged on the cooling garment and slapped the electrical harness into the EVA suit's upper torso. Then dragging the components of the suit into the crew locker with her, Claire closed the round hatch that linked the crew lock to the air lock.

She continued to pant into the oxygen mask. Lifting it for a second, she pressed the button on the intercom and shouted: "Lower pressure to 10.2 psi."

"It's too dangerous."

"Goddamn it, Anderson, Cole's gonna die!"

There was a pause. Then Anderson answered. "Lowering air lock pressure."

In the background, Hyun-Jin said, "You can't let her. She's risking decompression sickness. The only thing worse than one incapacitated astronaut, is *two*."

Her ears popped as the pressure in the crew lock dropped. Claire silently thanked Anderson for ignoring Hyun-Jin's protests.

She squirmed into the hard breastplate and attached the arm and leg components. It was awkward, working around the oxygen tank, but she wanted to give her body as much chance as possible to expel nitrogen. In her mind, she was back on Earth in the EVA training session. Dr. Banning stood before a whiteboard describing the symptoms of the bends: localized pain, dizziness, paralysis, shortness of breath, and—in serious cases—unconsciousness.

When the EVA suit was complete, Claire pulled off the oxygen mask and jammed on the helmet. With one swift motion, she sealed its locks. Her head pounded. Just stress, she told herself.

She pressurized the suit one psi above air lock pressure to check the seals. "Testing suit integrity. How's Cole doing?"

"Still can't get through to him. Hyun-Jin's trying, but we can't get a clear signal. Pulse and heart rate are maxed. Shit!"

Feeling blind because she couldn't see the screen, Claire shouted, "What is it? What's going on?"

"His tether broke." Anderson's voice was dead calm. The voice of a fighter pilot deciding whether to pull the eject lever. "He's holding onto the fuel line. But it won't last long."

Claire's eyes flicked to the suit readout. She clipped her tether into the ring next to the air lock door. "Suit pressure is good. Blow the hatch, I need to get out there *now*."

A half-second pause. "You sure, Logan?"

"Yes I'm sure! Blow the damned hatch!"

In the control module, Anderson keyed the emergency code for immediate evacuation of the air lock. Claire exploded outward with the expanding air. She saw the flash point of fog Anderson had mentioned during the rapid decompression of the lifeboat.

Then she hit the end of the tether—hard. Claire's teeth snapped together and intensified her headache. When the sparks cleared from her eyes, she scanned for Cole. He was easy to spot against the blackness of space, a white dot on the end of an unrolling fuel line.

Claire unclipped the tether, unfolded the joystick on her right arm, and used it to jet after Cole, full power. With her tongue she activated the external radio signal. "Cole, this is Claire. Can you hear me?"

No reply.

"Cole. If you can hear me, hang on. I'm coming to intercept." Her head swam with nausea, and she blinked to clear tears. There was no time for this. She had to reach Cole before the fuel line snapped and he was lost forever.

The distance between them shortened: twenty meters, fifteen meters, ten.

Cole's suit fired erratically, bobbing him left, then swinging him right. His legs were tangled in the fuel line. He jerked and spun like a fish caught in a net. Claire altered course to follow him: ten meters, nine. From here she could see his faceplate was fogged with exertion.

Cole's suit reversed direction towards the station. He passed over the Canadarm, snagging the fuel line under its elbow joint. It caught. Cole ran out of slack and hit the end of the line with a whiplash snap. His grip failed. Cole floated free in space—with no tether and a malfunctioning EVA suit.

"Shit." Claire poured on the acceleration and tongued the radio again. "Cole? Can you hear me?"

Anderson's worried voice broke in, ". . .'s . . . hap . . . all . . . ?"

There was no time to explain. Claire glanced back. She'd come this far. No matter what, she was going to save Cole.

Her sphincter clenched when she looked back and saw the station dwindling behind her. No umbilical cord attached her to its safety. She tried to mentally calculate how far she could chase Cole and still have enough fuel to bring them back to the station with the doubled mass of two suits.

Cole's suit jinked left, and Claire changed course again to intercept him. Cole was only six meters away, five, four. Claire could almost reach out and touch him, he was so close.

His suit fired again, driving Cole into her. Their suits collided with a sickening smack, and sent them into a wild tumble. The Earth and *Reliance* flashed through Claire's vision in parallel stripes of blue-green and silver as she spun end over end. Claire scrambled to grab hold of Cole. If she lost him now . . .

Cole's suit bucked like a bronco beneath her. It took all her upper-arm strength to grip his leg. She released the joystick that controlled her suit, shutting off her jets. Then, closing her eyes to blot out the disorienting blur of rotating space, she ran her hands up Cole's body to the controller box for his jet propulsion system. Her gloved fingers fumbled against the catch that locked it onto the space suit.

She prodded and probed. "Come on, goddamnit. I am *not* going to die out here."

There. Her fingers found purchase and she popped the controller free, deactivating it. The small metal box dangled from his suit like a cancerous skin tag.

Claire grabbed the end of Cole's tether and tied it into the clip, securing them tightly together with two sets of square knots. They were literally joined at the hip. She grabbed the joystick and fired quick bursts to stop their rotation.

It was all she could do not to throw up. Claire swallowed bile. The Earth and *Reliance* slowed in her vision, resolving back into round planet and elongated station, the latter too far away for comfort.

Claire angled toward the station and fired her jets full throttle. With one eye on *Reliance*, she glanced to her left to check on Cole.

She pushed up the gold visor so she could see his face. Beads of moisture jiggled on the inside of the faceplate. Through the clear spaces left in their tracks, his skin was almost as pale as the surgical whiteness of his space suit.

Claire checked her progress toward *Reliance*, then bent her head to touch helmets with Cole. "Cole!" she shouted. "Cole, can you hear me?"

The proximity of their helmets made sound transmission possible, but either there wasn't enough contact area for Cole to hear her, or he was unable to respond.

"This is Claire. I'm taking you back to the station. Just hold on."

Reliance loomed comfortingly larger. Claire adjusted the angle of her approach to match the station's path in orbit. She tongued the radio. "*Reliance*, EVA2. I've got Cole. I'm bringing him in. Meet me in the air lock with the medical kit."

She didn't know whether they received her message. Claire tried not to think about the radiation she and Cole were being subjected to. It was too late to worry about that now.

Claire jinked left to avoid the coils of fuel line that burst from the ATV supply ship like so many spilled intestines.

Claire loosened the slack on the tether joining them and crawled in through the hatch. Once inside, she clipped her retractable tether to the air lock u-bar and began to pull Cole in. Claire panted as she tugged his unresisting body. His mobility pack caught on the hatch, and she removed it and stowed it in the wall harness. Then she squirmed and tugged, bracing her feet against the side of the hatch to bring Cole through. She was sweating by the time she got him inside and sealed the hatch.

With both of them in the air lock in full EVA suits and Cole sprawling unconscious, it was claustrophobically close. Cole's chest wedged her hips against the wall and his arms were in her face. Claire could barely move.

"I'm in," Claire called over the radio. Then she checked pressure in the air lock. It was rising. When it hit 4.2 psi, she jerked off her helmet and gulped station air. The nausea and sharp chest pains that hit her outside began to ebb.

She pulled off her gloves and slid open the neck seal on Cole's helmet and carefully lifted it off his head.

Outside the air lock door, she heard thumps as someone ricocheted down the access tunnel.

Cole's lids fluttered as if he were in REM sleep. When the humid station air hit his skin, he convulsed. Cole's back arched, throwing Claire against the wall harness and causing one of its clamps to stab painfully into her kidneys.

"Cole! Can you hear me?" Claire clung to his arm as he jittered and spasmed. His blue eyes were wide with fear and shock. Claire shouted, "You're inside the station. We're going to take care of you." She turned her head towards the hatch that led to the equipment lock. "Anderson, I need that medical kit. Now!"

The psi inside the air lock was 13.8, almost station normal.

"Stand back!" Anderson shouted, his voice muffled by the layers of steel and glass. He popped the hatch and it slammed open, propelled by the higher pressure in the station. Claire and Cole lurched through the opening.

"What can I do?" Anderson asked.

Cole gave a groan that emanated from deep in his belly and went limp.

Claire pressed her fingers to the pulse point in his neck. "His heart's stopped." She glared at the inadequate palm-sized kit Anderson had brought with him. "We need the defibrillator—now!"

Half a missing heartbeat. Anderson's voice was somber. "It's in the lifeboat."

The lifeboat. That couldn't be reached from the station because the hull had ruptured. The lifeboat. That couldn't be reached from EVA because there was no time to depressurize and no time to cut the hole in its hull open large enough for a person to crawl inside.

"Manual compressions." Claire yanked off the arms of Cole's EVA suit and tugged at the hard upper-torso shell. With Anderson's help she got it over Cole's head. During training, they'd discussed how to do CPR in space, but she had never expected to use it. Anderson wrapped his legs around Cole's waist and pressed his fist against the point just above Cole's sternum. It looked like he was awkwardly performing the Heimlich. One jerk, two, three.

Claire grabbed Cole's head and gave two quick breaths.

Jo-Jo popped her head through the hatch. "Oh, my God. Is he—"

"Take over the breathing," Claire ordered. "I need to get out of this suit."

"But I-I-" Jo-Jo looked back and forth between Claire and Anderson.

"Do it!" Claire demanded.

Jo-Jo slipped between Claire and Cole. She pinched off Cole's nose and began breathing, two breaths for every fifteen of Anderson's chest compressions.

In the equipment lock, Claire took a deep breath to center herself.

Hyun-Jin hovered near the hatch to the access tunnels, his eyes wide with fear. Wordlessly, he helped her doff the EVA suit. Claire wracked her brain as they worked. Surely there must be a spare defibrillator on the station, tucked into one of the drawers they hadn't opened since the station was built. There was so much equipment stashed in every available cranny, surely there was something they could use.

When she'd untangled herself from the pieces of her EVA, Claire poked her head through the opening to the air lock. Anderson was red-faced and veins stood out on his forehead. Manual CPR on earth was exhausting, where the rescuer used the weight of their body to compress the chest. Here all the work was done by Anderson's straining biceps.

"We need to move him to the equipment lock," Hyun-Jin said, "Where there's more room."

Anderson gave an infinitesimal nod, and Jo-Jo let go and pushed Cole's head towards the hatch.

Claire and Hyun-Jin pulled Cole through, and Hyun-Jin took up the compressions where Anderson had left off. Jo-Jo continued breathing.

Between Jo-Jo's breaths, Claire reached up and touched Cole's neck.

"Anything?" Anderson asked, his voice full of dread and hope.

Claire held her breath, every ounce of attention straining to feel a pulse. After ten seconds she looked up. "No."

They tried for another twenty minutes, switching off roles as each became exhausted.

"It's no use," Claire said finally. "He's gone."

Jo-Jo and Hyun-Jin looked to Anderson.

Anderson bit his lip. His expression was angry . . . and defeated.

They backed away from the body, panting, sweating, faces set in masks of grief and despair.

Station Commander John Cole was dead.

CHAPTER 5

"I can't believe he's gone," said Anderson. He slumped in midair, hands drifting before him in a body neutral position.

Claire looked at the husk that had been her commander. His body was still warm, but something ineffable was missing. What had been a vital living human was now so much meat.

Tears bubbled and floated free from Jo-Jo's eyes, silver spheres that drifted across the crew lock. Claire thought someone should catch them, soak them up before they shorted out an electrical system. But she couldn't bring herself to move just yet.

Hyun-Jin put his arm around Jo-Jo.

She wiped her nose. "Wha-what do we do now?"

"We follow protocol," replied Anderson. "Store his body in the air lock for transport back to Earth."

If there *was* a shuttle coming for them, thought Claire. They hadn't heard anything from NASA since the satellites went down.

Claire said, "We should strip him of the EVA suit and cooling garment . . ." She kicked off towards Cole's body.

Anderson grabbed Claire's wrist and they precessed around their shared center of gravity. "Nobody's touching him."

Claire turned to face Anderson. "What?"

Anderson's pulled her close until they were nose-to-nose. "Not until this has been investigated."

She couldn't believe what she was hearing. "Investigated?" She pointed at the air lock door. "There's a nuclear war Earth-side. None of us may get home alive, and you're worried about an *investigation*?"

Anderson squeezed her wrist until the bones ached. "You were the last person with Cole. You helped him prep his equipment. What if you made a mistake?"

Claire whispered. "Are you saying Cole's death was my fault?"

"Of course he isn't," said Hyun-Jin, looking from Anderson to Claire.

But Anderson's grip was relentless and the look in his eyes steely.

Claire pressed her foot against Anderson's chest and pried them apart. "I went outside. I risked my life trying to *save* Cole."

"Guilty conscience? You were the most qualified to spacewalk. *You* should have done the EVA in the first place," insisted Anderson. "If you'd gone out—in *your* suit—Cole would still be alive."

"Stop it!" shrieked Jo-Jo. Her ponytail had come undone, and multicolored tentacles of hair wavered around her red-blotched face. "Cole's dead. What matters now is: How are *we* going to stay alive?"

Claire licked her lips. "First, we undress Cole. That's a ten-million-dollar EVA suit, not a body bag. We store him in the air lock. Then we get back to the shielded control module. Try to contact NASA, find out if the shuttle launched."

"We're not stripping Cole," Anderson persisted.

Claire fixed Anderson with a look she'd used on Owen when he wouldn't eat his beets. "Do I need to remind you, Captain Robert Anderson, that *Reliance* is a civilian vessel, and as lead Mission Specialist, I am second in line after Cole. *Reliance* is now my command." She stared at Anderson until he blinked. Then she turned her gaze on Hyun-Jin and Jo-Jo.

Hyun-Jin gave a nearly imperceptible nod.

Jo-Jo rubbed her puffy eyes. She didn't seem to care.

Anderson's mouth worked. "This is a military situation, it needs a military leader."

Claire felt hollow. She'd almost died, had lost her friend and commander, and now this. But she couldn't show weakness. Her private talk with Cole the night before had shown her what the crew needed from a leader: resolve. She silently forgave Cole his drinking. Steeling her voice, she said, "As a military man, I expect you to honor the chain of command."

Anderson balled his hands into fists. "I don't want him stripped naked in the air lock, wearing only that damned diaper. Cole deserves better than that."

Claire felt her eyebrows rise. Was that what this was about: Cole's dignity? Or was Anderson asking for a concession to save face? "Of course not," she said. "We'll dress him in a flight suit. Hyun-Jin, will you help Anderson take care of Cole?"

Hyun-Jin nodded.

Jo-Jo pushed past Anderson, swiping at her eyes, and said, "I'll try to contact Houston."

Claire followed Jo-Jo to the command module. It was her way of letting Anderson know she trusted him to carry out her orders. She listened to the recordings of their conversations with Mission Control Houston to familiarize herself with the details of the planned shuttle launch.

Jo-Jo repeatedly hailed an unresponsive Earth.

Ten minutes later, Hyun-Jin and Anderson entered the command module. Anderson's eyes were red-rimmed and his face was stony. "It's done."

Claire nodded and pinched the bridge of her nose. "No word from Houston."

At the radio, Jo-Jo jerked off her headset. "This is impossible. Nothing's getting through."

"Keep trying," Claire urged. "In the meantime, we need to calculate when we think the shuttle launched and predict a flight path. We need to verify the launch, even if we have to do it by looking out the window."

Hyun-Jin's eyes widened. "They wouldn't cancel the rescue mission. Would they?"

Mike Marshant stomped into Mission Control, his flight suit unzipped. Alice followed in his wake, eyes wide with worry.

"What the hell are you doing here?" demanded Hank. "You should be preparing for takeoff."

Mike's jaw clenched and unclenched. "They canceled the rescue mission. The ground crew's been told to go home."

"What the hell?" Hank picked up the phone. He jammed the button for the Ground Manager. "This is Hank. Tell your crew to stay put." Hank took a deep breath around the tightness in his chest. "The launch is going to happen." He listened a moment. "I don't care what Cas said. It's a misunderstanding. I'll straighten it out. We've got astronauts in jeopardy, and I promise you we're not just going to leave them up there."

Hank's phone rang. He picked it up and snapped, "What?"

"Uh, this is Allen, at the front desk. There's a driver down here from the Pentagon, he says he's here to take you to the airport."

"Not now." Hank combed his fingers through his thinning hair. "Tell him to wait."

Cas and four NASA directors stalked into Mission Control. "Stop the countdown clock," Cas announced. "The launch is scrubbed. We're going to wait until conditions are safe—"

"What is this bullshit?" Hank demanded. "We already decided to go through with it." His voice rose. "Mike and Alice are committed. The ground crew worked through round the clock. Everything's a go."

Cas said, "Emotions were high in the meeting. After the dust settled, we realized that a launch is not in NASA's best interest."

At Hank's side, Mike tensed. "What about the best interest of Cole and his crew?"

Hank's phone rang, an insistent jangle. He jammed his finger at Cas's chest. "What's not in NASA's best interest is for me to send a memo to the President and every congressman on how you five decided to let astronauts die in orbit, without even *attempting* to save them."

Amanda leaned over and hooked Hank's phone with one well-manicured nail. She put it to her ear.

"Do you want to be the focus of Woodward's next book?" Hank continued. He glanced down at Amanda.

She cupped her hand over the receiver and whispered, "It's your driver. He can't wait. He's got other people to pick up."

For a split instant Hank considered going. Considered walking out of Mission Control, flying to Virginia, and leaving Cas and her gang to make whatever mess of NASA they wanted. A tiny bottle of scotch would do much to soothe his nerves at thirty thousand feet.

But Hank's mother didn't raise him to back down from a fight. He snatched the phone from Amanda. "Go on without me," he said, then hung up the line. He pulled out his cell phone, and cursed when there was no service.

Using his landline phone, he dialed from memory the number of Bob Legaurre, the chair of the NASA Missions Operations Directorate. "This is Hank Rubin at NASA Mission Control. I'd like to talk to you about a situation we have here."

Legaurre said, in smooth, cultured tones, "Can you make it quick? I'm about to leave the office."

Hank imagined a Pentagon driver, identical to the one who'd come for him, waiting on Legaurre. For a split instant, he wondered what he'd given up by not going. Into the phone he said, "I understand, sir."

Claire surveyed her crewmates. Josephine worked the radio, trying to establish communications through UHF or VHF. Anderson grimly recorded Cole's time of death in the crew log. Hyun-Jin drifted near the window, watching for a launch. He kept mumbling: "They wouldn't abort the rescue mission."

Claire shook her head. It was the first rule of rescue: Don't contribute more victims to a hopeless situation. Hyun-Jin knew that as well as she did. If he chose to ignore it, that was his problem. "We need to be prepared for all contingencies."

"What about the EVA?" asked Anderson when he'd closed the log file.

Claire cocked an eyebrow at him. "What about it?"

"Cole didn't finish his mission. Without the fuel in the dry dock, *Reliance* won't make it to the rendezvous point."

"Cole just *died*. I'm going to make sure no one else does. No EVA. The shuttle will have to change course and pick us up here."

"If that's even possible at this point," said Anderson. "You'd just let the solar reflector project die? Let *Reliance* burn up in the atmosphere? Without the boost to mid-Earth orbit, she'll only survive in orbit a couple of months. If she goes down, there's no telling when—or if—NASA will get together the funds to build another like her. Congress is already saying we should shut her down and hire zero-gee research time from the Brazilians." He cocked his head belligerently. "Are you up here to sightsee or are you an astronaut?"

Hyun-Jin clung to the wall of drawers to the left of the hatch, staying out of the argument.

Claire poked her finger against Anderson's chest, pushing them slowly apart. "I *know* the ESR is important—I've spent the last three years of my life preparing for this launch. But I'm commander of this station now, and it's my responsibility to get the crew home safely. And that includes you—if I have to duct-tape your hands and feet together to do it. Do you understand?"

Anderson caught her forearm and they revolved around each other like partners in a square dance. "I don't need you to babysit me," he sneered. "I can make my own decisions. If you're too scared to EVA and finish what Cole started, don't go. *I'll* take your suit out."

Claire completed the forearm grip and pulled Anderson close until they were nose to nose. "No one—no one—goes outside. That's a direct order, Anderson. You understand?"

Anderson's face darkened. "No, you—"

"I got something!" Jo-Jo shrieked. "A radio signal." She fumbled the headset around her head and spoke into the microphone. "This is Space Station *Reliance*. Please repeat your message."

Claire dropped her grip on Anderson and grabbed a

handhold next to where Jo-Jo worked the radio. "Is it Houston?"

Anderson and Hyun-Jin crowded around behind, hanging off straps on the walls.

Jo-Jo listened, adjusted the frequency dial up and down. "I don't think so." She pressed the speaker button and it spewed a stream of agitated voices speaking something that sounded like a cross between French and Spanish. "*Estação de Espaço do Alliance. Está qualquer um lá? Nós estamos sendo atacados. Ajude-nos por favor. A estação—*"

"It must be the Brazilian space station," Claire said. She pointed at the transmit button. "Ask if they can switch to English."

Jo-Jo held the microphone closer to her mouth. She spoke slowly and distinctly. "*EEA*, this is *Reliance*. Do you hear us? Please respond in English."

The voice rose in pitch. "*Ajude-nos por favor! Nós pensamos que nos ajudariam mas . . .*" There was the sound of tearing metal, screams. The voice whispered hoarsely, "*Não confíe—*"

Claire's fingers dug into her palms. "What the hell's going on over there?"

"*EEA, Reliance.* Please respond." Jo-Jo urged. "*EEA, Reliance.* Please respond."

Everyone on *Reliance* held their breath. There was no answer.

Jo-Jo repeated the hail. Nothing.

From over Claire's shoulder, Anderson said: "It was the goddamned Chinese. They shot the Brazilians down with an ICBM."

"You don't know that," Hyun-Jin protested.

"It stands to reason. The Chinese started this war. If they take out the other stations—like *Reliance*—they'll have space superiority." Anderson narrowed his eyes at Claire. "Like I said, a military situation requires a military leader. If you don't start thinking 'war,' we'll all be casualties."

Claire tapped on her palmtop, bringing up the registry of objects in low-Earth orbit. "What we can't afford to do is jump to conclusions." She held up her computer for all to see. "The *EEA* was just over Canada." She cocked her head and looked at Anderson. "Unless you're suggesting the Canadians are collaborating with China? Or maybe you think China has missiles that can hit low-Earth orbit from halfway around the world?''

Anderson took the palmtop from Claire and studied the positioning chart. ''Then what the hell just happened?''

''I don't know,'' answered Claire. ''That's my point. We can't afford to make assumptions. Or whatever it was might happen to us.''

Anderson's eyes widened for a millisecond, and in that instant Claire saw what underlay his anger and bluster. He'd almost died in the decompression of the lifeboat, had seen his commander killed performing an EVA. Anderson was afraid.

Claire felt sorry for him. Anderson believed that if he were in command, he'd know what to do, be less fearful. But he was wrong. Being in charge would only add the fear of making the wrong choices. And they couldn't afford a leader who'd make decisions out of a need to prove to everyone and himself that he wasn't scared. The best thing she could do for Anderson, for them all, was be a strong leader.

''Anderson, estimate possible interception scenarios for the shuttle based on our last-known launch data and subsequent weather conditions. Jo-Jo, keep trying to establish radio contact, with Earth, the other stations, anyone who will listen. Hyun-Jin, I want you to make a survey of the food supplies on board and estimate how long we can go without resupply.''

Everyone stared.

Claire felt her face heat. ''In case the shuttle's change of course causes our rescue to be delayed.''

''Delayed,'' Anderson said. The word was a death knell.

Amanda looked up from her terminal. ''Just got a call from the Brazilian government. They've lost contact with their space station and want to know if we've heard anything.''

''You got a line to *Reliance*?'' Hank asked.

''Not yet. I'll keep trying. But I don't think anything can punch through the radiation polluting the upper atmosphere.'' She tapped keys. ''We don't even have telemetry at the moment.'' Amanda glanced at the count-down clock. It read 06:22. In an aside, she asked, ''Are you sure we're doing the right thing? We don't even know if there's anyone up there to save. With electronic systems going down everywhere . . ." She paused. "We might be sending Mike and Alice into danger unnecessarily."

Anger flared in Hank. He'd called in every chit he'd ever accumulated, turned down the President's order for him to relocate to NORAD, and Amanda had the nerve to question his resolve. He looked at her honest brown face, wide-eyed with concern for him and the shuttle's crew, and his anger faded. "The people on *Reliance* risked their lives to put up the solar generator and make things better here on Earth. The least they deserve is for us to *try*."

While the rest of *Reliance*'s crew went about their respective tasks, Claire typed a report of everything that had happened during the EVA. While she worked, Claire kept her headset on and the frequency scanner browsing, hoping to establish contact with Mission Control, or anyone on Earth. A gentle roar of static was punctuated by occasional words—some in foreign languages—as they picked up sporadic VHF transmisssions.

A panicked man's voice with an Indian accent made Claire stop.

"—ten thousand dead. Riots in Guwahati, Dibrugarh, and Digboi City. The people have gone mad with fright. Our presence only inflames them. The green ghosts in the sky predict our doom, I fear. This is Risaldar-Major Bisnu Rabha, in Assam—"

His transmission cut off, and despite Claire's efforts to recapture the signal, it was gone.

When her report of events was done, Claire printed it out and tucked it into the flight checklist. If something happened to her and the crew, she wanted a record left behind. It might provide answers as to what caused the accident that killed Cole. Claire prayed it wasn't her fault.

She wondered what they'd do if the shuttle didn't come. The hull could be welded; they could cut a patch from the station's hull if necessary. And they carried spare heat tiles and epoxy on board. It was the CEV's damaged engine that worried her. It looked hopeless: splayed and torn metal, crimped fuel pipes, crushed nozzles. But if they had no other choice, could it be repaired? Claire was deep in charts of engine specifications and welding technique three hours later, when a blood-curdling scream sliced the air.

Claire jerked upright, the instinctive reaction throwing her into a tumble. Heart pounding, she touched the wall to slow herself. "What the hell—"

"Did you ever see anything more beautiful?" Anderson was at the window. He kissed the glass.

Rising like a phoenix from the Florida peninsula was the telltale plume of water vapor left from a shuttle launch.

Claire sucked in the first deep breath she'd taken in ages. Thank you, she prayed to a God she didn't believe in. Thank you.

Hyun-Jin and Jo-Jo hugged and laughed. Then Hyun-Jin's grin faded. "I wish Cole could see this."

There was a moment of silence as they watched the shuttle's progress into space. A rescue vehicle packed with all the latest medical equipment, launching too late to save their commander.

Bisnu sat on a rise overlooking the city of Guwahati. In the center of town, the Central State Library and Assam State Museum were in flames. The sounds of gunfire came from the riverfront.

His short-range radio buzzed with reports from field commanders. Lieutenant Rasmussen's strident bellow: "Civilians do not respond to orders to return to their houses. Hysteria has taken hold. Three of my men have been hurt by people throwing rocks."

The sound of gunfire was echoed by a machine gun's staccato retort.

Dear gods, we fire on our own people.

In the sky, rockets shot from the west, cutting clouds into ribbons as they streaked towards the Chinese forces to the east.

Bisnu's driver, Iswar, craned his head to follow the rocket's flight. "Are those—"

His voice was cut off by a boom of thunder, followed by a flash of piercing light, the same that had temporarily blinded Bisnu when the Chinese first attacked.

Rubbing the afterimage from his eyes, Bisnu spoke into the radio. His voice was dead. "Recall the aircraft. They can do nothing more for us in the sky." He lowered the radio to his lap and felt its weight like a millstone across his legs. "This war is beyond us."

"What shall we do?" asked Iswar in a panic.

"Pray," said Bisnu. "All we may do is pray."

Reliance had hummed with excitement and fear since the shuttle's launch. Excitement that rescue was on the way, and fear they wouldn't be able to make the rendezvous.

The best cure for worry was work. Claire said, "Anderson, I want to check the calculations on the time until we contact the shuttle." She turned to Jo-Jo. "As soon as they're through the atmosphere, I want radio contact. We need to tell them about the change in plans." Nodding at Hyun-Jin, she said, "Download backups of all data, and estimate what we can take with us." Claire looked around at the metal bulkheads and white-painted walls that had been her lifelong dream, and home for the past three months. It killed her to leave it this way, in full retreat, but she had to be practical. "If *Reliance*'s going down, I want to salvage whatever we can before she goes."

An hour later Jo-Jo said, "I've got them on video." She pressed a button to route the incoming signal to the center monitor.

Mike Marshant and Alice Depuy appeared onscreen dressed in the orange space suits that NASA used for launch and reentry. Tight caps fitted over their heads. Mike looked like a marine recruitment poster, with flinty blue eyes and a square chin that hosted a Douglas Fairbanks cleft. Wisps of Alice's golden-brown ringlets peeked out around the bottom of hers, complementing her mahogany complexion.

The crew of *Reliance* crowded around the monitor, hanging from all angles, their heads like the spokes of a wheel.

"*Defiant*, *Reliance*. I can't tell you how glad we are to see you," said Claire.

The freckles on Alice's wide nose spread as she smiled. "*Reliance*, *Defiant*. The feeling's mutual. Hadn't heard much from you lately."

Mike looked up from the panel. "Tell Cole we're on schedule to rendezvous in ten hours."

Claire's grin faded. "*Defiant*, I can't do that. There was an accident during the EVA." She swallowed hard. "Cole's dead."

Alice's smile vanished. "Oh, no. Not Cole."

Mike frowned. "*Reliance*, what happened?"

"There was an equipment failure. His jets fired uncontrollably. We almost lost him to space. When we brought him back through the air lock, he went into a seizure and died. We tried resuscitation, with no success."

Mike shook his head sadly. "Cole was a good man, a good astronaut."

Claire swallowed. "This also means we can't risk the EVA to reach the Mars fuel platform. Can you change course to meet us in orbit?"

Mike and Alice exchanged an unhappy look. "I'm not sure. We'll check with Houston."

"*Defiant*, you still have communications with Houston?"

Alice glanced down at the panel. "That's affirmative."

"Good. I need to transmit details of what went wrong on the EVA to Houston." She loaded up her report and the file Cole had given her before he went outside. "There's also a personal message from Cole . . . to his wife."

"*Reliance, Defiant*. Received," said Alice. "We'll make sure these get where they need to go."

"Has NASA communicated with the other space stations?"

Alice cocked her head. "Not that I've heard. Why?"

"We received a strange transmission from the *EEA*." She transmitted it to the shuttle. "They may be in trouble."

"I'll pass it along."

"What's happening Earth-side?" asked Claire.

"Things are tense," said Mike. "India responded to China's aggression with nuclear strikes of their own. The United Nations is calling for both sides to stand down. President Tucker has threatened American involvement if President Mao Du Feng isn't removed from power."

Claire winced. Did Tucker really expect the leader of China to give up power during a war?

Mike shook his head. "It's scary down there. There are rumors the president's family has been relocated to NORAD."

"You don't think . . ." It was too absurd to even say.

No leader on Earth would risk a nuclear war. Scientists decades ago proved a nuclear conflict was unwinnable. The damage to the Earth's environment and weather would hurt everyone. And still, the world's governments hadn't dismantled their nuclear weapons. Despite disarmament agreements between the U.S. and Russia, each country still had enough bombs to destroy the world many times over. And now there were new nuclear powers: India, Pakistan, and North Korea.

Alice looked down, her thin brows knitting together. "That's odd. We're seeing something anomalous on radar."

"There's a lot of debris generated by the high-altitude bursts," Claire warned. "That's what hit our lifeboat. Watch yourself."

Alice's smile was kind. "Don't worry, I'm sure—"

The transmission ended midsentence. Static filled the screen.

Brilliant light filled the command module, streaming in from the window.

Claire's eyes watered. She blinked to clear them. Green retinal afterimages of the glowing window blurred her vision.

"What the hell just happened?" Claire demanded. Fumbling the microphone closer to her mouth, she said, "*Defiant*, this is *Reliance*. Do you copy?"

More static from the speaker.

"*Defiant, Reliance.*" Claire's voice rose in panic. "Answer me. Answer me!"

Hyun-Jin made a choking sound in his throat.

Claire looked at him, alarmed.

Mutely, he pointed at the window. In the distance, where the shuttle had been a bright pinpoint, was a streak of silver motes. Claire zoomed in the outside camera. A white-painted piece of debris with the letters NASA whirled in and out of view.

"But what—" Claire sputtered. "How—" Alice's wide smile was burned into her mind. Claire could see every freckle. Alice and Mike had been right there, alive, about to rescue *Reliance*'s crew.

The radiation alarm warbled as a new wave of X-rays and electrons hit them, blasted from the nuclear detonation that had destroyed the space shuttle.

CHAPTER 6

The spacecraft-tracking map dominated the central wall of the Flight Operations Room. On it, the line for the shuttle's trajectory went red.

Hank's chest tightened. "Tell me that's a communications malfunction."

Alex Yeung, the Propulsion Engineer in charge of in-space maneuvering said, "I don't know. We've lost telemetry on the shuttle."

"CAPCOM? Can we get a person on the line?" Hank ground his teeth together, and tried not to look at Cas, listening from the observation platform. "I'd really like to hear Mike or Alice's voice right now."

Amanda shook her head. "I've got nothing."

"Wait a second," Alex said excitedly. "I've got visual data from Keck Observatory in Hawaii. It's a few minutes old . . ." He tapped keys and the shuttle appeared, a blurry streak in the upper atmosphere. A second, smaller streak rose from the Indian-Chinese border to intercept it. As all nineteen engineers watched—the shuttle exploded into a hailstorm of debris.

There was a collective gasp.

"God, no!" Amanda screamed.

Hank sat down heavily in his chair. His chest felt compressed by steel bands. Sweat streamed down his forehead, stinging his eyes. He tried to raise his arm to wipe his face, but the pain nearly made him black out. His vision tunneled. In a hoarse whisper he asked, "Is . . . video confirmed? Was that a missile?"

Cas ran down from the observation platform, her high heels tapped out a fast rhythm. She grabbed Hank's arm. "This is all your fault," she hissed. "I told you the political situation was too dangerous. The last thing we need is an international incident in the middle of a nuclear exchange."

She continued speaking, but Hank couldn't hear her. He slid from his seat to the floor. His head thumped to the floor. He heard only the irregular beating of his damaged heart.

The buzz of *Reliance*'s radiation alarm snapped Claire out of her shock. The console flashed eight new red lights, indicating system failures in the rate gyro assemblies, fire detection and suppression subsystem, and the potable water processor.

"What's happening to the station?" demanded Jo-Jo.

Claire knew the answer in the pit of her stomach. Anderson had been right; she should have listened to him. This was a military situation. "X-rays inducing currents in *Reliance*'s hull; the shuttle was destroyed by a nuclear weapon."

"Damn," Anderson cursed. "I told—"

Claire spoke over him. "Hyun-Jin, try a reset on gyro assemblies one and two. Let's see what we can bring back online."

"Oh, my God. Mike and Alice . . . Mike and Alice are *dead*?" Jo-Jo's eyes widened with panic. "What are we going to do?"

Claire checked the collision early-warning system. In minutes they'd be crossing the debris field of the *Defiant*. Without looking up, she said, "First we survive. Then we go home." All looked functional. She routed the display to the laptop station. "Anderson, run our trajectory through a simulation of the expanding debris. I need your ideas on how to avoid impact."

Anderson looked like he wanted to argue, but said, "I'm on it."

Jo-Jo tugged at a blond-and-auburn strand of her hair. "And me?"

Claire tossed Jo-Jo a headset. "Get on the radio. Contact anyone you can. We need to let Houston know what happened."

Jo-Jo nodded, expertly caught the headset, and slipped it on. She began hailing up and down the radio frequencies.

It was a pointless task—there was too much interference for a signal to get through—but it would keep Jo-Jo occupied and prevent her from thinking about what had happened to Mike and Alice.

Anderson leaned close to Claire and murmured, "We're a sitting target up here. If whoever shot down the *Defiant* decides to take us out . . ."

Claire hated to think that the war on Earth had expanded into space. But she couldn't ignore what she'd seen, and heard from the *EEA*. "There's only one option."

Anderson looked at her, eyebrows raised in a question.

In the same low tone, she said, "We need to finish the EVA."

"Another eighty kilometers of altitude won't keep us from being shot down. Anyone with a telescope could pick up our new location."

Claire cut her eyes at Hyun-Jin and Jo-Jo. They were engrossed in their work and didn't appear to have heard.

She took a deep breath. Her idea was insane, but she couldn't see any other option. "Not if we use the fuel on the Mars platform to launch into mid-Earth orbit."

Mid-Earth orbit was twelve thousand miles above the surface of the earth, sparsely populated by global positioning satellites and the Japanese weather station.

Anderson pressed his lips together. "It'd make it that much harder for NASA to do an extraction."

Claire's voice dropped to a scant whisper. "There isn't going to be another rescue ship before the Argus effect hits. NASA can't scramble another shuttle in time." She pointed at the red indicators that wouldn't reset. "We're already seeing systems fail. In one, maybe two, days we're floating in a dead tin can."

"Goddamn it!" Jo-Jo flung the radio headset across the

module. It slammed into the silver rim of the hatch and ricocheted off, nearly missing Hyun-Jin's head before it hit a mesh bag holding a nest of cables, and drifted off.

"Jo-Jo, what the hell?" Claire asked.

The younger woman knocked her hand away and pounded the headset against the control panel. "The radio's shorted out. It's gone." She looked up and tears clouded her midnight-blue eyes.

Claire pushed away from the laptop station and took the younger woman into an embrace. She rubbed circles between Jo-Jo's shoulder blades. They'd all been awake too long, under too much stress.

"Cole's dead. Alice and Mike are dead," Jo-Jo sniffled. "We're going to die up here, too. I know it."

Anderson shook his head back and forth, as if amazed that women had been allowed in the space program.

Claire met his eyes over Jo-Jo's shoulder and dared him to make a comment. "It's going to be all right," she soothed. "They'll have seen the shuttle's destruction on Earth. Help is on its way. You have to believe that."

Hank Rubin woke when the medics loaded him onto the stretcher. What's happened? He intended to say. How are Mike and Alice? But his tongue was thick and unresponsive, yielding only: "Whaa?"

"It's all right," the flight surgeon knelt by Hank, as the EMTs lifted the gurney. "Just lay back, we'll take care of everything."

Amanda's hands covered her mouth. Her brown eyes were horrified with worry. "Is he going to be all right? I mean, a heart attack—"

Hank passed by his engineers on the way out. Their stunned faces turned to watch him go.

As he turned the corner to exit, he saw Cas at his station. She straightened her jacket. "We're all sorry about what happened to Hank. But our priority now is figuring out what happened, and whether we can do anything for the astronauts on *Reliance*. We're going to do things right," in a lower tone, Hank could hear her say, "for a change."

Matt Logan's mother lived in a low-slung ranch house in the Hollingsworth Hills neighborhood of Lakeland, Florida.

Her house had been built in the 1960s, with the low ceilings and modern lines of the era. It was an anachronism among the larger, Colonial-style houses built by newcomers to the area.

A hand-braided oval rug dominated the living room. At one end was an old cabinet television, on the other an avocado-green sofa that she'd bought when Matt's father was still alive.

Owen was on the floor, running a Hot Wheels car around the red-and-gold racetracks of the rug.

The television was on, tuned to CNN. Matt had called the Kennedy Space Center six times since Clarissa Henly, the Secretary of Astronaut Affairs, had alerted him that Claire's return might be delayed, but he hadn't been able to make it past Clarissa's platitudes that "everything was under control" to talk to anyone who would tell him what was really going on.

The television reception was spotty; the picture kept fading in and out.

"Mom, you've got to let me buy you a new television," Matt said.

"It works fine most of the time," Betty Logan answered from her kitchen. "There must be a thunderstorm coming."

"The rocket, the rocket, the rocket," Owen chanted, pointing at the screen with the toy car and bouncing on his knees.

Among wavering horizontal lines, the space shuttle *Defiant* stood at the launch site, strapped to the liquid oxygen and hydrogen tanks that would generate more than six million pounds of thrust and propel it into orbit.

The announcer explained that the space shuttle was launching two days early to evacuate the crew of *Reliance*. The space station had hit debris in orbit and suffered decompression, but the crew had followed procedures and the leak had been contained with no casualties.

"Fucking NASA," Matt grumbled beneath his breath. It was insane that he had to get information about his wife's condition from the evening news.

As the countdown ticked off onscreen, Betty brought sliced grilled-cheese sandwiches to the coffee table in front of the green couch. She scowled at Matt as if she'd heard his bad language.

Owen grabbed a sandwich dripping American cheese and hoisted it to his mouth. Matt caught an errant strand of cheese with a napkin before it hit the rug.

In a plume of white smoke, *Defiant* lifted off. Owen raised his free hand in the air and cheered. "Yay!"

The commentator described how the shuttle would catch up with *Reliance* in orbit, transfer the stranded astronauts, and bring them safely to Earth.

Thank God, Matt thought as he bit into the sandwich. Claire had been gone three months, longer than work had ever taken her away. Now maybe she'd reconsider an engineering job on the ground. Something safe, where he could count on her coming home every night.

Matt changed the channel to the cartoon network. They had nearly finished lunch when a banner appeared across the bottom of the screen. Matt caught only the words ". . . Space Shuttle." He flipped back to CNN.

On screen, a streak of white crossed the space shuttle's path. The spacecraft exploded in a hail of smoke and debris.

Owen screamed. His mouth distended in horror. He looked over his shoulder at Matt, and two tears dotted his cheeks. "Mom-Mommy's spaceship?"

Matt grabbed up his son and drew him into a hug. He rocked him. "Shh. It's all right. Mommy wasn't on the shuttle. She's on a space station."

His mother's hands shook as she lowered her sandwich to her plate. "Was that—?"

Carrying a clinging Owen, Matt turned up the volume.

"Not sure what's happened." The announcer's baritone said. "It looks like—dear God—it looks like the shuttle's exploded."

Owen buried his face against Matt's shoulder and wailed.

"It's all right," Matt soothed. "Mommy's all right." He thought about Claire, three hundred miles above the Earth, in a damaged space station, and wondered if that were true.

In *Reliance*'s command module, Hyun-Jin interlaced his arms above his head and stretched up and back, flexing the muscles that had held him hunched over the laptop. "I've got the rate gyro assemblies stabilized, but we've lost the water processor and the fire alarms are offline."

Still holding Jo-Jo, Claire asked Anderson, "What about the debris field?"

He pointed at the display, tracing an arc across the diagram. "We'll miss the bulk of the wreckage from the shuttle. There may be some secondary perturbations from space junk. I've plotted a course to avoid all recordable fragments. Anything under ten kilograms I can't track, so no promises there. But we've already closed off hatches to all nonessential modules. I think we're good."

Claire pulled away from Jo-Jo and shook her shoulders gently. "See, we're going to be all right. Pull yourself together. We've got some hard times ahead, and we all need to be ready to deal with them." She nodded at the radio. "Is it repairable?"

Jo-Jo shook her head. "It's the main circuit board. We don't have any replacements."

Claire thought a moment. "What about the ham radio the first crew used to talk to high-school students? Is that still on board?"

Jo-Jo wiped her finger under her nose. "Don't know. I'll check module one."

Module one was where all the extraneous equipment was kept. It was a pack rat's paradise of old experiments, cables, and obsolete parts. The drawers were packed full, and so many cargo bags were strapped to the walls that you had to remove half the module's contents to get inside.

Looking for the radio would keep Jo-Jo occupied.

Claire worried about her. Jo-Jo was only twenty-four. She'd been expedited through the training process to serve a three-month internship in space as part of her graduate work in propulsion physics. She didn't have the experience to deal with this kind of life-and-death crisis. No one had expected this space mission to be different from any other.

When she thought Jo-Jo was out of earshot, Claire said, "Hyun-Jin, I want to boost to MEO to avoid the Argus effect."

Hyun-Jin's eyes widened. "Mid-Earth orbit? There's no way a shuttle could reach us at that altitude."

"NASA isn't going to send another rescue vessel," said Claire. "LEO is too dangerous. We've already lost the radio, water recycling, and the gyro assemblies are fading in and out. No automated vehicle could make it through.

And if we wait any longer, we won't be *able* to boost out of harm's way. We can't sit here and wait to die."

Hyun-Jin bit his lip nervously. "We've only got food for two weeks. Moving to a higher orbit won't save us; it'll just delay the inevitable. What about the lifeboat? Can we repair it?"

Anderson shook his head. "If it was just the rent in the hull, maybe we could patch it. But you saw the engine—it's destroyed."

Claire thought about the capsules used by early astronauts to return to Earth. They also had the ATV. It wasn't designed for reentry, but perhaps—

"Found it!" Jo-Jo floated through the hatch carrying a gray metal box the size of a breadbox. Cables trailed behind her like the tentacles of a dispirited jellyfish. She saw the three of them huddled together. "What's going on?"

"We were discussing our options," Claire said.

Jo-Jo's brow wrinkled. "Without me?"

"I thought you could use some time to . . . calm down."

Jo-Jo's face pinked. She flicked the top of the ham radio. "So this was a snipe hunt to get me out of the way while you three figured out what to do?"

"You cracked under pressure," Anderson snapped. "We needed cool heads to discuss what to do next, and couldn't wait for the Midol to take effect."

Claire wanted to smack him. Anderson's retort was like smothering a fire with kerosene. "That's not it at all. We need the radio. It's our only link to what's happening on Earth. The options currently under discussion are trying to repair the lifeboat or boosting to MEO. What are your thoughts?"

Jo-Jo slammed the radio against the wall and secured it under an elastic strap. She punched in cables, connecting the radio to power and communication ports. "I'll get back to you when the Midol kicks in."

Claire sighed. She didn't have time to deal with Jo-Jo's drama or Anderson's antagonism. The clock was ticking, and every minute they wasted in senseless conflict might mean the difference between life and death.

"I've done some research," said Claire, "and I don't think we can repair the lifeboat—" she held up a hand to forestall Hyun-Jin's protest. "Not in the next twenty-four hours. We're losing electronics left and right and being exposed to elevated levels of radiation. A higher orbit will give us time to figure out an alternate plan. Jim Lovell made it back all the way from the moon with a crippled ship. We can come back from MEO."

Hyun-Jin looked at his hands. "What about using the engines from the ATV supply ship NASA sent us? We'll have a better chance in a patched lifeboat leaving now than navigating through the Argus effect later."

Claire's stomach twisted. There was no way to know which decision would save them—if they even could be saved. "Jo-Jo, what do you think?"

Jo-Jo looked up from installing the ham radio. She chewed the inside of her lip. "They're completely different engines. The ATV is hypergolic, it uses hydrazine with nitrogen tetroxide as an oxidizer. The lifeboat uses *monopropellant* hydrazine. We could try kludging them together, but it'd be dangerous—what if the nitrogen tetroxide ignited? She shook her head, sending her tricolored ponytail into oscillations. "It'd be a hell of a hinky fix. Give it a thirty to fifty percent survival rate. At best. And no way could the work be done in less than two days. I say go for MEO."

Claire's eyebrows rose. Everyone looked at Jo-Jo.

"What?" Jo-Jo shrugged. "Rocket science is my thing. What did you think I'd been doing in lab two, playing with myself? The title of my doctoral dissertation was *Optimization of Directional Xenon-Ion Propulsion in a Microgravity Environment*.' " She went back to connecting cables on the radio. "Duh."

Anderson looked stunned.

Hope lit Hyun-Jin's face, and the trace of a smile played around his lips.

"All right, it's decided. We'll finish the fuel patch and up-orbit to MEO. Anderson, I want you to plan a coplanar orbital transfer. We'll need to recalculate the two burn cycles; NASA's calculations didn't take astronaut mass into account."

"I—" Claire took a deep breath, "I'll go prepare for EVA." Her chest tightened with dread at the thought. She'd only been back at station pressure for a few hours; going out again so soon would intensify the pains she'd felt in her joints on the last EVA. The nitrogen bubbles from her quick exit last time hadn't had time to break up in her system. Add to that the worry about beta radiation affecting the electronics, increasing her radiation exposure, possible impacts from shuttle debris, and Cole's corpse . . . she'd have to crawl over it on the way out, a chilling reminder of her mortality before she stepped into the big black.

Claire kicked off towards the hatch.

Hyun-Jin followed on her heels.

Claire turned. "What are you—"

"You can't go out there alone." Hyun-Jin ran his hands through his thin black hair, and they trembled. "Not after Cole—it's too dangerous."

Claire smiled sadly at Hyun-Jin. They'd developed a camaraderie during the long hours of pool training for the EVA to release the solar reflector. She could tell he was terrified, and still he was willing to back her up. "I appreciate the offer. But the controller on the manned maneuvering unit for the second suit is damaged. You can't—"

"I'll leave the MMU off," Hyun-Jin said. Sweat beaded on his upper lip. "Take only the handheld emergency propellant."

Astronauts in the twentieth century had EVA'd using only their muscles and emergency handheld jets. It was exhausting and dangerous. She and Hyun-Jin had trained in the pool for such maneuvers—in emergency scenarios. But what was this, if not an emergency?

Claire felt a guilty sense of relief. "You're right." She wondered if Cole had secretly wanted her to insist on accompanying him. It hurt too much to think about what might have gone differently if she had.

Noise blared from the speaker Jo-Jo had patched the ham radio into. It sounded like a thousand voices talking at once. "I'm getting something—reflections off the ionosphere. Don't know how long it will last."

Occasionally English words rose above the international hubbub. "Conspiracy . . . shuttle explosion . . . bombs . . . Tucker's threatening to . . . international incident . . . not what *I* heard . . ." Other voices spoke French, German, and Russian, and there was a burst of polysyllabic singsong that caused Claire to look to Hyun-Jin.

Hyun-Jin shook his head. "It was a public service announcement. Warning people not to drink untreated water."

"Can we transmit a message?" Claire asked.

Jo-Jo shrugged. "There's a lot of background chatter, and there's no way to know if NASA will pick up a signal on the amateur bands." .

"Do it." Claire licked her lips. They were cracked from where she'd chewed them. "We have to let them know we're still alive."

Jo-Jo picked up the microphone and placed her hand on the transmit button. "What message?"

Claire thought a moment. She needed a message that would transmit the essentials without adding to the panic on Earth. Taking the handheld microphone from Jo-Jo, she spoke into it. "Houston, this is *Reliance* Space Station. Communications down. Argus closing in, please advise." Handing back the mike, Claire asked, "Can you repeat that for as long as the communication window lasts?"

"Will do," Jo-Jo said. "I'll also send the same message as text packets."

"It's a million-to-one that the message will ever reach Houston," said Anderson.

"Which is still better than doing nothing," Claire snapped. "It's either this or use the safety mirror from the bathroom to flash Morse code signals. If we're going to survive up here, we have to assume something we do *will* work."

Claire turned to Hyun-Jin. "You ready?"

He swallowed hard, then nodded.

"We'll be in the equipment lock. Anderson, use the intercom if anything happens."

When Amanda came back to work, the display from Keck Observatory displayed not *Reliance,* but a patch of blue sky. "What's happened to the space station?" she asked, taking her seat next to Cas Walker.

Without looking up from her terminal, Cas replied. "We're repositioning the observation telescopes. The Department of Defense needs them to track the debris cloud from the shuttle for possible threats to mission-critical satellites."

Amanda looked uneasily at the display. "What about *Reliance*'s crew?"

Cas looked up. "We're facing the possibility of *nuclear war*. *Reliance* will have to take care of itself."

Claire and Hyun-Jin said nothing as they pulled and kicked their way through access tunnels to the equipment lock. There they would begin the long process of prebreathing for the space walk, and assembling and testing the EVA components.

The small room was dominated by the two space suit forms that held the components during testing and dressing. With their protruding artificial arms, the forms looked like sentries warning Claire and Hyun-Jin to turn back, away from the dangers of the space walk.

Hyun-Jin hunched his shoulders up around his ears, as if fending off a cold wind. Without looking up from the elbow joint he was testing, he asked, "What do you think our chances are of getting out of this alive?"

Claire thought of Cole and all the times he'd reassured them that things would be all right. She'd admired him, relied on his judgment. But now he was dead, and she was in charge. "I don't know. But all the best minds in NASA are working on bringing us back. That's worth something."

Hyun-Jin's eyes flickered towards the sealed air lock where Cole's body was stored. "My daughter—" his voice trembled. "My daughter is only eighteen months old. For half her life I've been training for this mission." His eyes were moist when he looked at Claire. "And now I'd do anything to have those nine months back."

Claire knew exactly what he was feeling. Every time she'd dropped Owen off at day care, each night she'd come home to find him already asleep, she questioned her priorities. Claire closed her hand over Hyun-Jin's wrist and he covered it with his free hand, clinging to her like a man to a life raft.

"You'll see your wife and daughter again," she whispered. "I promise."

Hyun-Jin nodded and released her hand to dash at his eyes. "Of course."

Claire thought of Matt and Owen: the sweet way that Owen's hair stood up in little tufts when he first woke up,

Matt's eyes warm with desire over late-morning coffee. Claire closed her eyes and breathed deeply. She would see them again. Any other outcome was unthinkable.

Hyun-Jin changed out the controller on the suit that Cole had died in. He tested the replacement while switching out the arms and legs.

"I'll use that one," Claire offered.

Hyun-Jin shook his head. "Yours is already configured. It would only waste time."

He was right. Claire blew out a breath and nodded.

They took turns on the ergometer, working hard while breathing pure oxygen, to flush nitrogen out of their bodies.

A sharp clang startled Claire and caused her to lose her grip on the cycle. The rubber bands that held her legs down catapulted her over the top. Debris and dust floated out of the crevices where they had been hiding.

Claire kicked over to the wall intercom and, bracing herself with one hand, pushed the button to speak. "Anderson, what's going on?"

Anderson's voice was confident and calm. "Lab one got hit. Probably debris from the shuttle. It was already sealed off. We've lost some air mass, but the station is secure. If you're going to do this thing, I suggest you hurry."

Claire swallowed, thinking of her previous joint pain. But Anderson was right. They didn't have time for a leisurely EVA prep. "Understood. Anything more from the radio signal?"

"It broke up. Before we lost it, we heard speculation that the United States will enter the war in retaliation for *Defiant*. I'm not sure if that's good news or bad news."

"At least they know we're stranded," Claire said. "Was Jo-Jo able to get our message through?"

"No way to know. We haven't received confirmation."

"All right, we'll accelerate the prebreathing schedule to an hour and a half. I don't want to cut it any closer than that. I got lucky the last time I skimped on the nitrogen blow-off. I don't think we can count on that again."

While they waited, Claire went over the procedure for attaching the fuel lines and auxiliary thruster cones with Hyun-Jin. As the pressure in the crew lock dropped, her knee started to ache. She focused on the work ahead to distract herself from the pain.

"Is something wrong?" asked Hyun-Jin, seeing her wince.

Claire licked her lips. NASA protocol would have her report any physical ailment. She'd be sidelined and the EVA canceled. But they didn't have that option. Hyun-Jin's suit was crippled. She'd have to gut it out. "Just a stitch from the exercising."

While they took turns wriggling into the cooling suits and electronics, Hyun-Jin asked, "Do you think the U.S. will get involved with the war in China?"

"I don't know," Claire answered slowly. "China has used nuclear weapons, and if they shot down the *Defiant,* that's not something President Tucker can ignore." Tucker was a hard-line Republican, voted into office on a campaign of tough national security and tax cuts. Claire hoped that he would hold off on taking action until the crew of *Reliance* was safe on the ground. Escalation would only make their situation more precarious.

Claire wished she had a religion to call upon, but her mother's attempts to indoctrinate her in the Southern Baptist faith had failed. Claire's religion was science. It was a cold doctrine, one that offered little comfort.

No atheists in foxholes. Claire looked out the porthole at the infinite blackness of the universe. *Please, if anyone's listening,* she thought, *I'd like very much to survive to see my family again.*

The pressure gauge showed that the air lock was up to station pressure. Claire tucked the helmet of her EVA suit under her arm and opened the air lock.

Cole's corpse was wrapped in plastic sheeting and attached by Velcro straps to the wall. It swayed in the air currents from repressurization, giving it a ghoulish semblance of life.

Claire had never been around a dead body before. Like an accident on the freeway, it made her acutely aware of the delicate balance between life and death. She wished there was another way out of the station, or a more digni- fied place to store Cole's body. But the station had no provisions for housing a corpse other than the evacuated air lock. She silently saluted her dead commander. Out of the corner of her eye, she saw Hyun-Jin follow suit.

It was cramped in the air lock. More so with Cole's body.

But to move him into the crew lock would hasten decomposition, and subject the station to noxious gases the air system couldn't filter out. Claire was thankful that they'd wrapped his body in silver space blankets, so she didn't have to see his desiccated eyes.

They ran through the final stages of preparing for the EVA, overpressurizing the suits and checking for leaks. Everything was a go. The pump whined, sucking the last bit of recoverable air out of the lock. Then Claire opened the hatch and the last vestiges of air puffed out of the station.

Cole's corpse strained against its bonds, as if his ghost wanted to finish the job he died trying to complete.

Claire gasped. Earth was in daylight. They flew over northern Russia. On the edge of the horizon, obscured by the Earth's atmosphere, lay China and India. The Great Wall was shattered, the thin line of it broken like a child's sand fortress dashed by the surf. Even at this oblique angle, Claire saw craters where cities had been. Black billowing smoke rose from the ruins and trailed like streamers on a coffin. Seeing the explosions at night had made it seem unreal, a bad dream that would vanish upon waking. The damage exposed in full sunlight was undeniable.

Over the VOX radio, Claire heard Hyun-Jin swear. She hoped that, somehow, his extended family had escaped the destruction.

She tongued the ship-to-ship radio. "*Reliance,* this is *EVA 1.* Do you copy?"

The only response was an increase in the volume of static.

Switching over to VOX, Claire said, "Looks like we're on our own. You know what to do?"

Dragging his gaze from the damaged Earth, Hyun-Jin nodded. His job was to position himself near the ATV and control the slack of the fuel line so she didn't get tangled up as Cole had.

They crawled over the station, clipping tethers into new rings as they traveled until the ATV rose above them, a golden cylinder four and a half meters across and ten meters long. Four solar panels radiated from it like propellers on a stationary windmill. Coils of white fuel line billowed from its open hatchway, and a loop had wrapped around the ATV's docking pin.

Hyun-Jin pointed at himself, then the wrapped loop of hose.

Claire nodded to indicate that she understood he meant to untangle it. Then she crawled along the surface of the station, towards the hatch Cole had opened. Each time she pushed off a handhold, a knife thrust of pain jabbed her knee. When she paused to catch her breath, her whole leg throbbed. Claire gritted her teeth.

Hyun-Jin eased the tangled fuel hose from the docking pin where the ATV attached to *Reliance*.

Claire watched anxiously, praying the line wasn't kinked or punctured.

When the hose was free, he gave Claire a thumbs-up.

She took the free end and crawled into the open hatch. Bile rose in the back of her throat. Choking down nausea, Claire fought to stay focused. Just a little longer.

Claire's eyes teared with pain when she grabbed the handhold near the ATV's hatch. She blinked to clear her eyes and lashes and tiny droplets filled the inside of her helmet, jiggling in midair until they hit her skin or the inside of her helmet and adhered, or were drawn into the air filter.

The nausea worsened as she moved inside the dark interior of the ATV. The light from her helmet was the only illumination, dancing in fitful shadows over the four fuel tanks that had been bolted into the interior.

Claire swallowed. Her heart was pounding in her chest. If she threw up in her space suit, there was no way to clear the fluid from her face. She might drown, or it could clog her oxygen filtration system and suffocate her.

"Every . . . right . . . out there?" Anderson's voice was broken by hissing static, the interference testimony to the increased radiation hitting the station.

Claire stuck her hand outside of the hatch, thumb up, trusting Hyun-Jin or a camera to relay the image to the control room. Her eyes watered and she blinked rapidly, her gorge in her throat. She didn't trust herself to speak.

She wished the NASA engineers had the time to weld and test a direct feed into the ATV's main fuel tanks, then this EVA would have been unnecessary and Cole would still be alive.

But wishing wasn't having. And the longer she took, the

more radiation she and Hyun-Jin were exposed to, and the worse her symptoms would get.

When she'd applied to be an astronaut, one of her tests was to sit, fetal-position, inside a completely dark meter-wide rescue ball without a watch or anything to give her a sense of time, for twenty minutes. In claustrophobic darkness, with no reference of time except the pounding of her heart, twenty minutes had stretched into a subjective eternity. It had been the hardest part of her training.

This was worse.

Claire crept along using the friction of her fingertips on the nearest fuel tank to propel her towards the two dual-connectors that mated the four fuel tanks. Her first task was to test for leaks and make sure the connectors hadn't vibrated loose during the launch.

The ATV used hypergolic propellants for orbital maneuvers and refueling *Reliance*'s attitudinal thrusters. A combination of fuel, monomethyl hydrazine, and an oxidizer, nitrogen tetroxide, they would ignite on contact. Hypergols weren't as efficient as the cryogenic propellants liquid oxygen and liquid hydrogen, but they were easier to start and stop combusting, and easier to store and transport than the cryogenics, which required refrigeration to several hundred degrees below zero Fahrenheit.

Of the four tanks in the dry-cargo hold, two were hydrazine and two nitrogen tetroxide.

Claire squeezed along the inside of the ATV's cylindrical wall, up towards the top of the tanks. One hand held the free end of the fuel hose. Like welding hose, it had two lines attached together: one red, the other green. Surrounding that was a white nylon sheath that protected the inner hoses. The hose caught and released as Hyun-Jin, outside the ATV, fed her the hose slowly, controlling its slack.

More than five tons of highly toxic, highly explosive compounds pressed on Claire from either side as she eased herself into position. The simulation had shown three inches of clearance for her MMU; it felt like three millimeters. She scooted herself along like an inchworm, praying the friction against the tanks wouldn't damage her suit.

Two thirds of the way up the tank, Claire pointed her helmet light at the tank valves. They looked intact, but even a miniscule leak could cause an explosion when the ATV's main engines fired. She reached down along her body for the electronic leak detector. Her arm wedged between her chest and the tank in front of her. Claire tried to ease it free, but it was stuck. Instinct and the crushing mass of the tanks surrounding her urged her to jerk her arm free. But that would be foolish. It might tear her suit. Claire rocked her arm back and forth inside the casing of the MMU suit. She sucked in a breath reflexively, as if inhaling could deflate the hard casing surrounding her torso.

Claire tongued the radio control. "*Reliance*, MMU 2, this is MMU 1. Do you copy?"

Silence.

Claire repeated the call three more times. No answer.

In the dark, stuck without a safe way to free herself and a radio that didn't work, her hindbrain screamed at her to thrash herself free. But training and logic held. She would not panic.

She pressed her hips forward, levering her torso against the two tanks in front of her, hoping to free enough space to clear her arm. Her heart hammered in her chest. She concentrated on slowing her breathing so she wouldn't hyperventilate. Time stretched as she wriggled and pushed like a breech baby trying to be born. No matter how she moved, she was trapped, her arm acting as a wedge pinning her against the ATV's inner wall.

When something grabbed her ankle, Claire screamed. The high-pitched screech was deafening inside the confines of her helmet.

Hyun-Jin, she told herself. It was only Hyun-Jin. Not Cole's ghost come to exact retribution for his death.

Claire tried the radio again, "MMU 2, this is MMU 1. Do you copy?"

At this proximity, the signal came back clear, "MMU 1, is there a problem?"

Flushing with embarrassment, Claire said, "I'm stuck. My arm is wedged between my suit and the fuel tanks."

"Have you tried pushing your hips forward?"

"Everything. I've tried everything," Claire said. She fought to keep panic out of her voice.

Hyun-Jin's hand moved up her leg to her calf. New shadows flickered on the tank valves above her, cast from Hyun-Jin's helmet. She imagined him below her, trying to get a better view of her predicament.

"It looks like your mobility pack is caught on one of the brackets attaching the tank to the wall. Let's try removing it," he said. "I'm going to undo the bottom clips. Can you get the ones on top?"

Claire's left arm was free, and she worked to bring it down behind her helmet to her upper back. It was awkward using her off hand, and swathed in the eleven layers of her space suit, but she felt the emergency release clip below her fingers. "I've got it."

A gentle tug as Hyun-Jin undid the lower clips. Fumbling, Claire managed the nearest clip. Stretching until she felt her shoulder start to dislocate, Claire could barely touch the second. With the tips of her fingers, she scrabbled against the clip, until with a loosening of her whole body, it released and she slipped forward into the space above the tanks.

Relief flooded her veins, and Claire fought back tears. She hadn't realized until this moment how terrified she'd been. The nausea returned, redoubled, and she swallowed against bile.

"You okay?" Hyun-Jin asked, holding her mobility pack.

"Yeah," she replied hoarsely. "Thanks." She finished the move that had trapped her and brought out the molecular sniffer, waving its intake tube above each valve as she checked for leaks. Sweat that had bubbled on her skin during her ordeal floated free in tiny droplets and stung her eyes, making the gauge hard to read. Blinking to clear her vision, she saw the readout. There was no leak.

Thank God. At last, something had gone right. Claire attached the fuel hose to the two valves, one mating the two fuel tanks, the other the two oxidizers. She opened the valves and the fuel line went rigid, like a fire hose filling with water. Claire checked her connection. It was still tight.

Breathing another sigh of relief, Claire packed the sniffer in her thigh pocket and began the crawl back through the place she'd been pinned. It was an easier fit, now that her jet pack was removed, but still she held her breath for the second it took her to wiggle through the point where she'd been trapped.

The final task of the EVA was to hook up the free end

of the fuel hose to a port on the side of the ATV. Hyun-Jin and Claire clipped in their tethers. Then Hyun-Jin pried up a panel just above the engine cone and Claire screwed on the fuel hoses. That done, she opened the valve on the end of the fuel hose.

Reddish-brown bubbles of nitrogen tetroxide sputtered free from the brass fitting.

"Shit!" Claire swore, and cranked the hose valve. She'd acted instinctively and hadn't braced, so instead of closing the valve she swung around, hitting Hyun-Jin's helmet and bouncing off the side of the ATV. The oxidizer spilled out in an expanding stream of bubbles. *Reliance* swirled in her vision before she hit the end of her tether and bounced, recoiling towards the ATV. Claire put out her hands to brace herself and caught a handhold. Her wrist ached as it pulled on her entire mass to stop her motion.

Hyun-Jin had the valve and cut it off. "The fitting's not seated properly," he spoke over the radio. "Looks like part of the o-ring caught in the threads." He unscrewed and fiddled with the brass cap, and then retightened it.

Claire held her breath as he opened the valve again, hoping the o-ring hadn't been damaged to the point where it wouldn't form a seal.

The seal held.

Claire let out a shaky breath. What had happened to her? She was usually deft and efficient. How could she make such a stupid mistake?

Sore in every muscle of her body and dripping with sweat, Claire followed Hyun-Jin into the air lock. Her knee screamed pain.

Cole's corpse, still swathed in its cocoon of plastic, was a grim reminder of how close she'd been out there. Claire handed the sniffer to Hyun-Jin and he scanned the exterior of her suit.

It showed trace elements of nitrogen tetroxide clung to the exterior of her suit. The station's gravity was small next to that of the Sun and Earth, but even its small gravitational field was strong enough to keep a small halo of particles close to its surface. In the same way, their space suits attracted molecules. Nitrogen tetroxide was highly toxic, and even trace amounts could be deadly if introduced into the sealed atmosphere of the station.

"We'll have to flush the air lock," Hyun-Jin said, his helmet pressed up to hers so sound could transmit.

Claire wanted to cry. It would waste more oxygen they couldn't afford to spare. All because of a mistightened valve. Stupid. Stupid. Stupid.

Not trusting herself to speak, Claire nodded. The motion almost brought up her dinner from the previous night. She closed her eyes and forced her breathing into slow, regular patterns.

Flushing the air lock involved partially pressurizing it, then venting the air into space. The friction of the air molecules would clear away the toxic gas clinging to their suits.

Claire crawled in next to Cole's corpse and clung to a set of handholds. Hyun-Jin closed the air lock and pressurized it to .025 psi. Then he pushed the emergency button that would pop the hatch and let all the air rush out at once. The resulting pressure wasn't enough to overcome their grip on the handles.

Cole's body rattled and shook as the air exploded from the hatch. Then suddenly, the Velcro holding him to the wall ripped free and Cole shot out the open hatchway. Claire let go with her right hand to grab him. The silver sheet covering his face unwrapped, exposing the top half of his head. His vitreous humor had boiled in the vacuum of space. For an instant, Claire was frozen by Cole's stare: dried white eyeballs lay shriveled like raisins in their sockets.

Hyun-Jin moved too late to catch Cole's body.

Their air lock tethers were only three meters long. She and Hyun-Jin were too far away to reach him.

The space blanket encasing Cole's corpse unraveled further. It trailed from him like a New Year's streamer. The jet of air sent him tumbling perpendicular to *Reliance*'s orbit in the direction of Earth. The thin atmosphere at 300 miles altitude would eventually slow his orbit, and gravity would draw him into Earth's fiery embrace.

Claire was horrified . . . but also a little jealous. Cole, at least, was going home.

They repressurized the air lock and entered *Reliance*.

Anderson waited on the other side, in the equipment lock. "What happened out there? Why'd you flush the lock?"

Claire pulled off her helmet and glanced at Hyun-Jin. He said nothing.

She said, "We had some trouble getting a good seal. Had some nitrogen tetroxide pollution to clear from our suits." She swallowed. "Cole's body . . ." The sight of his shriveled eyes came back to her, and her body wracked with nausea. She groped wildly for a plastic equipment bag from a wall dispenser and threw up into it. The liquid hit the back of the bag and rebounded against her mouth. She vomited again and again until dry heaves shook her body and she felt as insubstantial as tissue paper.

Anderson left and returned with a packet of water and paper towel. The expression on his face bordered on sympathetic. Claire remembered bar talk about how sick Anderson had been on his first flight.

Claire drank gratefully, flushed her mouth, and cleaned her face.

Hyun-Jin removed his helmet. "Cole's corpse detached during the venting. There was nothing we could do."

Anderson stiffened, his eyes gone wide for an instant with shock and pain. Then he was back in control. He said nothing, but Claire felt his disapproval. After a moment's silence he said, "Hurry up and desuit. When you're back in the command module, I'll initiate the first burn." He turned and pulled himself through the access tunnels out of the crew lock.

When Claire finished stowing her suit, she and Hyun-Jin pulled themselves wearily along the access tunnel to the command module.

Anderson and Jo-Jo were positioned in front of both laptop stations. Claire didn't have the energy to ask one of them to move. Instead she settled with Hyun-Jin against the back wall, near the hatch.

The ATV controls were still on manual since the docking. Anderson used the joystick to position the ATV's main engines towards Earth. He entered commands that would fire the first burn for 6.4 minutes.

"Initiating first burn," he said. Then he pushed the execute button.

The station's hull vibrated as it accelerated against Earth's gravity in an elliptical path.

Inside her socks, Claire crossed her toes. Please hold together, she begged the station. Without a lifeboat, *Reliance* was their only chance of survival. If anything happened now, any serious breach, they would die.

The station shimmied. Dirt and missing parts vibrated out of crevices they'd been wedged into.

"Is this supposed to happen?" asked Jo-Jo in a tremulous voice.

The station had been designed for incremental boosts, enough to keep it in orbit. Its engineers had never considered this wild ride into a transfer orbit. Claire exchanged a scared look with Hyun-Jin.

The only sign of fear that showed on Anderson's face was the white rim of tension around his mouth. "She'll hold."

The acceleration grew and the hull groaned like a damned soul. Anderson and Jo-Jo were drifting sideways, pivoting around the ankles they'd tucked under handrails. Hyun-Jin and Claire lay against one of the station walls. A handhold dug uncomfortably between Claire's ribs.

After 6.4 minutes, the engines shut down and they drifted into constant velocity. Claire and Hyun-Jin floated free of the wall.

Anderson checked the control panel in front of him. "All systems nominal. We're in transfer orbit. When we hit apogee, I'll do another burn to settle us into an orbit matching the Mars fuel platform."

Hyun-Jin passed out plastic bags of cranberry juice. "It's not Champagne, but I thought we should celebrate."

The thought of drinking the sweet juice made Claire's gorge rise, but she took a bag.

Hyun-Jin held up his plastic bag. "To *Reliance*."

"To *Reliance*," Anderson and Jo-Jo echoed, sloshing their bags against hers.

"To *Reliance*, and the hero of the hour: Hyun-Jin," Claire added.

Hyun-Jin blushed as the others repeated Claire's toast. His color deepened to crimson as she described how he'd saved her life and helped her connect the fuel lines.

The sky was the brilliant blue of midmorning, but no birds sang. A harsh wind blew from the Himalayan Mountains. Bisnu and his driver, Iswar, huddled in the shade of the Humvee. His radio no longer worked. Gunfire echoed from the city, but Bisnu could see no point in trying to quell the madness any longer. It had gone too far, the city was burning.

Iswar pointed mutely to the sky.

Streaks of white—long bony fingers—clawed at them from the east, growing longer as the aircraft cut the upper atmosphere and caused water crystals to condense in their wake.

Missiles from the west rose to meet them, but too few. The arsenals of China were vast. For every missile interceptor India could muster, ten ICBMs flew.

"This is the end, Iswar," said Bisnu. Images of his children, little Sanjay and Indrani, flew through his mind. Their wide, trusting eyes, bright smiles. He wept to think how he and his people had failed them, failed to protect what was most precious. How could they have thought, for even a moment, that oil was their most valuable resource.

Iswar blubbered beside him, his arms over his head, as if mere flesh could ward off the coming explosion.

"Shiva, destroyer of worlds," Bisnu intoned, "we are in your hands. Forgive us our arrogance and foolishness."

The surviving missiles arced overhead. The grasping fingers of death stretched to the ground. Bisnu's world erupted in white light.

From their new altitude, *Reliance*'s crew could see more of the Earth at one time. No longer limited to a view of 1,200 miles, entire continents now filled their windows. White clouds glistened above electric-blue seas. The Pacific Ocean crept underneath them, unrolling a west-to-east view of North America.

It was Hawaii-postcard perfect, and Claire felt a pang, wishing she was down on the planet, lounging on a beach, the Argus effect and the ESR launch somebody else's problem.

"It looks so fragile," Jo-Jo said, swiping red and blond strands of hair out of her eyes.

"So far away, you mean," grumbled Anderson.

"Rescue is still possible," Hyun-Jin said. "They've got telescopes. They know *Reliance* is in a higher orbit. If they launch a ship carrying hardened electronics, it could survive the Argus layer to rendezvous with us at the Mars platform."

"Uh, guys." Jo-Jo's voice was breathy, as if she'd been punched in the stomach. Her arm extended towards the porthole, index finger pointing at the Earth. She twisted her neck to look back at them, a pleading expression on her face.

"Oh, God, no!" Hyun-Jin shouted.

Anderson's mouth worked, but nothing came out.

Claire forced her eyes to focus on the planet four hundred miles below. Brilliant fireworks blossomed over the northwest coast of the United States, followed by glowing embers and deadly phosphorescent auroras. It was pretty, like the fiber-optic toys of her childhood that changed hues as a light revolved past colored filters.

Not possible.

Her chest hurt, and Claire realized it had been more than a minute since she'd taken a breath. She reached out a hand to stop the bombs, to cradle and protect the planet. From space it was so obviously a miracle of green and blue life. An oasis in an endless black desert.

The earth rotated beneath *Reliance,* and they saw the bombs continue their southeast march, over the Rocky Mountains, across the central plains.

Not the East Coast, Claire prayed. Not Orlando. Not the home of Mickey Mouse, sunshine, and orange fields.

Not the city where Matt and Owen waited for her.

CHAPTER 7

Owen dangled from the lower branches of the grapefruit tree in his grandmother's yard. Matt had taken him outside, away from the television and the news broadcasts speculating on what had happened to the shuttle, and what might await the astronauts on *Reliance,* waiting to be rescued.

Laughing, Owen craned his head back to reach for a higher branch. His gesture stopped half-completed. He pointed into the sky. "Daddy, is those airplanes? Is Mommy coming home?"

"*Are* those . . ." Matt started to correct, then stopped himself. High overhead, five slender shapes cut contrails from the clouds. They didn't look like any airplanes Matt had ever seen. He hoisted Owen down by the waist and ran for the sliding glass door.

"Mother," Matt said as he closed the door behind him.

His mother looked up from the television with concern. "What? Is Owen all right?"

Matt grabbed her hand and, still carrying Owen, dragged her towards the bathroom.

"What's going on?" she asked.

He didn't have an answer for her. Matt felt foolish. Surely they were just jets from the Orlando Air Force Base, flying in formation. But a gnawing fear in his gut drove him toward the center of the house. "Mother, humor me."

He led her into the bathroom and set Owen down in the tub, then stepped in with him.

"What on Earth?" his mother protested, as he gestured she should join them.

Matt huddled with his four-year-old son and seventy-two-year-old mother in the cold porcelain. The bathroom smelled of the lavender baby powder his mother had used for sixty years.

His mother squirmed against him, her bony hip poking his ribs. "Matt, what is—"

Her words were cut off by the flash of the first explosion.

The air was lead. Claire couldn't move, couldn't breathe. Glittering explosions tramped across the United States.

Hyun-Jin wailed when Houston flashed and went dark. His wife and daughter were there. They'd declined to fly to Orlando for the reunion; Hyun-Jin's wife was too cautious to travel with their toddler.

Claire had met Hyun-Jin's family at a NASA barbeque, days before the launch. Elisabeth was a blond, round-faced woman, proudly cradling her then-fifteen-month-old daughter, Rachel.

Hank Rubin was in Houston, and Amanda, and all of the engineers in the flight control room. People she'd worked with for years—gone in an instant. Their bodies blasted to ash. Millions of Americans dead in minutes. It was impossible to fathom.

The bombs moved inexorably southeast, taking out Houston and D.C.

Please, God, no. Please not Florida. There's nothing of strategic value in Florida.

Atlanta disappeared in a plump of white smoke.

Claire wanted to squeeze her eyes shut, but the lids wouldn't move. They felt as dry as sandpaper. She wanted to go back into her sleep sack, to wake up from this unreality that must be a nightmare. Life couldn't be this—

The center of the state erupted in flame. Halfway up the

peninsula, a red fireball erupted into the sky; over the course of a minute, it spread into a white mushroom cloud.

Not possible, her heart pounded out the words. Not possible. Not possible.

Somewhere behind her, someone was screaming. The anguished pitch was too raw to tell whether it was male or female.

Owen's mischievous blue eyes grinning at her under his tousled sun-bleached hair. His cheeks still round with baby fat, and a smile missing a top incisor.

Her imagination blasted his tiny body to a skeleton in nuclear winds. Claire spasmed. Her body crumpled into fetal position around the pain in her chest.

Matt smoothing her hair after making love. The softness of his lips next to his stubbly cheek. His breath on her ear as he told her how much he loved her.

Gone.

Claire screamed until her whole world was one long shriek. Her breath went on and on. Every iota of her was discordant noise. As if she could rouse the gods in the heavens and make them take back this impossibility now. She screamed through the pain in her chest, screamed through the breath that wouldn't come. Screamed until the stars burned in the sky and winked out one by one.

Someone shook Claire's shoulders. They vibrated around their combined center of mass.

Hyun-Jin's face was puffy. Red rimmed his eyes and nostrils. "Claire?" His voice was hoarse. Was he sick?

In the corner, Jo-Jo precessed. A tight ball of humanity, she hugged her knees to her chest. Tears bubbled from her eyes, twin streams of glittering balls of quicksilver, drifting apart.

Anderson stared vacantly. His lips were pale and moved, though no sound came out.

"Claire," repeated Hyun-Jin, his voice louder. "We need you." He snuffled and wiped his nose on his sleeve. "What do we . . . what should we . . ."

The room spun around them. Claire reached out her hand to make it stop. Her fingers clenched around the handhold nearest the commander's station.

She knew. Her blackout hadn't been long enough to erase what had happened. But if they were going to survive, if there was any hope of life at all, she needed to forget. Just for a little while, she promised Matt and Owen. Just these few minutes.

And some part of her mind whispered, you don't know . . . Matt and Owen might have survived somehow. Decided at the last minute to visit Matt's mother in Lakeland, or taken a tour of the gator farm Owen was so excited about. Her heart clung to that hope. As long as there was a *chance* they had survived, she had to hold together. *Reliance* and its crew needed her.

Claire checked their location. Three minutes to apogee, when Anderson would need to make the second burn that would put them in orbit with the Mars fuel platform.

The skin of Anderson's shoulder felt clammy under her palm. She shook him gently. "Anderson, we need to make the orbital burn." He turned his head in her direction, but his gaze was unfocused, or focused on something far away. His lips moved in an inaudible murmur.

Claire leaned close to hear what he was saying.

"Gone. He's gone." He repeated the words in a breathless drone.

"What do we do?" Hyun-Jin asked.

Claire wasn't sure whether he was asking about Earth, Anderson's state of shock, or the upcoming burn. Something caught in her throat. No—they were still alive. She'd have felt it if they weren't. She had to deal with what was in front of her, to survive long enough to see them again.

Anderson had already calculated the timing of the second burn. All that was needed was to manually fire the engines of the ATV. His programmed commands would do the rest.

The timer to the second burn counted down on a display in front of Anderson. When it reached zero, Claire reached past him and pushed the button to start the second burn. If Anderson noticed her intrusion or the station's acceleration, he gave no sign, just continued his litany.

"They're in shock," Claire whispered to Hyun-Jin. She looked at his red-rimmed eyes and pale complexion. Who was she fooling? All four of them were in shock. "We need blankets, and something hot and sweet to drink."

"Cocoa," Hyun-Jin croaked. "Jo-Jo has cocoa on her meal plan."

There were no official astronaut dietary guidelines. Each team member was responsible for keeping fit enough to pass the physical examinations. She gave thanks for Jo-Jo's sweet tooth. "Prepare four servings. I'll get blankets from the sleeping quarters."

Claire unpacked a space blanket from one of the drawers built into the wall. As she closed it, her eyes fell on the picture of Matt and Owen wrestling in the grass. Her stomach clenched. She reached for the picture, intending to turn it over. Looking at it was too painful. Her fingers stroked her son's image. She couldn't bear to lose the last sight she'd have of Owen.

She turned her back on it instead, and wrapped the blanket around Jo-Jo. The young woman dragged it over her head, looking like a toddler trying to make the world go away by not looking at it. She wrapped her arms around the younger woman. "Shhh. Shhh. It's all right." Of course it wasn't. Things would never be right again. But what else was there to say? She took a drink packet from Hyun-Jin. The plastic was warm under her palm. Claire held the straw to Jo-Jo's lips. "Drink."

Hyun-Jin draped a second blanket around Anderson.

Anderson, who had been immobile for the better part of ten minutes, darted out a hand and grabbed Hyun-Jin by the throat. "Fucking Chinese," Anderson roared. He throttled Hyun-Jin, shaking him so hard Anderson they vibrated away from the control panel. "You killed my *father*. My brothers, uncles—my whole family!" He shook harder, until Hyun-Jin's teeth rattled together. "Freak. Animal. Monster."

Claire launched herself at the two men, shoving her way between them. She clawed at Anderson's fingers, trying to break his grip. "Hyun-Jin. Is. One. Of. Us."

Hyun-Jin gargled, unable to form words.

Claire grabbed Anderson's little finger and bowed it backwards. The joint at the knuckle popped.

Anderson shoved Hyun-Jin and Claire away, cradling his wounded hand. Through gritted teeth, he hissed, "This is your fault, Logan. The situation needed a military leader. If I had been in command—"

"You couldn't have done anything," Jo-Jo said in a snuffling voice. The blanket had fallen from her head and shoulders and drifted behind her. "This war wasn't about us." Her inflection was flat, devoid of any hope. "The bombs would have fallen anyway. This isn't about Chinese or American stupidity. It's about the stupidity of the whole human race. We made the bombs. Someone, sooner or later, was going to use them."

"You know nothing, little girl," Anderson spat.

Jo-Jo thrust out her chin. "Claire got us out of the elliptical orbit that would have taken us back into the line of fire. While you were staring off into space, she saved us."

"Stop it!" Claire shouted. "All of you. We can't undo what's happened on Earth, and we don't know how bad the damage is. Our best course of action is to figure out how to survive. We can't do that if we fall apart."

Anderson pointed at Hyun-Jin. "How do we know we can trust him?"

Claire let out an exasperated breath. "He was born in *Indiana*. Hyun-Jin is as American as you or I." She inhaled a deep sigh that touched the part of herself she'd locked away. Just enough to sting, not incapacitate. "His family . . ." she gestured at the Earth through the porthole, unable to finish the sentence she'd meant to say. Claire shortened the sentiment, removed any mention of what might have happened to Matt or Owen. Only then was she able to choke the words out: "His family . . . too."

It was enough. Anderson bowed his head and covered his face. "Oh, God. This can't be happening."

Claire pulled herself close to Anderson and adjusted the silver blanket around his shaking shoulders. She bound his sprained finger. His hurting was no different from theirs, just its expression. He deserved the same compassion. She pressed a plastic bag of warm cocoa into his hand. "Drink this."

Anderson took the bag and warmed his hands with it. He didn't meet Claire's eyes. He whispered, "I shouldn't— I don't want anyone to see me like this."

Claire wrapped the blanket tighter around the pilot who had always before seemed invulnerable. "What," she whispered back, "human?"

* * *

The overhead fluorescent light at Dr. Ronald Hadley's office at the British Atmospheric Data Centre flickered again. Its inconstancy was giving him a headache.

"Sir, have you heard?" his research fellow, Andy Ferrier, shoved his head in the door. A gawky man at thirty-seven, he was all spectacles, lanky arms, and legs, topped by a wild ginger profusion of curls. He gasped like a fish, trying to catch his breath.

Hadley looked up from the fallout predictions he'd been refining as an update to his report to Parliament. Green, yellow, orange, and red lines marked out radioactive contours across Europe and the U.K.

"China's bombed the United States," said Andy. "And the U.S. retaliated. Hundreds of megatons in all. It just came in over email."

"Impossible," said Hadley. "It must be a hoax." He opened his email program to prove the lie to Andy. There it was, sealed with the electronic fingerprint of the office of the Prime Minister. His hands sweated as he opened the file.

Thirty-two confirmed detonations in the United States. Possibly more. Another dozen in India and China. A death knell for an already wounded planet.

He plugged the estimated figures into his simulation and zoomed out to display the entire globe. Yellow, orange, and red lines crawled like deadly worms over every country on the planet. The damage wrought would take centuries to abate.

He looked up and met Andy's worried gaze. "They're insane," he said. "The Chinese, the Americans, completely insane."

Claire turned on the ham radio to monitor what was going on Earth-side. Reception was spotty, breaking through pockets of radioactive dust and interference from the Argus effect.

"CQ, CQ. This is N9UDS! Is anyone out there? Aw, Jesus, I don't know what's going on. It looks like the end of the world outside, the sky's gone black and I can't—"

"—answer me, this is Lou, I'm trapped in the barn. There's some kind of burning black snow—"

"—flames everywhere. The whole city's on fire—"

"—fever of 104, throwing up blood—"

"—God's vengeance. Sinners repent!"

"This is Dave in Wenatchee, Washington—"

Anderson's head whipped around. "That's near where my father lives. Ask him about Everett."

Claire had met Anderson's father once, at a reception honoring the astronauts who were named as permanent staff to the newly commissioned *Reliance*. In his eighties, Liam Anderson had once been a tall man, but years of carrying around a heavy burden of anger had stooped his shoulders and pulled the corners of his lips into a permanent frown. Claire had been standing near Liam when Anderson brought him a flute of Champagne: "And I'm one of only twelve who were chosen for permanent rotation," the astronaut son had bragged. The older Anderson had taken a sip of the drink, spat it out on the marble floor, and replied, "Maintenance crew, so that makes you what— a janitor?"

It was a painful memory, and she had only been a bystander. But Anderson's eyes were wide with concern for his father.

Claire pulled the microphone to her lips. "Dave in Wenatchee, this is NA3SS. Do you copy?"

"Yes." There was obvious relief in the man's voice. "Yes, I do. Damn, it's good to hear another voice. Where are you? Do you know what's going on?"

Claire hesitated. Amateur radio was a broadcast medium; anyone listening in could hear their conversation. She imagined Hank Rubin cautioning her not to create a panic. She looked down at the black clouds that swirled over North America. "What have you heard?"

"Nothing." There was frustration in Dave's voice. "The power's out. I can't pick up any signals on my portable televison. None of the radio stations are transmitting, not even the emergency broadcast signal. My cell phone reads NO SERVICE.

"All I know is there were explosions, a bright light, now it looks like the end of the world outside. I've made contact with Ellensburg and Cle Elum using ham radio, but they don't know what's going on either."

Anderson leaned over Claire's shoulder. "What about Everett? Heard from them?"

"Nope. Nothing west of the Cascades. Where are you, NA3SS?"

Anderson blew out a breath and leaned away from the radio. He bit the heel of his palm.

Anger and righteous indignation rose in Claire. The government that had played with nuclear weapons like model rockets now just left the survivors to their own devices? Damn NASA's publicity policies, Dave and the others needed to know what they were up against.

"I'm four hundred miles above you. I'm the commander of *Reliance* Space Station."

There was a pause. "For real? I'm talking to an astronaut? You must have a great view of the damage. Tell me, did Hanford blow or what?"

"No." Claire licked her lips. "There's been a nuclear war."

"What?" Dave's voice was incredulous. Then he chuckled. "You're pulling my leg, right?"

Claire grimly described everything: the bombs marching across the country, clouds of radioactive dust, and electrical interference.

"Damn!" His voice was full of horror. "That's worse than I imagined. Is anywhere safe?"

Claire looked at the ravaged country passing underneath her. "Maybe the Midwest . . . or Canada."

Dave moaned. "Dear God, it's the end of the world."

"No," Claire said sharply. "You're alive. That means there's still hope. Here's what you're going to do." She described sealing the windows and doors with duct tape to keep fallout at bay, how to purify water, and where the fallout clouds were drifting. She promised to transmit updates each time they passed over the United States. She couldn't prevent the people back home from suffering, but she would give them what she had to offer: information.

The second burn had raised their altitude to four hundred miles, an orbit just below the orbit of the Mars fueling platform. The speed differential of the two altitudes would allow them to catch up to the platform in its orbital path in two days.

With the situation on Earth, there was no hope of a rescue ship, manned or unmanned. And they only had food for two weeks. If they were going to survive, they'd have to rescue themselves.

Two hours had passed since the attack on the United States. The blankets and cocoa had stopped the shivering and crying. Hyun-Jin kept his distance from the others, his hands trembling, and stifling the occasional sob. Anderson plucked at his lower lip, until the skin split and bled. Jo-Jo drifted off into blank stares, tears welling in her eyes. The pain would take years to heal—if it ever did.

Tampa or Lakeland, Claire whispered to her own grief. They weren't in Orlando. It will be hard, but I'll find them. We'll be a family together again. She wasn't sure how, but she'd make it happen. She had to. Claire squeezed her eyes shut and rubbed them until she saw sparks.

Better to keep busy. She wanted them all to be occupied when they next passed over North America.

"Everyone," said Claire, "I want to look at ways to repair the lifeboat."

The crew looked at her with dull eyes and little interest. She knew what they were thinking: what was there left to go home to?

"Anything on the station is fair game," she continued. "I don't care if *Reliance* is completely disabled." She made eye contact with each one in turn. "We're going home."

At the mention of home, she saw determination, and saw despair flicker into hope. Jo-Jo wiped her eyes and Anderson let go of his lip. Hyun-Jin watched her warily, as if daring her to save him.

She pushed on. "Jo-Jo, look into converting the lifeboat's engines to use the ATV's fuel. Anderson, is there a way to manufacture a weld that will hold through reentry? Hyun-Jin, how can we shield its electronics from the EMP effects of the Argus barrier? Any idea, no matter how improbable."

Josephine's head jerked up. "I've got Moscow on the radio." She handed the headset to Claire. "Don't know how long it will last."

"Moscow, this is Claire Logan, commander of *Reliance* Space Station."

"It is good to hear you," said a Russian-accented voice. "We were not certain *Reliance* had survived."

"Moscow, I presume you know the United States space

program is out of commission. Can you could send a supply ship? We're running low on food and air filters."

A pause long enough that Claire began to wonder whether they'd lost the signal, then, "*Reliance*. We cannot get a Soyuz to you. The ionization of the upper atmosphere is too great. Our recommendation is to move to higher orbit. Perhaps in a month or two . . ."

"In a month or two," Claire said desperately, "we'll have starved"

"I am sorry, *Reliance*. It is a sad truth that not all things are possible." The signal faded out as *Reliance* crossed over the horizon, cutting off communications.

"What the hell are we going to do?" Anderson asked. "We can't get help from the ground, moving *Reliance* to MEO only buys us a couple of weeks, and fixing the life-boat is impossible."

"If there was ever a time to accomplish the impossible, it's now," said Claire. "The situation on the ground has changed. I was counting on mission control to figure out a way to extract us from MEO. I don't think that's feasible anymore."

A moment of silence as everyone's eyes turned towards the window. Right now it displayed a treacherously beautiful Atlantic Ocean and the lush green coast of Africa. Lost to the eastern horizon was the devastation of all they loved.

"What about the other stations?" asked Jo-Jo into the stillness. "Now that we're at a higher altitude, further from the electrons in orbit, we might be able to contact them. They're in the same fix we are—maybe we can help one another."

Anderson shook his head. "If we transmit a message, the Chinese station might overhear our conversation."

"So?" challenged Claire. "Do you believe the Chinese astronauts had anything to do with the war? If they haven't evacuated, they're as trapped as we are."

"Don't be naive." Anderson's face twisted with disgust. "Our nations are at *war*. They're not going to extend us a helping hand."

"And don't you let your prejudices blind you to a potential source of aid," shot back Claire. "We're astronauts, not soldiers."

"On *this* station. The Chinese station, *Shenzhou XI*, is

funded by the government. They manufacture nanomachine assemblies on board. Maybe even black ops research. The station is probably crawling with military personnel." Anderson looked past Claire. "Hyun-Jin, tell her I'm right."

Hyun-Jin's brows furrowed. "How would I know? A grandmother and a great-uncle living in China doesn't make me an expert on the Chinese space program."

"You understand the language. That gives you insight on how they think, what they value. You heard what their prime minister said on the radio, and how he said it." Anderson's chin jutted out. "*Tell* me he wouldn't direct his space station to attack rival stations."

Hyun-Jin scratched the top of his head, where a lock of hair floated up from a cowlick. "I don't know. I just don't know."

Jo-Jo bit her lip. "Anderson's right, what if *Shenzhou XI* offered to help us, then attacked when we got close? We have no weapons; there'd be no way to defend ourselves."

Claire wanted to tell Anderson he was being paranoid, but the shuttle's destruction had changed all that. "All right, if we aren't ready to risk radio communications, what about visual? We need to ascertain who's still in orbit, and the condition of their stations."

Anderson's eyes widened. "You're thinking salvage."

"If there's an abandoned station with equipment that can help us get home, I wouldn't be above it." She braced herself internally for Anderson's argument. Everything with him was a battle.

He didn't grin—there was too much grief for that—but the lines of disapproval around his mouth softened. "Good idea."

"We can use the Earth-observation cameras." Jo-Jo tapped her lip. "The new high-magnification lenses have an Earth-side resolution of three meters. We won't be able to pick up fine detail—"

"—but we'll be able to see if the lights are on," Claire finished. "Anderson, can you plot our nearest path of approach for the four other stations in orbit?"

"Will do," Anderson said, easing himself behind the navigational laptop with a half-salute.

It was the first sign of respect he'd given Claire since she took command. Maybe, just maybe, if they pulled together

they could get home. Then there'd be time to deal with the
thunderheads of emotion piling up in her mind.

Her worry about Matt and Owen's safety made it hard
to breathe. Claire shoved the pain back. She wouldn't
grieve, not until she was certain. Because once the rain
started falling, flash floods would wash her away.

The flash of light shone through the bathroom's tiny cel-
estory window, blasting sight into intolerable whiteness.
Matt was stepping out of the bathtub, sure the worst had
passed, when the pressure wave hit. The sound was deafening. The ranch house's walls reverberated with the blast.
Overhead the shower curtain rings chimed and danced on
the pole. Plaster fell from the ceiling.

"Daddy," Owen wailed, and tried to burrow into
Matt's armpit.

"Dear Lord," Matt's mother whispered in a quavering
voice.

Matt clenched his eyes shut and hugged his family to
him, trying to shield them from whatever was going on with
his body and the force of his will. Even through closed
eyes, the horrible light burned through his eyelids, turning
everything red.

Pounding blast after blast rang out. God's own thunder-
claps and Lucifer's lightning.

The noise stopped, all except for Owen's sobs and the
weeping of his mother. Matt opened his eyes. Everything
was bathed in a green afterimage. As his eyes focused, he
saw that the bottles of moisturizer and baby powder on the
sink had toppled. A hot wind blew in from the shattered
window high on the wall. Flakes of black soot fell like hellish snow.

One landed on Owen's cheek and he shrieked, clawing
at his skin.

Matt wiped it off.

A red welt blistered Owen's skin where it had fallen.

"Oh, God." Matt yanked the shower curtain down and
wrapped it over them like a blanket. While he protected
them, Betty helped Owen out of the tub. They stumbled
through the darkened house to the hallway, the only room
in the Florida house without windows. Matt began shutting
doors, locking them away from the deadly fallout.

A coldly logical part of his brain noted that the power had gone out.

His mother looked at him with fear-wide eyes. "What's going on?"

Matt wasn't sure whether to tell her about the missiles. She seemed so frail. He stuck with basics: "We need to store water, fill up all the Tupperware from the faucet in the sink. Power's out, so open the refrigerator as little as possible. We'll eat the food in there first. Do you still have that hand-crank radio in your hurricane kits? And duct tape? Is Dad's shotgun in the garage? We'll need it."

"Matt?" His mother's voice was a shriek, and she plucked at his sleeve. Despite his best efforts, flakes of fallout left a smattering of irregular burns across the back of her hand. With her free hand, she hugged a sobbing Owen to her side. "What's happening?"

Matt scrubbed his hand across his face, wishing he could wake up from this nightmare. When he'd shut the door to his mother's bedroom, he'd caught a glimpse of sky through the broken window. A red fireball the size of Orlando rose into the sky, trailing a column of smoke. "I don't know, Mom. Son thing bad."

Anderson tapped the navigational laptop's screen. "This is what I get using the last telemetry data received from Houston. Before . . ." Anderson rubbed his eyes and took a moment to catch his breath. "What I'm saying is, the other stations may have changed orbit. This is the best I can do."

Claire squeezed his shoulder. "It's a place to start. Thank you."

Anderson nodded without looking up.

On the screen four oscillating lines crossed a map of the Earth. The S-shaped paths were marked in red, blue, green, and black and represented the circular orbits of the four stations as plotted onto a flat representation of the globe.

"The black line is us," Anderson said. He pointed at three glowing dots along the black line. "These points represent our closest approach to the other stations." He touched the first of the dots with his finger and a pop-up window displayed two sets of coordinates, *Reliance*'s and the *EEA*'s, as well as the vector between the stations. "We'll be passing over the *EEA* in about an hour."

"Good work." She turned to Hyun-Jin. "What do we know about the *EEA*?"

Hyun-Jin grimaced. "Not much. There's a brief summary of the station in the onboard reference. Give me your palmtop." Claire unstrapped the device from her thigh and handed it to him. Hyun-Jin used the IR port to download the information he'd gleaned and handed it back to her.

The tiny screen scrolled with statistics, the weight and volume of the *EEA* station, its major components, when they were attached, mission commanders and crew, its total flight time. Claire scanned the list of components, looking for . . . there it was. The *EEA* was equipped with an ATV lifeboat capable of evacuating a crew of five. She checked the last mission. There were three astronauts on board: Paulo Santos, Mauro Kaleri, and Iara Oliveira. Two empty seats on a lifeboat. Claire prayed that whatever prompted their distress call had been dealt with and that they hadn't already evacuated orbit.

Two empty seats.

Claire looked around the control module, taking in Anderson, Hyun-Jin, Jo-Jo, and herself. Could two empty seats be extended to four? She'd worry about that later.

A dark thought whispered from the storm clouds in her mind: If the distress call had been a decompression so catastrophic that no one on the *EEA* had time to reach the lifeboat, two empty seats would be five. It was a horrible thing to hope for.

"What about the other stations?" Claire asked.

Hyun-Jin checked the screen in front of him. "Still running the searches on those. I'll let you know as soon as I have something."

"Anderson?" Claire asked. "Anything on repairing the lifeboat?"

Anderson chewed on his inner cheek. "We can scavenge aluminum from the hull of lab one, but I'm not sure spin-friction welds will hold up under reentry."

"Jo-Jo, the engine substitution?"

Jo-Jo tapped her fingers on her forehead. "I may have a way to patch in an engine, but we'll lose fine-control steering . . . and, well, it's dangerous." Jo-Jo chewed on a golden strand of hair. "I think there's like a thirty percent chance we *won't* blow up."

Claire blew out a breath. "I need answers, not excuses."

"I'm doing the best I can," Jo-Jo whined. "This is hard."

Lightning flashed in the storm clouds of Claire's mind. What did this little girl know about hard? Who had she lost: a few friends, siblings, her parents? That would have happened with time, anyway. Parents were supposed to die before children, not the other way round. Somewhere down there, *Owen*——

"It's hard? *Hard*?" Claire pointed at Hyun-Jin. "Do you think any of this is easy for Hyun-Jin? Or Anderson?" She choked on the words "or me?" and left them unsaid. "You *will* find answers. There isn't any room for failure. All the mistakes we can afford to make have already been made. Do you understand me?"

Jo-Jo's eyes blinked rapidly. "I understand—I understand that you're a complete bitch."

Claire slapped her. Microgravity softened the blow, using half its force to rotate Claire away.

Hyun-Jin grabbed Jo-Jo and restrained her from striking back. Anderson caught Claire.

"Anderson was right, you're not fit to lead us," Jo-Jo howled. "Cole wouldn't have let things get this bad."

The words echoed doubts Claire had harbored since she'd faced down Anderson. Maybe he had been right and she should have turned over command to him. What if she got them all killed?

Then she remembered Cole's drinking and Anderson's fear. There were no perfect leaders. Only earnest ones. Claire pulled her arm free from Anderson's grip. "We've all been on edge. Jo-Jo, I shouldn't take things out on you. I'm sorry. Gather whatever information you have, educated guesses, intuition, anything. We need to know if repairing the lifeboat is possible." Claire smoothed the front of her flight suit. "I'll be in the camera observation port, prepping the 70mm camera with a wide-angle lens. Use the intercom if anything comes up."

Jo-Jo's eyes were hot as she watched Claire go.

After she closed the hatch on the command module, Claire sighed, wondering if she'd still be in command when she returned. If the crew decided not to follow her leadership, there would be no consequences. No court-martials or danger of getting kicked out of the astronaut program. All the enforcements back on Earth were gone. The only thing standing between her and mutiny was their goodwill.

After several hours, the marks on Owen's head began to ooze blood. Matt pressed the back of his hand to Owen's cheek. The child was burning with fever, his face was pale.

"Daddy, I don't feel good. I want Mommy." He coughed wetly. The coughing turned into hacking and Owen bent forward, the grilled cheese sandwich he'd eaten that morning spewing forth all over his lap. There were streaks of red blood and tiny black flecks among the yellow chunks of cheese. Owen began to cry.

Matt stripped off his son's T-shirt and jeans and held the boy to his chest. "It's all right. We're going to be all right," he lied. Over Owen's shoulder, he exchanged a worried glance with his mother.

"We've got to get him to the hospital," she whispered in Matt's ear.

Matt nodded, setting his son down on a clean patch of hallway next to his grandmother. He took up the plastic shower curtain. "I'll try the phone."

The kitchen was aswirl in black flakes and soot. Matt pulled a clean dish towel out of a drawer and used it to pick up the handset. He dialed 911, and got a busy signal.

Taped next to the phone was a list of contact numbers. Matt dialed Lakeland Regional Hospital.

"Please hold," a woman said tersely, and transferred him into Muzak.

Owen's wailing was interrupted by the guttural sound of his vomiting. Matt was about to hang up when the woman came back on the line.

"Lakeland Regional. Please hold—"

"I need an ambulance," Matt said in a rush, before she cut him off.

"I'm sorry, sir, there're none available. If you'll give me your address, I can add you to the waiting list."

"There isn't time! My son is throwing up blood, and this black ash burned his face. He may have swallowed some of it."

Her voice conveyed the weariness of a woman trying to feed a multitude with a handful of grain. "All I can do is add him to the list. If you can bring him in yourself, I suggest you—" The line went dead.

Matt cursed and put the receiver back in the cradle.

He opened the door to the garage. His mother's year-old Toyota Electra was parked in its usual spot next to the garbage cans and piles of newspapers ready to recycle. The other side of the garage was filled with shelving units tidily stuffed with Rubbermaid containers that held his father's clothes and possessions. Twenty-four years after his death, his mother still hadn't the heart to get rid of them.

Matt picked the car keys off a hook inside the kitchen door and got in the driver's side. He slid the key in place and cranked the engine.

Nothing happened.

Matt buckled himself in, checked that the car was in park, and tried again.

Nothing. No dashboard lights, no starter grinding in an attempt to ignite combustion, not even the radio.

Cursing, he pounded the steering wheel.

He climbed out of the car and checked the battery. Laying a screwdriver across the terminals produced a spark. So why wouldn't it start? Matt had exhausted his automotive repair skills.

He crossed to the gun cabinet. The combination was Matt's own birthday. His father had bought it when Matt was three and had gotten into the dresser drawer where a pistol was stored.

All that was left of his father's gun collection was an old twelve-gauge shotgun that had belonged to Matt's grandfather. The rest had been given away to Matt's uncles. The gun was wrapped in oilcloth and gleamed in the low light when Matt uncovered it. There was a box of shells on the shelf above the guns. Matt lifted it, and the tagboard gave way, spilling yellow shotgun shells all over the concrete floor. Matt scrabbled to collect them all, then groaned. The price sticker on the side of the box was yellowed and bore the name of a gun shop that had closed two decades ago. These shells were at least twenty years old.

There were nineteen in all, *if* the powder had stayed dry all these years. He loaded three in the shotgun, and thought about shooting one as a test. But no, the neighbors had enough to worry about without random gunfire, and if the shells were viable, nineteen was too few to waste.

Hoisting the shotgun to his shoulder, Matt closed the door to the gun safe and saw a jumble of tubes and dials sitting on the shelf next to the safe. A swell of sadness and nostalgia hit Matt as he remembered summer nights as a child, staying up after dark with his father trying to reach distant lands with the ham radio they'd built together.

Matt ran a finger over the top casing. It was thick with greasy dust.

Owen's cries cut through his reverie. This was no time to dwell on the past. He grabbed a plastic container that held his mother's hurricane kit: bottled water, dried food, duct tape, space blanket, crank-powered flashlight/radio, and iodine tablets.

Back in the hallway, his mother had mopped up the vomit with Owen's T-shirt and relocated the boy to the other end of the hall. She draped her cotton cardigan over his shoulders and patted his shoulder, rocking him sideways in rhythm while humming *Brahms's Lullaby*, a song Matt remembered her singing from his childhood.

Her veneer of bravery was betrayed by the trembling of her hands, and the pale parchment of her face. She looked down and away from the gun.

Matt bent and wrapped the silver space blanket around them both. Then he squatted next to them, lay the shotgun out of Owen's reach, and cranked the emergency radio. It lit up as his kinetic force was converted into electricity by the generator.

"—mergency broadcast system. Please stay inside until further notice. Secure your windows and doors with plastic. Repeat, do not go outdoors unless absolutely necessary. If you require assistance, erect a red flag and National Guardsmen will assist you as soon as possible."

Matt cranked some more and listened. The message looped through again, repeating itself. No indication of what had happened, no explanation. Just a calm recitation to stay put.

Matt opened his mother's linen closet and rooted around until he found a red tablecloth. Donning his shower curtain, he hurriedly opened the door and slammed the cloth in the door, draping it over the top as a makeshift flag. He slapped at the burning flakes that drifted onto his arm, making sure they were gone before he returned to his mother and son.

He didn't tell them what he'd seen outside the door. They were scared enough without knowing that the sky had gone dark, Orlando was in flames, and the green ghosts of electric auroras danced in the sky.

The camera port on *Reliance* was a twenty-inch-diameter porthole of high-quality optical glass. It was shielded from light leaking in from the station by a two-meter-wide box built around the window. The inside walls of the box were painted black. Claire pushed the top half of her torso through a neoprene tube that clung to her waist and completed the seal.

Camera equipment was strapped into racks that lined the walls of the camera port: 35mm and 70mm cameras, IR filters, and a host of lenses. Geologists and meteorologists were always desperate for high-resolution images of Earth.

Claire pushed the button that caused a protective cover outside of the station to slide away from the window. The view was spectacular. Looking out the high-quality optical window always gave Claire the breathless feeling that she was floating in space without a suit.

They were passing over Australia in daylight. Iron content in the soil colored the deserts red, fading to tan and then green where it met the ocean. From here, she couldn't see the cities but she imagined life in them was much the same as ever. No bombs had fallen on this self-sufficient continent. Unreasoning hatred of the Australians welled up within her.

Claire wiped her hand across her face to clear her mind. She had to stay in control, or there'd be more mistakes like she'd made with Jo-Jo. The crew needed her. Right now she had a job to do.

Feeling leaden, Claire unstrapped a 70mm camera from the rack and attached a wide-angle zoom lens. She put it in a mounting frame that dampened the vibration from the station and swung the frame in front of the porthole. Once that was set, Claire checked the clock on her handheld. If the *EEA* hadn't changed course, *Reliance* would pass over it in the next ten minutes.

She looked through the camera lens to set the zoom on minimum, so she'd have the largest possible field of view to make initial line of sight to the other station.

The southwest coast of Australia lay beneath her, green land fracturing into cobalt ocean. Without intending to, her hands zoomed in on a coastal city. Maybe Perth? It was sprawling, and with the high-resolution lens Claire could make out buildings in tidy rows, cars moving on highways, and boats lolling at tie-ups in the harbor. Everything was heartbreakingly normal. The viewfinder of the camera fogged over. Claire dashed her eyes and carefully cleaned the viewfinder with optical cloth.

A beeping from her palmtop heralded the point of closest approach to the *EEA*. Claire zoomed out, moving the mounting frame to scan the space between *Reliance* and Earth. A bright point of light caught her eye, but turned out to be sun bouncing off a cloud.

Anderson's voice boomed down the access tunnel. "We're not getting any images, is the digital line hooked up?"

"It's not there," Claire shouted back. "There's nothing to photograph." Claire checked the ticks on the camera mounting rack. She was looking in the right place. She scanned the area again. Nothing.

A large white cloud mass swept across the Pacific Ocean west of the Australia coast. A black dot crossed it, catching Claire's eye. Claire zoomed in on it. She sucked in a breath.

The cylindrical station had been torn nearly in half. It looked like a giant had grabbed both ends and twisted, as if to open a stuck jar lid. The edges of the tear were ragged where the metal had failed. No lights flickered from the station. It floated dead in orbit. Debris drifted alongside it, white puffs of insulation, metal drawers, and a limp body, arms and legs flung wide like a discarded rag doll.

Claire snapped pictures of the wreck. The camera automatically transmitted the digital images to the command module.

What was left of the *EEA* tumbled gently in orbit. Hating herself, Claire hoped the accident had happened too quickly for the lifeboat to be used. She waited for the *EEA* to turn its docking port her way. Minutes that seemed like hours crept by. Claire continued to take pictures as new views presented themselves. It was ghoulish, but information about what happened to the *EEA* might save their lives.

The station tumbled; its docking port rose into view. For a second, Claire thought she saw the dorsal fin of an orbital space plane, but it was only the edge of a satellite dish. The station continued to turn, exposing an undamaged, but empty, docking pin.

The *EEA* was destroyed, and its lifeboat gone.

CHAPTER 8

Claire took dozens of pictures of the *EEA* as it tumbled through space. They would decide later whether the station was worth salvaging. So far, Claire didn't see anything that would make her risk radiation exposure and waste fuel on a rendezvous.

When she had what she needed, Claire checked her palmtop. The next nearest space station was the Chinese station: *Shenzhou XI*. In forty-five minutes *Reliance* would cross its point of nearest approach. When Claire traced the orbital line with her stylus, her stomach rumbled.

She couldn't remember the last time she'd had food. "I'm going to the galley," she announced over the intercom. "What does everyone want?"

Hyun-Jin responded. "We're not hungry. And shouldn't we . . . institute rationing?"

Claire pinched the bridge of her nose. They had bigger problems than food rationing. "We'll figure that out later. Right now, we can't afford to make mistakes because of low blood sugar. I'll pick something."

Claire squeezed out of the camera port, took the left tube to the galley, and grabbed four breakfast sandwiches.

There were small, easy to eat, and full of protein for long-term energy.

When Claire entered the command module, Jo-Jo was studying the images Claire had taken of the destroyed *EEA* and scribbling notes on her palmtop. Jo-Jo took the heated sandwich that Claire offered without looking up, and mumbled "thanks." The civility gave Claire hope that their working relationship could be salvaged.

"What's the word on the *EEA*?" Anderson asked, taking the sandwich from her hand. "We still planning to rendezvous with the Mars platform?" He pulled at the heated plastic to unwrap it, and steam vented into the air, carrying with it the scent of eggs, cheese, and Canadian bacon.

Claire tossed a sandwich to Hyun-Jin and then plucked at her own to open it. "I don't see anything on the *EEA* that changes my plans. But I haven't viewed *Shenzhou XI* yet. It comes into view," she checked her palmtop, "in half an hour." Looking at the graph, she frowned. "What's this plus sign on the Japanese orbital line mean?"

"Orientation. They're an astronomical research facility, studying the solar flares that affect communication satellites. They're in middle-Earth orbit. We'd have to flip the station to put the viewing port in line of sight."

Claire took a bite of the sandwich. The savory taste of cheese and ham wakened her hunger and she quickly took a second bite. After she swallowed, she asked, "With ten thousand miles of altitude separating us, would we be able to see any relevant details with the cameras?"

"I doubt it. The Japanese Weather Observatory is a small station. Only has a crew of five. Even if they haven't evacuated, they won't have much in the way of supplies."

Worse and worse. It was beginning to look like the Chinese—currently at war with the United States—might be their best hope of aid. Claire took another bite. She prayed Anderson was wrong about the Chinese astronauts' politics; that human decency and the fraternity of astronauts would sway them to help, and if not that, at least to cooperate against the deadly forces of man and nature.

The alarm she'd set on her palmtop bleeped, indicating ten minutes left before her viewing of the Chinese station. Claire finished her sandwich and stuffed the plastic wrapper into the canvas dry-waste bag strapped to the wall. The bag was full and she had to shove the new waste in forcefully. It was another reminder of how long it had been since their last resupply.

Reliance was over the Atlantic Ocean somewhere between South America and Africa. The war-ravaged continents of North America and Asia were mercifully out of view.

Claire used the 70mm camera to scan the cobalt-blue ocean for a silver dot. A gathering of clouds spiraled into a tropical storm. Sun glinting off the white clouds made Claire's eyes water. The dips and crenellations of the spiral could easily obscure the small bright point of *Shenzhou XI*.

A glint of silver caught her breath and Claire focused in. Disappointment washed over her. It was just a weather satellite, not *Shenzhou XI*.

"We're not receiving any images," Anderson called over the intercom.

"That's because there isn't anything to transmit," Claire sent back. "I can't locate *Shenzhou*. Are your calculations correct?"

A moment's silence. "They're correct according to the last telemetry data we received from Houston. They wouldn't have enough fuel on board to make a major orbital change. You should see them. Space stations don't just vanish."

Claire searched the sky again. "This one has."

A rustling sound over the intercom. "I'm coming down."

Claire's face heated at the implied assumption that he'd be able to see something she missed. She rubbed her tired eyes. Claire sighed, wishing she could go to sleep for a week. Maybe Anderson was right, a fresh perspective would help.

She wriggled out of the neoprene tube.

The hatch popped open and Anderson came in. "Let me take a look."

Claire moved away from the port and gestured to it. "Help yourself."

Anderson grunted as he squeezed into the light-sealing neoprene skirt.

Feeling redundant and useless, Claire hovered over his

legs, waiting while he searched. He made an interested noise, then snorted disappointment. She guessed he'd found the weather satellite.

After an eternity of waiting, Anderson pulled himself free of the isolation box. The skin above his eyebrows puckered with worry. "I don't get it. A space station can't just disappear. If it had been destroyed, there would at least be a debris field."

"Not if they deorbited into the atmosphere," Claire said. She thought of all the things that could wrong on a station, especially one under EMP attack from the residue of nuclear explosions. "It could have been accidental. The controller that fired the attitudinal thrusters malfunctioned. Drove them deeper into the Earth's atmosphere."

Anderson was silent a moment. It was a horrific thought, a station being dragged into reentry by the friction of the Earth's atmosphere. Space stations were delicate structures, built for weightlessness. They didn't have the strength or heat-shielding necessary to survive a return to Earth. If *Shenzhou* was on a collision course with Earth, it would take days to founder. The crew would be trapped inside a disintegrating vessel, burning alive.

"If that's what happened—and it's not certain—there's no way we could save them," said Anderson.

Claire nodded. It was speculation, not worth worrying about. They had too many real problems to waste time on hypothetical ones.

They returned to the command module.

Jo-Jo asked Anderson, "What's up with the Chinese station?" She didn't make eye contact with Claire.

"It's missing," Claire answered. "We don't know what happened. There's no debris, no wreckage. It's just gone. It may have reentered the atmosphere."

Hyun-Jin was at the pilot's station, studying the damaged Earth onscreen. He looked up, eyes stricken. After a moment he asked softly, "So what's our plan?"

Claire pulled herself over to the navigational laptop and checked the telemetry. "We rendezvous with the Mars platform. Once we fuel up, we decide whether to repair the lifeboat quickly enough in LEO to avoid the spread of the Argus effect—possibly using salvage from the *EEA*—or if we have to hide out in MEO with the Japanese."

"What will MEO buy us? We only have food for—"

"Three weeks," Claire said exasperated. "I *know*. But that's time we won't have if we sit in low-Earth orbit and wait for *Reliance* to fall apart." Claire put her hands on her knees. She had to give them hope. "Let me tell you a story. A thief was sentenced to die. On the day he was to be hanged, he went to the king and begged for his life. The king refused. Then the convict pointed to a nearby pig and said, 'If you give me a year, I'll teach that pig to sing. If I succeed, pardon me. If I fail, you can put me to death.' The king accepted his bargain. When his family asked how he could possibly teach a pig to sing, the convict replied, 'Either way, I've got a year more of life, and you never know . . . the pig might learn to sing.'" Claire clapped her hands against her thighs. "That's us. Trying to gain enough time to teach *Reliance* to sing. You got me?"

Hyun-Jin nodded, but his shoulders were hunched in defeat.

The Mars platform would solve two of their problems: fuel and air. But there was no food on board. The Mars mission was still years away, waiting for the huge liquid oxygen and liquid hydrogen fuel tanks to be filled. For the past three years, countries all over the world had been sending cargo ships bearing water to the fueling depot. There, solar-powered electrolysis units converted the water into the fuel that would power the long-range mission.

Claire felt guilty about raiding the Mars fuel depot. For the past decade, international enthusiasm over the mission had been growing. Sponsors had clamored to fund the development of a long-range ship; governments had pumped billions into the project. Mankind was preparing to take the next step out of Earth's cradle, after a lag of nearly forty years, to take up human space exploration again. What she was planning would set the project back years.

Then it hit her. There wasn't going to be any Mars mission. Not in four years, not in four decades. Earth's governments would turn their eyes from the heavens to rebuilding cities, repairing infrastructures, and trying to fix the ecological disaster wrought by the nuclear war.

Thunder rumbled in her chest, and Claire fought back a hailstorm of tears. Survive. Later there will be time to grieve. Or there wouldn't. Either way, now wasn't the time.

Claire checked Anderson's calculations on the pilot's screen. On their current course, *Reliance* would rendezvous with the Mars platform in three hours.

In the meantime, *Reliance* required routine maintenance. Since the bombs had fallen over India, no one had vacuumed the air filters or changed the CO_2 cartridges. The air quality on the station, never great, was now like trying to breathe through dirty sweat socks. The CO_2 levels were at 3 mmHg and rising.

"Jo-Jo?"

The young woman ignored her and continued to read her palmtop.

Claire moved until she hovered in front of Jo-Jo. Crossing her arms and legs, she waited like a hovering Buddha until Jo-Jo looked up.

The expression on the younger woman's face was sullen.

Claire knew she'd have to make peace with Jo-Jo. Things happened fast on a space station; there wouldn't be time to soothe emotions when events started flying. Claire held out her hand. "I need to check the CO_2 canisters. Will you help?"

Jo-Jo sighed. She stowed her palmtop in a pocket on the sleeve of her flight suit and unfolded herself without taking Claire's hand.

The air filters and carbon dioxide scrubbers were in the habitation module. A vacuum was built into the wall. Claire pulled out the retractable rubber hose and suctioned off the debris the filters had pulled in over the past few days: crumbs of food, a lost screw, dust, shed hairs. Larger items, a palmtop stylus, Band-Aids that had fallen out of the first aid kit when Jo-Jo wrapped Anderson's head, and a focus ring for a 35mm camera, Claire collected into a clear plastic bag to put away later.

Jo-Jo returned with a new desiccant and absorption unit for the CO_2 scrubber. Her eyes were wide. "There's only one left after this. It's marked with a black *X* of electrical tape."

A grim smile tightened Claire's lips. "I know. It failed last week. It's why I haven't worried about the food rationing." She lifted the plate from the wall to expose the old canister. "Three weeks of food, two weeks of air."

"You knew about this?" Jo-Jo accused. "And you didn't tell anyone?"

Claire stopped working free the old canister filter and met Jo-Jo's stare. "What good would it have done? Do you think Hyun-Jin or Anderson need anything more to worry about right now? Did you?"

Jo-Jo's eyes flashed. "You don't have the right to withhold information. Especially something this vital."

Claire sighed. This wasn't how she had intended their talk to go. "I'll tell them as soon as we get back. I wanted to speak to you first, privately."

Jo-Jo narrowed her eyes. "To chew me out?"

Claire pinched the bridge of her nose. "To apologize. I'm sorry I lost my temper and lashed out at you. It was wrong. I'm trying to be a good commander . . . but, well, this hasn't been the easiest command." She held out her hand to the other woman. "If we're going to make it home, we can't afford any bad blood between crew members."

Jo-Jo looked at the CO_2 canister in her hands and did not reply.

"Jo-Jo, do you accept my apology?"

Without looking up, Jo-Jo said, "I've always hated that name. It makes me sound like the dog-faced boy."

Claire blinked. It wasn't the response she'd expected. "Why didn't you say so before now?"

When Jo-Jo looked up, her eyes were bright with unshed tears. "Because I wanted to fit in. All my life I'd wanted to be an astronaut, and I wasn't going to let some stupid name keep me from being one of the team, but . . . I hate it."

The absurdity of it: their dying in space, the war on Earth, and Jo-Jo's foremost complaint was about her *nickname*? Claire failed to suppress a smile.

Jo-Jo looked wounded.

Claire covered her mouth. "I'm sorry, but with all that's going on . . ." With great effort she sobered her expression and fought off hysterical giggles. "What do you want to be called?"

"My name: Josephine." Her voice roughened. "If I'm going to die, I don't want that damned nickname to be the last thing anyone calls me." The tears she'd been holding back exploded, and Jo-Jo—Josephine—covered her face with her hands. Her back and shoulders shook as she cried.

And that quickly, Claire understood the strain the young woman had endured. She'd been promoted ahead of others because of her scientific successes, had endured envy from those passed over, had been the outsider in the station's crew: too young, too unconventional. Claire had thought her tough beyond her years. But it had all been an act. Inside Jo-Jo, Josephine had been suffering.

Claire took her into her arms. "Shhh, Josephine. It's all right. We're not going to die up here. We're going to to fix the lifeboat. We'll get home." She smoothed a strand of dark hair from Josephine's face. "It's a good thing you're on board. We need a specialist in propulsion physics."

Josephine took a few minutes to master her breathing, then gently pushed Claire away. She undid and retied her ponytail to catch the strands of hair that had escaped. Without looking up, she said, "You remind me of my mother."

Claire raised an eyebrow. "Ouch." She was only eight years older.

"No—I mean in a good way. She could face anything. Nothing got Mom down. Dad left her with six kids to raise all by herself. And she did. We never went hungry, always had new clothes at the beginning of the school year. No matter how bad things got, she made me feel hope." Josephine's lips pressed together and Claire knew she was remembering the bombs. Mother, siblings, even the wayward father, likely all were dead now.

"My mother's the one who convinced me to become an astronaut. She said I could do anything I set my mind to." Josephine nodded to herself, as if listening to an inner voice. Then she looked up. "Guess I'd better set my mind to fixing the lifeboat."

Claire grinned at her. "I'd guess you'd better . . . Josephine."

Matt moved his mother and Owen to the garage, laying Owen down in the backseat. The car wouldn't start, but it was free of the burning black flakes that filled the other rooms of the house.

Owen worried him. The boy was burning up with fever

and moaning incoherently. He said "Mama" so often it broke Matt's heart. Matt raided the freezer for some ice, wrapped it in a towel, and gave it to his mother to dab on Owen's forehead.

The waiting chafed Matt. Where was the National Guard? Owen was feverish, and there was nothing he could do to make him better. He'd braved the bathroom for Tylenol, but it wasn't working.

He had to *do* something. The crank-handle radio told him to seal off the windows and doors. But how to do that when the windows were shattered? His mother didn't have a supply of plywood.

Desperate for something to do, Matt pulled down his father's ham radio and brushed the dust off. If he could figure out how to power it up from batteries, he could use the radio to call for help. Tell the guard where to find them. Tell them his son needed help.

Or maybe he should run outside and try to steal a car. But how would he hot-wire it? And the burning black flakes were still falling like hellish snow.

Matt wiped his brow. He felt hot and nauseated. No. He couldn't get sick, his mother and son needed him.

He wished Claire was with him. She was the scientist, always good in a crisis. Matt looked up at the garage ceiling, imagining the stars beyond. No. He wished he and Owen were with her, instead of down here.

From a distance, the Mars fuel platform looked like a pair of enormous golden wings. They were high-performance solar cells that powered the electrolysis that separated water into liquid oxygen and liquid hydrogen propellants.

Between the solar arrays two huge white walls shielded the fuel tanks from the sun. The radiators prevented its rays from warming the depot's fuel back into its gaseous state.

Though the tanks were currently hidden, Claire had seen diagrams of the depot at a colloquium at NASA: twelve-meter-long tanks, eight of them, lined up abacus fashion along a central structure that housed the water docking port, water storage tanks, and the electrolysis system. The tanks were aligned with the Earth's gravitational field, orbiting so the long axis of the tanks pointed at Earth's center of mass. The microgravity gradient settled the propellant after production.

Beneath the tanks, pointing Earth-ward, was the oversized nozzle of the rocket engine designed to take a crew of five to Mars. Attached to the station, it provided periodic burns to keep the platform in orbit. It was like swatting a fly with a Buick, but when the Mars Transport was assembled in space, it would be transferred to that spaceship. The maintenance burns acted as a low-level stress test on the biggest engine mankind had ever built.

There were two ports at either end of the central structure. The down-orbit one was covered by a water-delivery vehicle. At the ends of each tank was a docking port used to extract fuel.

In addition to stockpiling fuel for the Mars mission, the fueling depot provided reboost propellant to communications satellites and orbiting telescopes.

It was an ungainly, blockish structure, built for strength, not architectural splendor, but to Claire it was more beautiful than a Gaudí cathedral. The fuel depot represented water, oxygen, and an escape from the Argus effect. It would be their salvation.

"Glorious," Anderson said from the pilot's station beside her.

Hovering behind them, Josephine tapped her lip with a finger. "We might be able to scavenge an engine from that water transfer vehicle. I believe it uses monopropellant hydrazine for its docking thrusters. It'd take a helluva kludge to make it work, though."

"Initiating burn to dock with the fuel depot," said Anderson. "Now." He pushed a button on the console and Claire felt the gentle resistance of inertia.

Hyun-Jin used a pair of binoculars to study the fuel depot from the porthole. It wasn't as optically clear as the camera port, but at this proximity, it was good enough. "There appears to be something . . . Oh, my God."

"What?" Claire turned to him, alarmed.

Hyun-Jin pulled the binoculars from his face. His eyes were wide. He handed her the bulky field glasses.

Claire took them and scanned the fuel depot.

Rising over the radiator panel was a collection of cylin-

ders of different sizes, attached end-to-end, and topped by
a set of four solar panels. At this distance, it looked like
the segmented body and wings of a dragonfly. Claire sucked
in a breath.

Another space station. *Shenzhou XI*. She recognized it
from NASA briefings. It was twice as massive as *Reliance*.
The Chinese used it to manufacture nanomachine assemblies in a weightless environment.

"What is it?" asked Anderson, hands hovering over command panel. "Should I abort the approach?"

Claire dropped the field glasses from her face. She felt
stunned. In a flat voice she said, "We just found the Chinese station."

She felt stupid for not anticipating this. Of course the
other stations trapped in orbit would head towards the only
fuel source: the Mars depot.

Claire kicked back to the commander's leg restraint and
reoriented the forward camera. She zoomed in on the
fuel structure.

The dragonfly body crested the fuel depot. Delicate script
formed pictographs on its side. Beneath, in Arabic lettering:
Shenzhou XI.

"Where *the hell*," said Anderson, "did the Chinese get
the propellant to move their station to the Mars platform?"

As they watched, the tail of the dragonfly detached,
turned, and showed its cylindrical profile.

"ATV," Josephine said dispiritedly. "No reentry capabilities." She scanned the station's image. "I don't see a lifeboat. But maybe . . ." She zoomed the camera in on a
detail along one side of the dragonfly's thorax. "Yes." Josephine's tone was breathless with excitement. "They're using
Russian-made EADS Model CHT 400 engines for attitudinal thrusters. They're the same as on our CEV." She
jabbed her finger at the screen. "With those thrusters, I
could fix the lifeboat."

The Chinese ATV moved towards the array of fuel
tanks. For a horrific instant, Claire thought it meant to
crash into the tanks and destroy the depot. At the last
moment the ATV fired jets and slowed to softly dock
with the transfer vehicle docking pin on the end of the
nearest tank.

"They're stealing our ride to MEO," Anderson said. He

half-pushed himself out of the pilot's station, as if he intended to intercept the ATV bodily.

"The Mars depot is an international effort," said Hyun-Jin quietly. "It's as much theirs as ours."

"Whose side are you on?" Anderson growled. He jabbed his finger at the oversized cone welded to the station's base. "There's only the one cryogenic engine. We can't let them take it."

"Let's find out their intentions," said Claire, "before we assume the worst. Josephine, can you establish line-of-sight communications?"

"Yes, Ma'am," answered the young woman.

Anderson raised an eyebrow. She wasn't sure if his surprise was at her use of Jo-Jo's full name, or the respect she'd shown Claire.

"*Shenzhou XI*, this is *Reliance*," Josephine called over the radio. "Do you read? *Shenzhou XI*, this is *Reliance* station, off your bow. Do you copy?"

The radio sputtered, then a grainy picture formed on the video screen. Through the static, Claire made out a man, mid-forties, with a smooth maple complexion. Above the flat planes of his cheeks, intelligent brown eyes gleamed under high-arching eyebrows. Short-cropped black hair came to a widow's peak in the center of his forehead. If his face had a flaw, it was a weak chin. His lean, whipcord body was dressed in shorts and a T-shirt sporting an arm patch of the Chinese Space Agency's logo: the corner of a red flag and stars superimposed over a black background, symbolizing China's entering space.

"*Reliance*, this is Zhang Rui, commander of the *Shenzhou*." His voice surprised Claire. It was deeper than she'd expected, and resonant, the Chinese lilt overlaid by round British vowels. James Earl Jones, if he had been the love child of the British consulate to China.

Claire leaned over Josephine. "This is Claire Logan, of the *Reliance*. We copy you, *Shenzhou*." She wasn't sure how to proceed. What was protocol when talking to an enemy commander, one whose help you desperately needed to survive? "Are you in need of assistance?"

A long pause. The video image froze.

"Have we lost the connection?" Claire asked Josephine.

Josephine shook her head, sending her ponytail into oscillations. "The carrier signal's still strong."

Zhang's image unfroze. "We are five. With no return capability. One of my crew holds a Ph.D. in aerospace engineering. He tells me your lifeboat is damaged, but may be repairable. Perhaps we may help one another."

"Five?" Anderson's voice was shrill with disbelief. He reached out and cut the connection.

Claire glared at her pilot. "How dare you—"

Anderson continued as if she hadn't spoken. "Our CEV only holds seven, max. We can't rescue them all. They've got to know that. We don't know what happened to their rescue vehicle, or the *EEA* station. They might help us repair the lifeboat then steal it out from us. We're better off doing the kludge repairs—"

"Anderson!"

He blinked, stunned at the force of her shout.

Claire moved close, until their noses nearly touched. In a deadly undertone, she said, "Never interrupt me when I'm speaking on the com. This is a delicate political situation. If you've got something to say, you *wait* until I'm done talking."

"I hate to agree on this," said Hyun-Jin in a soft voice, "but Anderson may be right. My Uncle Shen told me stories about life in Communist China. The government may have ordered them to destroy the other stations. If that were their goal, they would have no scruples deceiving us."

"This is crazy," Josephine said. "Those aren't soldiers over there, they're scientists and astronauts. They're people who—like us—have no way home. Sure I can kludge a fix that's got—maybe—a thirty percent chance of making it home, but with their engines, our chances are three times better. Five more passengers only puts us two over the recommended limit; we could remove some equipment, balance the weight. Find a way to strap in the extra passengers—it'd be dangerous flying without a seat, but a whole lot better than leaving them stranded in space."

They looked to Claire. She felt the weight of their expectation and wondered if Cole had felt the same when she had looked to him for answers. "We need more information. But please"—and she focused her next words on Anderson—"let me do the talking."

Claire smoothed her hair and forced a calm expression of concern on her face. "*Shenzhou, Reliance.* Sorry about that, we had communication difficulties. What happened to your escape vehicle?"

Zhang's image froze, and Claire wondered if he was having command issues with his crew. Even frozen in place, the set of his mouth and wisdom in his hooded eyes exuded confidence and authority. Probably not.

"We had a medical emergency. Two of our crew took the lifeboat and returned to Earth. The rest of us stayed behind to continue our research. A new rescue vessel was due to dock in three days. It did not seem an unreasonable risk." His thin lips nearly disappeared in a rueful smile. "At the time."

Claire wanted to believe him, to believe the whole world hadn't gone insane and people could still help each other, regardless of political affiliations. Zhang's expression was honest and guardedly hopeful. But some internal intuition nagged at her. There were details he'd left out about the loss of their lifeboat, and the mystery of where *Shenzhou* had gotten the fuel to boost into orbit matching the Mars fuel depot, and the unexplained destruction of the *EEA* station.

She froze the connection.

"We're going to work with them, right?" Josephine said, hovering over Claire's right shoulder. "I mean, we're not just going to let them die up here."

Anderson, squeezed in next to Claire, pivoted towards Josephine. "Are you insane?" he thundered. "China is—in case everyone *else* on this station has forgotten it—the country that blew the United States to hell. Killed our loved ones? Remember? I'd die before I'd work with them."

Adrenaline shot lightning through the clouds of emotion Claire'd repressed. She turned on Anderson. "Do you mean that? Because that may be *exactly* the choice we're facing."

Anderson leaned forward. She could smell bacon on his breath as he talked. "What makes you think his offer is legit? It could be a gambit to put us off our guard. The

U.S. did damage to China as well. Perhaps Zhang wants revenge."

"In his place," Josephine argued, "I'd want to survive more than I'd want revenge."

"And you?" Claire asked Hyun-Jin.

Hyun-Jin fumbled his fingers along the hem of his T-shirt. "I think we should proceed . . . with caution. He may be dangerous, but he is also our best chance of repairing the lifeboat."

On the main screen, the ATV remained docked to the Mars platform. Claire's eyes were drawn to something on the hull of the ATV. She slid in next to Anderson and zoomed in with the camera. The view swung left, centering on the ATV's call sign.

The black script on the side wasn't Chinese calligraphy, it was Arabic lettering. The words read: ESTAÇÃO DE ESPAÇO DO ALLIANCE. Beneath them, instead of the Chinese Space Agency emblem, was the blue-and-green symbol of the South American Space Alliance.

Anderson's voice was triumphant. "If they're good guys, what the hell are they doing with an ATV from a destroyed station?"

CHAPTER 9

Staring at the ATV, Claire remembered the *EEA* station, an aluminum can torn in half by a giant, its ragged edges gleaming in sunlight, contents spewed into vacuum. Spilled drawers, shattered equipment, splayed bodies, carelessly shoved into vacuum's harsh embrace. The lifeboat had been gone. Claire prayed the rest of the crew had evacuated; what was left of the station couldn't support life.

Anderson stabbed his finger at the tiny ship ferrying fuel to *Shenzhou XI*. "The *EEA* sure as hell didn't *give* Zhang that ATV."

Claire made a slicing motion across her neck to silence Anderson and reached for the transmitter. "*Shenzhou*, this is *Reliance*. We're noticing the ATV you're using bears *EEA* markings. How did you come by it?"

"Ah." Zhang's arched eyebrows drew together in concern. "That is a sad story." He wiped sweat from his forehead with his shoulder. "The *EEA* station was stricken by EMP from a blast that destroyed a U.S. spy satellite. We heard their distress call. One of my crew speaks Spanish, which was close enough to Portuguese to understand the message. They had lost power to their air-purification system and were choking on exhaled CO_2.

"Their orbit was close to ours, so we did a burn to catch up and rescue them." Zhang's voice softened. "It took sixteen hours to reach them. When we arrived, the station was destroyed. It looked as if a canister of pressurized oxygen had exploded like a bomb and torn the hull in half. Perhaps they tried to rig a temporary breathing apparatus and damaged the tank's nozzle.

"Using EVA suits, my crew searched for survivors, but found none. We salvaged the ATV and enough fuel to boost *Shenzhou XI* into orbit with the Mars platform."

Claire took in the information, seeing the destruction anew through Zhang's description: the flared-out metal from where the EEA had explosively decompressed. But there was one thing unexplained. "What about the *EEA*'s lifeboat?"

The skin between Zhang's brow puckered. In his rich, slow voice he said, "I don't know. It was missing when we arrived. We can hope some of the crew evacuated before the hull ruptured."

Claire remembered the panicked message they'd received from the *EEA* crew. They hadn't understood the words, but it had clearly been a distress call. Guilt cramped her stomach. If *Reliance* had tried to help the Brazilian station, could they have prevented the explosion?

Anderson put his hand over the transmitter to cut off video and sound. "Bullshit. Don't believe a word of it. *Shenzhou XI* destroyed *EEA*. If we let our guard down, they'll do the same to us. The Chinese started the goddamned war by invading India." His voice thickened and his hands clenched into fists so tight his arms trembled. "They killed our family, our loved ones. I say it's time for payback. We take them out, then salvage the thrusters we need from the wreckage."

Anderson's hate was palpable in the small command module. Claire felt it wash over her like acid. For a long moment, nobody spoke.

Owen's chubby hand as he patted her face and told her "all better" after she'd twisted her ankle skating with him. Lightning struck thunder in Claire's mind.

"Fortunately, it's not *your* decision." Claire snapped. "*I'm* in command. I say we proceed"—she held up a hand to cut off Anderson's protest—"with caution. This isn't a military station; we have no weapons. But most of all, killing Zhang and his crew won't bring back," she swallowed hard, "the people who died Earth-side." She couldn't say "our families," wouldn't face that until she had to. "Until we have evidence that Zhang was involved with what happened to the *EEA*, I'm inclined to believe him."

Anderson looked at her incredulously. "The Chinese are our *enemy*."

"The Chinese *government*. These are individuals, astronauts, just like us. They need our lifeboat, we need their thrusters, or we all die. It's a strong motive to cooperate."

"Yeah, they'll cooperate until the lifeboat is repaired. Then we'll see."

The radio blinked, waiting for her reply.

Claire pushed back her hair, trying to calm herself. It immediately sprang back into its weightless Afro position. "I don't like relying on Zhang, but it's our best option."

"You're going to get us all killed," Anderson rumbled.

Claire felt a pang of indecision. He might be right. But they might also die if they tried to repair the lifeboat without Zhang's help. There was no way to know ahead of time. With faked resolve, Claire said, "We're going to work with the Chinese. I want ideas: What do we need from them? How can we expedite the repairs with their help?" She pointed at Anderson, "You figure out how to mitigate risk if they turn on us."

"We need a patch for the lifeboat's hull," Hyun-Jin said. "We've got the stir-welding guns used during *Reliance*'s construction, but a TIG or electron-beam welder would be better for cutting the patch."

"Great. Since you're fluent in both Mandarin and English, I want you relaying the construction plan to *Shenzhou*. I don't want any miscommunications. We can't risk anything else going wrong."

Claire pointed at Josephine. "You're in charge of planning the engine repair. Make a list of tools, which engines off *Shenzhou* you need, extra fuel lines, anything you can think of. When you're done, give the information to Hyun-Jin to relay to Zhang."

"What's your job?" Anderson asked.

"I'm going to figure out what we can pull out of the lifeboat without crippling it. If we're going to take on two extra people, we need to get the weight down. Maybe install extra oxygen tanks."

The com light still blinked. Two hundred and fifty meters away, Zhang waited for his reply. Claire hit the transmit button. "*Shenzhou,* this is *Reliance.* We believe we can fit your people into our Crew Escape Vessel."

Zhang barked a few words in Mandarin over his shoulder. A ragged cheer went up from his crew. When he turned back, the taint of a relieved smile tweaked his lips. "That is good news."

"We need your help, however, in repairing our CEV. Mission Specialist Hyun-Jin will describe what we need."

Claire traded places with Hyun-Jin and he repeated their request for equipment in Mandarin.

Zhang's left eyebrow rose in surprise and he uttered a long sentence in lilting Chinese.

Hyun-Jin looked over his shoulder. "He says our requests are quite reasonable. He will direct the two crew members who are already EVA to stop work on the Mars platform, return to *Shenzhou,* and disassemble the engines we need. He regrets, however, that he does not have a welding device."

"We can make do with the spin-friction welder," Claire announced.

Hyun-Jin relayed the message.

When he finished transmitting, Anderson pointed at the Mars fuel platform through the window. "What about that? Do we still let them modify the platform to boost *Shenzhou* into MEO? Have we given up the idea of saving *Reliance* from the Argus effect?"

"Anderson, my goal is to get us home alive. If that means *Reliance* burns up in the atmosphere . . ." Claire closed her eyes against a black cloud of grief and pinched the bridge of her nose. "So be it." Unshed tears clogged her throat— *the flash in Owen's eyes when he proudly declared that one day, he too would be a 'stronaut*—no, couldn't think of Owen. Not now. When her crew was safe on Earth, she'd have whatever was left of her life to grieve.

Claire remembered Cole's vodka spilling across the habitation module. She cursed her puritanical impulse that had caused the accident. Right now, she could use a drink . . . or many.

Claire swallowed the pain and turned to Josephine. "Come on. We'll grab a snack from the galley on the way to the equipment lock to prebreathe."

"Me?" Josephine pointed at herself. "I'm going EVA?" Her eyes gleamed with enthusiasm.

The sight brought a half-smile to Claire's face. "You're the only rocket-engine expert we have. I want you on-site for the repair. You've trained to back up the EVA team, and I'll be there to help you." She pointed at Anderson. "While I'm on EVA, you're in charge." Claire wished she could leave Hyun-Jin in command, but he didn't have command experience and Anderson had seniority. "Don't do anything I wouldn't do." Claire stared him down. "I mean that."

The crew lock smelled faintly of vomit and shit. The scrubbers hadn't been able to erase the telltale scents of Cole's death. Claire squeezed her eyes hard against an image of corpses littering the streets of Orlando.

Josephine's knee caught Claire in the ribs, disturbing her morbid thoughts. "Sorry." Josephine handed Claire a tofu burrito. "I'd forgotten how tight it was in here." Thirty-four cubic meters in volume, the equipment lock was crowded with EVA suit parts, an ergometer, oxygen masks, jet packs, and hand tools used in previous spacewalks.

Claire checked the list of equipment stored in the toolbox outside the station, making sure it contained the items they'd need on the space walk: spin-friction welders that looked like oversized hand drills, replacement reentry tiles and epoxy, and a multiwrench and cutter for the rocket repair.

Exhaustion dragged at Claire, making her feel as if she moved through syrup instead of air. She hadn't slept in hours, but there was no time. The Chinese astronauts would arrive within the hour, and the eighty-kilometer buffer they'd put between themselves and the Argus layer was eroding as the electrons spread outward. Electrical systems would begin to fail, making it impossible to fire the lifeboat's engines if they waited too long.

"How are you doing?" she asked Josephine. "We've missed the last three rest periods. You up for this?"

Josephine beamed the grin of a twenty-year-old hacker who, at 4 a.m., had just cracked the Department of Defense Web site. "I'm good. I couldn't sleep now if I tried."

Ten years ago, Claire thought, that was me.

Josephine slipped an oxygen mask over her face and began breathing deeply. They would spend thirty minutes breathing pure oxygen, while they traded off on the ergometer. While she waited her turn, Josephine pulled a palmtop out of her thigh pocket and studied the thruster's schematics.

Claire donned an oxygen mask, strapped her feet onto the pedals and cinched the Velcro straps tight over her instep. As she pumped her arms and legs, her mind wandered to the welding job ahead. They would sacrifice the hull integrity of lab three. It had been sealed off from the station and evacuated during *Reliance*'s initial lockdown, and contained the biomedical experiments. They were least likely to be useful during the repairs.

Claire would help Josephine remove the damaged engines, then Josephine would be her backup as Claire used the spin-friction welder to cut a patch from lab three's 7mm aluminum hull.

The spin-friction welders used a new technology: A rotating pin heated the aluminum to a plastic state and then mixed the two edges together. Hopefully it would be strong enough to survive reentry. Returning to Earth in a repaired hull had never been tested.

The ergometer upped the resistance of the flywheel and Claire pushed harder with her hands and feet, sweat bubbling on her forehead and upper lip. The knee that had bothered her on the last EVA, when she had skipped prebreathing, ached dully.

It was stupid to go EVA so soon after suffering a mild case of the bends, but there was no one else to back up Josephine. Anderson didn't have EVA experience, and Hyun-Jin was needed to translate. She wouldn't risk Josephine in a solo walk. Not after Cole.

Claire pumped harder and breathed deeper, willing nitrogen out of her bloodstream. She tightened her jaw against the aching joint. Her knee would have to make do.

After a half-hour of exercise, Claire took a break and, through the muffling silicon of her oxygen mask, called over the intercom, "Any new developments?"

"No new communications. We're monitoring *Shenzhou*'s suit-to-ship frequency, picking up the chatter between his crew who were already EVA and the station. Hyun-Jin tells me it's routine checklist stuff. They're starting to disassemble the engines." Anderson's voice was weary. "I've been scanning *Shenzhou* with our cameras. There's something strange in the infrared band. They're leaking heat all over the place. I'd have expected them to shut down nonessential modules, like we did. But no."

Claire wondered why Zhang would have kept so much of his station online in an emergency situation. But then, if his plan had been to up-orbit to MEO and wait out the Argus effect, perhaps it made sense. "Have you been able to contact the Japanese?"

"I've tried. No response. My bet is they've already evacuated."

Claire had to agree. The Japanese solar weather observatory was in MEO, ten thousand miles above the Earth's surface—too high to have been affected by the EMP of a nuclear explosion or damaged by debris or Earth-launched missiles.

Still, Claire would have expected an automated message, some response from the station's computer, even if the observatory had been shut down.

Fifteen minutes later, Anderson called back. "Lowering to 10.4 psi."

Claire's knee twinged in response to the drop in pressure. "Acknowledged." Claire tapped the screen of her palmtop to save the CAD drawing she'd been working on, a patch for the CEV's hull. "How's *Shenzhou*'s crew doing with the engines?"

Hyun-Jin answered, "First engine is removed and in the ATV's cargo hold. They're having a problem with a stuck connector on the second one."

"Have they said anything that makes you distrust them?"

Hyun-Jin was silent for half a minute. "Not really . . . They have concerns about us. There's anger that the U.S. got involved with the war. But it's just talk."

"So far," Anderson grumbled in the background.

Claire wondered if Zhang had to rein in his crew's emotions the way she did with Anderson. If so, she hoped he was better at it.

Josephine finished her exercise and, with Claire's help, began the laborious process of donning her EVA suit. Between the endless safety procedures and seal checks, Josephine grinned in flashes of glee, the war temporarily forgotten in her joy at the prospect of stepping outside to confront eternity in its primal aspect.

Claire put on her helmet and slid the seal closed. She felt only cold dread. EVA was dangerous under any circumstances, and working around torn metal to remove the damaged engines would be doubly so. But they had no choice. Claire envied Josephine her first few hours of EVA, and hoped they wouldn't also be her last.

Together they completed the checks on the suits' integrity. All systems were nominal. Josephine would be working without an MMU, but with triple tethers, Claire thought she would be all right.

Claire stepped out of the air lock and felt again the enormity of space. Normally the sight thrilled her; now it felt like a giant black glove, poised to crush her and the station. To punish them for the hubris of leaving Earth.

The Mars refueling platform loomed in the foreground, and beyond it lay the elongated cylinder of *Shenzhou XI*. NASA's mission control would have panicked to have so many collisional objects in proximity to *Reliance*. Their presence added to Claire's feeling of claustrophobia.

Josephine uttered a squeal of delight, which transmitted over the voice-operated suit-to-suit frequency.

As they used the handholds to transverse the station, Earth was behind them, hidden by *Reliance*'s curving bulk. Claire was glad not to have to face it, to see the fires burning across what was left of North America. The fifty-foot tether that connected them to the air lock reeled out behind them, a white lifeline.

The CEV's engines were further than that from the lifeboat, and Claire double-checked Josephine's procedure as she completed the tether transfer, clipping off the fifty-foot tether and starting a new twenty-foot tether. The young woman moved with practiced ease, the hours spent in pool simulations paying off.

Claire performed her transfer and followed Josephine to the engines. There were no handholds on this part of the station.

Josephine unpacked a ball restraint from the mesh bag she carried with her. Like an oversized Tinkertoy, ball joints attached rods that could be moved over a 270-degree range, enabling Josephine to brace herself into the various positions she'd need to remove the thruster assemblies.

Josephine snapped her treads into the brace's footpads and began shutting down the thruster assembly, flipping up the covers that protected connectors, disconnecting them, and unbolting the fuel lines.

Claire hovered nearby, ready to receive the engine parts as Josephine dismantled them, and to stow them in a second mesh bag tethered to the station. They couldn't risk sharp edges floating free in their EVA space. "*Reliance*, we're clipped in, about to begin removal."

"We copy," Anderson acknowledged. "Be careful out there."

Josephine began with tin snips, cutting away the flared metal where the debris had scraped alongside the engine.

Claire caught the strips with tongs, careful to angle the sharp edges away. Then she wrestled with the mesh bag, trying to insert the scraps without tangling in the fabric of the bag.

Josephine worked in silence, needing all her concentration to bend the pressurized space suit into position and to avoid the sharp edges that waited to catch and puncture her suit.

After she had unbolted a broken fuel hose, she stopped and wiped the back of her glove against her helmet, for an instant forgetting that she was in a suit. Josephine straightened and arched backwards, stretching the abdominal muscles that had held her in a forward crouch over the last engine. "I had no idea EVA-ing took this much strength," she panted.

Claire gingerly accepted the wild twist of pipe. "It's different than in the pool, that's for sure."

"*Reliance* to *EVA 1* and *2*," Hyun-Jin's voice called over the radio. "Zhang's team has finished removal of engine two and is starting on the third."

"Glad to hear it. They have an ETA?"

"They should be done in another hour. Then Zhang and all of his crew will fly over with the engines in the ATV. The two crew who are EVA will stay suited and help with the install."

Claire wished she could speak privately with Hyun-Jin, find out how Anderson was handling news of their impending guests. But there was no privacy in the command module, and *Shenzhou* was certain to be monitoring their ship-to-suit communications, as Hyun-Jin had monitored theirs. Any shift to a secured channel would be noticed and raise suspicion. "Hyun-Jin, I'm putting you in charge of making our guests welcome. It'll be some hours yet before I can get inside. Make sure Anderson knows what to do."

A pause. "That's a copy."

Claire imagined Anderson fuming about their security and possible Chinese attacks. She hoped he would take prudent, but nonoffensive, precautions.

Josephine had finished removing the body of the first engine and, shifting her braces, positioned herself to pull it free. She strained, and the engine moved. Inch by inch it crept out of the housing. Then its progress stopped.

"It's stuck," Josephine said over the radio. She angled her helmet to look up along the engine. "I think it's stuck on one of the fuel connectors." Her arm disappeared up to the elbow inside the engine cavity. "Almost got—shit," Josephine cursed. "I'm caught. One of the pipes I cut away. There's a ragged edge. Oh shit. Oh shit. Oh shit." Her feet thrashed in the beginnings of panic.

"What's going on?" asked Hyun-Jin. "Jo—Josephine's heart rate just jumped through the roof."

"Not now," Claire snapped. She bent forward and put gentle pressure on Josephine's back. "I'm here. Your suit's intact. We will get you out of this. Take a deep breath."

"My *first* EVA," Josephine wailed. "God, I'm useless."

"A deep breath," Claire urged. "Breathe with me." She inhaled slowly and noisily.

Josephine sighed in and out, a ragged breath, but a step away from panic.

"Good." Claire encouraged her. She pressed her helmet against Josephine's, bringing them almost eye-to-eye. The vibration of air in her helmet transmitted through the faceplates, allowing them to speak without the radio. "Look at me," Claire commanded, holding Josephine's gaze. She watched fear and self-recrimination fade into watchful attention. "Good. Now tell me. Where are you caught?"

"Hard to tell through the suit. Oh, God. Feels like my elbow."

"Okay, hold still." Claire slid her hand along Josephine's arm, all too aware that the ragged pipe that had snagged Josephine might catch her as well. Her fingertips encountered pressure. Now, how to free Josephine's arm without ripping her suit. Claire steeled her face not to show her anxiety.

Feeling for the sharp edge of pipe with the pressurized gloves was like trying to pick up rice wearing an oven mitt. Claire pushed gently on the fabric of Josephine's sleeve and felt something give.

The younger woman's eyes widened with fear. "What was that?"

"Stay calm," Claire ordered sharply. "I think I've got it." She pushed outward on the pipe her fumbling fingers had encountered, praying she didn't rip Josephine's suit. Helmet-to-helmet, she asked, "Can you retract your arm?"

Josephine licked her lips, then in glacial movements, pulled back her arm. Claire could see her tensing against any resistance, any sudden loss of pressure. The arm came free. The younger woman breathed hard, hyperventilating and clutching her arm to her chest.

Claire extended the arm and inspected the suit's fabric. A few of the fibers were puckered and broken on the outside of the elbow joint. The space suit fabric, a mix of Kevlar, Teflon, and Nomex, was incredibly strong and flexible. That it was scuffed at all was an indication of the friction Josephine had endured.

Claire asked, "How's your pressure?"

Josephine checked her suit's readout. "It's 3.8 psi and holding."

"Good." Claire looked inside the hole Josephine had been working in and bent the culprit tube out of the way. "Let me know when you're done."

Josephine looked at the hole that had almost ripped her suit and cost her her life. Emotions played across her face— incredulity, fear, and resignation. There was no choice. They had to fix the lifeboat. She extended her arm back in.

Josephine removed the damaged thrusters and prepped the engine housings to receive the thrusters from *Shenzhou*. She moved slowly, taking care around the dangerous sharps. Even with Claire's assistance, the work took more than an hour to complete.

Claire strapped the last of the damaged engines to the station's hull. Then she radioed the command module. "We're done with the removal. How's Zhang's team doing?"

"They're about to leave *Shenzhou*," Hyun-Jin said. "They'll be here in forty-five minutes."

Claire felt a qualm of fear. She hoped she was doing the right thing in trusting Zhang and his crew. "Is Anderson prepared?"

Anderson's voice came over the radio. "I'll make sure nothing goes wrong." There was an implicit threat towards the Chinese crew in his words. Claire hoped Zhang wouldn't pick up on it.

"Good."

Claire touched Josephine's shoulder. Inside her helmet, the younger woman sweated profusely. The dehumidifier in her suit was having trouble keeping pace with her exhalations. A light misting of fog obscured her mouth.

"You all right?" Claire asked.

"Yeah," Josephine panted. "I will be."

"Eat some of your power bar and drink some water. We can't afford to have you fatigued."

Josephine used her teeth to pull up the power bar strapped inside the collar of her space suit.

Claire took small sips of water while she waited for Josephine to recover; enough to quench her thirst, not enough to make her need the maximum absorption garment.

"While we're waiting for our guests," Claire said, "I'd like to inspect the heat tiles on the front of the CEV. See how difficult the repairs are going to be."

Josephine nodded and unclipped her boots from the brace. "I'll leave this in place for the installation."

Claire nodded and began the trek up-station to the nose of the CEV. The top of the escape vehicle was docked to the station, so only the top of the tiled nose cone was easily accessible. The bottom of the nose, and the rest of the heat-resistant tiles were on the belly of the CEV, beyond reach.

The tiles in view were undamaged. The chipped surfaces were all on the underside of the CEV, a smooth surface without handholds or the bolts that could accept foot restraints.

"How are we going to get out there?" Josephine asked. "Use the MMU?"

Claire shook her head. The MMU's jet pack was suitable for a fly-by inspection, but it wouldn't provide the stability needed to replace the broken tiles. She looked over at the broken Canadarm. There was a foot-restraint bolt on the end. If it were operational, she could attach her feet to it and have Anderson use the arm to position her over the bottom of the CEV. Claire swallowed, remembering the damage she'd uncovered just before the first bombs fell. "We'll have to fix it."

CHAPTER 10

The housing was still off the Canadarm's elbow joint from when she and Hyun-Jin had abandoned the repair. A gash cut across the interior disk of the joint. Claire shone her flashlight into the crevice while Josephine, tethered to a nearby handhold, floated above.

A black piece of metal, no bigger than the tip of Claire's finger, had wedged between the plates. It was one of the thousands of pieces of space junk too small to track that circled Earth. Some coincidence of trajectory had caused it to hit the arm with enough velocity to jam but not puncture the plates.

Claire looked over her shoulder. "Can you hand me a screwdriver?"

Behind Josephine was the incoming ATV. Claire took the tool, then pointed with her free hand. Josephine turned to watch it come in. It loomed overhead like a jetliner coming in low over the freeway. Claire felt vulnerable with just her suit and a thin nylon tether protecting her. They shouldn't be outside during the docking maneuvers. There was too much danger from collision and thruster backwash. More NASA protocols broken.

"Tell them to hold off until we're back in the air lock," Claire radioed to Hyun-Jin.

Hastily they unclipped the positional tethers and reeled back to the unpressurized air lock. They crawled inside and pushed the hatch shut. "We're in place."

From the air lock's porthole, Claire and Josephine watched the ATV bob into position and dock to the port opposite the CEV. When the engines shut down, they opened the air lock door.

Claire and Josephine jetted over to the ATV's external cargo hatch. As they got there, the first of the Chinese taikonauts emerged. He looked disarmingly ridiculous in his bulky Russian-designed EVA suit. The hard joints and carapace looked like the Pillsbury Doughboy after baking, or an overweight suit of armor.

Claire spoke over the suit-to-suit frequency. "*Ni hao,*" she said, exhausting her command of Mandarin. "This is Claire Logan, commander of *Reliance* station, do you copy?"

"*Ni hao,*" a man's voice replied, sliding more expertly over the intonation. The closest of the two figures waved. "Greetings. I am Hu Liai and this"—he gestured at a second taikonaut emerging from the hold—"is Bai Ling-Sheng." His nasal English pronunciation was not as crisp as Zhang's.

"Why do you not open the station-side hatch?" demanded Zhang in his cultured tones.

"The station-side door is stuck," Anderson drawled. "We're working on it."

"This is intolerable. We are cooperating with you. We disabled our station to bring you replacement engines, and you imprison us in our ATV?" Zhang's voice slipped into singsong tones in his anger, reverting to his native Chinese. "I do not believe the hatch is malfunctioning. This is a deliberate action. This is not the cooperation I was promised."

"Anderson, what seems to be the difficulty?" Claire asked.

"It's stuck. I'm working on a—"

"This is not the way to gain our trust." Zhang insisted. "We came in good faith—"

Claire wanted to strangle Anderson. She'd specifically

asked him to find a way to protect the station without offending the Chinese. "Hyun-Jin, what's going on?"

There was a pause, then Hyun-Jin said, "Anderson's working on the door. We should have it free by the time you finish your EVA."

"Zhang, I'm afraid you and your crew will have to sit tight until we can fix this malfunction. We'll reverse the pumps to blow air into the ATV through the docking pin. I'm sorry for this inconvenience. We will complete the repairs to both the CEV and the station's hatch with all haste. I assure you—"

A spat of Chinese cut her off. She didn't need Hyun-Jin to translate.

A third taikonaut came out of the cargo hold, pulling behind him a mesh bag filled with the replacement engines. Even through the bulky space suit, Claire could see anger in his movements.

Zhang transmitted, "Two of my taikonauts will assist with the engine replacement, the third will oversee the hull welding." His voice was slightly cooler, as if he held his temper at bay by force of will. "It is important the repairs be done correctly."

Claire touched her helmet to Josephine's, and pointed to indicate that the younger woman should turn off her voice-activated radio as Claire did. When they could speak in private, Claire asked, "Are you up for doing the engine repair with only taikonauts as backup? It will save time if we work in parallel."

Two taikonauts tugged the replacement engines towards the back of the CEV. They worked slowly, so as not to damage the fragile inner workings of the engine by banging them against *Reliance*'s hull. Josephine watched them for a few seconds, then said, "Yeah. If they mean us any ill will, they won't make their move until after the repairs are done. I'll just make sure my repairs take longer than yours."

As much as Claire hated to admit it, Anderson's locking the unsuited taikonauts in the ATV was a smart move. If they were sincere in their effort of cooperation, it would only be a temporary inconvenience. If not, the crew members trapped in the ATV were hostages to the others' good behavior.

Claire waved the third taikonaut to follow her back to

the Canadarm. There, she pointed to the elbow joint. "I have to repair this, so I can use the arm to position myself over the patch area."

The taikonaut peered up into the elbow joint, but said nothing. Claire wondered if he spoke English. It was the language of aviation, but as a mission specialist or visiting scientist, he might not have enough for general conversation. Claire pointed at the arm, then pantomimed an arm looming over the side of the CEV. The taikonaut nodded, but whether it was comprehension or acknowledgment, Claire couldn't tell.

"How are you doing?" Claire radioed Josephine.

"Good," Josephine replied. "Hu and Bai have engine one in position, and I'm just tightening down the interior bolts."

Claire was relieved that the communication problem wasn't affecting Josephine's work. This being her first EVA, Josephine needed good backup—assuming the Chinese taikonauts would help in a crisis.

With the screwdriver, Claire wiggled the scrap of metal free. She snagged it delicately between thumb and forefinger and handed it to her taikonaut.

He pulled a plastic bag out of a hip pocket and secured the dangerous sharp.

At least he was trained in EVA procedures and knew what to do. Claire relaxed a fraction.

The plates of the elbow were scored from where the metal had passed through.

"Anderson, I've removed the obstruction. Can you please test the elbow joint of the arm?"

"EVA-1, activating elbow joint . . . now."

Please work. The arm was her best hope of being able to fix the CEV's hull. Trying to weld from a jet pack would be impossible. If this didn't work, they'd have to build a scaffold to hold her into position.

Nothing happened.

Claire felt her heart fall into her boots. "Increase power to the elbow joint."

"Increasing . . . now," Anderson echoed.

With a spasmodic twitch, the arm folded at the elbow joint, flexing away from the station.

"It's working, Anderson." Claire's heart pounded in her chest. For the first time she really believed they could fix the lifeboat. They might actually go home. Anxiety about what they might find there pressed on her like an incoming storm front, but Claire clung to her optimism.

"Anderson, I'm going to attach a foot brace to the end of the arm. When I'm locked in, I'll need you to position the arm over the rent in the hull. Do you have camera coverage of the rupture?"

"EVA-1, that's affirmative. I'll get you there."

Claire climbed along the Canadarm and stopped short of the pinchers where a bolt suitable for attaching a foot brace lay. From this height, she looked back at her taikonaut. He'd climbed up the base assembly of the arm to the elbow and was inspecting the damage.

"Taikonaut on the Canadarm . . ." Damn, she didn't even know his name, and his name patch was an unreadable Chinese character. "Josephine, can you ask Hu or Bai who I'm working with?"

"That is Sheng," said Hu. "He has Ph.D. in materials science. Very knowledgeable about metal welds."

Reassuring, but she still couldn't talk to him. "Hu, can you ask him to keep clear of the elbow joint? We'll be moving soon."

Hu spoke quickly in Mandarin. Sheng gave a curt reply, then moved away from the elbow joint, halfway down the first strut to the base of the arm.

Claire understood why Zhang wanted his crew involved in the repairs, but how could he send a taikonaut who spoke no English? EVA was dangerous enough with good communication. "Hu, tell him to stay there. I don't want him to get hurt."

Another Mandarin exchange, this one longer, and with a pleading tone in Hu's voice. Sheng gave another curt reply, then gestured a thumbs up to Claire.

"Anderson, I'm in place."

The wheels of the Canadarm's base rolled in their track along the station's length until the arm was next to the CEV's damaged hull. Claire crouched to keep her balance as the arm swung out over the lifeboat.

Now the tricky part. Anderson, using the joystick and

external station cameras, would have to position her close enough over the CEV's hull to cut away the flared edges of the rent without slamming her into it.

The damaged elbow joint began to bend. It jerked and sputtered as damaged plates ground over one another. The vibration traveled up from her boots and rattled her teeth.

"EVA-1, the elbow is a bit sticky," Anderson said. "But don't worry, I'll get you there."

The arm jerked forward, then eased back. It rocked sickeningly as Anderson inched her towards the CEV's hull.

Suddenly she was moving fast, too fast. "Stop the arm!" she shouted.

"On it. Catch, damn you, catch!" Anderson's voice was a tense whisper.

The jagged hole where the CEV had decompressed loomed larger. Claire was approaching the solid surface of the CEV's hull. She twisted, trying to reach the foot braces. Her fingers fumbled against the quick release.

The arm accelerated as the joint broke free. Claire would smack into the hull headfirst. The white hull was the only thing in her field of view. She was half a meter above the surface, about to make impact. Would her faceplate shatter? Her neck snap?

"I can't get—" transmitted Anderson.

Claire closed her eyes as the hull rushed up. A jolt—

Her faceplate was an inch above the hull's surface. She could see the overlapping spray patterns where the aluminum had been painted.

Another jolt shook her body like a rag doll. Then a third. Claire strained to twist her head and look back along the arm.

Her breath caught. Sheng had jammed his arm into the elbow joint, preventing it from closing. But the Canadarm was still fighting to finish its maneuver. Each time the arm slammed into Sheng's suit—even a Russian-designed hard suit—the suit risked rupturing.

Another pounding vibration as the arm tried to close.

"Anderson, shut down the arm. Now! Emergency power off!" Claire shouted.

"Got it," Anderson said. "Lucky the arm jammed—I thought you were going to hit the CEV."

Claire pushed her hands against the CEV's surface for

leverage and twisted her waist until it felt like her back would snap, but her fingers were able to touch the quick release on the foot brace. She fumbled it open and tumbled free.

Sheng was still caught in the elbow of the Canadarm. Claire crawled down the arm to him. She braced her feet and hands against the arm and pried it open.

He floated free, motionless, his armored arm joint crushed.

Fearing the worst, Claire pushed up the golden sun shield covering his helmet.

Zhang opened his eyes. His golden face was pale. "I'm still alive, then?" he said in his round British vowels.

"You?" Claire said. She looked at the quarantined ATV. "But I thought—"

Zhang pulled his arm to his chest and inspected the damage. He flexed his wrist. "Suit's damaged, but I'm not. Pressure looks good." He spoke a few sentences in Chinese, apparently reassuring his crew.

"Ms. Logan. What kind of commander would allow his crew to EVA, in an emergency situation, with people of unknown motives, and not take part? I suited up for EVA and transferred over in the cargo hold. I meant no disrespect, but I had to protect my crew. As Hu said, I earned a Ph.D. in metallurgy from Oxford University. I can help you patch the hull." He nodded at the Canadarm's damaged elbow joint. "I suggest we weld the plates in place, to prevent further catastrophe."

Claire didn't know what to say. She was still in shock from her near accident and Zhang's revelation. She didn't know whether to feel angry, surprised, or grateful. At last she nodded. With Zhang holding the Canadarm in the desired position with his undamaged arm, Claire spot-welded the joint into place with the spin-friction welding gun.

When it was secure, Claire and Zhang climbed down the arm to where the CEV's hull had ruptured. Metal blossomed out along the edges of the hole. It started off shallow at one end, then deepened as the shrapnel had dug into the hull.

Claire said, "My plan is to use the spin welder to perforate an oval area around the hole, use leverage to break the perforation free, then to cut a patch from an unpressurized section of *Reliance*'s hull. Overlap the oval opening, and use the spin welder to seal it in place."

Zhang's intelligent black eyes scanned the damage. "There is a better way. Cut a rectangular opening instead. Cut two patches. One, slightly larger than the hole, is welded from the inside. A larger patch overlaps the hole from the outside. The edges of the interior patch add strength when the hull is pressurized. The exterior patch protects the interior weld during reentry."

Claire liked the idea, but saw a problem. "How do we access the inside of the lifeboat for the interior weld? Even it we undock if from the station, our EVA suits are too large to fit through the hatch."

Zhang thought for a moment, his dark eyes troubled. "I had not considered that."

"Wait, I've got it," Claire said. "Weld a handhold to the center of the interior patch, then pass it through the hole diagonally. Rotate it into position, then pull on the handhold to keep it in place while you perform the weld from the outside."

"Brilliant," said Zhang. "Where did you learn that technique? Graduate school?"

"Actually," said Claire, "I learned that repairing wallboard in my house." Owen had been playing with the baseball bat Matt had given him for his fourth birthday. Claire had directed Owen away from the lamp when his backswing took out a fist-sized chunk of the wall. She and Matt had fought about that. It seemed so trivial now. Tears prickled her eyes. She'd give anything, let Owen and Matt demolish ten houses if she could see them again.

Something brushed her arm. Behind the bubble of his helmet, Zhang's black eyes were concerned. "Are you well?"

Claire sucked in a snuffling breath, swallowing tears and grief. She nodded. "Let's get this done." Whatever awaited them on Earth, they had to get safely on the ground before they could deal with it.

After the near disaster with the Canadarm, cutting the two patches went relatively smoothly. They'd gotten lucky: The hole was small enough that the difference in curvature between the station's hull and that of the CEV wasn't a problem.

Zhang watched as she attached the outer patch with the spin-friction welder. Looking like an oversized power drill, it had a retractable pin that spun at thousands of revolutions per minute, heating the two sides of the weld to a plastic consistency, then feathered them together. It enabled the astronauts to weld aluminum, which could be tricky with older welding technologies. The spin-friction welder had been standard equipment ever since the disaster on MIR III.

When she had the external patch tacked in place and could let go of it, Claire stopped to stretch her shoulders and hands. She'd been spacewalking for hours, working muscles against her inflated space suit. Her suit reeked of sweat, she was light-headed with hunger, and her knee throbbed in time with her heartbeat, something she tried to ignore. As much as she would have liked to call a break, to go inside the station and rest, there was no time. The SIRAD radiation-sensing strip built into her suit was navy blue, indicating that she'd exceeded the maximum allowed dose.

Claire radioed Josephine. "How's your progress?"

Josephine grunted. "Just tightening the last bolts on engine three. One left to go. You?"

"I've got about another hour's worth of work. How do the replacement engines look?"

Josephine made an equivocal noise. "They're ten to twelve years old, but Hu and Bai assure me they're in good condition. I don't see any obvious flaws, though we won't know for sure until we start them up."

Claire stretched again, then bent her aching muscles to the laborious task of sealing the perimeter of the patch.

"If you would allow me," Zhang offered, "I can do that while you rest."

Claire felt a twinge of fear. She had never worked with Zhang before, and the patch had to be done right. On the other hand, in her current state—exhausted, hungry, and distracted by the growing pain in her knee—she wasn't able to do her best work.

Popping her boot treads free of the brace, Claire climbed down the arm to Zhang. She was glad the Chinese had modeled their space gear after the Russians, so the treads of his boots were compatible with *Reliance*'s foot braces.

Zhang climbed up the arm with practiced ease and snapped his feet into position. Drawing the spin-friction welder smoothly along the edges of the patch, he sealed it against vacuum. When he had completed the circuit, he pulled the stop trigger, which eased the spinning pin out slowly, sealing the join so there was no keyhole.

Claire crawled down to check his work. The seam was smooth, a slight feathering where the two different types of aluminum met and merged. "Good work."

Zhang nodded in acknowledgment. They climbed off the arm and clung to handholds near the lifeboat's docking pin.

"Anderson, I need you to back the Canadarm away from the CEV. The elbow joint is frozen in place, so be careful when you get near the solar panels."

She and Zhang watched as the Canadarm rolled away from the CEV. It stopped halfway up *Reliance*'s cylinder, silhouetted against the solar panels in the sunlight rising over Earth.

"Good job, Anderson. How are things inside *Reliance*?"

"Not great. The controller for the water-recycling pump has stopped working. We haven't been able to restart it."

Another casualty of the Argus effect. Claire could all but feel the electrons building up around them. "Copy that. Hopefully we'll be ready to leave in little over an hour. Any luck with radio communications?"

"Nope. Nothing from Earth. Nothing from MEO."

It was disheartening news, but no more than she'd expected. "Josephine, I'm done with the exterior repairs. How're the engines coming?"

"Just," Josephine gave a grunt of effort, "opening the fuel lines now. As soon as I'm—" Another grunt. "—done here. They'll be ready to test. There. That's got it."

"Good. Meet you in the air lock."

Claire packed up the welding gun and scraps of metal and returned to the air lock. She stowed the welder in the box of equipment just outside the air lock and tied the mesh bag of scrap metal to a ring built into the station's hull.

It would be too dangerous to test the thrusters while the astronauts and taikonauts were on *Reliance*'s surface. Claire waited until Josephine crowded into the evacuated air lock.

There was only room for two people in EVA suits in the small room. "Zhang, are your people in position?"

"We are," Zhang radioed from the confines of the ATV's cargo hold.

"Anderson, commence thruster test procedures."

"Firing thruster one," Anderson reported.

Claire felt the station shift almost imperceptibly around her. She gave Josephine a thumbs-up.

Josephine grinned. She touched her helmet to Claire's. "I think we might actually make it home."

"Good work," Claire said, her heart lightening at the other woman's pleasure in a job well done.

"Thruster one. Nominal function. Firing thruster two."

The station hiccupped, a stuttering vibration that shimmied their tethers into oscillating white snakes.

"Thruster two reports intermittent outage."

"Damn." Josephine's eyes looked off into the distance, obviously replaying the steps of the engine's replacement in her imagination.

"Thruster three. Nominal operation."

They waited. Inside her space suit, Claire crossed her toes.

"Thruster four, offline."

"Damn. Damn. Damn. What did I do wrong?" She chewed her lip; drops of blood welled from the corner of her mouth.

Claire put her hands on either side of Josephine's helmet and brought the other woman's gaze to hers. "You'll figure this out. You *will* get the engines working."

Claire's stomach roiled. Every minute outside was more radiation, more time for the Argus effect to chew away at the electronics they depended on. She wanted to shake Josephine for her failure to get the fix right the first time, to push her aside and do the work herself—except Josephine knew more about rocket engines, and wouldn't work well with Claire hovering over her.

Claire forced a smile for Josephine. "You can do this. Zhang and I will check the exterior of the hull for other damage. Let me know when you're done." She relayed the commands over the ship-to-suit frequency for Hyun-Jin and Anderson.

Josephine, Hu, and Bai returned to the engines. Zhang met Claire outside the open air lock door.

"You heard?" she asked.

Zhang nodded. "Has your pilot considered deorbiting on two thrusters? A longer burn? Perhaps using *Reliance*'s thrusters to start the acceleration before undocking?"

Claire relayed these ideas to Anderson.

Anderson said, "It wouldn't be the optimal flight path, but it could—"

"I've got it!" Josephine crowed. "I hadn't hooked in the igniter on four." Her voice lost enthusiasm. "Thruster two has a crimped fuel hose. I can't straighten it. The hose would have to be replaced. It would mean either welding into the fuel line—which is dangerous—or a trip back to *Shenzhou*."

"There's no time," Claire said. "Anderson thinks we can get home on two engines; three should be more than enough. You've done good work, Josephine. Clear the work area."

When Josephine, Hu, and Bai were clear, Claire had Anderson repeat the test on engine four.

"Engine four nominal," Anderson said. "Good work, Jo—I mean, Josephine."

Josephine's fist punched vacuum in triumph. Hu and Bai clasped arms.

"I agree, good work all," Claire radioed. "Anderson, begin pressurization test of the CEV. Go slowly. If there's a problem with the patch, we don't want to lose any air unnecessarily."

Seconds ticked by. Claire felt her heart pounding in her chest. Her knee throbbed in sympathy.

"Raising CEV pressure to point-five psi," reported Anderson.

Claire glanced at the patched hull, as if she could see microscopic leaks that might threaten its integrity.

"Pressure appears to be holding at point-five. Increasing pressure to four-point-two."

Claire crossed her toes. So much had gone wrong on this mission. Was it her imagination, or was she seeing tiny ice crystals extruding from the edges of the patch? Claire squeezed her eyes shut to clear them. No. There was nothing there.

"Pressure holding at four-point-two. Increasing to full cabin pressure."

Claire couldn't breathe.

"Pressure appears stable at full cabin pressure," Anderson reported.

Claire let out her breath, slowly. Relief flooded her. They could go home.

Claire led the procession of space walkers to *Reliance*'s air lock. Standing open, it was a small cave in the side of the station, too small to accommodate them all once the hatch was closed.

"There isn't room to process all of us at once," Claire said. "Josephine and I will go first, then you three—"

Zhang raised both hands to interrupt her. "I am not comfortable with my crew entering the air lock second. You have cooperated with us as necessary to repair the CEV, but my people remain locked in the ATV. If we do not join you in the airlock what assurances do I have?"

"You think I would let your people die?" Claire was incredulous.

Zhang winced at the last word. "These are desperate circumstances. And some of my crew believe the hostilities on Earth should affect what happens here. It is possible some of your crew feel the same."

Anderson. With Zhang's command of the nuances of English, Anderson's suspicions had not escaped his notice. Nor, she suspected, was he fooled by Anderson's claim that the controller of the docking hatch connecting the ATV to *Reliance* was malfunctioning.

But on the other hand, if Zhang was untrustworthy, Hu and Bai might have weapons concealed under their EVA suits. They could overpower Anderson and Hyun-Jin and take over the station. Either way, one of them was going to have to trust the other.

"You, Josephine, and I will go in first," Claire said. "When you verify your safety, Hu and Bai can follow."

Zhang considered, then nodded slowly. "I will trust you." He spoke swiftly to Hu and Bai in Mandarin. Claire hoped Hyun-Jin was tuned in. She thought she could trust Zhang—he had saved her life with the Canadarm. Still, these were cautious times.

The air lock was a tight fit. Claire had to squeeze in

against Zhang's hard suit in order to close the hatch behind her. It was like crawling into a metallic womb. The hissing of oxygen flowing into the air lock was balm to her frayed nerves. It signaled the successful end of a dangerous space walk. One more time she'd walked into the black infinite and come back alive.

The pressure equilibrated with the station pressure and Josephine was able to open the hatch to the crew lock. Claire felt it as an easing of the pressure of Zhang's hip against her kidneys.

Josephine pulled off her helmet and sucked in a lungful of tepid station air. Despite the stench of unwashed bodies and fear-sweat, she was beaming. "We did it. The lifeboat's fixed. We can go home."

Claire pushed past Zhang. Hyun-Jin was inside the crew lock, helping Josephine out of her EVA suit. In contrast to Josephine's happiness, he looked worried. His hands worked to unlock Josephine's shoulder seals, but his eyes were on Anderson.

Anderson's eyes were bright with an emotion Claire couldn't name: fear, anticipation, joy. It could have been any or all of those.

Claire popped off her helmet and began the process of removing the components of the EVA suit. Unlocking seals. Anderson assisted her and, to her surprise, helped Zhang find places to stow his helmet and gauntlets. He hovered between them, helping each in turn.

Anderson turned to help Zhang wiggle free from the torso carapace of his hard suit when Claire saw something glitter dull silver in Anderson's back pocket. Horror widened her eyes. A knife?

Zhang's arms were raised, the torso unit pulling over his head. He was helpless, made vulnerable by his EVA suit.

In a swift movement, Anderson grabbed the silver from his back pocket.

Claire reached her hand to stop him, missed the grab, tumbled forward.

Silver duct tape ripped from the spool like the sound of rending flesh. As Anderson pulled the torso unit over Zhang's head, he wound the tape around Zhang's wrists.

Zhang thrashed like a caught fish, kicking with his legs, still in the hard plates of the lower half of his EVA suit.

A gold medallion of Buddha snaked free from the collar of his T-shirt. He cursed in Mandarin, his eyes flashing at Claire.

Anderson looped the duct tape through a drawer pull and tied Zhang to it.

"Stop it," Josephine shrieked. "My god, what are you—"

"Anderson, cease and desist." Claire ordered. "Release—"

"Listen to this," Anderson said. He held up his palmtop and pressed a button.

Matt's voice, tinny and rough with static, was still recognizable. "CQ, CQ. This is Matt Logan. I don't have a call sign." He sounded exhausted. "I'm in Lakeland, Florida. My little boy is sick. I think it's radiation poisoning. We need a doctor. Are there any doctors in the area? CQ, CQ. Looking for doctors in the Lakeland, Florida, area. Anybody? Is there anybody out there who can help?"

Claire couldn't breathe. She snatched the palmtop from Anderson and replayed the message. Alive! Matt and Owen were alive! It was everything she had hoped for. Tears of thanksgiving bubbled her eyes and blurred her vision. Then the words sank in. Owen was sick. Images of the survivors of Hiroshima and their horrific burns flitted through her mind. Not her Owen. Please, no. She had to protect him. "We have to get on the ground—now!"

Anderson nodded and pulled her through the hatch. "Thought that would change your mind."

Claire reached back towards Zhang. "No wait—we can't abandon the taikonauts."

"You don't know what the Chinese government is like, Claire," said Hyun-Jin. "My Uncle Shen told me stories. You don't know—"

Zhang's cursing became more urgent, louder, more controlled.

Hyun-Jin's face went pale.

"What is it?" Anderson demanded, looking over his shoulder at the imprisoned Chinese commander.

A tinny voice replied from Zhang's helmet.

In his haste to desuit Zhang, Anderson had neglected to disconnect the radio wires that ran from the helmet to the power supply on the torso.

"Zhang just told his crew that he's been captured,"

Hyun-Jin said in a terrified, hoarse whisper. "He told them to attack, breach the hull, and take the lifeboat."

Claire scraped the edge of her palm against Anderson's fingers, trying to loosen his grip. "Let me go. Stop this insanity—"

A clanging started against the air lock hatch. Claire thought of all the tools in the box just outside the air lock. Bolt cutters, socket wrenches, and the spin-friction welder.

Anderson's grip tightened painfully. "There's no time. We've got to get out of here—now."

CHAPTER 11

The clanging grew louder as Hu and Bai reached the outside door of the air lock. Hu's helmeted face loomed in the porthole, his rubbery lips moved, shouting words that couldn't be heard across the vacuum of space.

More Chinese spilled from Zhang's helmet radio.

Zhang writhed against the duct tape tethering him to the wall and yelled a reply.

"They're arguing," Hyun-Jin translated, pausing in the hatchway, "that if they breach the station, he'll die." His eyes flicked to Zhang. "He's telling them to do it anyway."

Zhang looked in Claire's direction. "You are their commander. Make them stop."

Claire braced her feet against the rim of the hatch and resisted Anderson's grip. With each jerk and twist she grunted out words: "Stop—there's no need—we can all—"

At the porthole, Hu raised the spin-friction welder into view. Then he pointed at Zhang. A Chinese command came over Zhang's helmet radio. Even without translation, the meaning was clear. Release Zhang, or they would breach the hull.

Anderson shook Claire so hard her teeth rattled. She lost

her foothold on the doorway and he pulled her through. "No. We can't all. The CEV is a glider. The Chinese crew would add too much weight, change the glide path, threaten the landing. I looked over your list of equipment to remove to get the weight down: the medical kit, emergency rations, and water canisters." He held her by one shoulder, pressing his face close to hers. With his free hand he slammed the hatch between the air lock and the crew lock closed. "What kind of world do you think we're returning to? A major nuclear exchange between the U.S. and China isn't a police action. It's the end of fucking civilization."

As he spoke spittle flew into Claire's face. She smelled the musk of his fear.

"Hyun-Jin and I discussed it while you were EVA. We decided the American lifeboat should be for *Americans*. Look at them." He grabbed her face and twisted it towards Zhang, Hu, and Bai. "You'll need the medical kit to help your son: iodine supplements to ward off thyroid cancer, bandages for his burns, penicillin for secondary infections. Are you willing to leave it behind to carry a potential enemy back to Earth?" He squeezed her jaw to hold her in place. "Which of them is worth your son's life?"

Hyun-Jin fought to restrain Josephine. "We put a sound pickup on the ATV's docking pin." He grunted as her foot connected with his stomach. "Picked up the crew's private conversation. They were talking about whether to attack and steal the lifeboat."

"So you beat them to it," Claire said through gritted teeth.

"Yes," said Hyun-Jin. Then with more force, "Yes, we did."

Anderson and Hyun-Jin dragged Claire and Josephine through the crew lock. Anderson stopped only long enough to seal it off behind them. He yanked Claire through the access tube. He kicked hard, and they bounced off walls in a blur. A handhold caught her chin. Tears of pain blinded her.

They passed the hatch where *Shenzhou*'s ATV was docked. A screwdriver was jammed into the door mechanism, locking the Chinese astronauts in their craft. Muffled shouts and the hammering of fists came from the other side of the hatch.

Claire tasted blood from where her teeth had caught her lip.

A vibrating whine keened down the hall. Hyun-Jin and Anderson exchanged a look.

"What's that?" asked Claire.

"The spin-friction welder. We heard the same sound when you cut the patch out of lab three."

"Come on," Anderson jerked Claire down the tunnel. "There isn't time to argue." His movements were panicked, desperate to reach the lifeboat before the hull breached.

The station shook and rattled like a freight train passing by. Then all was silent.

Hyun-Jin whispered. "They're through the air lock."

"Zhang," murmured Claire. She felt a pang for the man she had worked with to repair the lifeboat. Despite Anderson's paranoia, she didn't believe Zhang would have turned on them.

While everyone was distracted, Josephine pulled her arm free and cracked her elbow against Hyun-Jin's temple. The blow was softened by Newton's third law; half the energy spun Josephine away in reaction.

Claire didn't make that mistake. She clasped the thumb and forefinger of her free hand around Anderson's wrist and squeezed a pressure point Claire's mother had shown her when she started dating.

Anderson yelped and lost his grip.

Claire kicked off towards the crew lock, unsure how she could convince the Chinese crew this was all a mistake. She only knew she had to try.

Anderson threw himself between her and the door.

"It's too late," Anderson said. "When they get through the crew lock door, they're not going to listen to reason. They were willing to kill their commanding officer to get to the lifeboat. Your death won't make them blink. This is our only chance. You have to come with me and Hyun-Jin."

"I can't believe you decided—we're talking about *lives*." Claire panted. "You would strand the Chinese crew? Just leave them to die?"

"A lot of people"—Anderson's brow furrowed with anger—"people we *love*, are dead. Killed by Chinese missiles." He looked over her shoulder in the direction of the crew lock. "There isn't time to argue. We have to leave—now."

Hatred burned through Claire, anger so hot she could barely see straight. If Anderson had been on the other side of an air lock door, she would have flushed him into space. But for better or worse, his actions had committed them to a course of action. They had to get to the lifeboat before Zhang's crew destroyed *Reliance* around them. She had to get back to Earth, to help Matt and Owen. Claire jabbed her finger in Anderson's face. "You'll pay for this."

"Yeah." Anderson kicked off in the direction of the lifeboat. "Explain it to me when we're on the ground."

Josephine's eyes were wide and her lower lip trembled. "You don't mean . . . you can't possibly mean—" She looked back at the corridor where the Chinese crew trapped in the ATV pounded on the hatch.

Claire grabbed the younger woman's sleeve and pulled her along. "Right now, we don't have a choice." As soon as they were safely in the lifeboat, she could deal with Anderson. Then, maybe, she could get the Chinese crew to trust her again. Zhang had been a good man—she owed it to him to try to save his people. But first, they had to reach the lifeboat. She kicked hard against a handhold, bruising her foot to get more acceleration.

Reliance shuddered around them. Claire felt something no space dweller wants to feel—an unexpected draft. The decompression alarm sounded.

In front and behind, bulkheads slammed down.

"Move!" Anderson shouted. The hatchway to the lifeboat was just ahead. The bulkhead between it and them was closing. Anderson got his arm and head through, then pulled back just in time. He sucked on the end of his ring finger, pinched by the falling bulkhead. Then he slammed his fist against the unyielding aluminum. "Goddamn it!"

Hyun-Jin stared at the walls around them. "They breached the hull. We're trapped."

Josephine grabbed a handful of hair on the back of Anderson's head and snapped it back. She jammed her finger in his face, scratching his left cheek. "This is all your fault! If you had stuck to the plan—"

Anderson backhanded her away. "They were planning

to kill us and take the lifeboat. You and Claire didn't hear what they were saying. We did."

All eyes turned to Hyun-Jin. He visibly shrunk in on himself. "They want the lifeboat for themselves. They wanted to take it, but Zhang forbid—"

"That's not what you said before," Anderson accused. "You said they were going to attack."

Hyun-Jin's eyes flashed. "No. That's what you heard. I never wanted to go against Claire, but you—"

"Stop!" Claire ordered. The others fell silent. Claire pointed at the sealed bulkhead. "Right now, I don't care who said what or why. If we want a seat on that lifeboat, we have to stop the Chinese from stealing it. What's their next step?"

"They have to load the crew," said Hyun-Jin.

"The taikonauts in the ATV are as trapped as we are. They can't move through *Reliance* if there's a breach."

"And the taikonauts on EVA need an air lock to process back into atmosphere," said Josephine. "The CEV doesn't have an external lock."

"Since they just destroyed our air lock, that means *Shenzhou*. Can they pilot the CEV remotely?"

"Sure, if they had a transmitter able to send the command codes," said Anderson. "It's not a secured channel. NASA didn't build *Reliance* with piracy in mind."

Claire pulled her palmtop out of her thigh pocket. She tossed it to Anderson. "Get there first."

There was a scraping noise from the walls. Claire imagined Hu and Bai climbing over them from the outside. While her crew was trapped in a corridor, they had free access to the exterior of the CEV.

Josephine had her palmtop out. "The air lock and module two are in vacuum. The atmospheric controller is testing all bulkheaded areas for the ability to hold pressure."

Claire pointed at the door in front of them. "What about the bulkhead in front of us? Can you raise it?"

Josephine bit her lower lip. "The station isn't through testing pressurization. We lost a lot of atmosphere in that last rupture. Station pressure is down to 2.8 psi. Another decompression, and we might not have enough to support life."

"If that lifeboat leaves and we're not on it, it doesn't matter," Claire shouted. "Get that bulkhead open. Override and run the test routine."

Josephine's face was stricken. "But there might be vacuum on the other side."

"Oh, shit," Anderson breathed, looking at his palmtop. "They just gave the order for the CEV to prepare to undock."

"Open it now!" Claire ordered.

Josephine tapped keys, her fingers trembling.

The bulkhead rose with a groan of protesting metal. But no wind. Claire and tumbled forward, kicking in their haste to reach the lifeboat. "Stop the CEV," she shouted at Anderson over her shoulder. "Jam their communications. Keep the lifeboat here."

The hatch to the lifeboat was closed, still sealed from when Anderson had barely escaped its decompression. Claire caught it and threw the latch to open the lock. She pulled on the round handle. It wouldn't budge. She fought to tear it open, bracing her feet against the wall, tugging until veins stood out on her neck.

"It's too late." Anderson's voice was uncharacteristically gentle. His warm hand cupped her neck.

Claire unclenched her eyes and met his. He pointed out the porthole set in the center of the hatch.

The lifeboat was gone.

It had undocked. The white-and-black stub-nosed space place was headed towards *Shenzhou XI*. A figure in a Russian-built hard-plate EVA suit clung to the docking pin. His other hand held the space-hardened handheld computer he used to control it.

Claire clawed at the glass, as if she could capture the ship with sheer will.

"*Shenzhou*'s ATV is undocking," Josephine reported. "I'm restarting the pressure test."

The golden ATV flashed by, en route to a rendezvous with the CEV at *Shenzhou XI*. As it turned, Claire saw another figure clinging to the inside of the open cargo hold.

Hu and Bai saw what happened. They knew it wasn't on her orders that Anderson had tried to steal the lifeboat. If she could make contact with them, get to them in time, they might listen.

The ATV was too far away for ship-to-suit radio.

Turning away from the window, she pointed at Hyun-Jin. "Patch through *Reliance*'s radio controls from here to contact *Shenzhou*'s ATV." Next was Anderson. "We've got to get to our ATV. Follow them over there. It's our last chance. Make it happen."

"And me?" Josephine asked.

"Check the pressure between here and our ATV's docking hatch and, if it's pressurized, raise the bulkheads between here and there."

Josephine chewed her lower lip. " 'Pressurized' is a relative term. *Reliance* lost 73 percent of its remaining air in the last decompression."

An invisible hand clenched Claire's heart. They'd been so close, if Anderson had only—no time for recriminations now. To Josephine, she said, "Find a way."

"I've got radio contact," Hyun-Jin said.

Claire swallowed. She spoke into the tiny microphone built into the side of Hyun-Jin's palmtop. "This is Claire Logan, commander of the *Reliance*. I regret the actions taken by one of my crew. He is in custody." She glared at Anderson. "I assure you he will do no further harm."

There was no reply.

"Are you sure we've got a signal?"

Hyun-Jin nodded. "Got a ping from the ATV's transceiver. They hear you all right."

"Please. We have no other way to return to Earth." Claire didn't know what to say, how to convince them.

"You promise help, but you lie," Hu said harshly. "Commander Zhang dies because of you."

"You can't leave us here!" Claire heard panic in her voice. Her cheeks flushed with shame that Hu couldn't see. "We'll die."

"That may be your karma. I do not know."

The connection went dead.

Claire punched the icon to reconnect, but *Shenzhou*'s ATV was either out of range, or wasn't responding.

"Here goes," said Josephine, sounding less than confident.

The bulkhead behind them rose.

A gentle breeze flowed over Claire, towards the opening door, taking her breath away. She and the others gasped, sucking hard on the thin atmosphere like landed fish.

"Pressure—low," gasped Josephine. She waved them to follow her towards the ATV docking point.

Claire felt light-headed and nauseated, but followed Josephine.

"Shit!" Josephine gasped in a thready voice. Her hands fumbled for a grip on the hatchway.

Claire pushed past her, clutching to the ring that opened the hatch to the docked ATV.

It was empty.

"Global—undock—command," Anderson gasped out. He panted trying to recapture his breath. "Chinese must have—sent global command."

Claire flattened her nose against the porthole, trying to see out. The ATV was there, hovering a meter away from *Reliance*'s hull. It had undocked, but been given no command to move away from the station. Inertia had kept it in lock-step with the parent station. Good in that, given time—and air—they could reclaim it. Bad in that any perturbation could sending it crashing into *Reliance*'s 7mm-thick aluminum hull.

Josephine was bent over her palmtop, desperately tapping icons with her stylus.

"Need—go—command—module," Anderson wheezed. He pounded weakly against the bulkhead separating them from the access tunnel.

"Can't tell—pressure," Josephine panted.

White flashes and blackness crowded Claire's peripheral vision. The low air pressure had them close to blacking out. "Do it," she gasped, her voice no more than a whisper.

Josephine crossed the fingers holding the stylus and tapped.

The bulkhead rose.

Free air blew over them. It stank of months-old sweat, but to Claire it was nectar. She inhaled deeply. Her vision cleared.

Anderson was already on the move, clawing his way along handholds towards the command module.

Claire grabbed Hyun-Jin and Josephine's elbows, preventing them from following. "When he docks the ATV, we'll need to board immediately if we're to have a hope of catching the lifeboat."

Hyun-Jin looked in the direction of Anderson. "But what about—"

"We'll come back for him," Claire promised.

"I don't see why," Josephine grumbled, not quite under her breath. "This is all his fault."

Hyun-Jin looked alarmed and moved towards the command module.

Claire increased her grip on his elbow. She made eye contact. "We'll come back. I promise." As angry as she was at Anderson, and much as she might agree with Josephine's muttered comment, it wasn't how she ran things. "But we can't save anyone, until we get that lifeboat."

"Damn ATV isn't responding," Anderson announced over the ship-wide intercom. "Radio interference. Same as before." He grunted with effort.

Outside the porthole the ATV's thrusters fired weakly, and it listed towards the solar panels, nose cone canted off at an angle.

"Are you sure it's safe to wait here?" Josephine asked, looking over Claire's shoulder at the ATV. "If the docking goes wrong . . ."

"We're dead," Claire finished, her eyes never leaving the ATV. "Either now from decompression, or later from radiation and starvation. Only question is, do you want to die quick, or slow? Anyone who wants to go to the command module with Anderson, feel free. I'm staying here."

Hyun-Jin and Josephine exchanged a nervous glance, but neither left.

The ATV twitched and bobbed, like a fish fighting a line.

Claire looked past the malfunctioning ATV to the two ships converging on *Shenzhou XI*. The CEV was already docked, and the Chinese ATV was sliding into position.

"Anderson, get that ATV docked," Claire ordered. "We don't have time—"

"I know. The rightmost thruster is firing erratically. I can't shut it down, and I can't risk docking if the ATV might jump left at any moment."

Claire's hands clenched and unclenched. Three white figures in EVA suits crawled like white dots out of the docked ATV. Once they were through *Shenzhou's* air lock and unsuited, they would enter the CEV and take off towards Earth. If that happened, there was no way to catch them. Their only hope of evacuation would be gone.

"Risk it," Claire ordered. "Over there." She pointed Josephine and Hyun-Jin to move to the other side of the nearby bulkhead. That way, if the hull was breached, they'd have a chance.

"I'm not going to—" Anderson protested.

"They're entering the air lock," Claire countered. "How fast could you desuit if your life depended on it? We've got minutes—not hours—to get there and stop them from doing the reentry burn."

Anderson blew out a breath. "Brace yourself, this is going to be rough."

The ATV rotated its nose cone towards the docking pin. It staggered like a drunk on approach, jigging left suddenly, then straightening out, only to jig left again.

Watching the ATV's unsteady progress, doubt crept into Claire's mind. It might already be too late to catch the Chinese; the ATV might be too unstable to safely dock. But it was too late, and there was no other choice. She glanced left at Josephine and Hyun-Jin.

They looked scared.

Claire nodded with confidence she didn't feel. "If anyone can bring this ATV home, it's Anderson."

The approaching ATV filled the porthole. Still it did its wandering dance.

Muffled curses came over the intercom that Anderson had left on VOX. Imprecations for the ATV's approach to straighten out, condemnations of the defense contractor whose lowest bid had skimped on radiation-hardening the ATV's electronics, and pleas to a higher power.

Seconds stretched into minutes.

Claire clung to the round ring of the hatch and pressed her face flat against the glass, peeking sideways at *Shenzhou XI*. There was no visible movement on the Chinese station. Both small craft were docked and the space walkers had gone through the air lock.

Would the Chinese take their time, confident that *Reliance*'s crew couldn't recover their ATV? Claire didn't think so. Burned once, the crew of *Shenzhou XI* wouldn't dawdle.

"Got it!" Anderson crowed.

The ATV slid into dock with a thump and a clang of the docking pin's capture.

Claire pulled open the hatch and shot inside. She clawed her way to the pilot's seat and wrapped her arms through the five-point safety harness. Behind her, Josephine and Hyun-Jin tumbled in and closed the door.

"Grab something," Claire said. Without further warning, she opened the ATV's thrusters up full throttle, jetting away from *Reliance* towards *Shenzhou XI.*

Anderson was their best pilot, but all of them had put in simulator time on the ATV. Claire's hands flew over the controls, adjusting pitch and yaw, checking the ATV's functions. Running on manual, its controls were responsive, and all systems—save the automated pilot—seemed nominal.

Behind her, Hyun-Jin and Josephine scrambled against acceleration to climb into the other two seats.

Shenzhou grew larger as they approached. The tiny black-and-white dot that was the CEV resolved into a miniature snub-nosed plane. Claire's eyes fixed on it like a laser. That CEV was hers, and she wouldn't let—

The lifeboat detached from *Shenzhou*'s docking pin and rotated away from the station.

Claire pushed the button to transmit over ship-to-ship frequency. "CEV, this is *Reliance* ATV-1. Please return to *Reliance* station."

There was no response. The lifeboat's thrusters glowed briefly as it accelerated away.

There was no threat she could offer the CEV. The only action she could take against them was to ram the lifeboat with her ATV, which would kill them all. And at this point, it was unlikely she could reach the CEV before it made its deorbit burn.

"Please. There are four of us. If you take the lifeboat, we'll die up here." Images of Owen's chubby face rose in her mind: contemplative, laughing, wailing. Claire glanced at the ruined Earth. Somewhere down there Matt and Owen were suffering, needing her help, and failing that, her comfort.

"Please," her voice broke. "I have a little boy—he's only four years old—he needs his mother." Shame filled her chest, but she couldn't stop herself from sobbing. She'd been up for thirty-seven hours, six of that hard-labor EVA, working her muscles against the constant resistance of a pressure suit. She was tired and scared, and had nothing left to give except her grief.

"What happened to Zhang is a tragedy," she said, pleading, "but it was the action of one crew member. *One*, and he's back on the station. Please . . ."

Hyun-Jin glowered at Claire. In a hoarse whisper, "You promised—"

Josephine shut him up with an arm around his throat. Her lips near his ear, sotto voce: "Shut. Up."

"Please." Claire was openly crying now. She knew it was wrong, she should show strength. Bargain. Think of something she could offer the Chinese crew. But they had already taken everything they wanted from *Reliance*.

Claire waved Hyun-Jin over. "Tell them in Chinese. Make them understand."

Josephine let him go and pushed him towards the radio.

Hyun-Jin glared at Claire and Josephine, then took the headset and said a few words. Claire checked the radio. There was acknowledgment from the CEV's transceiver. But no response from the crew.

The CEV's main engine lit. It grew smaller, a black-and-white toy plane the size of her little finger, dwindling into its reentry orbit.

Claire scraped tears away from her eyes with her thumbs. "Come back, you goddamned cowards!" She pounded the ATV's control panel. "Come back!"

Sobs wracked her body.

Beside her, Hyun-Jin looked stricken, in shock, as if he didn't believe what he was seeing.

Josephine wiped moisture from her eyes. "That's it, then," she said in a dead voice.

Claire wiped her face on the sleeve of her flight suit. It was over. Too little, too late. The realization that she'd never see her husband or son again was like burning lead in her chest.

Her hands and eyes on automatic, the product of hundreds of hours of drilling in the simulator, Claire piloted the ATV back to *Reliance* and docked it without incident. The thought "I will kill Anderson" formed in her head.

Not in anger, but as a cold dead certainty. This was his fault. All his fault.

Anderson relinquished the commander's station when Claire and the others entered. He said nothing, only moved to the back of the room.

Josephine glowered at him as he passed her.

Hyun-Jin was silent, eyes staring ahead at the screen where a camera showed the departing CEV.

Claire didn't look at Anderson. She was afraid to let down the wall of ice that had formed around her heart. Years of trained professionalism constrained her. She was an astronaut. There was a way things were done, a protocol. But all that had been stripped away in the minutes she'd spent in the ATV begging for her life, for the right to see her son again. Everything she cared about was gone. All that was left for her was to die among people she worked with.

On the largest viewscreen, the lifeboat was a shrinking black-and-white dot. There was nothing she could do. No way to bring it back. But she couldn't look away.

Josephine zoomed in on the CEV with *Reliance*'s forward cameras, enlarging it from pinpoint to stubby-winged space craft.

It was well within the atmosphere now. A ball of flame engulfed the CEV as friction against the Earth's atmosphere slowed the craft and produced temperatures as high as 2,300 degrees Fahrenheit. The video monitor washed out to yellow and orange, all detail lost.

Josephine zoomed out.

A fiery chariot carrying *Shenzhou*'s crew to the safety of Earth.

Claire glanced at Anderson out of the corner of her eye and saw tears bubbling on his lashes. His hands were balled into fists.

This was all his fault. Owen would die without the comfort of his mother or the life-saving medicines in *Reliance*'s medical kit. While on *Reliance*, they would starve to death, and he would be the reason for their bleeding gums, their atrophied muscles, the fatigue that would overcome them. The baking-bread smell of the malnourished. All of it his fault.

If she didn't hate him so much, Claire might have pitied him.

"No!" Josephine screamed, her horror drawing the word out into three syllables.

Claire focused on the screen. A series of black specks flaked away from the tiny CEV. The reentry blaze surrounding it brightened suddenly.

Claire grabbed the control and zoomed out. The flaming trajectory of the CEV was gone, in its wake, a fireworks display of shrapnel. White contrails exploded from the CEV, shooting up, then arcing back down to Earth, dragged low by gravity.

The patched hull hadn't held.

For a long moment, no one said anything.

"Hell, yeah!" shouted Anderson, pumping the air with his fist. "That's what I call fried wontons."

Hyun-Jin glared at him.

"Hey!" Anderson slapped Hyun-Jin's shoulder playfully. "Those bastards stole our ship. They got what was coming to them."

Claire's stomach knotted. The hope she had harbored during the repairs was gone. She knew for certain they would never reach Earth. They would die up here, either from equipment malfunction, lack of oxygen, or starvation. But the open spaces of Earth were gone forever. The hated faces of her crew members would be the only ones she would see between now and the moment of her death. The dam of denial and repression that had kept her emotions at bay dissolved. Flash floods of grief tore through her veins. She screamed with all her might: "God damn you, Anderson! Damn you to hell!" She grabbed his throat, intent on crushing the life out of him. She would die, but he would go first.

Anderson choked and pushed at Claire's hands. He thrashed and got an elbow up in front of her face. Hyun-Jin pried her fingers apart.

"What the *fuck's* the matter with you?" Anderson accused, wiping spittle from his mouth.

Hyun-Jin stared at Claire in open-mouthed shock.

"You don't get it, do you," said Josephine in an empty voice. "The CEV was our best hope at creating a ship that could survive reentry. And it failed. We're trapped up here until we die."

CHAPTER 12

Josephine's prediction of doom hung in the air. No one could dispute it. The CEV was gone, and with it, any hope of returning to Earth.

"If the goddamn Chinese hadn't—" Anderson began.

Frustration boiled up in Claire. Owen needed her, and she couldn't help him. Her anger found a target: "No." Claire jabbed a finger into Anderson's chest. "I had things with Zhang under control. This is all *your* fault."

"You don't know what they would have done," said Hyun-Jin with quiet heat. "If Anderson and I hadn't acted, they might have killed us to steal the CEV."

"We are dead," Josephine murmured to no one in particular.

Claire whirled on Hyun-Jin. "Zhang was a good man. He saved my life on the arm. He would have kept his word."

"He helped you," Anderson said, "because it was in his best interest. You were about to crash into the CEV."

"None of which," said Josephine in her flat, hopeless voice, "answers the question, 'what do we do now?'" She pointed at the command panel. Three more systems had gone red: the water recovery subsystem, the step-down transformer from solar array one, and attitudinal control. The last controlled the thrusters that kept *Reliance* from sinking into the atmosphere and burning up.

Claire looked out the window at Earth, so tantalizingly close and yet unreachable. Her skin itched with her need to return, to save her family. "Is there any way we could create an ablative shield? Something that would dissipate the heat of reentry and last long enough to see the ATV safely back to Earth?"

Josephine shook her head. "Not before the Argus effect shuts us down. We're already past the safe time period Houston outlined. If we stay in LEO, we'll die sometime in the next twenty-four hours; with the atmosphere we lost in the battle over the lifeboat, probably less. The atmospheric recyclers aren't efficient at low pressure." A morbid half-smile crossed her thin lips. "Of course, with low supplies, we're dead in MEO in a couple of weeks."

"Oh, god." Hyun-Jin clasped both arms on top of his head. "We're going to die. *Really* going to die."

Anderson placed a hand on Hyun-Jin's shoulder and gave it a shake. "Pull yourself together, man."

Claire heard Matt's worried voice in her head: "My son is sick. I think it's the radiation." It played over and over in her head. Claire remembered how she felt when Owen was two days old, so tiny and delicate. One of his tiny red hands rested in her palm, and Claire knew she no longer had the option to die easily. Whatever fate threw at her now, disease, sorrow, physical disability, she would have to fight and stay alive—for Owen's sake. Because a little boy needed his mother.

She couldn't afford Josephine's bleak depression or Hyun-Jin's fear. There was only one way to proceed. To go down, she would first have to go up. Claire locked eyes with Anderson. "We'll have to finish what we came here to do. Launch us and the solar reflector into MEO."

"The solar reflector?" Josephine asked. "It's all we can do to stay alive and you're worried about finishing the mission NASA gave us?"

Claire kept her eyes locked on Anderson. He was the one she had to convince. NASA was defunct. There was no punishment waiting on the ground for mutiny, and he didn't like taking orders from her. The only way he would work with Claire instead of against her, was if he agreed with the plan. "When the U.S. rebuilds, it's going to need energy. There's not a lot of good we can do from up here, but we can put the solar reflector in place. If we're going to die, let's make it mean something."

Anderson nodded slowly. "By God, yes."

Hyun-Jin still looked scared, Josephine uncertain.

"Not that I intend to die up here," Claire reassured them. "From MEO we can deploy the solar reflector, build a new lifeboat, and find a way to safely return to Earth."

Josephine raised an eyebrow. "In three weeks?"

Claire pointed into the porthole. *Shenzhou*'s dragonfly shape hovered on the other side of the Mars fuel platform, a cylindrical ATV still attached to its central docking pin. "A crew of five, and they'd just rotated in fresh supplies."

Hope animated Josephine's face for the first time since the CEV was stolen. "You mean . . ."

"The depot was stockpiling fuel to travel to Mars. There's plenty to take us, the platform, and *Shenzhou XI* into MEO—if we can rig it up before the station goes dark around us. We'll have to move fast. But if we can pull it off, with two stations, two ATVs, and the largest stockpile of fuel in space, can you honestly tell me that we won't be able to find a way home?"

Josephine bit her lower lip. "It'll be hard to maneuver the *Shenzhou* into position. It's missing four thrusters and we won't be able to read the characters on the controls." Then her eyes lit up with the challenge. "But maybe . . ."

That was the secret to motivating smart people, Claire realized. You didn't have to make it easy, you just had to make it possible.

"Hyun-Jin," Anderson asked. "Can you read Chinese characters?"

"I—I don't know many," Hyun-Jin said, as the long main cylinder of *Shenzhou* loomed in the fore window. "My Uncle Shen tried to teach me when I was a kid, but I never got into it the way my sister did."

"You'll do fine," Claire said. "The Chinese station was built using Russian blueprints, which were designed to be compatible with U.S. systems ever since the collaboration on the ISS."

Hyun-Jin wasn't as certain. "How can we EVA? Hu and

Bai destroyed our airlock. There's no way to connect the stations to the fuel depot."

"Actually . . ." Josephine tapped on the control panel's touchscreen. "I'm getting a pressure reading in the air lock." She frowned. "How is that possible? I thought Hu and Bai—"

Claire's eyes opened wide. "Zhang." She kicked off down the corridor, and caught a handhold to arc her body into a side access tunnel and into the crew lock. Anderson and the rest of the crew were right behind her. Claire pressed her face against the glass separating the crew lock from the equipment lock.

The Chinese commander hung from his duct-taped bonds, not the desiccated husk of a man exposed to vacuum, but struggling and kicking.

Despite herself, Claire grinned.

Josephine still looked puzzled. "I thought Hu and Bai broke into the air lock when were trying to stop us reaching the CEV. We heard the drills."

"They had no need to break into the air lock," Claire said, looking at the man who could help her pilot *Shenzhou XI* into MEO, "since their crewmates in the ATV hacked into our command codes and got the CEV to undock. They punctured the hull farther up to drop the bulkheads and keep us from reaching the lifeboat."

Anderson's hand reached towards the control that would purge the air lock to vacuum.

Claire grabbed his hand and dug her thumb into the pressure point between the bones of his wrist. "Don't even think about it. Zhang is a now a vital member of our crew. He knows the systems and capabilities of the *Shenzhou XI*."

Anderson shook off her grip. "He's the enemy. Even if he was working with us before, he won't trust us now. First chance he gets he'll turn on us. We're the reason he's still up here."

No, thought Claire. *You're* the reason he's still up here. Claire held up her forefinger. "You screwed up once, Anderson. Up here once is all you get—if that. From now on, you don't make a move unless we're all in agreement— understood?"

"We don't need him." Anderson glowered. "He'll just

be a drain on our resources, an angry, resentful drain. Like you said, we can only survive one mistake. Don't let this be yours."

Claire moved between Anderson and the button that would evacuate the air lock. She couldn't believe what she was hearing. "Are you suggesting we cold-bloodedly kill him?"

Anderson thought about it. "Better to kill him now than give him a chance to kill one of us. It isn't pretty, but that's what war is. I wouldn't expect a civilian to understand."

"NASA isn't a military—"

Anderson pressed his face close to Claire's. "This isn't about NASA. There *isn't* any NASA anymore. By the time the Chinese finish bombing North America, there may not be a United States. This is about four people who want to survive."

Hairs on the back of Claire's neck prickled. This was a side of Anderson she'd never seen in training. Of course, they hadn't prepared for a situation like this. For the first time, Anderson scared her.

"Before you go all *Lord of the Flies*," Josephine interrupted from behind Anderson, "that guy is our best chance at connecting *Shenzhou* to the Mars platform, and *Shenzhou* is bigger, better equipped, and doesn't have several holes in its hull. We need him."

"We can do it without him," Anderson growled over his shoulder, still leaning in to intimidate Claire.

Josephine advanced, poking her finger into his shoulder blade. "Using him improves our chance of success. The way things are going, we'll need every advantage."

"He won't help us," said Hyun-Jin. "We betrayed him."

Josephine snorted. "That was then, this is now. He wants to live as much as we do. It's in his best interest to help us. If he turns on us—*then* we kill him."

Claire couldn't believe her fellow crew—people she thought she knew well—discussing whether to brutally murder a man who had done nothing but help them. Had they lost their minds? Hyun-Jin was afraid. She'd seen the depths Anderson was willing to go to survive. But Josephine?

Josephine pushed passed Anderson and Claire to the window that separated the crew from the equipment lock.

When her gaze was hidden from everyone but Claire, Josephine winked.

Claire eased out a breath. She still had an ally. And if Zhang could be made to understand what had happened, perhaps two. "The only way to find out is to ask." She unlocked the hatch between the two locks.

Zhang immediately became still. His eyes were wide, taking everything in. He looked like a rabbit sizing up his chances against a jackal. The Buddhist medallion floated near his chin. "You're here." His deep voice was smooth. "My crew must have escaped with the lifeboat." A glint of satisfaction creased the corners of his eyes.

"Didn't do them any good—" Anderson lunged forward.

Claire caught his chest on her arm, and braked them both by catching the arm of the nearest EVA-suit valet. "Anderson. To the command module. Now."

He wavered. The cords in Anderson's neck stood out. He outweighed and could outfight Claire. They both knew it. Only years of military training in obedience to authority kept him in line.

When he had confronted Claire earlier, she'd seen through his macho bluster. Anderson was terrified and couldn't admit it. That made him dangerous.

If he didn't back down, if he crossed the line of insubordination, he'd take command, and the only way Claire would be able to wrest control from him would be to kill him. Recognizing his threat wasn't something she'd learned from NASA. It was thirty-three years of on-the-job-training, being female.

"I'm going to check the filtration system." He glowered at Hyun-Jin. "Don't let them cut him loose."

Claire let out a long breath when he left. He hadn't given in, but he hadn't attacked. Anderson was on a thin tether. She hoped he could keep it from breaking long enough for them to get safely home.

Zhang's black eyes followed Anderson out. When he was gone, his gaze shifted to Claire, appraising. He didn't speak. Just hovered there, wrists tied together.

Claire licked her lips. "I won't ask you to forgive Anderson. What he did was unforgivable. But now that the lifeboat is gone, the only way we can survive is to transfer to mid-Earth orbit. That might buy us enough time to devise a way home. Right now the Argus effect has taken out half the systems on *Reliance*, and it's getting worse."

Zhang shifted position and looked at Claire, Josephine, and Hyun-Jin in turn. His eyes settled back on Claire. "What did that man mean: 'it did my crew no good'? What happened to them?"

If she expected him to trust her, she had to begin with the truth. Claire kicked over to Zhang and began undoing the tape that held his wrists. "The lifeboat exploded on reentry. Our patch didn't hold. I am sorry."

He didn't react immediately. His black eyes scanned her face for clues as to whether she told the truth. Apparently he found it. His face sobered. "They were . . . a good crew."

Claire gave him a moment with his grief. But a moment was all she could spare. "The Argus effect is closing in on us. We've lost three more systems in the last hour. The only way we can survive is to transfer to MEO. Will you help us?" With a jerk she pulled the tape free of the EVA-suit restraint. The last strip of duct tape clung to Zhang's skin.

He tore it off angrily, the glue leaving red welts on his wrists. He glared in the direction Anderson had gone. "That man has much to answer for." His gaze slid towards Hyun-Jin. "As do you."

"It seemed like the right thing at the time," Hyun-Jin said defensively. "And it wasn't all bad. If Anderson and I hadn't captured you, you'd be dead now."

Zhang said a phrase in Chinese.

Hyun-Jin paled.

Claire didn't ask for a translation. Zhang's tone was clear enough. "We're going to MEO, and we're taking *Shenzhou XI* with us. We need its supplies and raw materials. The only question I have is: Are you going to help us?"

Zhang looked at the air lock's porthole. Earth was visible on the other side of the Mars platform. Tons of dust had been thrown into the air by the nuclear explosions, and dull beige clouds hid much of the intensely blue Pacific Ocean. A heavy sigh lifted and dropped Zhang's shoulders. "I have no choice." He looked back at Claire and his eyes were hot. "But that man, Anderson, he will answer to me for what he has done. If he had not rushed my crew into hasty action, we would have tested the repairs. We would have found the fault, fixed it. We would all be alive on Earth, even now."

The truth of his words rang in the tight confines of the air lock. Anderson's fear, his rash actions, had killed Zhang's crew, and unless brought into check, could kill them all.

Hyun-Jin bowed his head, his cheeks red with shame.

"You screwed up." Claire clapped an arm around his shoulder. "That can't be undone. But don't make the same mistake twice. You have to help me reel Anderson in." She looked up at Josephine.

"We should lock him in a lab." Josephine's cobalt eyes were murderous. "We can't afford a loose cannon. Not now."

"Yes," Zhang echoed. "I can—"

"No." Claire felt weary. Somehow she had to balance all these personalities and get them working together as a team. She wished Cole was there to take the burden from her, but he wasn't. And no one else could do the job as well as she—if she could at all. "We'll need every hand free to get this done as quickly as possible. Josephine, Hyun-Jin, you go with Zhang to *Shenzhou XI* and make the necessary arrangements. Zhang, I assume your crew had a plan for connecting *Shenzhou* to the Mars platform."

Zhang nodded. "The necessary equipment is collected in a case outside our air lock."

"Good. I'll stay here with Anderson. Work out a way to get *Reliance* connected." The words fell like lead into her stomach. She wasn't looking forward to the confrontation that was sure to develop with Anderson, and without backup. But if she was going to prevent another outburst like the one that had destroyed the lifeboat, it had to be done.

"Are you sure that's wise?" Zhang asked. His right hand clenched and unclenched into a fist. It looked like an unconscious gesture. "The girl is right, that man is too dangerous to—"

"I'll handle Anderson. You three get *Shenzhou* hooked up to the Mars platform."

For three seconds, nobody spoke. Then Zhang said, "As you wish."

*   *   *

Matt shut down the ham radio. He'd been able to run it off the car battery and had broadcast messages. The only replies he'd heard were other people trapped in their houses, asking for aid. Between pleading for help were the conspiracy theories and dire predictions of more bombings—nothing he needed to listen to. Reality was hard enough right now without imagining worse.

The car door opened, startling him. His mother crooked a finger to draw her son close. "Matt," she whispered, "he's getting worse."

Dried blood caked the corner of Owen's mouth. His eyes were sunken and dark purple bruises had appeared on his arms. He chest rose and fell so shallowly that Matt watched for long seconds before he believed that his son still breathed.

It had been hours, and still no sign of the National Guard. "Damn," he breathed. "We've got to get him to a hospital."

There was a clatter from inside the kitchen. Adrenaline shot through Matt's nervous system.

Betty, wide-eyed, turned towards the door that led from the garage to the kitchen. Her wrinkled face looked ashen in the low light.

Matt put a finger to his lips and picked up the shotgun. He crept to the kitchen door and eased it open.

Three youths in hooded raincoats stuffed canned goods into a rucksack.

"Get 'em all," said a red-haired boy whom Matt had seen playing basketball in a driveway three doors down.

"Oh, shit!" said another boy as he turned and saw Matt with the gun.

Matt leveled the gun at the boy with the sack. "Put the food down."

The boy dropped the bag and backpedaled, his arms raised in surrender.

"Matt?" Betty's quavering voice came from directly behind him. She stood in the doorway.

Matt turned his head, "Mother, go back—"

The red-haired boy grabbed the bag of food from the ground and swung it at Matt, knocking him backwards. He snatched for the gun, but Matt held on.

The motion pulled the trigger and a chunk of plaster fell from the ceiling.

The boy shoved Matt's mother down and ran out through the living room.

Matt heard his mother scream. He pushed himself to his feet.

Betty lay on the ground near the door, weeping. "I think—I think I broke my hip."

Matt picked her up, careful not to touch her wounded leg, and settled her in the backseat next to his son. Then he went back to the kitchen and gathered the canned food that was left. The boys had taken most of it. What was left was a smattering of vegetables: creamed corn, peas, green beans. He gathered it in a plastic trash bag and threw it in the passenger's floor well.

Then he crawled into the backseat and cradled his mother and son. Tears crept down his face as he listened to his mother's weeping and the rattling breaths of his son.

What was humanity coming to when junior-high students stole food and pushed old women down? Was this desperation, or had this violence always been there, waiting for calamity to bring it to the surface?

Claire found Anderson in the control module. The amateur radio was on in the background, a low surf of static that occasionally heaved up the driftwood of phrases: "Conspiracy by the government to—Saddam Hussein's grandson—effects of global warming—another blackout, can't tell you—"

His back to Claire, Anderson cast his own message into the waters. His voice was low and urgent: "CQ, CQ, this is NA3SS, calling for Everett, Washington. Anyone in Washington state—" When he caught a glimpse of Claire he broke off and clipped the microphone back onto the radio. He did not meet her eyes.

The amateur radio filled the silence between them with a cacophony of languages, static, and the international call for an answer: CQ, CQ. A hundred different voices called out for people who would never answer.

Claire's anger at Anderson was tempered—just a little—with pity. "How's the filtration unit?"

He didn't look up. "Struggling. The reduced station pressure means the pump has to work harder to keep the air flowing through the carbon-dioxide filters. I'm trying to find a way to increase the throughput, maybe have Hyun-Jin—"

"He can't," Claire said, staring at the back of Anderson's crew-cut head. "I sent him and Josephine over with Zhang to connect *Shenzhou XI* to the Mars platform."

Anderson whipped around. "You cut Zhang free?" His expression was equal parts incredulity and anger.

Claire kept solid eye contact. "I put Zhang in charge."

"You're insane." Anderson untucked his legs from behind the laptop station and kicked off towards the hatch. "He'll take what he needs from *Reliance*, then sabotage—"

Claire caught his upper arm and they spun around each other in the weightless cabin. "No. You're staying here. We're going to hook *Reliance* up to the platform."

Anderson scraped her hand off his arm. "Like hell. You may have lost your mind, but I haven't. I'm going to sto—" He kicked towards the hatch again.

Claire kicked harder, got there first. She blocked the hatch with her body. "As your commanding officer, I'm telling you to stay here."

Anderson clawed at Claire's ribs, trying to push her aside. "If you've let Zhang free, you're not fit to command. You'll get us all killed."

"Like you almost did." Her sharp words slapped back.

His eyes narrowed. "I did what I had to do, and it would have worked if you and Jo-Jo hadn't slowed us down."

"Then we'd all be dead now. The lifeboat blew up, remember? Because you rushed things, we didn't have time to test the integrity of the repair. We can't act impulsively. There's too much at stake."

"That was pilot error. *I* could have—"

"No," Claire snapped. "You couldn't. A rupture during reentry isn't something you can pilot around. Going back to Earth isn't something you can solve alone. It's going to take all of us." She pointed out the window at *Shenzhou XI*. "That includes Zhang."

"Cole wouldn't—"

"Cole's dead. You fucked up. And *I'm* the only person who can hold this team together long enough to have a *chance* at going home."

Anderson's head snapped up. Claire wasn't sure whether it was the obscenity or her claim.

"Yeah." Claire jerked her thumb at her chest. "Me." She leaned forward until her nose nearly touched Anderson's.

He ground his teeth. "You don't have the training for a military situation like this."

"And *you* don't have the people skills. That little stunt you pulled—think Josephine will ever trust you with her back again? Hyun-Jin admits you two screwed up. And Zhang—better not go there.

"I'm the only one they'll all listen to. Josephine's too young and inexperienced to lead. Hyun-Jin doesn't have the personality for it. Zhang's foreign, and you're a loose cannon." She jerked her thumb into her chest again. "There's just me."

Claire was out of breath. She panted and waited for Anderson to either agree or punch her.

Anderson ran his hands along the side of his head and balled them into fists.

Claire tensed, not sure what she would do if he attacked.

In the stillness, the amateur radio continued its monologue of desperation and hope. A little girl's voice broke out of the hubbub: "CQ, CQ. Daddy, are you there? It's all dark outside and I'm scared. Please come home. Daddy?"

Anderson glanced stricken at the radio. The tension slumped out of his shoulders and he looked lost. "I just can't . . . believe he—they're all gone." Anderson bit his lip until it bled. "I'm smart and I'm strong and I'm the best pilot in NASA. But none of that matters. There's nothing I can do . . . to save them—I had somebody special in Houston, my father in Everett, and they're all gone." His voice cracked and he turned away. In a hoarse whisper he said, "Nothing makes sense anymore."

The flood behind Claire's eyes rose in answer, but she forced it back down. Anderson needed her to be strong. She let out the breath she'd been holding. Claire touched Anderson's shoulder. "I know what you mean. Sometimes none of it seems real. Then I see Earth, and it's all I can do to breathe."

"At least your people are all right. You know they're alive down there. My brothers—my father—I have no idea."

Claire caught his chin and made him look at her. "My son is sick, probably dying of radiation poisoning, and there's not a damn thing I can do to help. It's killing me. The only thing I can do—the only thing any of us can do—is take care of this moment. One step towards home, then another." She held out her hand. "Will you work with me?"

Anderson took her hand. "All right." His grip was firm, but there was a hollowness behind his eyes.

Claire slapped his shoulder. "Good. Then let's figure out how to get this station mounted to the Mars platform."

They discussed every possible option and decided to use the Canadarm to clamp onto a girder of the Mars platform.

"Will it hold through the transfer?" Claire asked.

Anderson checked the computerized simulation of the transfer orbit. "Maximum acceleration will be point-eight gee. If you weld the joints in place and lock down the track, it should be good."

The radio crackled: "*Reliance*, this is Josephine on *Shenzhou XI*. Do you copy?"

Claire donned the headset and toggled the microphone. "We read you, Josephine. What's your status?"

"We've docked to *Shenzhou*. Hyun-Jin and Zhang' are preparing for EVA. I'll be piloting the ATV. We're going to use its engines to maneuver, since *Shenzhou*'s a few thrusters short at this point. You?"

"I'm prepping for EVA. Anderson will handle communications while I'm outside. Good luck, Jo. See you on the platform." Claire pulled off the headset and handed it to Anderson.

As she kicked off a handrail, heading towards the hatch, her knee twinged. It made her pause long enough that she heard what she'd tuned out. The background hiss and pop of the amateur radio, a babble of a dozen different voices: "CQ, CQ—is—there?—lost power—bombs—blackout—army maneuvers—clouds of dust—Armageddon—"

Claire caught the rim of the hatch and pivoted back towards Anderson. "While you're searching for your father, will you send a message for me?" She nodded at the radio. "Will you try to contact Matt? Tell him I'm alive, that I love him." Her voice cracked with emotion. "Tell him to hold on, stay inside, I'll be home soon."

Anderson's lips compressed, but apparently he thought better of what he'd been about to say. He nodded. "You bet."

Hank Rubin felt like he'd been kicked in the chest. He was in a room with concrete walls, the lines of cinder blocks visible under white paint. A thin hospital blanket covered his body. The green glowing line of a heart monitor traced his pulse.

A man in army fatigues with a Red Cross patch on his shoulder adjusted his IV.

"Where am I?" asked Hank, plucking at the silicon tube running into the back of his hand.

"He's awake," shouted the medic over his shoulder.

President Tucker walked into the room. He wore an oxford-cloth shirt and khaki pants. He crossed to the hospital bed and clasped Hank's free hand in both of his own. "Hank, it's good to see you up and around."

Suddenly Hank understood: the recycled taste of the air, the cinder-block walls, the President. "We're in a relocation center. One of the bunkers in Virginia."

President Tucker nodded. "We need your perspective on the low-orbit situation. When satellites might come back online. What's out there we can use."

"How . . ." Hank choked on the words, thinking of his daughter in Kansas City and—oh, God—his three grand-children! "How bad is it? How many bombs?"

Tucker looked down at his hands. "Not good. More than sixty percent of China's retaliation made it through our defenses." A bitter smile cut across his face. "You always told me that our anti–ballistic missile defense was inadequate."

"We have to help them." Hank tried to sit up.

The medic grabbed his shoulders and eased him back towards the bed. "Easy. You've had a major coronary event."

Hank slapped his hands away and stripped the IV from his hand. "We have to help people. Protect them—"

President Tucker pushed Hank back to the bed. "You always were stubborn. Even in college. Only man on the rowing crew that wouldn't give up, not even after another team crossed the finish line."

Hank scowled at the man responsible for destroying the United States, perhaps the world. "And you always were an idiot."

The medic readied a syringe, drawing clear fluid out of a glass bottle.

"We've done all we can," said President Tucker. His florid jowls gave him a hangdog look, like a dyspeptic basset hound. "The National Guard has been deployed to set up field hospitals. The emergency broadcast system is telling people to stay inside, drink bottled water. We'll get through this. Right now we need you to rest, to build your strength." Tucker nodded at the medic.

Hank struggled as the medic held him down with a knee and injected him in the arm. Lassitude filled his arms and legs almost immediately. Hank lay back on the bed and began to doze.

As he fell asleep, he heard voices:

"Why did you want this guy?" came the cultured tones of the Speaker of the House.

"He's a genius," answered Tucker. "We need him to rebuild satellite communications."

"Yeah, well," said the Speaker, "if he becomes a drain on the shelter's resources, we're putting him outside."

Claire used the accelerated protocol, breathing deeply, driving nitrogen out of her bloodstream and the joint of her right knee. Matt and Owen were alive. It was a miracle. The reckless despair she'd felt when she thought they were dead had been replaced by a desperate will to live. She had to get back to Earth.

She exited, feeling very alone in the enormity of space. By space-walking standards, the local area was dangerously crowded with other ships and stations. But beyond that, in all directions, was endless black, dotted with stars, going on forever.

Claire was careful with the tether transfer she had to make between the air lock and the Canadarm. She checked twice to make sure she was about to disconnect the right tether. There was backup propellant in her suit, but she didn't want to waste it with unnecessary maneuvers.

The arm was folded near the docking port that once housed the CEV. Claire stared at the empty docking pin and her heart clenched. If only Anderson hadn't—no. That was the past. Time to deal with the present.

The Canadarm had nearly killed her during the positioning to weld the lifeboat patch, would have killed her if Zhang hadn't intervened. But now there was no one near to help if things went wrong, and only a tense truce with Anderson, who would control the arm from the command module. He had acted precipitously once. Could she trust him? Did she have any choice?

She spoke over the radio: "EVA-1 to *Reliance*. I'm in position."

"Copy that," Anderson responded. His voice was all business, like this was a simulation they'd practiced hundreds of times, not a dangerous maneuver to fly a delicate space station over to the Mars platform and attempt to dock to it using a malfunctioning arm. This maneuver went against so many safety guidelines that NASA administrators—if there had been a NASA anymore—would have been apoplectic.

"Firing attitudinal thrusters," Anderson said.

From her position clinging to the arm's base, Claire saw the glow of the thrusters and felt the acceleration as a vibration under her palms. The Mars platform loomed larger.

She and Anderson planned to dock to the side of the platform, using the pincher of the Canadarm to grasp one of the struts that held the fuel tanks in place. It would keep them well away from the exhaust of the platform's oxygen/hydrogen engine, and give the combined structure a reasonable moment of inertia for maneuvering in and out of the Hohmann transfer orbits necessary to up-orbit to MEO.

Unfortunately, this positioning also meant that if Anderson overshot his target, in addition to whatever damage he might do to *Reliance*, he could rupture one of the pressurized fuel tanks and put the Mars platform into an uncontrolled spin. The approach had to be perfect the first time.

Until they were within twenty meters of the platform, all Claire could do was wait, watch, and worry.

The radiative panels protecting the liquid oxygen and liquid hydrogen from solar heat were made of crenulated polished aluminum. As *Reliance* drew nearer, the white wall rose and blotted out the stars. It was oppressive; Claire felt like an ant watching the approach of a descending boot.

"Forty meters," Anderson recited. "Thirty. Initiating braking thrust."

Thrusters on the side of the station facing the Mars platform fired, producing tiny wisps of gas that didn't seem substantial enough to stop *Reliance* from crashing into the platform.

"Twenty-five meters, twenty-one . . ."

Claire could only see the wall of black. *Shenzhou* was hidden on the other side, Earth behind *Reliance*. She could see individual rivets now from the platform's assembly. They were growing more slowly in size, but still growing.

"We're still drifting," she reported, keeping her voice level, as if they weren't about to smack into the Mars platform and destroy all hope of going home.

"I'm on it," Anderson said with a quiet intensity that indicated an unexpected problem was being handled.

Claire continued to breathe slowly in and out; holding her breath during EVA would be dangerous. But she couldn't prevent raising one arm to ward off the impending impact.

"Sixteen meters," said Anderson. "Relative drift is down to two to three centimeters. I should be able to contact the station with the arm now."

Claire moved to the base of the arm. "I'm in position. Go ahead."

The two-pronged pincher at the end of the arm opened and closed a couple of times.

"I'm getting slow response times," Anderson said. "The joystick feels mushy."

Claire bit her lip, considering the cranelike arm that towered above her and the oppressive white wall of the Mars station. "Can you make the grab?"

"Only one way to find out." His tone was uncertain.

The arm extended from the elbow joint, jerking as the damaged joint repeatedly bound then broke free.

Claire unpacked the spin-friction welder and checked its battery. It was fully charged, as it had been the two times she'd checked it in the air lock.

Waiting was the worst. Waiting and knowing that it all depended on Anderson.

Anderson's target was an exposed section of girder that connected the two radiative panels into a box around the fuel tanks. It ran perpendicular to the panels and in front of a tank of liquid oxygen.

The arm jerked forward in centimeter increments. The pincher fully open.

"Almost," Claire whispered. "Almost there." Anderson was running the arm with feedback from the cameras mounted along its length, but she couldn't help herself from giving play-by-play encouragement.

The two ends of the open pincher straddled the girder.

"You're there," Claire said excitedly. "Make the grab."

"Acquiring the girder," Anderson echoed.

Suddenly the wrist joint of the arm snapped forward. The pinchers hit the oxygen tank with enough force that Claire felt it in the motorized base of the arm. The arm rebounded from the tank, trapping her under the upper arm as the wrist gyrated against *Reliance*'s hull.

Claire pushed against the unyielding metal. He's trying to kill me. Trying to kill me and make it look like an accident. Shock, anger, and despair warred for supremacy.

"Goddammit," Anderson swore. "Come on, you motherless arm. Respond."

The arm continued to squeeze her. The hard plastic encasing her upper torso flexed. "It's crushing me!" she screamed. "Get it off! Get it off!"

"It's not responding," Anderson said hurriedly. "I'm going to shut it down and reinitialize the controller. Hang on."

Inside her suit, Claire heard her hard upper-torso unit creak. Pinned to the station, all she could see was the dull silver skin of *Reliance*'s hull, and a tiny patch of space dusted with stars. When she'd been in astronaut training she'd joked that if she had to die, doing it furthering space exploration was the way she'd want to go. Faced with the reality, she wasn't ready.

"What's happening?" she called over the suit-to-ship radio.

"Powering up the arm," Anderson said.

Claire tongued the heads-up display that projected on

the inside of her helmet. She craned her eyes to read the glowing letters. Tiny green numbers counted down. "Shit. My suit's leaking. I think one of my seals has a microscopic rupture."

"What's the rate of decline?" Anderson asked.

Claire counted off seconds. "Point-seven-five mmHg a second." She did a quick estimation. "I've got maybe five minutes of air."

"Arm's up. Sending command to return to neutral position."

The pressure pinning Claire to the hull eased. She pushed against the long shaft of the upper arm and scrambled from under it. Her suit's pressure was still falling, but not as fast. One of the o-rings was likely damaged by the increase in pressure while she was pinned.

"Preparing air lock to cycle you in."

"No." Claire checked that the spin-friction welder was still strapped to her hip. "The leak's slowed. I've got ten more minutes. I can do this, just acquire the target—and hurry."

"You sure?" Anderson asked.

It would take hours to cycle her back in, fix the suit, and cycle her back out. Hours they didn't have. "Yeah. I'm sure."

The arm moved towards the platform, faster this time. Claire guessed that Anderson was hurrying for her sake. The open pinchers grabbed at the girder, scrabbled off, then swung back around and clamped around it.

"Got it!" Anderson crowed. "Tack that thing in place and get back in here."

Claire moved quick, scrambling up the arm's length to the wrist joint. She worked quickly, soldering the plates of the joint in place with five spot-welds around their perimeter. "Wrist is tacked down."

She checked her pressure. Down to 1.16 psi. Claire did another quick estimation, then crawled farther up the arm and welded the face of the pinchers to the girder. "Welded girder to—"

"Claire," Anderson was excited. "Can you hear in the background? It's Matt."

Claire froze and listened with every fiber of her being. A rustling in the background; was that a voice? "I'm not getting anything," Claire tapped the side of the helmet that housed the speaker.

"Hang on, let me transfer it to ship-to-suit."

Silence.

"Damn. Lost the signal. Sorry, Logan. I think I got a recording before he went off the air."

Another spike of adrenaline coursed through Claire's veins. She was both delighted and desolate. Matt had been right there—right there—and she had missed him. Yet . . . "He and Owen are alive? They're well?"

Anderson cleared his throat. "I captured some of it. I'll let you listen to the recording when you get back in."

Claire looked at Earth, hidden behind *Reliance* save for the polar cap. Six thousand miles south lay Florida and her husband and son. Not within arm's reach, but still alive.

The pressure alarm in her suit bleeped, indicating less than five minutes' worth of air. "Returning to air lock."

Claire rushed the trip back to the air lock, fumbling the tether transfer and only a lucky grab kept her from floating off the station. The air in her suit was thinning, each breath more labored than the next. Twinkles of light that were not stars danced in her peripheral vision.

Claire ducked through the air lock hatch and slammed it closed. When it was locked, she gasped, "I'm in." It was all she had breath for.

The pressure gauges on the air lock steadily rose. When they crossed .5 psi, Claire popped her helmet. She drank in the oxygen in gulping breaths.

Anderson was on the other side of the crew lock when she emerged. "You all right, Logan?"

"I will be." She let him help her doff the EVA suit, watched him stow its components, wipe down the LCVG, replace the food and water supplies. The paranoia she had felt about him when the arm was malfunctioning faded. If he had wanted to kill her, he could have waited until the welds were done and simply been slow to cycle the air lock.

Claire felt as if her body had been beaten with hammers. She drifted limp and concentrated on breathing. When she felt better, she asked, "Where's the recording of Matt?"

"Command module. I put it on your palmtop." Anderson nodded at the hatch. "Go check it out. I'll finish up here."

Claire crawled through the hatch to the command module. The tiny room was dim and cluttered with controls, switches, drawers. Almost every surface was covered with an indicator or piece of equipment. But after her near-death outside, its cluttered closeness was comforting, like a metallic womb.

She retrieved her palmtop from its Velcro pad on the command console. On the desktop was a sound file. Claire tapped it with a stylus.

"CQ, CQ. This is Matt Logan, no call sign, in Lakeland, Florida. I'm trying to reach my wife on the space station. I don't know if anyone can hear me, but if you can, please rebroadcast this message."

Claire's eyes filled with tears at the sound of Matt's voice. The recording was fuzzy and low in volume, but he was alive. She pressed the palmtop to her cheek, putting the microphone as close to her ear as possible.

In the background, she heard the unmistakable sound of Owen crying. It pierced her heart.

"Mama!" Owen sobbed. "I want Mama!" The sound devolved from a four-year-old's speech to the inconsolable blubbering of a toddler. "Where's Mama? Mama!"

Claire crumpled inward into a ball, wrapping herself around the tinny recording of her family, alive, but in pain. She was helpless, too far away to comfort, too far away to protect, too far away to console.

Claire replayed the recording, this time listening to Matt's message.

"Claire, I hope you're still alive up there. Things down here . . . aren't good. The power's out. Looters broke in to steal food. I chased them off with Dad's shotgun, but one of them pushed Mother down. I think she broke her hip. And I don't know what to do about Owen." Matt's voice broke into a sob. "He's getting worse. Today he vomited and there was blood. I—I don't what to do anymore, the whole world—"

The message ended abruptly, fissioning into static then obliterated by a voice speaking in rapid Italian. Matt's line-of-sight connection must have fallen behind the horizon as *Reliance* circled the globe. In ninety minutes they'd be back over the U.S. Claire prayed that they could reestablish the connection.

If she could just talk to them, reassure Owen she was coming home soon. Whatever it took, she was coming home.

CHAPTER 13

Claire turned on the ham radio receiver. It was inconceivable that she would hear Matt's voice. Only a trick shot of radio waves bouncing off the ionosphere could bring his transmission over the planet's horizon. But she'd grasp at any chance now. And more, she needed to hear voices from Earth, to assure herself that other people lived besides her, Anderson, Hyun-Jin, Josephine, and Zhang.

The first voice she heard spoke rapid Spanish. From her college-language courses she could pick out a few words: help, danger, cold. Then two French speakers were interrupted by a third voice in German. Finally, the cultured round vowels of a British speaker.

"—exchange completely down. No one can get a call through with the satellites offline. Internet is completely jammed. Might as well come home and power up the telly. Rumors that both Asia *and* the U.S. have been bombed. The bloody hell of it is, no one really knows what is going on."

A second voice, more nasal and with a cockney twang, said, "Chinese took 'em out. Did 'em in good and proper."

A gentle cough behind Claire alerted her that Anderson

was back. She wiped her face on the shoulder of her T-shirt.

"You all right?"

Claire nodded without looking up. Another swipe at her eyes. "Let's see what Josephine and Hyun-Jin are up to."

She reached out and turned down the volume on the ham radio. The words of speakers continued to babble in a myriad languages in which phrases of English leapt out like shining fish before disappearing back into the stream of unintelligible speech.

"*Shenzhou XI,*" Claire transmitted. "This is *Reliance*. Do you copy?"

The forward screen filled with Josephine's grinning face. Her EVA suit was off; she answered from the cabin of the Chinese ATV. "We're ready." She sounded excited and happy. "*Shenzhou* is spot-welded to the platform in eighteen places. Zhang is a wizard with a welder." Her grin faded. "Something went wrong with hooking *Reliance* up?"

"No, I got it done." Claire's voice choked up and she swallowed rapidly to clear it. "We just got a radio message from Matt—"

"But that's great!" Josephine's grin returned, even wider. "That means he and Owen are all right—"

"Not really. Things are bad planet-side. I'm afraid they're going to get a lot worse before they get better."

"Hyun-Jin and I are ready to come back to *Reliance* for the transfer."

Claire thought about the trouble she'd had on EVA, and the small number of patches she'd been able to make with her compromised seals. "No. If you're secure, stay on *Shenzhou*. Anderson and I will transfer over once we hit MEO."

Claire looked over her shoulder at Anderson. "You ready to do the burn?"

"As ready as can be," Anderson said. "I've only got estimates of the platform's mass. I can't promise an exact positioning. I'll try to insert us into orbit near the Japanese station, but this whole thing is one big kludge."

"Understood. Can you give me a countdown?"

Anderson reached over and clicked off the transmitter. "Why don't I run the calculations one more time? In the meantime, you could fire up the ham radio, see if you get lucky. It might be a long time before the next call."

Claire hesitated, weighing her desire to check on Matt and Owen against the danger piling up against them in low-Earth orbit.

"Go ahead," Anderson urged, nodding at the amateur radio equipment. "If I had anyone left to call, you couldn't keep me away from it."

Claire unhooked the radio handset. "You'll let me know as soon as the calculations are done?"

Anderson chuckled, a wry soft sound against the background hum and whine of the station. "It'll take me about thirty minutes. By that time, we should be line-of-sight to Florida." He turned the transmitter back on. "I'm going to rerun the calculations and do some preliminary tests of the platform's engine."

Josephine's brow lowered and her midnight-blue eyes flashed. "What happened to Claire? Why this delay? The Argus effect—"

"It's all right," said Claire. "Half an hour won't make much difference." She hoped. "If we can insert closer to the Japanese station, it'll be worth the delay."

Josephine looked mutinous, but didn't argue. "I'll be waiting for a countdown."

With guilty hope, Claire tuned the ham radio, searching for English-speaking voices.

The minutes ticked by as she waded through a surf of foreign voices, unfamiliar call signs. "CQ, CQ" she repeated endlessly. Giving the call sign she had learned in seventh grade, asking for Matt Logan in Florida in the United States.

"Is it true about the bombs, Miss?" asked a stranger with a thick Australian accent. "That the U.S. was wiped out by the Chinese? Can't get anything sensible out of the BBC World News. Signal's garbled."

Claire hesitated before answering. NASA protocol would have kept her silent, let the U.S. State Department release the information in a politically measured way. But that all seemed irrelevant now. Her government was in shambles. In the aftermath of the nuclear war, all humans were survivors.

"Yes," she said. "There were nuclear strikes all over North America. I know because I saw—"

"You *saw* it?" His rough voice was incredulous.

"I'm one of the astronauts on *Reliance* Space Station." Now it was out. If anyone in whatever was left of NASA heard about this, she'd be in for it. People all over the globe were listening to the amateur bands.

"Crikey? For real?"

"For real. The reason the radio's down is that excess radiation in the atmosphere has disrupted the satellites."

"When will that clear up, Miss?"

"Two, maybe three years."

"Please copy. It sounded like you said two, maybe three *years*?"

"That's affirmative. You'll have to fall back on presatellite communication. It's called the Argus effect."

"Never heard of it." His voice was fading as the signal drifted over the horizon.

"You will," Claire answered, not sure if he could still hear her. "Everyone will." She told him everything, about the attacks in India, the retaliation against the Chinese, the destruction of the United States. NASA would have had a fit, but people needed to know what had happened, and with the satellites defunct, international news channels were down and planetary surveillance was impossible. Military leaders might know, but the populace had no idea a nuclear war had been waged half-way across the world.

Thirty minutes later, Claire had talked to three other people, giving them what information she could about the disaster. None of the hams had spoken to a Matt Logan, though one thought he had heard him calling CQ earlier in the day and promised to keep an ear open, to relay a message that Claire was well and would try to come home soon.

Anderson looked up from his calculations. "Any luck?"

Claire hung up the mouthpiece. "That's it. Can't delay any longer. I'll call Josephine and start the countdown." She leaned over the command module.

"CQ, CQ."

The words made the hair on the back of her neck rise. It was a voice she'd thought she'd never hear again. Claire kicked off and launched herself back to the ham radio, grabbed the handset.

"Matt?" Tears flooded her eyes. "Is that really you?"

"Claire. Thank God you're alive." His voice was void of inflection. He sounded desperately tired, as if he'd been up for days.

"How is Owen?" Claire asked fearfully.

"He finally fell asleep. But I'm worried. He's sick: high fever, vomiting. I tried to get him to a hospital but there's too much fallout and the National Guard hasn't come for us. Mom's hurt her leg. And the damn car—" he choked back a sob "—the damn car won't start."

"Oh, God. I'm so sorry. I wish there was something I could do to help."

"What about you? I heard on the radio there was something wrong with your lifeboat, and the rescue shuttle sent to evacuate you exploded. Is that for real?"

Claire cradled the microphone in her hands. "Don't worry about me. We're working out a way home."

Matt sobbed hoarsely. Claire had never heard him cry like that before. "Stay up there. Stay there. You don't know what it's like down here. The things I've seen. People are turning into animals. There's nothing good down here."

Claire's heart constricted. Her arms ached to hug him so tight no grief could touch him. "There's you and Owen. I'm coming home."

A wailing started in the background. Claire heard it rise between a keening high-pitched sound and whimpering.

"Owen's awake. I have to go to him."

Claire was suddenly aware this might be the last time she got to talk to her husband and son. It was possible to catch a ham radio signal at 10,000 miles above the Earth, but very unlikely, as the surface area to intersect the signal increased as the square of the radius. Not to mention that any signals would have to punch through the growing radiation in the ionosphere. If her plans failed, this conversation was all they would have to remember her. "Can I talk to Owen?"

There was a fumbling, then a sniffling. "Mum-mum-mommy?" Owen's high-pitched voice sounded congested, like he had been crying for some time. "Everything *hurts* Mommy."

"Oh, honey, I know. I know. Mommy loves you, Owen, do you know that?"

"Uh-huh."

"Remember, no matter what happens, Mommy loves you."

"When are you coming home?" asked Owen.

"As soon as I can."

"Promise?"

Claire's heart broke. She wouldn't lie to him. "I can't promise. It's dangerous up here. But I'll do everything I can to get home. Everything. I can promise that. Can I speak to Daddy?"

More fumbling. Matt's tenor voice: "I love you, Claire."

"I love you too. You know I might not make it. We're about to do a transfer orbit to buy us some time, but it might not work." She touched the microphone with her fingertips. "This might be the last time we talk."

"I know." His voice was rough. Owen still whimpered in the background, his voice wavering as Matt patted his back. "But I also know my wife. If anyone can find a way home, it's you."

"Love you. Love you both. Take care of Owen for me."

"You know I will."

Claire kissed the handset and pressed it to her forehead. There were no tears; it hurt too much to cry.

The main control panel bleeped. An incoming message.

Josephine's face appeared on screen, cocked to one side, brows furrowed. "What's the holdup? We were supposed to start burn seconds ago. We're losing our window while you're scratching your dick over there."

Anderson caught up the headset. "Sorry. Communication issue came up. It's resolved now. Strap down for first burn, starting in thirty—" he pointed at Claire "—twenty-nine, twenty-eight . . ."

Claire reluctantly placed the handset back on the amateur radio. Her chest ached, but she had to go. Leaving now was her only hope of making it back to Earth. She was strapped in before Anderson reached single digits.

"Eleven, ten, nine . . " His hand hovered over the button that would transmit the fire command to the engine on the Mars platform.

Claire worried whether her hasty spot-welds would hold through the acceleration. If *Reliance* broke free, there'd be no way to shut down the platform; they'd be drifting in orbit until friction from the Earth's upper atmosphere pulled them into a fiery embrace.

"Eight, seven, six . . ."

There wasn't anything she could do about it now. An EVA during acceleration would be too dangerous. Lose her attachment for an instant, and instead of bobbing alongside *Reliance*, able to recover with her jet pack, she'd be left behind as the platform hurtled towards MEO.

"Five, four . . ."

Claire closed her eyes and crossed her toes.

"Three, two, one—ignition."

Nothing happened.

"Shit," Anderson cursed.

Claire opened her eyes.

He jammed his finger repeatedly against the button that transmitted the ignition command.

"What's going on?" asked Josephine's voice over the radio.

"Got a malfunction. The transmission signal either isn't firing or the controller on the Mars platform isn't receiving."

The Argus effect. While she was trying to contact Matt, it had slipped in and damaged the remote controller of the platform's engine. Guilt washed over Claire as she watched Anderson try to reestablish contact with the station. This was all her fault.

"I told you this would happen." Josephine sounded frantic. "We should have left a half-hour ago."

"The past is done." Zhang's deep voice resonated over the speaker. "We must find a new solution. Can the engine be started manually?"

"Hang on," Anderson said. "I'm re-sending the transmission through channel two. See if the problem's on our end. Try again in: three, two, one, and ignition."

The acceleration built swiftly, growing from a gentle tug to a fierce hand shoving Claire against the wall. Bangs sounded in other areas of the station as unsecured gear hit the walls. Her cheeks pulled towards her ears.

"Way to go, Anderson!" Josephine crowed over the radio.

Claire turned her head sideways, and for the first time in days, saw Anderson grin.

* * *

Reliance's orientation on the Mars platform was such that Earth was visible in the forward window as they shot away from it. As their altitude increased, it dwindled, shrinking so that continents that had once filled the screen now took up only part of its real estate.

As the curve of the horizon became visible in the window, the blackness of space and the stars beyond illuminated what a tiny spark of life Earth was in the vast desert of the universe. It made war seem so petty. How could mankind threaten it so, when a vast inhospitable darkness surrounded them all? They should be stewards of this miracle of amino acids and oxygen, not its destroyer.

"We've got a problem," Anderson said.

Claire's attention snapped back to the command module. She scanned the indicators, and among a sea of lights that had gone red as the Argus effect nibbled away at their electronics, saw nothing new. "Where?"

Anderson tapped one of the LCDs in the laptop station. A gray-and-black blur filled the screen. "After I started the engines, I maneuvered external cameras to monitor the welds that attach the Canadarm to the platform. This," he pointed at the irregular black stripe that crossed the gray background, "is a close-up of one of the welds. It's beginning to separate."

Claire squinted, trying to bring the image into focus. "What about the others?"

"Solid as far as the cameras can see. But this one"—he tapped the screen again—"this one is the weld that holds the pincher closed. If it goes, the other welds won't matter. It survived the first acceleration—barely. I doubt it will hold through the next burn to settle into MEO."

Claire clawed her hands through the dandelion halo of her hair. "So our alternatives are: stay in the transfer orbit, alternately zooming out to MEO and then back into low-earth in a wildly elliptical orbit, each revolution dipping into the radioactive sea caused by the Argus effect, or risk the second burn and possibly separate from the platform and end up adrift in space, without enough fuel to get anywhere."

"That or reattach the weld."

"We don't have an EVA suit," Claire reminded him.

"The neck seals on mine ruptured during the last maneuver and the other one went with Hyun-Jin and Josephine to *Shenzhou XI*."

Anderson handed her the headset. "Then ask for help. Aren't you always saying we have to work as a team?"

Claire called *Shenzhou* on the ship-to-ship radio. "*Reliance* to *Shenzhou XI*. We've got a situation over here."

Zhang's face appeared onscreen. "*Shenzhou* to *Reliance*. We copy. What is your difficulty?" It was hard to read his expression under his heavy-lidded eyes.

Claire explained the situation as well as the problem with her EVA suit. "The next burn is scheduled in five hours. If we don't get it fixed before then . . ."

"When the acceleration ends," Josephine said, poking her head sideway into view, "I'll go over in the ATV and pick up Claire and Anderson. The relative velocity makes an EVA too dangerous."

"No," said Hyun-Jin off-screen, "we calculated *Reliance*'s mass into the first burn. If we lose *Reliance*, it will throw the transfer orbit off. We won't be able to rendezvous with the Japanese station."

"I will go." Zhang's resonant voice was just loud enough to cut through their argument. "Hyun-Jin is correct. We need *Reliance*. I will EVA to fix the weld."

"You?" Claire said, surprised by his offer.

"My suit has a more advanced propulsion system, and I have facility in creating welds that do not break."

Anderson clicked off the radio. He told Claire, "You can't let him do that. Zhang's an unknown. He's as likely to cut us free as help us."

"He wouldn't do that," Claire insisted. "Zhang wants to survive. You heard him, a fix maximizes all our resources."

"He wants to survive. I've already been a threat to him. Perhaps he'll decide that losing what's left of *Reliance* is worth getting rid of me."

"But Josephine and Hyun-Jin would—"

"He could make it look like an accident. Go EVA, play the hero, then—whoops—his weld didn't hold. You and I drift off into oblivion, and suddenly all the supplies on *Shenzhou XI* have to feed only three, not five."

It made cold-blooded sense. Claire wanted to trust Zhang—he'd played fair with them so far—but could she?

"Both ATVs are already docked to *Shenzhou*," Anderson continued. "He has most of what he needs already."

"So far he's been as good as his word."

"Nothing's he's done has been counter to his goal of getting home safely. But you didn't hear the conversation Hyun-Jin and I heard among *Shenzhou*'s crew. He translated it for me while they were talking. They discussed taking over *Reliance* and stealing the lifeboat. Don't tell me Zhang knew nothing about that. He was their commander."

The incoming message light blinked, indicating *Shenzhou* was trying to connect.

"So what's your suggestion?" Claire asked him. "Sit tight and hope for the best? Abandon *Reliance* and transfer to *Shenzhou*, accepting a less than optimal orbit?"

"We should transfer to the Chinese station. I don't like leaving *Reliance*, but it's safer than trusting Zhang."

"What's to stop Zhang from triggering the second burn himself, as soon as Josephine departs in the ATV? He's just as able to send the command as we are. She'd never be able to redock, we'd fly off into space, and he's down to only two mouths to feed." Claire shook her head, sending her blond halo into oscillations. "This kind of paranoid thinking only leads to the kind of mistake you and Hyun-Jin made in the air lock." She held up a hand to forestall his protest. "The only way we're going to get out of this alive is by trusting one another. I don't care what's happening on Earth; up here we're just people, trying to get home."

"People trying to get home on limited resources. If he has to choose between us and him, Zhang's going to choose him."

Claire stared at Anderson, wondering if he realized how much those same words applied to his own behavior. "It's my decision. I say we go with Zhang's plan."

"I could transfer over while Zhang's outside—"

"No." Claire didn't want Anderson at *Shenzhou*'s controls while Zhang was outside. She didn't trust him. If Zhang could trigger the second burn, so could Anderson—getting rid of Zhang and an annoying commander in the process. "You'll stay here, with me."

Anderson inhaled, and there was a moment when Claire realized he could overpower her. He appeared to weigh the possible outcomes, then slowly released his breath. "I hope you know what you're doing."

Me too, thought Claire.

They monitored Zhang's work on the weld using *Reliance*'s surface cameras. From all angles, his work looked legitimate, but for a materials-science expert it would be easy to form a weld designed to break under stress.

He too was taking a risk. It would be easy for Anderson, after Zhang completed the work and was on his way back to the air lock, to do the second burn. A nylon tether was little security against two gees of acceleration, and it would be impossible for Zhang to crawl back to the air lock. He would either break loose, and drift free, or suffocate as his air ran out.

Claire cut her eyes sideways at Anderson, wondering if this possibility had occurred to him.

Onscreen, Zhang finished the weld and began to pack up.

Claire positioned herself between Anderson and the button that would send the fire command to the platform's engines. She tapped one of the many red lights on the board. It was overhead, on the side farthest away from the transmitter.

"How long has this water pump been down?"

"About eighteen hours," said Anderson distractedly. He glanced back at the screen, where Zhang was starting to reel back to the air lock on his tether.

"And how will that affect our reserves of drinking water?" She tapped the red light again to draw his attention.

Anderson shifted position, moving across the control panel.

Claire tensed, ready to throw herself bodily between Anderson and the transmitter.

Zhang was ten meters from the air lock, five. He was reeling his tether in at maximum speed.

Anderson reached out to the command panel.

Claire grabbed for his arm—and missed.

Anderson finished his motion, retrieving his palmtop from the Velcro pad. "Hey!" he shouted as Claire's shoulder bumped him. "What?" He looked up and met her gaze. "You still don't trust me."

Claire returned his stare. "Should I?"

"Why is it you can trust *him*"—Anderson pointed at Zhang's armored body onscreen—"the commander of a station owned by an enemy nation, and you can't trust *me*?"

Claire didn't answer, just continued to stare.

Anderson ran his hands over his stubble. "All right, I may have acted precipitously, but that's in the past, and you yourself said if we were going to pull through this, we had to trust each other. Doesn't that include me?"

In her peripheral vision, Claire saw Zhang slip inside *Shenzhou*'s air lock. She fought to keep relief off her face. "All right, Anderson. You're right. Trust includes you." She sighed. "You ready to do the orbital burn?"

"Yeah." He slipped a foot under the handrail below the navigational laptop and pulled up the burn program he'd written. She'd said the words he'd asked to hear, but he still didn't look happy. Maybe he sensed the truth: that she'd lied.

While Anderson double-checked his program, Claire called over to *Shenzhou XI*. "We're about to initiate orbital burn. You strapped in?"

Josephine's face was anxious, "Zhang is still getting out of his suit in the airlock."

Claire looked over at Anderson's hunched back. "Tell him to hurry. We need to do the burn in . . ."

Anderson held up seven fingers.

". . . seven minutes for the best chance to insert into orbit near the Japanese station."

Six minutes later, Zhang called back. "We're ready." His heavy-lidded eyes were serious.

Claire wanted to ask him how the repair weld went, but there was no time. She pointed at Anderson and he began a thirty-second countdown.

Anderson's intonation of the numbers washed over Claire as she watched Earth, trying not to think about the delicate framework of metal that held them to the platform.

". . . three, two, one."

The engine ignited, spewing water vapor as hydrogen and oxygen combined in the combustion chamber. Claire felt the acceleration as an increasing pressure in her back and the seat of her pants.

Camera seven was trained on the weld Zhang had repaired. It looked solid, but as Anderson said, it would be easy for Zhang to fake a solid weld. The thin line of metal vibrated as the platform accelerated up to speed.

As their cobbled-together craft moved higher into orbit, the Earth dwindled in the window. Claire could see the whole arc of the horizon now. It was the relative size of a beach ball, shrinking like a deflating balloon as they traveled farther. Everything she knew and loved was so far away.

This is what the Apollo astronauts saw, she thought, only they went farther—with slide rules. You can do this. Yes, a tiny voice from the back of her mind whispered, but they had a strong country and a support staff back on Earth waiting for them.

The orbital burn lasted six minutes. Exhausted, Claire dozed through most of it. She woke to Anderson's monotone:

"Entering stable orbit. Radiation levels are at normal background. Our solar exposure is higher, but we're above the Argus effect."

"We copy that," piped back Josephine's young voice.

Claire opened her eyes. "How's—"

"We've got company," said Anderson. He tapped a silver line on the forward screen and zoomed camera four in on it.

The sleek lines of the Japan Weather Association observatory filled the screen. Four cylinders, each three meters long, formed an equilateral cross. Those four arms bristled with radio antennae, parabolic dishes, and telescopes. The nearest telescope pivoted in their direction.

Claire felt a prickle down her spine. She had expected the Japanese to have evacuated when the first bombs hit. "And somebody's home."

CHAPTER 14

Draped in a shower curtain, Matt pounded on the door of a two-story house. "I need to use your car," he said. "My son's sick and my mother's broken her hip." It was nightfall. Some of the houses had the flickering flames of candlelight glowing in the windows, others were dark as the grave.

"Please, I know you're in there. I can see the light."

No response.

Black ash no longer rained from the sky, but what had fallen blew around Matt's ankles in fitful gusts. There was a red glow in the sky in the direction of Orlando.

"Please. My son's going to die without medical treatment." Matt fought back exhaustion and hysteria. This was the eleventh house he'd tried. "Please. Owen is only four."

There was a scuffling on the other side of the door. It opened a crack, the chain still attached.

A woman's blue eye appraised him from the safety of the door.

"Shut the door, Janice," a second woman's voice called. "We can't help him."

Janice ignored the voice. "What are his symptoms?"

Matt frowned, confused. "I just need your car. Please."

The door closed. For an instant Matt thought Janice had changed her mind about helping him. Then it opened fully, the chain removed. Janice was short, five-foot-two, with light brown hair cut in a chin-length bob. Her heart-shaped face was pretty in the way of a healthy thirty-year-old. "I'm a nurse. Tell me what's wrong."

A wave of hope flooded Matt. "Can you come look at him? He's listless and has been coughing up blood. There are bruises under his skin. I don't know what's wrong with him."

"Janice!" the unseen woman's voice was strident. "Close the door!"

A shot rang out in the distance. The door slammed shut in Matt's face. There was an argument from the other side of the door. Two women and a man.

"Janice can't help you," the man said. "Go home."

"Please. I'm Mrs. Logan's son, from down the street. Please help us." Matt pounded against the unyielding oak. But it did not open.

Matt lifted the shower curtain over his head and scurried to the next house.

A Japanese woman with long bangs and buzz-cut sides appeared on the central monitor. "JWA station to . . . spacecraft." Her voice was soft and breathy. To Claire's ears, it was inappropriately feminine for an astronaut, but the woman's demands were plain enough: "State your name and country of origin, *kudasai*."

Claire wrapped the headset over her ears. "Claire Logan, United States. I am the commander of *Reliance* Station. We used the Mars platform to up-orbit out of the Argus effect."

"But also is the station *Shenzhou XI*," the soft voice insisted. "Explain, please."

Claire wondered what Zhang made of her assumption of command. But there hadn't been time to discuss a hierarchy, and hell, her crew outnumbered his four to one. "We are working with the survivors of the Chinese station. We plan to construct a lifeboat that can survive reentry. Will you assist us?"

The woman's black eyes widened. "We watched the conflict. China fires nuclear weapons at U.S.A., and U.S.A. retaliates. And you work together? With free will?"

"Yes. The conflict on the ground is between politicians, not astronauts."

"This," the woman onscreen reached forward, "will be considered." The transmission ended.

"That's it?" Anderson thundered. "What the hell does she mean: 'this will be considered.' "

Claire put a hand on his wrist to stop him from reaching for the control panel. "She's probably trying to ascertain if we pose a threat. In her place, I'd do the same."

Kagome Tsushima cut the transmission to the Mars platform. Her crew had watched the progress of the LEO space stations, watched the destruction of the Brazilian station, the converging of the U.S. and Chinese stations on the Mars platform. With their long-range weather telescope, they had even seen the fiery destruction of the lifeboat. Where *Shenzhou XI* traveled, destruction followed, and now it had come to her door.

Mutsuo Hitomi, her second-in-command, currently manned the communications station. "Are we within visual of Japan?"

Mutsuo checked the blue trace line on the central display. "In fourteen point three minutes."

Kagome grabbed a joystick and used it to orient telescope five at the Mars platform. At high magnification she could see the spot welds that joined the cobbled-together structure. The work had been hurriedly done. Combined with what she knew about radiation effects in low orbit, they had likely suffered medical and electronic damage as well. "They must be desperate to take such risks," she said aloud.

"If they succeed, they offer us a way home. Our lifeboat—"

Kagome was annoyed that he would bring up again her decision to delay evacuation. The delay had cost them an avenue of escape. Their lifeboat was too delicate to punch through the layer of electrons that surrounded the Earth in a radioactive halo. "Staying was the right decision," she said. "We have a duty."

Mutsuo readjusted his feet under the restraint shelf, and

Kagome knew he wanted to argue further. His family was Westernized, with an imperfect understanding of their place in the universe.

Kagome was grateful the other two crew members were busy taking observations of the radioactive dust clouds migrating over central Asia, and did not hear Mutsuo's insubordination.

"My duty is to my family," Mutsuo argued. "My wife is pregnant with our first child. If we join with the Americans, some of us could go home. Those who remained would have more resources, be able to continue observations longer."

"There will be a supply ship," Kagome insisted. "Mission control is working on a delivery vehicle that can survive the radiation."

Mutsuo did not respond to the polite lie.

Kagome pointed to the display of the Mars platform assembly. "They cannot be trusted. Even if they could, what help would it be to your wife for you to land in the United States or China?"

"Depends on where in China," Mutsuo countered. "I could pilot a boat—"

"I forbid it." Kagome turned away from him. "We serve our people best by staying here. With the satellites down, we are Earth's only global eye." She waved a hand at the controls. "Lock the laser for transmission to Earth. We will see what mission control thinks of this new development."

The central screen lit up with the Japanese woman's face. "Kagome Tsushima to Mars platform. We regret that we cannot assist you. Our resources are sufficient for our needs, and no more. Ground control orders us to—"

Claire couldn't restrain her excitement. "You still have contact with the ground? How? What's going on Earthside?"

Kagome frowned. "I am not authorized—"

Claire felt her face heat. "For crying out loud! There's been a major nuclear exchange. Surely protocol can be set aside long enough to let us know how the world is faring."

"Perhaps discipline is a tool *you* can set aside," Kagome said in her breathy, little-girl voice, "but for us, it is all." She reached forward to end the transmission.

"Wait!" Claire shouted.

Kagome halted her reach, waiting.

"If you can't give us physical assistance, what about design ideas?" Claire pleaded. "Perhaps your crew has expertise that can help us."

A man's face hovered into view in the background behind Kagome. His wide dark eyes watched the camera. Claire could see a play of emotions in tiny twitches at the corner of his eyes and mouth, but what he was trying to convey, she couldn't say.

"My crew," said Kagome, "already have a full schedule of duties. They cannot be distracted with auxiliary work."

"But, Commander—" said the man in the background.

Kagome cut him off with a rapid-fire stream of Japanese that held none of the breathy quality of her English voice.

Claire felt a momentary surge of sympathy. Did female commanders everywhere have to deal with the second-guessing of their male crew members?

Turning back to the forward screen, Kagome snapped the connection off.

Claire turned off the now blank screen. "How are they communicating with Earth? Any radio signal would be blocked by atmospheric radiation."

"Pulsed laser," Anderson said. "Has to be."

Claire tapped her lower lip. "But why would they have a long-range laser?"

Anderson frowned. "Communications with moon-based satellites, maybe? Or thermal readings of high-atmosphere effects? The JWA is a weather station."

Motion caught the corner of Claire's vision. She looked out the porthole at the JWA station. The cylindrical station pivoted, end-facing the Mars platform, and dwindled in size.

"Damn it!" Claire swore. "They're moving away. You think they'd at least take a moment to consider our offer."

Anderson snorted. "It's not much of a deal for them, is it? Help us and we'll go away." He pointed at the sleek shape docked to the side of the JWA's central hub. "They've still got a lifeboat, after all. Perhaps they're afraid we'll try to steal it."

Claire zoomed camera three in on the lifeboat. "That's one of the new ERVs." Highly computerized, the tiny planelike craft seated five. It was designed to come in on autopilot, completely controlled by ground-based computers. The blackout period of reentry had been eliminated by the TDRS satellites in the 1980s, making complete automation possible. But those satellites were now inoperable, due to the high levels of ionized radiation.

Anderson frowned. "An ERV can't make it through the Argus layer. It's too dependent on radio communications and automated systems. And any passengers would take a huge beta particle hit. It's a one-use craft; it's only got minimal shielding." He scratched a patch of hair above his temple. "If they can't use their lifeboat to get home, why wouldn't they help us?"

Claire pursed her lips, looking at the retreating station. And why, she wondered, didn't the Japanese evacuate when they could? Their commander had mentioned their duty to Earth—an eye on the planet would be invaluable now that the satellite network was down. But the crew, to have given up any hope of returning home. It was hard to believe.

Claire shook herself out of her reverie. "Worry about them later. Right now we need to load up our supplies and transfer to *Shenzhou*. *Reliance*, bless her, doesn't have the atmosphere left for extended life support."

Claire called over to *Shenzhou* and explained her intent. Zhang didn't look happy. She imagined he wasn't looking forward to sharing an atmosphere with Anderson, but he didn't voice his doubts. "And can you send back Josephine's EVA suit with Hyun-Jin? There's one last thing we need to do."

Zhang looked curious. "As you wish."

Claire disconnected the radio. She nodded at Anderson. "You wanted to go EVA; here's your chance."

Anderson's brows drew together in a puzzled frown. "What?"

Claire looked out the porthole. Earth was a lapis lazuli beach ball. "We've got a solar reflector to deploy."

While they waited for Hyun-Jin to arrive, Claire replaced the neck seal on her suit. She tested the repair three times before she was confident it would hold.

Hyun-Jin piloted *Reliance*'s ATV back to the station, docking to the pin nearest the galley. He crawled out of the hatch wearing a portable breathing mask. Claire and Anderson met him, wearing similar masks.

Claire took the EVA suit from him and told him what she and Anderson intended to do. She shouted so he could hear her over the twin barriers of their masks. "While we're EVA, can you load the food into the forty-gallon mesh bags?"

Hyun-Jin nodded and gave her a thumbs-up.

Claire and Anderson used the accelerated prebreathing protocols, and Claire helped him through the preparations: blowing out nitrogen, reconfiguring an EVA suit to fit him, and planning how two astronauts would complete a procedure originally planned for the Canadarm.

"Helluva view," Anderson said as they stepped outside. His bulky white space suit was outlined against the blackness of space.

Claire's knee twinged, and she tried to ignore the pain and what it might mean about the nitrogen levels in her blood. "That it is." She paused for a moment and looked at the Earth. It rose behind Anderson like a blue-green gibbous moon. At their new altitude it looked so much smaller, so far away. The sight gave her a lonely sense of melancholy.

They crawled over *Reliance* to the cargo bay doors. Inside lay the solar reflector, waiting to be deployed. The scaffolding, controllers, and square miles of golden foil were all encapsulated in a cylinder a meter across and two meters long. It was packed into a space barely big enough to contain it. White nylon cargo bags filled with equipment and station waste were crowded around the ESR. There were handrails everywhere on the walls, at least twenty in all, and in all orientations. Before they could remove the ESR, they'd have to shift the other cargo out of the way. It was a three-dimensional sliding puzzle.

Gritting her teeth against the dull ache in her knee, Claire said, "Let's get this bird fledged."

They wrestled the canister containing the solar reflector free of the cargo bay. It was weightless, but still had inertia. Once started in motion, it was hard to stop. They had to be careful not to hit the solar reflector's delicate mechanism against the cargo bay doors or get pinned beneath it.

Claire was sweating by the time they got it out.

Unclipping socket wrenches from their tool belts, Claire and Anderson unfolded the wing struts and tightened them into their extended configuration.

Claire paused, took a swig of water from the tube in her helmet, and surveyed their work. It looked like a half-opened golden dahlia. Six wing struts ringed the central cylinder. When it was in orbit, the struts would unfold, stretching the 400-micron-thin film into a twenty-kilometer-wide parabolic dish to collect solar radiation.

After more than an hour of work, the solar reflector was ready to release.

"You think the engine's controller will still work?" Anderson asked.

The solar reflector had been shielded from the worst of the radiation by the cargo bay. Claire hoped it would function properly. "Only one way to find out."

Carrying the reflector to the end of the Canadarm, Claire and Anderson gave it a final shove to release it into space. When it was fifty meters from the station, Claire activated the controller.

If all worked as engineered, tiny gyroscopes inside the solar reflector would determine its altitude and orientation towards Earth, and initiate a burn that would carry the reflector into geosynchronous orbit, where it would await further commands from Earth.

Inside her bulky space boots, Claire crossed her toes for luck.

Twin green LEDs lit up on the side of the solar reflector. The struts expanded and retracted like a fledgling bird trying its wings. Then the struts froze. One of the green LEDs turned red.

"Shit!" Claire ran through the ESR launch procedure in her mind. There were so many systems that could go wrong: the servos on the struts could misfire, the nagivational computer could be fried, the radiation could have damaged the embedded launch program.

"What's wrong?" Anderson asked over the radio.

"Hang on." Claire cleared and restarted the test. She held her breath as the ESR reset its position and started again.

Please work, she prayed. She hadn't spent the last two years of her life training for this, endured three months in

space preparing for the launch—survived a nuclear war—
to fail now. If she had to, she'd *throw* the damn satellite
into orbit.

The struts retracted and opened: once, twice—

Come on, damn you, Claire implored the machine.

—three times. The test complete, the golden film folded
back into its body. All three LEDs were green.

With a trembling finger, Claire pushed the button on the
remote controller to launch the ESR.

Jets on its sides fired, orienting it to the stars. Then the
main jet fired and it shot off into the dark.

Anderson gave a cry of victory and pumped his fist into
the air.

Claire's heart rose. She watched the solar reflector until
it was no more than a golden speck among the stars.

Tears bubbled in her eyes. In all the tragedy of the last
few days, something had finally gone right. Whatever else
happened, she'd completed her mission.

Once the Argus effect subsided, there would be a clean
energy source available to replace the exhausted oil supplies. The war-ravaged United States would have a hope
of recovery. If she never made it home, at least she'd done
something to help Matt and Owen.

The exhaustion she'd fought off in her push to launch
the ESR overwhelmed her. Sobs clenched her throat and
her helmet steamed with humidity from her tears of relief
and pain. Her body felt as if she'd been beaten with rattan
sticks, and her knee was a throbbing pulse of pain. Worse
was the thought she might not live to see her husband and
son. It felt like bands of iron were constricting her chest.
Each breath was a struggle.

She felt motion and opened her eyes to see Anderson's
glove clamped around her wrist. He was towing her back
towards the air lock. Claire's face heated with shame at her
breakdown. There was no way to wipe away tears inside
her helmet, no way to blow her nose.

Anderson's voice was surprisingly gentle over the suit-
to-suit radio. "Come on, Hero. You've saved the world. It's
Miller time."

The corners of Claire's mouth quirked up in a grudging
smile, and she let him help her back to the air lock.

Once inside *Reliance,* they used the emergency breathing

apparatus mounted on the wall of the crew lock to traverse the evacuated bulkheads to the command module. There, Claire shut down all the most rudimentary controls needed to keep *Reliance* going—enough heat to ward off condensation, the controllers that moved the solar panels to maximize collection, remote automation controls—so *Reliance* could be controlled from *Shenzhou*.

Claire ran her hand along the pull-out shelf that housed the laptop station. Five days ago *Reliance* had been a grand adventure, Cole had manned that console, and Claire had considered herself, and the United States, invulnerable. Now, with her country in ruins, her commander dead, she left *Reliance* in defeat, a refugee to an enemy's station. A stone lodged in her heart, some part of her unable to take in all that had changed in the course of a few days.

Claire detached the amateur radio.

Anderson raised one eyebrow, started to make a comment, then closed his mouth. He opened the mesh bag and let Claire put the radio in.

Claire followed Anderson out the hatch, closing it behind her. She felt like a traitor. *Reliance* had been their haven, had survived puncture and hostile attack and kept them safe. Now they were abandoning it.

They climbed through the mostly evacuated access tunnels, breathing through the depleted air masks. Hyun-Jin waited inside the ATV, opening the hatch when they knocked. They waited while the ATV replenished its atmosphere from *Reliance*'s nearly exhausted stores.

Reliance looked like a crippled hermit crab clinging to the Mars platform. Its single arm locked in place around a girder, holes in its hull, solar panels ragged from debris hits.

"It was a good station," Claire said to no one in particular.

Anderson followed her gaze. "*Reliance* did all right by us," he agreed. "Better than most."

Hyun-Jin was too busy docking the ATV to *Shenzhou*'s first port to comment. He brought the craft home with a jolt. "Sorry," he mumbled.

Compared to *Reliance*'s efficiency apartment, *Shenzhou* was a three-bedroom rambler. The walls were still cluttered with drawer pulls, and every possible surface stored equipment or display screens, but the walls were farther apart, and that space made Claire feel like a pot-bound plant finally transplanted and spreading its tendrils.

They were in the torso of the dragonfly, the largest cylinder that housed the command center and the crew's quarters. The latter was more cubicle than room, but each partition held a sleep sack, a locker for personal items, and a fold-down work surface.

"Welcome to *Shenzhou*, Commander Logan." Zhang held forth his hands, taking Claire's right hand in both of his and squeezing it in welcome.

"Please, call me Claire."

Anderson exited the hatch behind Claire, towing the mesh bags of supplies like a buzz-cut Santa Claus. "Where do you want these?"

Zhang's smile faded at the corners. Without looking at Anderson, he said, "Hyun-Jin, will you show him the galley?"

Anderson raised an eyebrow at Claire as Hyun-Jin escorted him to an adjacent room.

She knew what Anderson was thinking: two commanders, one station. Who was in charge? It was the kind of hierarchical chest-pounding she expected from him. But it was a necessary evil. In the days to come, there might be a time where the crew had to follow orders—and quickly. They couldn't afford confusion about the chain of command.

"Commander Zhang, this is your station, but Hyun-Jin, Anderson, and Josephine are still my crew. You understand me, don't you?"

Zhang fingered the Buddhist medallion around his neck. "Of course. As you must understand that—despite recent events—*Shenzhou XI* is still Chinese property, and I her commander." His face was composed, but his eyes flashed with some emotion—resolve, anger . . . fear?—Claire couldn't tell.

An uneasy compromise, she decided, would have to do.

"Claire, wake up!" Josephine's whisper was urgent.

Claire jerked, banging her head against the wall her sleep sack was Velcroed to. The dream of chasing Matt and Owen through an ever-expanding oven faded as she opened her eyes. For a moment, Claire was disoriented. The wall she usually slept facing was gone. This wasn't *Reliance*. It was *Shenzhou*. After she and Anderson had boarded, Claire had insisted that except for a one-man watch, everyone should catch up on their sleep. They'd been going hard for hours, and couldn't afford any mistakes during the construction of the reentry craft.

"What is it?" asked Claire, fear churning her stomach and jolting her awake. "What's happened?"

"Easy," Josephine whispered. She glanced over at Anderson and Hyun-Jin, who still slumbered. "We got a call."

"From Earth?" It was implausible that a radio signal could reach them. There was too much interference from radiation, and the area to intercept expanded as the radius squared. But it wasn't impossible.

"No," Josephine said in a low tone. "It's the *Japanese*. Or at least, one of them."

Claire pushed the sleep sack off her body and pivoted at the waist to slip past Anderson's sleeping body. She followed Josephine into the adjoining command module.

The flat-screen monitor in front of the radio was lit up. The man who had been in the background during the previous transmission to the Japanese filled the screen. His face was distorted by his proximity to the camera, as if he huddled around it. His brown eyes were hooded with worry, and he glanced over his shoulder.

"I am pilot Mutsuo Hitomi," his voice was a barely audible whisper. "Are you the commander of the Mars platform?"

It was complicated, so Claire just said: "Yes."

"You should know," he glanced over his shoulder again, "that not all of us agree with Commander Kagome's decision. Some of us wish to go back to Earth. Will you help us?" His wide eyes were pleading.

Claire heard a rustling behind her. Without looking back, she replied, "Yes. Of course."

Mutsuo's head turned again. "Someone is coming." His soft voice was nearly inaudible. "I have to go." He reached forward and the screen went blank.

"You can't be serious," Anderson said, his voice groggy with sleep, but still angry, "about taking on refugees. We barely have enough for ourselves."

Claire turned, hand on her hip. "I'm not going to strand people in space if it's in my power to help them."

Anderson drifted closer, looming over Claire. "This isn't about doing the right thing: It's about surviving. If we bring deadweight on board, it jeopardizes us all."

Josephine balled her hands into fists. "You've got a lot of nerve, after what you—"

Anderson reared back his hand, as if to strike.

A golden-brown hand grabbed his wrist. "As a guest on this station," Zhang's rich voice drawled, "eating food provided by the Chinese government, I do not think it is your decision who comes or goes."

Shaking off Zhang's grip, Anderson shoved the Chinese commander backward.

Zhang kicked out a foot to prevent himself from slamming into the ceiling and whirled, anger creasing the space between his brows.

Claire dove between the two men, hands pressing out on their chests. "Stop. Fight—if you must—on Earth. Now is no time for this." Turning towards Anderson, she said, "Zhang is right. This is his station, and it is his decision whether we welcome members of the Japanese crew on board." To Zhang, "My apologies if I overstepped my bounds, and for the rash action of my crew."

"Don't apologize for me." Anderson pushed her hand away.

Claire held her breath, afraid that he would initiate another attack.

Anderson merely swiped at his nose and floated in a half-kneeling position in the corner of the command module.

"Will you extend your hospitality to the Japanese crew?" Claire asked Zhang.

Zhang pulled his T-shirt straight. "Yes. It will strain our resources, but additional crew means the work may be completed more quickly. And like you, I would not strand those who seek asylum." He glanced angrily at Anderson. "Only animals would act so."

To Claire's relief, Anderson let the comment pass.

"One thing I don't understand," Josephine said in a tremulous voice, "is where, exactly we are going to land the lifeboat."

"The Gulf of Mexico," Claire said without thinking. "We bail out of the lifeboat over Florida, and let the craft splash down in the water."

Zhang choked with disbelief. "That puts us right next to a radiation hot zone. I agree we need a water landing for the lifeboat, but a better target is the Mediterranean, it's—"

"The Gulf of Mexico," Claire insisted. Logic had no part of this; she had to get to Matt and Owen.

Josephine's worried glance flitted between Zhang and her commander. "Claire, Zhang's right. Florida . . ." her voice choked up. "Florida's gone. The people there . . ." Her hands fluttered through the air like wounded birds. "We can't save them. We should try for southern Italy or Greece, dump the craft in the Mediterranean."

Claire wanted to wring the traitorous girl's neck. Logically, the Mediterranean was the right decision. Claire could see that. But if they landed in Europe, she'd wouldn't be able to arrange transport to Owen, not through a nuclear war zone.

"You are such a pussy, Jo-Jo," Anderson drawled. "You'd write off the whole U. S. of A. because of a few bombs?"

"You were the one about to sacrifice the Japanese crew to save resources," Josephine snapped back. "Don't talk to me about cowardice."

"Yeah, I'd sacrifice *them*." Anderson shouted back his nose nearly touching Josephine's, his arm outstretched to point at the screen where Mutsuo's face had appeared. "I wouldn't turn my back on my own."

Hyun-Jin appeared in the hatchway of the command module, his sleep sack still around his waist. He looked at the confrontation between Anderson and Josephine, Claire's barely suppressed anger, and Zhang's wariness. "What happened?"

Claire wiped a hand across her forehead. How had things gotten so out of control? She wished she had Cole's trick of making a joke to break the tension. But she was so angry, so desperate to convince Zhang and Josephine to land the lifeboat in Florida, that she could barely speak without screaming. "Nothing. Go back to sleep. We'll talk in the next work cycle."

Zhang tucked the gold Buddhist medallion floating at his neck under his shirt collar. "I agree. This is not the time to decide the landing point. We are exhausted and tempers are high. The craft in question is not even built." He gave

Claire a significant glance and his high brows drew together. "But we shall discuss this further, at a later time."

Matt tried the amateur radio again. Claire was out there
somewhere. There was a ham radio on *Reliance*. If only he
could talk to her again. He needed to hear a friendly voice.

The night was cold, down in the forties. He'd raided the
house for cotton blankets and a wool granny-square afghan
his grandmother had made. Owen was quieter now, and
the vomiting had stopped, but Matt didn't know if that
meant Owen was getting better, or just that there was nothing left in his stomach. He'd thought about building a fire
out of some old wood crates his mother had in the garage,
but fire might attract more looters.

As soon as he'd thought the word, he heard a noise from
inside the house. A rhythmic tapping. Heart in his mouth,
Matt picked up his shotgun and slipped out of the car,
easing the door back into position.

His mother woke as the car rocked on its tires.

Matt held a finger to his lips. "Be right back," he
mouthed silently.

The house was dark, lit only by moonlight through the
broken windows. The rapping sounded again, near the
front door.

Matt lowered his shotgun from his shoulder and moved
towards the sound. Someone was knocking on the front
door. "I'm armed. I don't want any trouble, but if I have
to, I'll shoot," he announced.

"It's Janice Coerr, from down the street. Please, let me
in."

Matt put his eye to the peephole. Janice wore a yellow
rain slicker with Mickey Mouse emblazoned on the chest.
In her right hand was a black medical bag. She shifted her
weight from foot to foot and looked over her shoulder
anxiously.

Matt shouldered his gun, pulled open the door, and drew
her inside. Her head came up to his mouth. Her hair
smelled of sweat and cinnamon.

"Carol and Bob—my sister and her husband—didn't
want me to come, but I told them it was wrong to let a
little boy and an old woman suffer because they were
afraid." There was a Southern twang in her voice. She

talked as Matt led her through the house. "Just my luck to be visiting from Atlanta when a power plant blew."

Matt stopped walking and looked back at her. "Is that what you heard?"

Janice looked up at him. "Yeah. That's what Bob said."

"I saw missiles before the explosions. Lots of them." He pulled open the garage door. "I don't think being in Atlanta would have helped."

The nurse stepped down into the garage. "You mean, the whole country's like this? No. That's impossible."

Matt opened up the back door. "Mom, this is Janice from a couple of doors over. She's a nurse. She'll take a look at you and Owen."

"Bless you," Betty said in a quavering voice.

Janice slid her hands along the old woman's leg, probing.

Betty sucked in a breath as she neared the hip, and bit her lip to keep from crying out.

Janice removed her hands and repositioned the leg. "That better?" When Betty nodded, she pulled out of the car. "Her hip's broken. I can give her something for the pain, but she needs to get to a hospital."

Matt rubbed his eyes. It felt like his eyelids were sandpaper. Every muscle in his body ached with fatigue, and now this. "Please."

Janice shook two Demerol out of a bottle in her bag and gave them to Betty. Then she turned her attention to Owen. She peeled back his eyelids and shone a pen light in them, scraped the bottom of his foot, palpated his abdomen, checked his gums.

Matt hovered behind Janice, trying to see what she was doing. "How is he?"

"He's unconscious, but his reflexes are good. There's some bleeding subcutaneously and around his gums which worries me. How did he get these sores on his forehead?"

"After the explosions. The black flakes. They burned as soon as they hit. He may have swallowed some, I don't know."

Janice nodded. She fumbled in her black bag and pulled out a red paperback copy of the *Physician's Desk Reference*. She thumbed through its pages. "I don't know much about radiation sickness. It's not something I've ever seen at the hospital."

Matt lifted a lock of hair to show her the wound on his own forehead. "If it's the fallout, why aren't I as sick?"

"His bodyweight, I'd guess. And if he took it internally . . ." She flipped through the index. "Damn. Nothing here. I can start him on an IV to replace his fluids, but he really needs a hospital as well."

"I tried calling an ambulance," Matt said, squatting down beside Owen as Janice hooked the IV bag over the handhold above the backseat window. "But they were all busy, and then the phone went dead."

"Your car won't start?" Janice asked, slipping the needle expertly into Owen's arm and taping it down. Owen's eyes fluttered as the needle pierced his skin, but he didn't wake.

"The engine won't even turn over."

"It was fine yesterday," his mother said. "I drove to the market that morning."

Matt dragged his hands through his hair. "It's last year's model, with a fully electric engine—maybe the bomb messed up its computers. Isn't there some kind of pulse when there's a nuclear bomb?" His hands clenched into fists at his temples. "God, I wish I knew what was going on."

Janice looked at Matt, her blue eyes wide with concern. "He can't stay here. You'll have to find a way."

"I know." He looked down at his hands. He'd always been good with his hands, cooking, building furniture, playing basketball. Now they seemed useless, unable to protect his mother and son.

Janice packed her medical supplies back in the case, handing Matt six more Demerol. "You can give her one of these every four hours for the pain."

"You aren't going?" Matt felt his heart lurch.

"I promised Carol and Bob I'd be back as soon as I could. They'll be worried."

Shots rang out in the street.

"It's not safe out there," Matt said. "If you stay the night, I'll walk you home in the morning."

Owen turned in his sleep and made a mewing sound.

"Please."

Janice looked from Matt, to his mother, to the sleeping child. She sighed. "All right. But at first light, I'm going back to my sister's."

"Thank you," Matt said. He was so grateful his knees were weak. He wrapped her in his grandmother's afghan and settled Janice into the passenger's seat, where she could keep an eye on Owen and his mother. Matt squeezed in behind the steering wheel.

Owen's breath rattled with each exhalation.

Matt leaned against the seat, terrified that each of his son's breaths might be the last.

"You should sleep," Janice said after a few minutes. "You look exhausted."

"I can't," Matt said. "I have to make sure he's breathing."

Janice touched Matt's arm and sighed. "I can't sleep either. Tell me about the missiles. We were inside watching the game. We missed it. Tell me what you saw."

Claire watched the Japanese station from the porthole in *Shenzhou*'s air lock. It looked impossibly far away, no bigger than her thumb. She'd offered to move the Mars platform closer, but in a surreptitious email, Mutsuo had refused, warning that it would alert Kagome and the other members of the crew.

It was eleven hours after Mutsuo's initial contact. Josephine, Hyun-Jin, and Zhang had spent the time working on a design to create an ablative shield for reentry out of the radiative shielding used by the Mars platform. Anderson developed flight plans for a variety of reentry locations. Tension about the landing point underlay every crew interaction, but no one had mentioned it since the blowup in the command module.

Now all eyes were on the camera display showing the JWA. Zhang was positioned at the navigational workstation, and Josephine operated the radio. Claire, Anderson, and Hyun-Jin hovered above.

The flat-screen monitor showed the Japanese station. The lights on the four cylindrical modules of its cross were muted. Inside, Mutsuo's friend had the watch, while the rest of the Japanese station slumbered. Any minute now . . .

The JWA's air lock slid open, a black pit in the silver curve of its hull. Two blue-and-white figures emerged. They wore the new slim suit designed by the Japanese. It was scarcely thicker than a ski suit, laced with thermally reactive polymers that kept the astronaut's environment a stable temperature. Each sat in a mobile maneuvering unit. The first one out, presumably Mutsuo, moved the joystick. Propellant shot from the MPU and jetted Mutsuo into the void between the JWA station and the Mars platform.

Claire was struck by Mutsuo's bravery. Even with a jet pack, there was a lot of space between here and there, and the propellant tanks had been designed for maneuvering around the station, not for crossing long voids. If Mutsuo ran out of propellant and missed the Mars platform, there was little Claire or any of her crew could do to help him.

The second figure took off from the station.

Josephine transferred the radio output to the central video screen. "You've got to see this."

Kagome wore a white tank top and panties, and her hair was tied up in a kerchief. She spoke in rapid-fire Japanese, all traces of womanly refinement burned off in the heat of her anger. Claire couldn't understand the words, but the tone of fury and betrayal was universal.

"Do you think there will be reprisals?" Josephine asked, looking over her shoulder. She chewed on a tricolored strand.

"With what?" Claire countered. "The *EEA* is a research station. None of the space stations carried weapons. Ordinance is too heavy to be worth transporting, and until very recently, there was no need for defense in space."

Mutsuo and his crewmate continued their sputtering approach: fire, correct angle, fire, correction. The directional controls on their jet packs weren't designed for long-distance jumps, so the angle of each forward burn took half a dozen corrective jinks.

A mechanized arm on the central body of the JWA came to life, reaching out.

Mutsuo's crewmate didn't see the approaching arm until a course correction blundered him into it.

"Josephine!" Claire shouted, pointing. "Get on the radio, you have to warn—"

Too late. The arm closed around his backpack, pulling the reluctant crewmember back towards the JWA station. The man twisted and turned in the MPU, trying to unlatch the safety harness that held him pinned.

Mutsuo looked over his shoulder, saw the problem. He pivoted his MPU and jetted to help his crewmate.

"No!" Claire pounded on the top of the display screen. It was a futile gesture, satisfying only her need to do something, anything.

Josephine transmitted the three-way argument going on over ship-to-suit radio communications. Kagome's outraged voice interleaved with Mutsuo's and his crewmate's. The latter's voice was high-pitched and hysterical. Mutsuo's was low and tense, repeating the same phrase over and over.

The crewman worked an arm free of the restraints and hacked at the harness with something that flashed sliver in reflected sunlight.

Mutsuo screamed a warning in Japanese.

A sudden jolt. The arm slammed sideways. The crewman hung limp as a broken doll.

Radio silence. Neither Kagome nor Mutsuo spoke.

Mutsuo tugged on the lifeless body, but it was held fast in the mechanical arm's grip.

He pivoted his MPU and jetted full speed towards the Mars platform. There were fewer corrections as he burned longer and accelerated faster towards *Shenzhou*.

Claire moved out of the air lock, sealing the hatch between it and the rest of the station. Mutsuo had just witnessed the death of his crewmate; she hoped he wouldn't let grief drive him into recklessness.

Kagome's face appeared onscreen. The bandana was gone. "You must return second lieutenant Mutsuo Hitomi to me at once. He has mutinied and led a fellow crew member into death. He must face charges for his actions."

"What should I reply?" Josephine asked Claire and Zhang.

Claire watched Mutsuo's approach. It was impossible to see his face behind the silver sheen of his faceplate. "Say nothing for now. Once Mutsuo is on board, we can discuss how to handle the JWA."

Matt snuggled into Claire's warmth. If she was here, in his arms, then everything else must have been a nightmare: the bombs, his mother's fractured hip, Owen's illness. Relief washed through his body like warm rain. He pulled her into him.

A contented sigh, then a yelp, small hands pushing him away.

Matt opened his eyes. It was dark. Only a thin sliver of dawn crept in under the garage door. He was trapped behind a steering wheel and his shoulder was stiff and sore. "Claire?"

"No. Janice."

Embarrassed, Matt pushed himself back, getting as far from her as the interior of the car allowed. "I'm sorry, I thought . . ."

Janice ignored his apology. She used her penlight to check on Owen.

A pitifully small bundle in his cotton blanket, Owen's chest rose slow and even. Sweat gleamed on his forehead.

"I'm sorry," Matt repeated. "I was dreaming of my wife. I'm married, you know."

Janice pulled an ear thermometer out of her bag. "I know, to the lady astronaut. You told me last night." She pushed the thermometer into Owen's ear. "I was married once. He lives in Dallas, runs his own used-car lot."

The thermometer beeped. Janice frowned at the reading and checked the other ear. "His temperature's 103." She pressed a stethoscope against Owen's laboring chest. "It sounds like he might have fluid in his lungs. Damn." She looked up at Matt. "We need to get him to a hospital—now."

Matt turned the key in the ignition again. As before, nothing happened. "The hospital's twenty miles away."

"We have to find a way."

CHAPTER 15

Mutsuo Hitomi crawled into the air lock, pulling the hatch shut behind him.

"He's in," reported Claire over her palmtop.

"Sealing hatch, pressurizing air lock," replied Zhang. He was the only one who could read the characters on the controls. Hyun-Jin's knowledge of written Chinese was spotty. Anderson was grimly memorizing the controls by position, his eyes watching Zhang intently whenever the man touched one.

When the pressure inside the lock was equal to his suit, Mutsuo removed his helmet. Beneath it was an attractive Asian man with a wide nose, square jaw, and blue-black hair. His eyes, however, were glassy and dull, and his movements as he took off the space suit listless.

Claire recognized grief. She'd had much experience of it lately. She popped open the interior door and helped Mutsuo stow his high-tech suit in a locker. She marveled at the play of light over the blue-white microfiber. It had a rough texture reminiscent of shark's skin. That such a thin protection could keep back the vacuum of space was incredible. With one last fondle of a sleeve, she closed the locker door.

"Welcome, Mutsuo Hitomi," Claire said solemnly. "I am sorry for the loss of your crewmate."

Mutsuo's mouth tightened and he nodded: once, twice. "A good man. He will be missed."

"This is where we eat and sleep." Claire led him through the tunnels to the crew quarters off the command module.

Zhang, Anderson, Hyun-Jin, and Josephine clustered around the door between the rooms.

"Welcome to *Shenzhou XI*," Zhang intoned.

"Ni hao," Mutsuo replied, executing a half-bow in midair by contracting his abdominals. "It is an honor."

Anderson's upper lip twitched with disgust and turned back to the control panel. As he went, he grumbled, "Ten thousand miles from home, no chance of resupply, and she's picking up strays. Unbelievable."

Mutsuo's eyes widened.

Josephine put a hand on his arm, startling him further. He raised one eyebrow at her tricolored hair and nose piercing.

"Don't worry about Anderson. He's the minority view." A genuine smile lit her face. "We're glad to have you aboard."

Mutsuo looked around again at the people he had thrown his lot in with. A muttered phrase in Japanese included the word *anime* when he looked at Josephine.

"Do you need food? Rest?" asked Claire.

"Thank you." His chin set with resolve. "I wish to begin work on the lifeboat immediately."

Claire and Zhang exchanged a glance over Mutsuo's head. "There will be time for that later," Claire said. "Building the lifeboat is so important that we must all be at our best. Fed, rested, and in a calm frame of mind."

"I came to work, not to sleep," Mutsuo snapped. "Toshiro did not die so I could eat and rest. Do you question my readiness?"

"No, I—"

The radio beeped insistently. Another incoming message from the *EEA*.

Anderson thumped the top of the radio. "What about this?"

Mutsuo kicked off, caught a handhold and hovered over

the radio, inches above Anderson's right shoulder. He tapped a key and Kagome's face appeared onscreen.

Her eyes narrowed and she spat a low invective of Japanese.

"Speak English—I will not insult my new crewmates," Mutsuo insisted.

Zhang and Claire rushed to Mutsuo's side. Claire was startled at the newcomer's decisive action. She'd always thought of the Japanese as calm and cultured, not desperately impulsive.

"They are not your crew," Kagome snapped. "We are. Your actions caused the death of Toshiro. For this you must return."

"You trapped Toshiro!" Mutsuo shouted back. "Forced him to try to cut himself free. Your restraint led to his accident. You are the only one of the JWA who clings to the old ways of self-sacrifice. The rest of us want to go home."

Kagome's eyes glanced to the right, seeing something or someone off-screen. "That is not true. The rest of us understand duty and honor. We are not cowards." She waved her hand across her face. "*Shenzhou* commander, get this traitor out of my sight. I have words for you."

Claire started to take Mutsuo's place in front of the video camera, but Zhang was there first.

"Mutsuo has asked for, and received, asylum," Zhang said. "Others of your crew are welcome, should they come of their own free will."

Kagome's eyes opened so wide, white showed all the way around her irises. "You invite my crew to mutiny?"

Zhang lowered his pitch to a bass rumble. "Commander, there will be no resupply. The Argus effect will destroy the electronics of any ship your mission control launches. I invite your crew to evacuate with us." A ghost of a smile touched his full lips. "That includes you, Commander."

Kagome pressed the heel of her hand to her forehead. "Impossible. Our reports are too important on Earth. I would not sacrifice the thousands of lives that may be saved by our reports of weather patterns carrying radioactive fallout for the four of us that remain." Her head turned and she asked a question in Japanese.

Three voices replied, *"Hai"* in unison.

Mutsuo bowed his head, sorrow and guilt etched in the fetal posture his body assumed.

"I respect your decision," Zhang said. "If we may render assistance, let us know. Once we are gone, you may have our salvage."

Kagome nodded stiffly. "There can be no peace between us as long as you harbor the traitor Mutsuo."

"That is your misfortune," replied Zhang. He reached forward and cut the connection.

Anderson studied Zhang speculatively, and, Claire thought, with more than a little respect.

Matt lined his mother's wheelbarrow with cotton blankets and gently set his mother and Owen into it, side by side. He gave his mother two Demerol and turned her so that her wounded hip was up. Owen lay on his back. His eyes fluttered open as they settled him in.

"Mama?" Owen reached towards Janice.

"Your mama's not here, honey." Janice said. "But your father and I are going to take real good care of you."

Owen's eyes widened and rolled until they settled on Matt. Then, as if that was the answer he'd been searching for, Owen fell back asleep.

They covered the wheelbarrow with the plastic shower curtain. Matt wore his father's old raincoat. He shifted the shotgun's strap higher on his shoulder.

"Bob will loan us his car," Janice said.

Matt wasn't so sure. Bob hadn't seemed generous when Matt had showed up on his doorstep last night. But what other option did he have? Surely the man would give in once he saw how badly off Owen was.

Matt pulled open the garage door and eased the wheelbarrow out. Gently, he steered it around the house and into the street. It was Wednesday, but there was no traffic. Few cars were on the street. An overturned Honda billowed black smoke.

Above the dawn was dark and bloody. Scant light filtered through clouds of soot and ash. The sun was a faint yellow disk in the sky.

Janice craned her neck to follow Matt's gaze. "Is your wife up there?"

Matt licked salt from his upper lip. "Yes. If anyone could survive this, it's Claire."

The plan was simple, in theory: cut a disk out of the white radiative shielding that protected the liquid hydrogen and liquid oxygen tanks from solar radiation. Claire and Zhang worked out a schedule of two-man work crews, round the clock, with each team working no more than six hours at a time.

But what was simple in concept was grueling in practice. Claire was covered with sweat from fighting the pressurization of her suit when she returned to the air lock. Her muscles ached from constantly fighting the mass of the TIG welder: accelerating it to move to a new position, decelerating it into place, holding position while Mutsuo used the welder to cut through the twelve-millimeter-thick radiative plating.

Claire envied him the Japanese suit. Its thinner surface made it easier for him to maneuver in EVA. While she looked and felt as if she'd just run a marathon, he was barely sweating.

She was jubilant under the layers of grime and exhaustion. The past eighty-four hours of work had borne fruit. Two hundred and thirty-four centimeters of circumference had been cut. Zhang and Josephine met them on the other side of the air lock, going out as Claire and Mutsuo came in. Their shift would make the final cut and begin the process of moving the enormous disk in place to be welded onto the base of the ATV.

Claire tapped gloves with Josephine as they passed. "Good luck," she mouthed.

Josephine raised her hand in salute as the hatch between them closed.

Inside the crew lock, Claire popped her helmet off, freeing droplets of sweat from her hair in the process. "I call first in the shower."

"Yes," Mutsuo said, looking in dismay at the shivering silver droplets.

Claire grabbed a paper towel from a dispenser on the wall and soaked them out of the air, wiped the paper across her forehead, then stuffed it in one of the nearby trash bags.

The shower was in the hygiene room just off the crew lock. The controls were in Chinese calligraphy, but the design was similar to the shower on *Reliance*. An accordion of opaque plastic that expanded to make the shower stall, a control panel on its side containing water and vacuum hoses.

Claire expanded the shower, stripped naked, and after a bit of experimenting discovered which hose was which and how to regulate the water temperature.

She was soaping her hair when the alarm began. A whooping bellow that made Claire open her eyes and curse as shampoo stung her eyes. She clawed at a towel and wiped her face clear.

An orange light flashed in time with the siren, bathing the hygiene room in a Halloween glow.

"Anderson," she yelled in the direction of the command room. "What the hell's going on?"

She snagged the flight suit she'd brought to change into and kicked through the access tunnel to the command module.

"Goddamn it, can't read the display—Hyun-Jin, what's that symbol?" Anderson jabbed at the screen.

Hyun-Jin bent over the display screen. "Two rocks together, in motion—collision, that must be the proximity alarm."

"It's broken free—" Josephine's panicked voice was breathless over the suit-to-ship radio. "Zhang's trapped, he's trying to—"

"Oh, shit!" Anderson enlarged camera one to the main screen. A white disk spiraled away from the fuel tanks. Half a dozen white tethers trailed from it like sewing threads on a manhole cover. Zhang was a white dot clinging to the edge.

"Sir, we've got a sit—" He looked up at Claire in the hatchway, and stopped speaking midsentence. He swallowed. "A situation."

Hyun-Jin's eyes were saucer-sized.

Claire looked down. She was naked and covered with soap suds. She jerked the face towel around her hips and gestured at the screen with her free hand. "Can you get a connection to Zhang? What's his status?"

Anderson bent to the task. Hyun-Jin turned away, cheeks flaming.

Claire stuffed her soapy wet legs into the flight suit, wriggled like a caterpillar molting backwards until she could zip up the front.

". . . pack . . . bring it back . . . not enough . . . lleration." Zhang's voice was smoothly modulated, but there was an edge of panic. The signal was breaking up.

"He's trying to use the jet pack on his suit to bring the disk back," Anderson said, still not looking up. "It'll never work, the disk's too massive. We're going to lose it."

Claire leaned over Anderson and pushed the talk button. "Zhang, abort. You can't save it."

". . . ghty-six hours . . . waste . . ."

"I'm going after him," Anderson announced.

"What?" Claire grabbed at his sleeve. "You can't EVA in—"

Anderson brushed off her hand. "Not going to. I'm taking the second ATV."

"But how will you pilot it? You can't read Portuguese."

Anderson's feet were already disappearing around the bend in the access tunnel. His voice Dopplered as he moved farther away. "Same manufacturer; how different could it be?"

Claire pushed off to follow Anderson.

Hyun-Jin grabbed her ankle. "Let him go. Zhang's expended too much fuel to return on his own. If Anderson doesn't bring him back, Zhang's dead."

"If Anderson can't pilot the foreign ATV, or hits the plate with too much force, they're both dead." Claire chewed on her lower lip. What would Cole do? Trust Anderson to do the right thing? Stop him? "Train good people," he always said, "then stay out of their way." Her heart aching, Claire took up the headset that Anderson had abandoned. "Anderson, are you there?"

"Just undocking from *Shenzhou*—damn!"

A clang resonated throughout the station.

"What's going on?" Claire asked breathlessly.

"Just a—" Anderson sounded as if he talked through clenched teeth, "momentary glitch. Grabbed the wrong control. The panel is laid out similar to our ATV, but some things are wired backwards."

Claire ran her hands through her hair, clenching them into fists at her temples. She would not scream. "Do you have Zhang and the shield in visual range?"

"He's just off my starboard, turning . . ."

Hyun-Jin punched several controls before camera two displayed its output on the front screen. On screen, the Brazilian ATV pivoted left, then swung right, homing in on Zhang.

"I'm getting a feel for her now," Anderson said.

Claire crossed her toes. "You going to match velocities?"

"That's the plan. Get in front. Match speeds, then ease the shield back towards the Mars platform. Tell Zhang to stop firing his jets. He's wasting fuel."

Claire changed over to the ship-to-suit frequency. "Zhang? Are you all right?"

"Can't get enough thrust to—" Zhang broke into Chinese. Then a sharp breath. "What is that idiot—"

"Anderson is going to stop the forward acceleration of the disk. Please. Stop firing your jet pack. You're wasting fuel."

"Is he drunk?" Zhang asked. "His flying is erratic."

Claire licked her lower lip. "The controls are wired differently than *Reliance*'s ATV. But don't worry, Anderson is our best pilot."

On screen, the ATV dipped and bobbed, clipping the white disk with a corner that crumpled the side of the ATV. Claire sucked in a breath. The ATV's hull was only seven millimeters thick.

Hyun-Jin was already changing frequencies. His hands seemed glacially slow. When the ship-to-ship frequency was up, Claire said, "Anderson, you there?"

"Almost . . ." He dragged the word out into four syllables, half-made it a prayer.

The disk spun. Zhang clung to the edge. A white beetle on a spinning turntable, his legs flung out into space. If he lost his grip, it was unlikely Anderson would be able to recover him. Given their history, it'd be even less likely that Anderson would try.

The ATV was in front of the disk. From *Shenzhou*, camera two had a side-on view. The ATV pointed nose-on at the center of the disk. Delicately, it slowed, letting the disk come to rest, like a Frisbee spinning on the finger of a college sophomore.

There was a grinding sound over the radio, as the air

inside the ATV vibrated in response to the contact. The ATV bounced back and to the side. The disk wobbled and began to flip end-over-end.

Hang on! Claire prayed for Zhang's strength to hold.

"He's losing his grip," Hyun-Jin said, pointing at the screen.

Zhang flopped from a single handhold on the edge of the disk. His legs flung wide into space, his free arm flailed for purchase.

The newly cut disk had sharp edges from where the welder pulled scraps of metal into sharp peaks. Any puncture of Zhang's suit, and there would be no time to react. The 4.3 psi of his suit would explode into space with the force of a car wreck.

"You've got to slow the disk's rotation," Claire transmitted to Anderson. "Zhang can't hold on much longer."

"I'm doing," Anderson grunted, "all . . . I . . . can."

The ATV bobbed closer. The side of its nose cone caught the edge of the disk. Momentum transferred, and the ATV was tossed off at a tangent to the disk. But the white circle slowed.

Zhang's free hand made contact with the handhold. If he was moving, he was still alive.

"Anderson, are you all right?"

"I'm going offline," he said. "I need to concentrate."

The radio went dead.

Claire wanted to pound the front display. There was nothing she could do now but watch.

The ATV stopped its wild tumble, gathered itself like a bumblebee thrown off course, and darted towards the now slower-spinning disk.

Too fast, Claire wanted to shout. Too fast.

The ATV tapped the center of the disk: once, twice, thrice. Each time, more of the disk's momentum transferred to the ATV, spinning it in place.

"Anderson must feel like he's in a centrifuge," Hyun-Jin said.

After each tap, the ATV's side jets fired, counteracting the spin.

The disk barely rotated now. The ATV tapped down once more on its center of gravity. This time the two masses stayed connected. Both revolved in tandem. The rear jets of the ATV fired. Ever so slowly, both it and the disk eased back towards *Shenzhou* station.

"I can't believe it," Claire said.

"Hoo-yah!" Anderson's voice was triumphant. "What a ride!"

"Zhang, you okay?" Claire transmitted, switching channels.

A moment of silence. "Yes." His deep voice was shaken. "I will be."

The ATV drew near to *Shenzhou XI*'s docking pin, lowered itself towards the port, floated back, lowered again. "I can't acquire a lock," Anderson reported.

"Hold on," Claire said. In a stage whisper, "Hyun-Jin, can you reorient camera five to point at the ATV?"

Hyun-Jin pushed several buttons, camera views slid in and out of the main screen: the receding Japanese station, the Earth—small and blue against the endless black sky—then Anderson's ATV.

Claire blew out a breath. "Your docking clamp is damaged." All the pressure on the ATV's nose cone had torqued it into an oval.

The ATV had no air lock. If it couldn't dock to *Shenzhou*, Anderson had no way back to the station, and no way to refuel . . . or replenish his air reserves.

But what he did have, Claire realized, was an EVA astronaut. Switching channels: "Zhang, Anderson damaged the docking pin on the ATV. Do you have enough fuel left in your jet pack to fly up there and see if it's repairable?"

"Will be there directly," Zhang replied. His voice was steadier.

The view from camera two went white as Zhang passed over it. He jetted over to the tip of the ATV, turned off his jets, and clung to the ring, inspecting it. "Looks like it's just the protective ring that's out of round. If I remove it, the ATV may be able to dock. But it will be a fragile dock. If the ATV doesn't come in straight and true, the pin could break."

They didn't have a lot of options. "Do it."

Claire relayed Zhang's plan to Anderson. "Think you can dock without a guide ring?"

Anderson replied, "On my worst day, during a solar storm."

Claire wasn't fooled. Sweat beaded his upper lip.

While Zhang removed the ring, Josephine retethered the ablative disk and hauled it towards *Reliance*'s ATV, which was already prepped to have it welded on to its base..

"The disk is off," Zhang transmitted. "Good luck."

"It isn't about luck," Anderson grumbled back.

"Close bulkheads around the docking pin," Claire told Hyun-Jin. She licked her lips. "Just in case."

Hyun-Jin looked at the array of buttons with their unfamiliar Chinese characters. "Sure. How?"

Claire punched the button in the same location as the one that controlled the bulkheads on *Reliance*. A touchscreen map displayed onscreen. Claire touched the corridors around the docking pin, and in the back of the station, bulkheads thumped into place.

Claire warned, "Remember the controls are different than those you're used to."

Anderson took a deep breath. "With every breath." He touched his lips. "See you on the flip side." Then he pressed his fingers to the camera lens. The blurry image disappeared as he turned off the com with his other hand.

"Why'd he do that?" Hyun-Jin asked.

"Didn't want the distraction." Claire said. "It's all up to him now."

The ATV, its delicate docking clasp exposed, bobbed towards *Shenzhou*'s docking pin. It was off center. Side thrusters fired. They burned too long, the ATV passed over the pin. Reverse thrusters carried it away from the station. Anderson pivoted the craft and turned for another try.

"What's he doing?" Hyun-Jin asked.

"He's lost the pressure sensor on the ring," Claire said. "There's no automated system to tell him when to acquire. He's got to do it on visual only, and within split seconds."

The ATV eased towards the station again. Scant millimeters at a breath. Claire's chest hurt, and she realized she hadn't taken a breath in over a minute. Please, she begged Anderson, don't screw this up. He was a troublemaker, and a bigot, but she didn't want to see him dead.

The ATV's nose cone blotted out the view from camera

two. Claire held her breath. She waited for a collision to shake the station and send debris skittering out of the crevices. The hairs on the back of her neck stood up in fearful anticipation.

A green light lit on the command panel. Anderson's face appeared on the central screen. "Acquired." Rarely had she heard so much pride in a single word.

Hyun-Jin cheered.

A sleepy Mutsuo appeared in the doorway. "What has happened?"

Claire felt her mouth stretch into a grin. "Way to go!" To Mutsuo, she said, "Tell you later." Switching over to ship-to-suit. "Anderson's docked the ATV. Is the disk secure?"

Josephine replied, "Locked down tight. Waiting for the final weld."

"It'll have to wait. Zhang's suit was stressed. I want you both inside."

"But there's another hour on my shift," Josephine argued. "I'm good for it. I could start—"

"I'm not leaving you outside alone." Claire was firm. "We've had enough excitement for one shift. Mutsuo and Hyun-Jin can start the welding."

Zhang's helmet was fogged with condensation when he came through the air lock, excess sweat from his exertion to stay on the disk.

Anderson met them in the access tunnel outside the command module. It was impossible to swagger in zero-gee, but there was a jaunt to his movements.

Claire stuck her finger in his face. "I'm glad you're alive, but if you ever go off half-cocked like that again—"

"He was right." The baritone voice cut through her reprimand.

Claire whipped around. "You agree with his decision to ignore a direct order?"

Zhang's hair was plastered to his skull with sweat, and he looked gaunt. "It was a desperate act, but these are desperate times." He held out his hand to Anderson. "And I, for one, am grateful."

Anderson's grin went nuclear-bright, and he returned the Chinese commander's grip.

Claire suddenly realized that the only thing worse than Anderson and Zhang at each other's throats, was Anderson and Zhang on the same side.

Bob's pickup truck had been built in the 1970s and belched smoke like a dragon with indigestion. But unlike the late-model cars lining the streets, it started.

Matt loaded his mother and Owen into the passenger's side of the bench seat. Janice surprised him by jumping in next to them.

"You're coming?"

Janice didn't answer, just mopped Owen's brow and cuddled him into her lap to give Betty more room on the seat.

Matt climbed in next to Janice, stowed his father's shotgun in the gun rack lining the back window, opened up the map, and unfolded the hospital listings he'd torn from this mother's telephone book. "Lakeland Regional Medical Center," he said, and put the truck in gear.

Betty moaned as the pickup truck's rumbling jolted her broken hip. She bit the side of her palm to keep from crying out.

Janice gave her another Demerol.

The suburbs were deserted, but as they merged onto the highway it was littered with stalled and wrecked cars. A Ford Taurus was overturned in the center lane. The few cars moving on the highway crept along at thirty miles an hour, dodging the debris and abandoned cars.

"Mother of God," breathed Janice, looking at the wreckage.

"Light from the explosions must have blinded the drivers." Matt looked away from an arm outflung from the overturned car. No way could the driver of that crumpled car still be alive. Besides Matt had to take care of his own.

As they traveled north, the traffic on the highway became more dense. People were packed into cars, their clothes and possessions blotting out rear windows. The stream of refugees clogged the highway to a trickle.

Owen woke up coughing blood.

"Damn. Damn. Damn." Matt pounded the steering wheel and honked at the slow car blocking his way. At this rate, they'd never reach the hospital in time. He worked his way to the median.

"What are you—" Janice started to ask.

Matt put the pickup in low gear and veered off the road. "Shortcut." He headed east, towards the hospital.

It was Claire's rest cycle, but she couldn't sleep. Adrenaline coursed under her skin with tiny ant feet, prickling her into vigilance. She crawled out of her sleep sack, past Hyun-Jin's sleeping form, along the access tunnel to the nearest porthole.

Ten thousand miles away, Earth no longer filled the window. It was small enough to encircle with her arms. Blue and white swirls of ocean and clouds were surrounded by an impossibly thin layer of atmosphere.

We're like infants, Claire realized. We think our mother is invulnerable, that nothing we can do will harm her, and really she's so fragile.

The unyielding black of space stretched for as far as the imagination could see. If Earth became inhospitable, there was no other haven. Megatons of nuclear bombs had fallen during the conflict. Claire prayed the Earth's ecosystem could recover. Or rather, that it would recover fast enough for mankind to survive. Or, failing that, die slow enough that Owen could live out his life.

A hand touched her shoulder.

Claire jumped and spun around.

It was Anderson. "We'll get there." His triumphant grin was gone. There was melancholy in the downward turn of his mouth.

"Your people?" Claire asked. He had mentioned someone special in Houston, and there was his father in the Pacific Northwest.

Anderson blinked rapidly. "I found Matt because I spent time on the ham radio listening for word of my dad or brothers." He looked down at his hands. "Gone. Quick, I hope."

There wasn't anything to say, so Claire touched his upper arm.

Anderson wiped his nose with the back of his hand, then pointed to the Japanese station in the far corner of the window. "Reentry would be a whole lot easier with their communication equipment. We could use telemetry—"

"No."

"With Mutsuo's help, we could—"

"No!" Claire scowled. "We're not wolves to fall upon each other when resources get tight."

"Aren't we?" Anderson cocked his head at her. "If something on that station could help your little boy, could any argument—moral or otherwise—keep you away from it?"

Tears blurred Claire's vision. "Don't bring Owen into this." Her voice was low and hot. "Don't you goddamn mention him."

Anderson leaned close and his breath tickled her cheek. "I don't have to. He's in your every thought. Don't think the others and I don't know what your real motivation is. You can talk about favorable wind conditions and known trajectories all you want. We all know the only reason to land in the Gulf of Mexico is your need to get to your son."

Claire said nothing.

"Cole put the needs of his crew first." His voice was a fist inside a velvet glove. "Maybe that's why he's dead and you're not." Anderson held up his hands to ward off her protest. "So don't call me selfish and opportunistic, Momma Bear, because I've got nothing on you."

Anderson pushed off. At the hatch to the crew quarters he turned, hands on the entryway. "If a time ever comes when you have to decide between doing what's right and saving Owen, I hope it's not my head on the chopping block."

CHAPTER 16

"To the *Phoenix*," Claire toasted, holding aloft a plastic packet of sports drink.

"The *Phoenix*," came a chorus of voices and the slap-slap of packets hitting each other as Anderson, Zhang, Hyun-Jin, Mutsuo, and Josephine echoed Claire's toast.

They were in the galley. Portholes inset in the curving cylindrical wall gave a three-sixty view of the environs outside. Earth's blue-green was dulled by thousands of tons of brown dust thrown into the atmosphere by the bombs. The Japanese station was a silver speck in the distance. But all eyes were on the newly finished reentry vehicle that Claire had dubbed "*Phoenix*."

"It's an unlucky name," Anderson grumbled.

"No, it's perfect," Josephine countered. "A bird rising from the ashes, triumphant, flying high."

"Streaming flames . . ."

"The name is not important," Zhang interrupted. His dark eyes scanned the craft. Only the tail end was visible in the window, since the nose was still docked to *Shenzhou*. The enormous white plate was welded to the end, a half-dollar glued to a pencil eraser. "Do you think it will work?"

"All our calculations," Mutsuo said, "indicate that the ablative shield will last long enough to protect the *Phoenix* through the worst of the reentry heat. As long as we maintain the correct orientation for insertion—yes, it should survive."

Zhang's hands tightened at his sides, and she knew he was remembering the flames that had killed his crew. They had been traveling in a craft much less improvised than this one.

"The tricky part," Josephine said, her hands echoed her words, pantomiming their descent, "is that the ATV doesn't have a drag chute. After reentry, when we hit the appropriate altitude, we'll have to bail out and use our personal emergency chutes to land."

"What concerns me," said Mutsuo, "is the landing point. Commander Zhang and I have calculated a sensible trajectory that lands us in southern Italy, and crashes the lifeboat into the Mediterranean." His eyes flicked to Zhang, seeking support. "But shortly before this celebration, Commander Logan asked me to plot a second course for southern Florida and the Gulf of Mexico."

Zhang cocked his head at Claire. "You still cling to this madness? I weep for the loss of your family as I weep for my own, but our deaths will not help them."

"I agree," said Mutsuo. "The United States has been devastated by war. Our observations on the JWA indicate that power is out over eighty percent of the continent. They will not have the infrastructure—"

"What do you know about it?" Anderson interrupted. "Your spy telescopes can't measure the American spirit."

Claire was surprised at Anderson's support. He was the last person she'd expected to back her, especially after their confrontation in the access tunnel.

"With all due respect," Mutsuo's words were crisp and his expression offended, "The Japanese know much about recovering from nuclear attacks. It is a slow process. Landing in the Mediterranean is the best option. The Europeans will surely—"

"We're landing in the Gulf of Mexico," Claire blurted

out. She was surprised at her own vehemence. She made an effort to reel in the adrenaline pounding in her veins. "The Europeans have no reason to help us. If we land in Spain, we'll be powerless to—"

"You put your desire to help your son ahead of the safety of this crew." Zhang's black eyes flashed. "This is irrational. The boy is already dead—"

Claire's hand cracked across his cheek like a gunshot. Though his neck absorbed most of the momentum, they pivoted away in reaction. "We are going," she panted, "to Florida."

Zhang raised a hand to cover his reddening cheek. Anger tightened the lines around his mouth, but he said nothing.

Hyun-Jin cleared his throat loudly. All eyes turned to him. He stuttered, "I—I agree with the reasoning behind Zhang and Mutsuo's plan. The Mediterranean is the safest option." He swallowed, his glance dancing between Claire and Zhang. "But I vote with Claire. I would rather die helping my people recover than live a long life in exile."

"Your people?" Zhang looked incredulous. "But you are Chinese!"

"No," Hyun-Jin linked his arm with Anderson, who looked startled. "I am American."

"Josephine?" Claire asked, extending her hand. "What about Luke?"

The younger woman's eyes widened at the mention of her fiancé. "He's dead," she whispered, shaking her head as if trying to rouse herself from a bad dream. "He was in Houston when the bombs fell."

"Do you know that for certain?" Claire urged. "Is it possible he flew to Orlando to meet you on the ground? Could you live your life in Spain, never knowing?"

"Oh, God." Josephine reached for and clung to Claire's shoulder. "You're right. We can't leave them."

"It's decided," Anderson said. "Two thirds of this crew votes for Florida."

"One third of this crew does not," Mutsuo countered. "Why should we go with you to pursue this folly?"

Anderson pointed his hand to the back of the station, where the second, somewhat damaged Brazilian ATV was docked. "You want to make a second lifeboat, land in the

Sea of Japan, go right ahead. We Americans are taking our ATV and going home. Democratic rules."

"A majority does not make you right," Zhang said in a deadly soft voice. "Think about what you will land into. A destroyed city, fallout, unsafe drinking water, looters. Even with the best of intentions, how much help will you be?"

Claire tried to keep her expression neutral, but she could feel the skin on her neck and shoulders heating up. It was foolish, irrational—Zhang was right—but the *Phoenix* was landing near Orlando. She couldn't do anything else.

After years of putting Owen's needs second—behind her drive to space, behind planning the launch of the ESR, behind her career as an astronaut—it was time to put Owen first.

Failure was not an option.

Landing in a foreign country and fighting through customs officials while her son died in a hospital without a mother's comfort was not an option.

Owen needed her, and she *would* be there for him. His safety was the most important thing in her world, and she would endanger herself and all these people to protect him. For the first time she understood the impulse behind Hyun-Jin and Anderson's mutiny. If she couldn't convince the crew to follow her plan and land in Florida, she was willing to steal the lifeboat and leave them here.

"It's insane!" Mutsuo shouted. "The radiation levels alone—"

"I don't know what it was like for you and the others in MEO," Claire said, fighting to keep her voice calm. "But those of us in LEO—we've already spent days in elevated radiation. We're probably already breeding the cancers that will kill us. There's nothing we can do to stop that, and nothing we can do to repair the damage done to the Earth. The *only* thing left is to go home and spend our remaining days with the people we love." She jabbed her finger at the porthole where the *Phoenix* was visible. "My crew and I are taking that ship to Florida." Her voice lowered. "You're welcome to join us. But I promise you—that's where we're going."

A vein in Zhang's temple throbbed. "You would steal the *Phoenix*?"

Claire raised her chin. "I'm commandeering it in the name of democracy. Four against two."

His hands clenched into fists. "You would take it by force?"

Claire braced the ball of her foot against the wall, ready to launch into a fight. "If I have to."

The truck's wheels spun in mud. Instead of crossing a short greenbelt and heading back into Lakeland, Matt's shortcut had led them into ever-swampier ground. Matt got out and inspected the tires. The rear right tire was more than half mired in the mud that sucked at Matt's shoes with every step.

Mosquitoes swarmed around him, humming in ecstasy at having such thin-skinned prey. It was dark; the sun had set early.

"Can you free the wheel?" Janice called from the cab.

Matt shook his head. "Not without a tow truck." He wondered if there were water moccasins in the cattails behind him. Ten yards away, something entered the water with a splash. A big something.

"Just leave me," his mother said when Matt climbed back into the truck. "You can move faster if you just take Owen. He needs a doctor more than I do."

Matt kissed his mother's velvety-soft face. "We're not leaving you."

"You can come back for me later. I don't want anything to happen to Owen because I slowed you down."

Matt took the old woman in a gentle hug. "It's not your fault, Mama. It's mine. I'm the one who took that damn shortcut." He fought to keep from screaming.

Janice pushed past him and stepped into the mud. She sank a few inches and took an experimental step. Looking back, she said, "I can carry Owen." There were no reprisals in her voice, no guilt, no shaming. Just a simple statement of fact. She couldn't weigh more than a hundred and ten pounds, soaking wet, and here she was offering to carry his son through a night-dark swamp.

In the reddish gloom, wearing a yellow Mickey slicker, Janice looked like an angel.

Matt carried his mother as if she were a child, careful not to put any pressure on her hip. Her skin felt hot and dry to the touch, and Matt tried not to think about the pain he was causing her with every step, or the possibility of infection.

Owen's head lolled against Janice's neck and shoulder. She carried him piggyback, hunching forward so his dead-weight draped over her back.

It felt to Matt like they had been walking all night. He had no idea if they were walking into or out of the swamp. More bombs could fall at any minute. All that existed was the four of them and the need to walk.

A hairy root cut across Matt's ankle, and he lost his balance. Matt clutched his mother to his chest. With an effort of will that pulled a muscle in his back he managed to fall to his knees instead of toppling headfirst into the water.

His mother grunted with pain.

As Matt pushed himself up, he encountered what he'd thought was a root. It was a rope, thick and made of jute. Pulling on it made the cattails to his right sway. He pushed them aside and saw a sight that made his breath catch—an empty airboat danced on the end of the rope.

Hope flared in his chest. "Janice," he cried, "look." He pointed to the craft.

They lowered their charges onto the cargo platform of the boat. Matt climbed into the driver's seat and extended a hand to Janice and she climbed up next to him. By some miracle, the keys were in the ignition.

Matt turned the key and the engine turned over. "Thank God." Something was finally going right. He reached for the clutch.

The cattails rustled off to the right. Matt looked, expecting a snake or an alligator.

Moonlight gleamed off a rifle barrel. "I don't know what the hell you think you're doing, but you can stop it right now," said the man holding the gun. He was whipcord thin, wore a tattered gas station attendant's uniform with the name "Howard" in script and an orange-and-blue "Union 76" patch.

Matt raised his hands. His shotgun was on the floor of the airboat, too far away to reach. "We didn't mean any harm. I thought the boat was deserted. My mother's hurt and my son's very ill. We need to get them to a hospital."

"What's the world coming to?" the man asked rhetorically. "Man goes to take a piss and city dwellers crawl out of the swamp to steal his ride."

In the back of the boat, Owen started to cough wetly. Janice turned towards him.

"Ach-ach!" The man made a warning sound like machine gun fire. "Tell your wife not to move."

"She's not my wife," Matt said. "She's a nurse. Like I said, my son's sick and my mother fell and hurt her hip." He felt foolish babbling at the wrong end of a gun, but found he couldn't shut up. He had the crazy idea that as long as he was talking, the man couldn't shoot. "My wife's an astronaut. Great career, but not a lot of help now." He was sweating; drops fell into his eyes, but Matt didn't dare lower his hands to wipe them away.

Howard scowled. "An astronaut? Where is she?"

Matt curled one of his raised hands to point to the sky.

A low whistle. "No shit?" Howard cocked his head. "What's your name?"

"Matt Logan."

Howard shouldered his rifle, stepped forward, and offered his hand. "I'm proud to shake the hand of Claire Logan's husband. Well, shoot, if it weren't for her, none of us would know what the hell was going on." He pumped Matt's hand like he was drilling for oil. "My wife listened in on your conversation. Made her weep harder than *Days of Our Lives*. If I let anything happen to Claire Logan's son, Missy would never let me hear the end of it." He shooed Matt out of the pilot's seat and climbed on board. Howard revved the engine. "I'll take you to a fishing buddy of mine. He can help your boy."

Images of mud poultices and leeches ran through Matt's mind. "He needs a doctor. I think he's got radiation poisoning."

Driving at an alarming speed with his left hand, Howard pulled a snuff tin out of a pocket with his right, deftly opened the lid one-handed, pinched out a bit, and tucked the tin back into his shirt. He stuffed the snuff between his cheek and gum. "I know what you're thinking. But Larry ain't no root doctor. He's a Yankee medical man from one of them big schools. Comes down year twice a year to hunt gator. He works on the cancer and I'm thinking he could help your boy." He tongued the tobacco deeper into his cheek and waved at the off-color sky. "Hell, I'm guessing he could help a lot of folk right about now.

Matt, not sure whether he could trust the man at the wheel and knowing he didn't have much choice, only nodded. He was cold, hungry, and desperately afraid that Owen would die. He'd tried to get them to the hospital and had gotten them lost in the swamp instead.

What had saved them? Not Matt, no. It was Claire. It was always about Claire. Her accomplishments were somehow supposed to be enough for him, to make up for the fact that his wife was more married to her work than to him. He'd thought Owen would bring them closer together, make her work less. But no, it had only given Matt company when Claire was gone on yet another work-related training or publicity tour.

He'd thought love was infinite, that there was always enough to go around. But it wasn't. Once Owen was born, Matt got only half as much of Claire as he'd had. Between the boy and her job, there was little left for her husband.

Shame colored Matt's face. I can't even save my own son without invoking her name.

Zhang entered the command module; his brows were lowered and he did not look happy. Mutsuo trailed on his heels. "We have discussed the matter. We will go with you, to Florida." His tone made the last word a curse.

"It's the best choice," said Claire.

"It's the only choice," Zhang spat. "Anderson's actions with the Brazilian ATV have compromised its hull. It cannot serve as a reentry vehicle."

"Hey, bud," Anderson shouted from the pilot's station, pointing over Claire's shoulder at Zhang, "my actions saved your ass. If I hadn't 'compromised its hull' you'd be halfway to Mars by now."

Claire pushed Anderson's arm away. "Stop helping," she whispered. Louder, to Zhang and Mutsuo. "I'm sorry our landing location does not meet your approval. Once we're on the ground, we'll do everything in our power to help you get home."

Zhang pursed his lips. "That would be appreciated. I am

the only son. My mother and sisters in Shanghai need me. . . ." His voice trailed off. Claire knew what he was thinking: They needed him . . . if they were still alive.

"My wife in Tokyo," said Mutsuo, "is pregnant with our first child—a son." The thin brows that arched over his heart-shaped face lowered. "I do not want to die in a radio-active hell."

Claire bridled. That hell was where her husband and son were. But were their positions reversed, she would have felt the same. "I'm sorry, Mutsuo, but I don't trust the Japanese government to transport me halfway across the world, especially when the destination would put their pilots in danger. Your son is safe." She stretched out her hands to him, pleading for understanding. "Mine might be dying."

Mutsuo nodded curtly and said no more.

It was the night before their reentry. Claire checked the trajectory in the computer dozens of times. She ran the simulation Josephine wrote to predict the heat and strain the ATV's hull would be subjected to. Come in too steep, and the parachute wouldn't brake them; too shallow, and they risked skipping off the atmosphere like a stone. In the current simulation, hull temp was 970 degrees Fahrenheit—only a couple of hundred degrees below the melting point of aluminum.

"That's enough," Hyun-Jin said, gently taking her hands and pulling Claire out of the command leg restraints. "You've tested every possibility. All you're doing now is scaring yourself." He blew out a breath and gave her a shaky half-grin. "And me."

Claire wanted to ask him what he thought the odds of their surviving tomorrow were, but she didn't. As commander, it was her job to put on a confident front, even as her insides were churning with doubt and fear. "You're right." She squeezed his hand and released him. "We've done our best. Tomorrow night we'll be on the ground."

Josephine's dark eyes darted from her palmtop over to Claire and Hyun-Jin. "Do you really think it'll survive? I mean, the ablative shield—"

"It'll hold," Anderson said without opening his eyes. He

was in a sleep sack Velcroed to the wall. "You've got the best pilot in the world—me—so stop worrying."

"But after what happened to the lifeboat . . ."

Claire squeezed Josephine's hand. "It's be all right. Don't worry about the journey. Think about what we'll do after we land."

The cockpit grew silent. Claire pictured the city of Orlando in ruins, skyscrapers toppled, abandoned cars clogging the streets, no power, looters running the streets. She was glad Owen and Matt were in the relatively quiet suburb of Lakeland.

Josephine picked at a fingernail. "Maybe Zhang's right. Maybe we should land in the Mediterranean. Things are bad in Florida."

Claire felt her chest go tight. "What about Luke?"

When Josephine looked up, her blue eyes were filled with worry. "He's probably already gone, dead. He would want me to live. Perhaps we should—"

"We're parachuting into central Florida and ditching the craft in the Gulf of Mexico," Anderson grumbled. "It's decided. Don't go soft on us now, Jo-Jo."

Josephine scowled. "I'm just saying—"

Claire covered Josephine's hand with her own. "If you want to stay here, work on another way home, you're welcome to. But I know Matt and Owen survived the blast. I can't abandon them."

"How can you help?" Josephine's eyes were wide. "You're no doctor. You can't undo the radiation damage. What can you do? Lie down alongside them and die?"

Claire breathed out. "We'll have medical kits, iodine supplements, and knowledge about radiation, weather patterns, and what's happened in the rest of the country. With the satellites and many of the emergency broadcast transmitters down, they may not even know the extent of the damage.

"In Japan, yes, we may be safer, but we'll just be four more people in a country of millions. Curiosities, maybe even celebrities. In America, we can make a difference."

Mutsuo came back from the galley and passed out steaming white buns. Claire bit into one and found it filled with barbeque pork.

As he handed the last bun to Josephine, Mutsuo said, "I

would like to contact the JWA. See if any of my crewmates
have changed their mind about returning to Earth."

"Now? At the last minute?" Claire asked.

"There will not be another opportunity. Zhang says we
could carry two more passengers."

Claire raised an eyebrow at Anderson.

He was half out of his sleep sack to eat. Between bites
of *hum bao* he said, "Have to redo the reentry calculations,
but yeah, we could take two more."

Claire suppressed surprise at Anderson's complacency
about changing the mass parameters at the last moment.
"Go ahead." She pushed away from the radio to make
room for Mutsuo. "But they'd have to get here in six hours.
I won't delay the launch."

Mutsuo took her place and powered up the radio.

As Claire backed across the command module, Zhang
came in through the hatch. They nearly collided. Claire
caught his upper arm to brace herself and settled at his
side. He smelled of cardamom and sweat.

Zhang grabbed for and caught the palmtop he'd dropped
in the impact. "You still plan to land in the U.S.A.?"

She met his gaze levelly. "Yes. Are you coming with us?"

He turned the palmtop so she could see the screen. The
Chinese characters were illegible to her, but she recognized
the radiation symbol overlaying a human figure.

"Medical documents," Zhang said. "If I must face danger, I would do it informed."

Claire nodded her approval.

Mutsuo spoke hurried Japanese into the radio.

The figure onscreen was not Kagome, but a thin, long-
faced man who kept looking over his shoulder. The skin
under his eyes sagged, giving him a tired look. He shook
his head and whispered a reply.

The exchange ended a few minutes later. Mutsuo's
cheeks were red and his hands clenched and unclenched.

"I take it we won't have company," Anderson said.

Mutsuo glared at him. Then breathed deeply. "No. They
prefer to die."

Claire felt Josephine's gaze turn on her, but she stead-
fastly refused to look at the other woman. "I'm sorry, Mutsuo. At least you tried."

"*Bakara,*" he muttered.

Claire opened one of the mesh bags that was clipped to the lee wall. It held equipment they'd brought from *Reliance*. She dug through it until her hand encountered the smooth metal case of the ham radio.

Anderson tossed the plastic wrapper off his pork bun to Hyun-Jin, who stowed it in a garbage bag. "There's no way you're getting a signal this far away."

Claire ignored him and plugged the radio into station power. A crackling hiss filled the room. Claire put earphones on and began whispering into the microphone: "CQ, CQ. This is Claire Logan in mid-Earth orbit. CQ."

She stopped and listened. Radio signals from Earth were electromagnetic energy and traveled endlessly through space. But the chances of intercepting one fell as the surface area around Earth expanded. It was nearly impossible that she'd hear Matt's voice—and yet, like Mutsuo, she couldn't help trying.

There. A pattern in the static. Some sort of modulation. Claire adjusted the frequency to make the signal clearer.

". . . fall of man . . . days . . . repent . . ." A man's voice. It was hard to tell above the static, but it sounded like a New England accent, possibly Maine.

The signal washed back into static, and all her efforts could not bring it back.

Sleep was hard to come by. Claire climbed into her sleep sack at twenty-three-hundred hours, and was still staring at the LED readout two hours later.

She tapped the zipper pocket of her shirt and felt the vial of iodine supplements she'd taken from *Shenzhou*'s medical kit. If she could get these to Owen, it would help prevent his developing thyroid cancer. Hold on just a little longer, sweetie, she pleaded, Mommy's coming.

When she finally did doze, her dreams were filled with fire and smoke. Mushroom clouds billowed over Disney World, blasting the brightly painted rides into scrap metal. Children evaporated in X-ray shots, skin, muscle, and bone dissolving in the heat, leaving behind only shadows on concrete.

Claire woke up screaming Owen's name. The sleep sack had tangled around her torso in her thrashing, and constricted her chest. Shaking and pánting, she untwisted the nylon fabric and pushed it down her legs.

"Wha—" Anderson groaned sleepily.

Claire's eyes were adjusted to the darkened command module. Hyun-Jin and Josephine slept in sacks near the controls. Mutsuo and Zhang's sacks, near the hatch, were empty.

She was instantly awake. "Oh, God. No." She kicked the remnants of the sack off her feet. The checklist for the ATV's undocking and reentry had been under one of the elastic bands on the wall. It was gone.

Claire grabbed the zipper on Anderson's sack and peeled it open like a banana.

"What?" He grabbed her arm. "What the hell's going on?"

Claire nodded at the empty sacks by the hatch. "Zhang and Mutsuo—they're stealing the ATV."

CHAPTER 17

Claire kicked off from the wall, caught the rim of the hatch, and pivoted down the access tunnel, left at the T-intersection towards the ATV dock. But this wasn't *Reliance*. She was in a dead end. Cursing, she kicked off the wall, changed direction at the intersection, and nearly collided with Anderson.

They scrabbled for traction on the walls, kicking handholds, grabbing drawer pulls to accelerate. Claire didn't let herself consider the possibility had it was already too late.

Claire turned the corner and caught her breath in disbelief.

Zhang and Mutsuo hovered around the hatch over his palmtop. Mutsuo swore softly in Japanese and touched his stylus to the screen.

Zhang looked up. His cool eyes widened slightly with surprise.

Then Claire was on him. Her elbow connected with the side of his head as she drove all her momentum through him and against the wall. They bounced off at forty-five-degree angles to each other.

"What the hell do you think you're doing?" Claire shouted. The Austin twang she worked hard to suppress rang through the corridor. "You bastard—you were going to strand us!"

Zhang didn't waste breath on a denial. He caught a handhold and lashed out at Claire with a kick. The zipper pull on his ankle sliced her eyebrow, sending quivering droplets of blood into the air.

Claire blinked rapidly, trying to clear her vision of a stinging bubble.

Anderson roared a primal battle cry and tackled Zhang. The smaller man folded at the waist, driven back by Anderson's force.

Through a haze of blood and tears Claire saw Mutsuo disappear in a ball of arms and legs as Josephine and Hyun-Jin grabbed him.

"Shit!" Hyun-Jin swore. He sucked in a breath. Mutsuo broke halfway free, and clawed at the walls of the hallway before Josephine wrapped her legs around the man's chest and restrained him.

Like most real fights Claire had seen, it was over in less than a minute.

Pressing on her forehead wound to stem the flow of blood with her left hand, Claire used her right to tickle a roll of duct tape out of a plastic bag of tools Velcroed to the wall. She bit off a piece, slapped it on her forehead as a temporary bandage, then used the roll to bind Zhang, taping wrists and ankles together, then hands to feet. She tossed the tape to Hyun-Jin to secure Mutsuo. Once they were both hog-tied, she floated back, taking the scene in view.

Mutsuo's palmtop was caught in a return vent at the end of the hall. Claire grabbed it and looked at the screen. A decryption program. She shook the computer at Mutsuo. "What's this?"

"To open the lock. The passcode was changed." Mutsuo spat blood. "Partners? You never trusted us."

Claire wanted to laugh. They'd been about to steal the only ride home, and Mutsuo accused her of betraying *his* trust. She nodded at the hatch. "This your idea, Anderson?"

His mouth widened in a lopsided grin. "Just another example of my counterproductive paranoia."

Claire clapped his shoulder. "Good work." Bending forward, Claire touched Zhang's chin with her hand, and pivoted him until they were eye-to-eye. "Why?"

Zhang didn't blink. "For the same reason you would have us land in Florida. Our families are as important to us as yours is to you." He indicated the hatch. "And there is only the one lifeboat."

"But we planned to send you home as soon as possible."

The corners of Zhang's mouth turned down. "A war-torn nation. What priority would they place on returning a foreign national—from the very country that had bombed them—to his home?" A soft snort. "Likely, I would not survive the evening."

"Americans aren't like that," Claire protested, but her eyes slid sideways to Anderson.

He hovered, arms folded behind Zhang's hog-tied body. "We can't take them with us now." He cocked his thumb at the hatchway to the ATV. "We can't trust them. If I hadn't changed the lock on the hatch, we'd be stranded."

"Leaving them here is as good as killing them," Josephine protested. Her blue eyes were wide with indignation. "There aren't going to be any more supply ships—not in a time frame that would save them."

Mutsuo looked down at his hands. Softly, he said, "Please, my wife is expecting our firstborn. He should know his father."

His plea, so similar to what Claire had said when the Chinese stole *Reliance*'s lifeboat, decided her. "They're coming with us."

"You can't be—"

Claire held up a hand and spoke over Anderson's protest. "I don't forgive their actions. She looked at Mutsuo. He wouldn't make eye contact. His body quivered with tension, digging the duct tape into his wrists. "But I understand their motive. We'll take them with us, as prisoners, and release them when we're on the ground."

Mutsuo pressed his chin to his chest, the constricted bow all he could manage in his bonds. "Thank you," he whispered.

"We could be more help," Zhang said, "if we were freed."

"I'm sure you could," Claire replied, bending down until her face was level with Zhang's. "I'm just not sure whom you'd be helping."

Anderson's hand rested on the control that would undock the ATV from *Shenzhou XI*. He looked over at Claire, strapped in next to him in the copilot's seat. "You sure about this? We're going to take a ship never designed for reentry, hope that the radiative shield will last long enough and deflect enough heat that we don't burn up, then bail out of the ATV using emergency parachutes because the thing has no landing capabilities, hope we hit land and the ATV hits water. It's a plan with so many holes to be damn near suicidal."

Claire ground her teeth together. They did not need Anderson's little pep talk. Looking straight ahead, she asked, "You got a better idea?"

Anderson shook his head. "Not a damn one." He leaned forward and pushed the button that started the deorbit burn. The ATV moved smoothly away from the docking pin, pivoted so its base pointed towards Earth, and fired all four side thrusters to push it towards the planet.

Three minutes later, the engines stopped. Anderson tapped the pilot's screen. "That wasn't four minutes, seventeen seconds." He whipped around in the pilot's seat and jabbed a finger at Mutsuo and Zhang, still tied up in the rear of the cabin. "You changed the programming," he accused, "from *Shenzhou*'s command module, and you didn't tell us."

Zhang blinked his golden eyelids with exaggerated slowness. "The destination you chose," his gaze moved to Claire, "for sentimental reasons, is not suitable. Landing in the Mediterranean benefits us all."

"Goddamn it." Anderson pulled up the navigation program and hastily entered numbers. Over his shoulder he shouted, "You changed the burn time, but not the insertion angle. You've got us coming in on too steep a glide path. If I can't flatten us out, we're going to burn up in the atmosphere."

Zhang's head snapped towards Mutsuo. "You didn't change the entry angle?"

"I-I—" his eyes widened. "I don't know. We were moving quickly—in the dark."

Zhang swore softly in Chinese.

"Shut up, you goddamned gook," Anderson shouted. "I'm trying to concentrate."

"Is there anything—" Claire started to ask.

"No." Anderson cut her off. His hands were blindingly fast on the keyboard. Blue navigation lines plotted and replotted on the screen, and each flashed red as it hit the Earth's atmosphere. "I'm trying—" he tapped more keys "—to brake the ATV." A frown creased his forehead. "This is like trying to fly a teacup powered by a model-rocket engine."

The ATV whirled into a spin. Claire and everyone else in the capsule was thrown to the walls. Only Anderson's harness kept him in place.

Air whuffed out of Josephine's chest as she hit the wall. Hyun-Jin's head cracked against a handhold.

The capsule filled with the red-orange glow of flames streaking past the porthole.

Claire licked her lips and tasted sweat. The temperature climbed: eighty degrees, ninety, one hundred. Inside her flight suit and parachute harness, Claire was smoldering. "We're too hot."

"Doing. My. Best," Anderson grunted out. More jets fired. The spin morphed into a stomach-lurching wobble.

The capsule shook so hard Claire's teeth rattled in her skull.

A loud bang nearly deafened her. *We're dead*, went through Claire's mind. She was that sure the hull had split.

"Motherfuck," Anderson swore. "The heat's loosened the welds. The ablative shield is only holding on at two points. It's banging against the hull." He checked the altimeter. "Better get ready to jump. If this bird holds together past fifteen thousand feet, I say risk it."

"Cut us free." Zhang demanded, holding forth his hands. "We can't bail out like this."

"This is all your fault. If you hadn't tried to steal the

ATV—'' Anderson shouted over the now-constant banging of the shield against the hull. "You deserve to die."

"Claire," Zhang shouted. "Help us."

She felt like she was in a cement mixer. Her neck ached with whiplash and she was nauseous. Her whole body vibrated with the friction of ATV against atmosphere and the rhythmic bangs of the shield slamming against the very craft it was meant to protect. She crawled, hand over hand, against the atmospheric deceleration to where Zhang and Mutsuo were tied up, and peeled back the edge of the duct tape, unraveling it from their wrists.

White-hot sparks glittered in the porthole.

"Hull's too hot. It's close to losing structural integrity," Zhang said. "Won't last much longer."

"Twenty-thousand feet," Anderson shouted. "Almost time to bail out."

"Where are we?" Claire yelled. Zhang's tampering with the burn had thrown them off course.

"Somewhere over the Atlantic," Anderson screamed back.

Claire's stomach lurched. A water landing. The plan had been to land east of Orlando in the upwind town of Lakeland. Her worst-case scenario had included parachuting into the warm, tame waters of the Gulf of Mexico, not being plunged into the middle of thousands of square miles of empty, wild Atlantic Ocean.

The altimeter dropped below fifteen thousand feet. Anderson pointed at Hyun-Jin. "You're good. Go!"

Hyun-Jin clawed his way to the hatch on the side of the ATV. His hand roamed quickly over his parachute rig, checking the straps and pull cords. Then he popped the hatch.

The air blew out of the ATV into the thin air of the Earth's upper atmosphere. The ATV fell uncontrollably. The roar of the air rushing past the hatch was deafening.

"See you on the ground," Hyun-Jin mouthed. He pushed off through the hatch, kicking off from the rim to get above the ATV. There wasn't enough air pressure at this altitude to catch a chute, so he free-fell, traveling with the ATV towards Earth.

Josephine's eyes were wider than Claire had ever seen them. Clear white all the way around the midnight-blue irises. They'd learned how to use parachutes as part of the astronaut training, but that had been under optimal conditions, with a fully functional plane and solid ground below.

"Go!" Claire shouted over the roar of the air. She waved Josephine through the hatch.

Pressing her lips together so hard they turned white, Josephine nodded and jumped.

Claire pointed for Mutsuo and Zhang to go next.

Mutsuo went without comment, businesslike in his motions and with only an instant's hesitation at the hatch.

Zhang saluted her with two fingers against his brow before he jumped.

"Thirteen thousand feet," Anderson shouted, unbuckling the harness that held him in the pilot's seat. "We've got to go."

Fear clenched Claire's sphincter. She'd hated the parachute training, every jump. But it was jump—or die.

"You first," she shouted.

Anderson's hands fumbled over his gear. Then he climbed up the handholds to the hatch, looked outside for a moment. He held his hand out to her. "Come with me."

Claire couldn't hear him over the wind, but she read his lips. Checking that her straps were tight and her pull cords accessible, Claire climbed up to where he stood. They faced each other, gripping each other's forearms.

When she felt him tense, Claire jumped.

They fell into a cloud. Everything was white and damp. Claire couldn't see a thing. She'd lost her grip on Anderson and flailed wildly, losing her perspective of where the ground, the ATV, and her crewmates were. "Anderson!" she shouted at the top of her lungs, but couldn't even hear her own voice over the rush of wind.

A hole opened up in the cloud beneath Claire and she saw dark blue water. Not a good sign. Shallow ocean water was blue-green. Zhang's tampering had cast them into the middle of the cold, barren Atlantic Ocean. There were thousands of empty square miles between them and land, and no recovery vessel.

Breathing deeply to control her fear, Claire opened her arms and legs into skydiving position, maximizing her drag on the air. The ATV tumbled off to her left, and Claire used the little she knew about shifting her weight and changing her falling profile to move farther from it. She didn't want to hit its steaming hull on the way down.

In the rush of air, Claire thought she heard her name. She craned her head wildly, looking for any of her crewmates, but saw no one. It might have been her imagination.

Lightning lit up the cloud to her left, and Claire realized she was falling through one of the summer storms that arose so quickly in Florida. Please, she prayed silently to a God she didn't believe in, please, let me live to see my boy.

Claire checked the altimeter clipped to the front of her flight suit. She counted off twenty-eight seconds and pulled the cord to release her main chute. The drag hit her like a front-end collision, slamming her forward against her harness and knocking the wind from her chest.

She looked around again through the cloud, hoping to see the blue and red of another NASA canopy. There—to her left and above her. A flash of red. It might be Zhang's parachute, with its Chinese insignia, or Mutsuo's rising sun. The cloud between her and the other flyer lessened, revealing the NASA stars and jets.

Claire shouted and waved.

The other flyer waved back.

She wasn't alone. From this distance she couldn't make out whether it was Josephine, Hyun-Jin, or Anderson. It didn't matter—she was glad to no longer be alone.

Claire popped beneath the cloud layer with only a thousand feet between her and the whitecaps. She recalled her training on water landings. The most important thing was not to get tangled up in the chute. She needed to hit the water with her chute behind her and drop it before its nylon folds could encase her and drag her under.

Claire pulled the steering toggles to angle her chute. She bicycled her legs, as if she planned to run along the tops of the whitecaps. Cold salt spray blew into her mouth, acrid and alive with the taste of seaweed.

When her feet touched cold water, Claire pulled the cutaway handle to release her chute. She dropped like a stone into the sea, and submerged. For a panicky instant Claire was covered by ocean; she couldn't see, and her clothes dragged at her as she tried to swim to the surface. Three months of living in space had left her muscles weak and her mind unused to the concepts of up and down. She floundered. It was not fair—*not fair*—to have survived so much, come so far, and die by drowning. Claire's right hand fumbled at the front of her flight suit, found the flat ribbon attached to the side, and pulled.

Air canisters in the life vest built into her flight suit inflated the vest and pushed against her ears. She was above water now, and took a shuddering, gulping breath of air. After the tang of salt and fear, it was sweeter than cotton candy. The second breath followed fast on the first.

Claire bobbed on the waves as wind from the summer storm whipped them into whitecaps. A spattering of fat round drops hit the top of her head and streamed down her face. Claire licked the rain and seawater from her mouth and shouted: "Anderson, Josephine, Hyun-Jin, Zhang, anyone? Can you hear me?"

Her ears were still ringing from the roar of skydiving. Thunder rolled across the waves and lightning lit the sky.

"I'm here!" Claire shouted again. She waited, ear pricked for a reply. The cold water already set her teeth to chattering.

A muffled sound that might have been a seagull—but there were no birds flying in this gale. The sound came again: "Claire!"

It was Anderson. He was low in the water, waving with his right hand. He hadn't inflated his life vest.

Claire waved back, then bent forward to swim to him. It was awkward, maneuvering around the life vest. Her arms and legs felt leaden, pushing against the water after months of free fall.

She was puffing by the time she reached him. "Inflate your vest," she said, pointing at her own.

Anderson shook his head. "Ripped when I popped my chute." A wave crested over his head and he spluttered. "Won't hold air."

"Share mine." Claire held out her arm to grab him.

Anderson clasped her hand and pulled close to Claire, clutching at her shoulders to keep his head above water. His boyish face was gray and his eyes were wide. For the first time since she'd met him, Anderson looked frankly scared.

His weight overloaded the life vest, and they both began to sink. Claire sputtered as her nose sank below the surface.

Anderson let go. "Too heavy." He glanced around desperately.

There was nothing that could help them. No floating driftwood, no other crew members to share flotation, no nearby shoreline. Even the parachutes, that would have held air for some time, had sunk between the waves.

They were lost in the middle of the Atlantic Ocean with no hope of rescue. Just Anderson, Claire, and a single life vest.

CHAPTER 18

Anderson trod water. Blood trickled down his forehead from where the salt water had reopened his scalp wound. "Remember when I said I never wanted to come between you and saving your boy—here I am."

"Conserve your energy," Claire said. "Do a self-rescue float." She dug in the side pocket of her life vest until her fingers found four slender cylinders. She pulled out a flare, tugged the cord to fire it, pointing high overhead.

The flare lit with a pop, shooting a ball trailing orange smoke high into the sky. The growing winds tore the line of smoke into streamers.

"It's no use," Anderson said. "There isn't anyone looking for us." He wiped blood and salt spray from his face. "We're going to die out here."

Claire grabbed the straps of his parachute harness and dragged him close to her. "No, we *aren't*." Overloaded, her life vest submerged. She sputtered bitter salt water. Claire slipped under the waves, Anderson's hand on her head. A primal urge for air gripped her. Claire clawed her way along his body, pushing him down in her fight for the surface.

Coughing, Anderson broke the surface, an arm's distance away. His hair was plastered to his forehead under the fitted cap of his parachute gear. "Your life vest can't support us both."

"Then we'll take turns," Claire said, reaching for the clips on her chest.

Anderson shook his head. "No. We can't. Sooner or later, one of us will fall asleep. Sometimes there isn't enough to go around. It's what got the planet into this mess. When resources are limited, some people have to die so others can live."

Fear trickled down Claire's spine. She remembered how Anderson had been willing to sacrifice the Chinese crew and the Japanese stations to get home. Her scalp still felt the imprint of his palm, pushing her under the waves as he fought for purchase. She paddled her hands through the water, getting distance from him. Heavy drops fell from the sky. It was beginning to rain.

"It's always been this way," Anderson said. There was more water on his cheeks than the ocean spray and storm could account for. "You want to live—so do I."

"No," she said, tensing for his attack. "When night comes, we'll pull the lights on our vests. A plane will see us."

Anderson went under the waves again and came up spluttering three feet away. "You don't get it. This isn't the world we left. Houston is gone. There's no ground support, no Coast Guard looking for us. There won't be a plane."

"We can help each other," Claire called to him over the rising wind.

Anderson disappeared behind another swell. When the wave crested, he was gone.

"Anderson!" Claire swam towards where she'd last seen him. Visibility was low in the now-driving rain. "Anderson!" Her voice was faint against the pelting rain and the crashing waves. "Anderson!" She flailed around in frustration. "Anderson!"

Her hand brushed something like hair beneath the water. Her breath caught. When she reached for it again, her life vest's buoyancy kept her on the surface. Anderson might be drowning, he might be a threat. She had only seconds to act. "Goddamn it!" she swore at the punishing sky. With numb fingers she unlatched the catch on her life vest. Clutching the vest in her left hand, she sank below the waves, groping with her right.

There. Silky strands slipped through her fingers. She grabbed at them, but they dropped lower. Claire couldn't reach them without letting go of her life vest.

Claire was more afraid than she'd been in her life. Her lungs burned for air and the weight of water all around her was smothering. She had only seconds to act before Anderson was lost forever.

She let go of the life vest.

Claire kicked towards the bottom of the ocean, both hands extended, feeling her way through dark water. Her pulse pounded in her ears. Fingers touched something solid. She grabbed. Kicked for the surface with all her might. Gulped sweet-tasting air, gasping it in until she was drunk with oxygen.

In her hands were filaments of seaweed.

Claire looked around desperately, seeking fluorescent orange through the haze of gray sky and blue swells. Like Anderson, her life vest was gone.

Claire swam to the top of a wave, hoping to sight it. Nothing but churning surf as far as she could see: no land, no boats, no other astronauts, no life vest.

She felt for the inner pocket of her flight suit. The iodine supplements for Owen were still zipped inside, nestled against her heart. Tears dripped down her face, mingling with the salt spray.

She didn't know what happened to Anderson: whether he'd stolen her life vest, chosen to drown, or been dragged under the waves. But he was right: They were going to die out here.

"Owen," she blubbered, treading water. "I'm so sorry. I tried. I tried so hard."

Exhausted beyond reason, Claire ler her rescue training take over. She floated face down in the water, lifting her head to breath, conserving her energy. Periodically, she rolled onto her back and floated, staring up at the empty, darkening sky.

The sun set in a three-hundred-sixty-degree panorama of

burning oranges, orchids, and dusky purple. She'd never seen a sunset so vivid. It reminded her of accounts of the magnificent sunsets after Krakatoa erupted.

When the sun dropped over the horizon, the air turned cold. She bobbed up and down on the waves, the stars her only companions. Claire began to shiver. She drifted in and out of consciousness, waking up choking on seawater and when something brushed past her leg.

It was then Claire remembered sharks hunted at night. And Anderson's sudden disappearance under the waves. She jerked her legs up to her body, started to sink, then turned on her back to float, forcing her breath into a slow, even rhythm.

There were no lights on the horizon. No glow over Orlando or Daytona Beach. Anderson was right. There wouldn't be a rescue plane. She had survived space and reentry only to drown hundreds of miles from the people she loved.

Owen looked ethereal under the plastic incubator of the ICU. Twin clear tubes piped oxygen to his nostrils, IV bags trailed fluids and medicine into his veins, and a catheter removed waste.

Larry, the gator-hunting oncologist, had been a surprisingly large, soft man. Like a quarterback gone to fat, but with dark, intelligent eyes. He ran the tent hospital on the north side of town. He'd taken Betty into care, but insisted that Owen be taken to Children's, where there was a pediatric intensive care unit.

Matt had agonized over leaving his mother in the hands of strangers, but she insisted that he take care of Owen first.

Rubber-soled footsteps made Matt turn. It was Dr. Aversano, the oncologist consulting on Owen's case. He was a slender man with a beaked nose. There were dark circles under his deep-set eyes. The children's ICU was filled with cases of radiation poisoning.

Owen writhed in his sleep. "Ma-maaa," he cried, drawing the last syllable out into a wail. "Ma-maaa."

"Can't you do anything for him?" Matt pleaded.

The oncologist shook his head. "He's on as much pain

medication as I dare give him. Any more could suppress respiration."

Matt's gut twisted in response to Owen's pain. "Is he?" he whispered. "Is he going to be all right?"

The oncologist sighed, removed his glasses, and rubbed the bridge of his nose. Putting his glasses back on, he said, "We've done all for him that we can. Sometimes it comes down to a patient's will to live."

The oncologist moved on, to another hushed conversation with a set of parents hovering over another child in a plastic coffin.

Matt leaned over his son and put his hand to the plastic. "Owen, sweetie, shh. It's all right."

"I want Mommy," Owen wailed, arching his back and straining the IV line in his left elbow.

"Shh. Settle down. I need you to stay calm. Give Mommy time to get here. She's hurrying to see you, but it's a long way from space."

Owen turned bloodshot eyes on his father. His face suddenly seemed ancient. The sunken eyes and despair etched in them made him look like an old man. "Mommy's dead." It was a statement of fact.

He lay back, tears leaking out of the corners of his eyes. In a world-weary voice he said, "The sky's gone all black and ugly, and Mommy's dead."

CHAPTER 19

A half-moon rose, blinding her salt-raw eyes.

Claire drifted with the waves. Exhaustion weighed down her limbs. The rocking sensation combined with sleeplessness reminded her of the first few months after Owen had been born. Long nights she had rocked his tiny body, soothing him to sleep with his little head against her chest.

Through salt-cracked lips Claire hummed the opening bars of Brahms' "Lullaby."

He'd been so fragile, so helpless. She'd bent down and kissed his downy head and promised that she would always be there to protect him, keep him safe.

Tears streamed down Claire's face. She felt as helpless as Owen had been. No boat was coming to save her. All she had done, all she had risked, hadn't been enough. Owen still lay sick, possibly dying. The possibility that she might only be a few miles off the coast—less than a hundred miles from her son—made her crazy with frustration. For all her ability to reach him, it might as well have been light-years.

Sobs choked her throat. "Goddamn moon," she cursed it. The ribbon of light unrolled like a highway before her.

Her foot brushed something submerged . . . and big.

Claire sucked in a breath and jerked her foot away. Wrong move. She should have stayed still. If it was a shark, sudden motion might attract it. Claire tried not to hyperventilate, all her attention on her right leg, waiting for an attack, the searing fire of tearing teeth.

She waited to die.

Claire had never been good at waiting. Frustration and anger welled up in her. She'd been scared and afraid of dying too long. This last tension took her beyond endurance. "Come on, you fucker," she dared the shark. She thrashed in the ocean, kicking arms and legs violently. "You want to kill me—come on!"

Nothing happened.

Claire sagged in her rescue float, water covering her face. She lifted her head to breathe.

The moon highway stretched before her, leading west towards the east coast of Florida, and sixty miles beyond that, Lakeland, where Matt and Owen waited. She had no idea whether the ocean currents were with her or against her.

Exhausted, without hope of success, and abandoned by a quick death, Claire began to swim.

It was timeless, the rising and falling of her arms, the scissor motion underwater of her legs. Claire had no idea how long she'd been crawling over and through the waves. The moon rose above her, and Claire kept swimming. It fell behind her, and still she was nothing more than motion, without thought, without emotion, without hope. Each breath filled eternity.

Claire was so focused on swimming, she didn't hear the shouts until her hand struck wood.

"Who are you?" a man's voice asked. He shined a flashlight in Claire's face.

She lifted her hand to block the light. The motion raised her arm, making visible the NASA emblem on her upper arm.

"Holy shit." The man crouched lower in his boat to stop it rocking. "I think it's an astronaut," he said over his shoulder. To Claire: "You an astronaut?"

"I'm Claire Logan." Her mouth was so dry from salt water and exertion that it came out as a whispered croak. The man leaned closer and she whispered it again.

The light crawled across her face. "*The* Claire Logan? The one on the radio?"

Claire didn't know what he was talking about. She grabbed the edge of the boat. "Help me."

Strong hands grabbed her armpits and lifted her into a flat-bottomed rowboat. Claire's body felt leaden as they lowered her onto the floor of the boat. Rough fingers held a Nalgene bottle to her lips. Water had never tasted so sweet. Claire drank until the thirty-two-ounce bottle was empty. She licked her cracked lips. "Thank you."

"Say: 'This is Claire Logan of *Reliance* Station,' " said the first man. In the dim dawn light she saw a week's worth of beard beneath wire-rimmed glasses.

Claire repeated the words.

The man broke into a grin. He looked up at the man with the water bottle. "Ho-lee shit! It *is* her! The real Claire Logan." He grinned and pumped her hand. "I'm honored to meet you, ma'am."

"Wha—what's going on?" Claire searched from face to face. In the days of Apollo, astronauts were celebrities, but in the modern era of routine space flight, only the most devoted of space enthusiasts knew their names.

"Your radio transmission, over ham radio. It was the first information about the bombs. I must have heard it a dozen times. The land-based stations picked it up. There's no satellite communications, and the local stations had no idea what was going on—you were the only one telling the truth. The government wouldn't tell us anything until your broadcast came out. National guardsmen moved in. They wouldn't say what was going on. Some people thought terrorists had hit Disney World; others thought it was an industrial accident. We didn't even know we were at war. No one told us how bad the country had been hit—until you."

Claire looked up at the lightening sky from her vantage point in the well of the boat. "Aren't you worried about fallout?"

The man with the bottle shrugged as he screwed the cap back on. "Some. But with all the radiation we've taken so far, not sure a little more will hurt. Plus, the Gulf Stream keeps bringing in clean air from the Atlantic."

"And if we're going to die," the first one said, "might

as well go out fishing." He held out his hand again. "I'm Bob Richardson."

"Aaron Wells," said the other man, stowing the bottle in a cooler.

Claire shook Bob's hand. "Thank you. Thank you for saving me. Have you seen anyone else on the water?"

Bob and Aaron looked confused. Aaron nodded at the waves. "There's more of you out there?"

"Six of us left the station," Claire said. "I'm not sure how many of the others survived."

Aaron squinted up at the fading stars. "If you were safe up there, why come back to this hellhole?"

Claire rubbed her tired eyes, thinking of all the ways to answer him: the Argus effect, low supplies, and inhospitable space. What she said was, "Family. I have family here."

Aaron and Bob took turns rowing and calling across the water. They saw one other fishing boat, also oar-powered, but no astronauts.

Guilt gnawed at Claire. I can't be the only one who survived, she thought.

The sun was high in the sky when Aaron shook his head sadly. "If they're out there, we're not going to find them. Best thing is to tell the Coast Guard—what's left of them—to keep an eye out."

Claire nodded. She could do nothing for the others except pray. But Matt and Owen, she needed to see them, to tell them she was alive. "How far are we from Lakeland? My little boy was sick; he'd be in a hospital. I have to get to him."

Aaron removed the baseball cap from his head and scratched his thinning hair. "That's Melbourne. It's what, forty miles to Lakeland? But you'll have to take back roads. The highways are all clogged with cars." He lowered his voice. "And corpses."

Bob shook his head as he dug a beer out of the cooler. "Best way is to get her to the National Guard. They've been setting up emergency hospitals all over the state. Most likely your boy is at one of those."

Lieutenant Greerson of the National Guard was less impressed with Claire than Bob and Aaron had been. A bulky six-foot-two, he scowled at her from behind a portable desk that held a laptop and a cup of coffee. "You're the Claire Logan on the transmission? The one that panicked the populace?"

Claire needed his help to find Matt and Owen. "That wasn't my intention, sir. I was trying to help—"

"Your 'help' caused panic and looting. Three of my men were shot trying to defend a sporting goods store."

Claire licked her lips. Perhaps coming to the Guard was a mistake. She wondered if it was too late to slip away, to try to make it overland to Matt's mother's house. "I'm sorry. If you want me to rebroadcast a new message, ask people to calm down and cooperate, I'd be happy to. But right now I need to find my son. Please, he's only four years old. He's sick and he needs me."

Greerson continued to scowl. He dragged the laptop and punched keys. The portable desk shook with the force of his typing.

"Sir," a sergeant burst through the tent flap, his hat askew and eyes wild. He pointed over his shoulder, "We've got a—"

"What's this interruption?" Greerson's brows drew together.

Before the sergeant could answer, two men burst into the tent. Between them was a struggling captive. He resisted them, refusing to stand. They dragged him on his knees and deposited him in the middle of the room. One of the men drew a gun and aimed it at the captive's head.

The captive raised his head, anger flashing from his black eyes.

"We caught this spy—"

"Zhang!" Claire pushed aside the man with the gun and knelt next to the Chinese commander. She grabbed him by his shoulders and shook him until his teeth rattled. "I nearly drowned because of you. I think Anderson *is* dead. What about Josephine, Hyun-Jin, Mutsuo, did they make it?"

"Commander Logan," said Zhang. His cultured tones were thick through his swollen upper lip. His wrists were lashed together with cable ties that dug into his golden skin. "It is good to see you alive." He shook his head sadly, exposing bruises on his left cheek and temple. "I do not know about the others."

Greerson came from behind his desk and stood over them. He squinted at the Chinese emblem on Zhang's sleeve. "You know this man?"

"He's a spy—or a downed reconnaissance pilot," the sergeant said breathlessly. "We pulled him out of the water near Fort Pierce."

"He's *not* a spy," Claire spat at the sergeant. She turned to Greerson. "He's an *astronaut,* like me. He and his crew helped *Reliance* when we were damaged. He's no more your enemy than *I* am."

Greerson raised an eyebrow. "That cuts both ways, Logan. Maybe you were working with the Chinese, trying to spread panic with your broadcast."

The man with the gun had it pointed again, this time at Claire.

Claire was outraged. "Are you going to shoot me? Is that what America has come to—shoot first and ask questions later?"

"This is a military situation, we can't—"

Claire stood up and pointed at the crumpled figure of Zhang. "Does he look like a threat? This man has spent months living in zero-gee. He can barely stand, let alone bring down a battalion. Without satellite communications, he can't even tell his government he's alive, much less send them sensitive information. He's an astronaut, a specialist in materials science."

Greerson looked from her to Zhang.

"The space stations didn't have anything to do with the war. We were as much victims as you were. The reason we bailed out is that the radiation from the nuclear explosions was spreading into space. If Zhang's crew were expecting the war, they would have evacuated before the first bomb fell." She pointed at a radio in the corner of the tent. "If you don't believe me, contact your superiors. They'll tell you we weren't involved."

Greerson followed her gaze. He dismissed the privates and the sergeant with a wave. "I'll handle this."

When they were gone, he squatted next to Zhang. "Is what she says true? Did you help American astronauts?"

Zhang's golden eyes blinked. "Yes."

Greerson bounced on his heels. "We'd just blown up your country. Why would you do that?"

Zhang looked into Greerson's eyes, perfectly still. "Because it was the right thing to do."

Greerson snorted, pulled a pocketknife out of his back pocket, and sliced the cable ties around Zhang's wrists. "My grandfather was a fighter pilot in World War II. When he bailed out over Okinawa, his parachute got stuck in a tree. He hung there, feet over head, until he passed out. A Japanese family cut him down and gave him food. Afterwards he asked why: 'Because it was the proper thing,' they said." Greerson stood. "I guess we're even." He pointed the knife at Claire. "That doesn't mean that if he does anything suspicious, I won't have him shot. I'm releasing him into your custody, Logan. See that he behaves." He folded the knife and slipped it into his back pocket. "And keep him close. I've already had to court-martial five privates for beating up Chinese immigrants. A lot of people have lost family; they're looking for someone to blame."

Zhang stood shakily and rubbed the chafed red lines on his wrists. "Thank you."

"What about central command?" Claire asked. "Can you contact them and arrange a flight home for him?"

Greerson shook his head. "Might as well ask for a flight to the moon. I haven't got a signal from FEMA in three days. Best I can do is have a man fly you and your sidekick around to the local field hospitals. You can look for your son." His face was grave. "Got to tell you, though, so many people are hurt, I can't imagine you'll find him."

Claire nodded, her eyes full of tears of fear and gratitude. She pumped Greerson's arm. "Thank you, sir. God bless you."

Greerson glanced at the closed tent flap. "Just tell me . . . when you were up there looking at the damage and where the bombs fell"—his voice thickened to a hoarse whisper—"how was Minnesota?"

Downtown Orlando was a black crater. Claire could see it off to the right as the helicopter flew her west, towards Lakeland. Flattened utility poles spread out from the blast zone like obscene petals. Skyscrapers had tumbled into piles of rubble, and here and there cars had been tossed like dying fish on dry ground.

They traveled away from the impact zone, crossing over I-4. As Greerson had said, it was glutted with cars whose tires had melted to the asphalt during the subsequent wave of heat and light.

Claire held Zhang's hand, crushing it between her own as each new landscape told the tale of horrors she had only guessed about from orbit. That Matt and Owen had survived was miraculous. She prayed for another miracle: to find them.

Lakeland was a sprawling suburb community nestled between Tampa and Orlando. It was far enough away from the impact zone to be largely intact. They dipped low over downtown and Claire saw landmarks from her visits to Matt's mother: the 1920s Polk Theatre still stood, though its neon marquee was unlit and broken glass littered the sidewalk. Plywood over the lobby windows hinted at looting.

Few cars crawled the streets. Claire spotted four men carrying rifles over their shoulders and toting canvas sacks in their free hand. They jogged down the street. When they ducked into an alley, Claire saw each wore a bandanna over their nose and mouth, whether as a precaution against radioactive dust or to avoid identification, Claire couldn't say.

"What kind of world have we come home to?" she asked no one in particular.

"A world designed by our fears," Zhang said, patting her clasped hands, "and our hatred."

Matt's mother lived in the Lake Hollingsworth neighborhood. Few cars were parked on the street. No lights were on, no TVs illuminated, flickering blue light against filmy curtains. No one was out watering flowers or clipping the lawn. Smoke rose from a few houses with decorative chimneys, a frivolous luxury turned necessity.

Claire leaned over the pilot's shoulder and directed him through the winding streets to the house Betty had lived in since her husband's death. It was a low-slung brick ranch house with an orange tree in the front yard, surrounded by larger two-story houses.

The helicopter put down in the street, whipping the orange tree's branches with its backwash. Claire climbed down from the helicopter and gasped.

The front door hung from the bottom hinge. The lock had been shot off, probably by a twelve-gauge shotgun. Claire ran inside.

The kitchen had been ransacked. The cupboards were open, utensils scattered on the floor from upended drawers, dishes broken in the sink. All the food was gone, as was the bottled water dispenser that normally sat by the fridge.

"Matt!" Claire called, as she wandered through the small ranch house. "Owen? Betty?"

The furniture in the living room was broken. The couch lay boneless and dissected in the middle of the room, green velour mixed in with bushels of stuffing and springs. It took Claire a minute to realize what she was seeing: the wooden frame of the couch, the TV cabinet—all the wooden furniture was gone.

The back bedroom was the same: the dresser was gone, the clothes in a heap on the floor, mattress propped against the wall. No one was there.

A wailing from behind the leaning mattress made her heart stop. Claire lunged and pulled it away from the wall: "Owen?"

Clarabelle looked up at her with golden-green eyes. She was the Siamese cat Matt had bought his mother for her birthday. She put her paws up on the mattress and yowled again.

Claire picked up the cat and buried her face in its fur. Hot tears ran down her cheeks. She'd been so scared—so hopeful—that she'd found Owen. The cat wriggled against the tight embrace and Claire relaxed her grip. Clarabelle climbed onto her shoulders, licked the salt off Claire's cheek, and settled into a machine-gun purr.

Claire scritched Clarabelle behind the ears. She remembered when Matt had given Clarabelle to his mother. Owen had been three. His face lit up when he saw the "kit-tee" and he'd patted the kitten's fur with reverential awe.

A motion caught her eye. It was Zhang in the doorway. "Your family is not here?"

Claire shook her head. She walked out into the garage. The non-power tools were gone, as was the shotgun Matt's father had owned. But what she was looking for was still there. Claire edged around Betty's car to pull the beige cat carrier from under an acrylic storage container filled with holiday decorations.

Before Clarabelle could catch on, Claire had the carrier down and the cat safely ensconced.

Cat in hand, Claire knocked at the house next door. There was no answer. Nor at the other three houses she tried. The neighborhood was deserted, either ransacked by looters or—she hoped—evacuated by the National Guard.

The helicopter pilot shook his head when Claire climbed on board with the cat carrier. "I'm not authorized—"

Claire leaned close and shouted over the noise of the helicopter. "This is all the family I've found so far. The cat's coming with us."

The helicopter pilot blew out a breath, looked at the copilot, who shrugged, and then nodded. He gestured them back to the cargo area and lifted the helicopter into the air.

The emergency hospital was set up on the baseball field of Lakeland Middle School, four sixty-foot-long tents surrounded a courtyard of stretchers. The helicopter set down in the school's parking lot. The breeze from it flapped the canvas, causing medics and patients to crane their heads at the newcomers.

Claire stepped down, shielding her face from the gravel kicked up by the helicopter. Zhang followed close behind, toting the Siamese's carrier.

A harried-looking woman in green fatigues met them at the edge of the ball field. She carried a clipboard, and there was a Red Cross badge on her arm. She pointed at the carrier. "You can't bring an animal into the hospital." She looked suspiciously at Zhang, still in his Chinese taikonaut uniform.

"I'll wait here," Zhang said, setting the cat's box on the ground.

"You sure?" Claire asked. The female medic wouldn't be the only one curious about Zhang.

Zhang noted her glance at his insignia. "I am sure. But perhaps you could loan me your jacket?"

Claire handed him the hunting jacket she'd been given by Bob and Aaron when they transported her to shore. He looked absurdly festive in the red-and-black checked flannel, sitting next to a Siamese cat.

The medic was already walking back to the hospital. Claire ran to catch up with her. "I'm looking for my family. They're from the Hollingsworth Hill neighborhood. They might have been brought here."

The woman handed Claire the clipboard. "Knock yourself out." It held eleven pages filled with handwritten names. "It's our admittance list. The ones struck through, didn't make it. Need it back when you're done. It's our only record."

They were at the periphery of the hospital now. Groans rose from the patients lying on cots under the tents. The smell of charred flesh and putrefaction hit Claire like a blow. There were bandages everywhere, wrapping faces, hands, covering the legs that ended just below the knee.

The medic moved among them, adjusting IVs, checking bandages for seepage, taking pulses. At one cot she pulled the sheet over the patient's face and motioned for two men in army fatigues to help her move the body.

Radiation burns were everywhere, scattered across damaged human flesh. A little girl with the hair half-burned from her face whimpered and tried to nestle under the arm of an unresponsive woman.

The sight made Claire sick. She turned and ran from the hospital. At the edge of the encampment, she bent double and vomited. Fell to her knees and heaved until her stomach was empty.

"Hey, now!" The female medic snatched the clipboard from Claire. "Careful with that. I told you it was our only record."

Claire wiped her mouth on her sleeve. "I'm looking for my mother-in-law, my husband, and my son. Last name Logan. Can you help me?"

The medic scanned the sheet, crossed off a couple of names. "We've got an Elisabeth Logan."

Claire's heart leapt. "That's my mother-in-law. What about a Matt Logan, or Owen?"

The medic scanned further. "Nope. Just Betty." She pointed to the other side of the courtyard. "She's in tent three."

Matt's mother lay on an army cot. Her face was red and blistered, and her hands were bandaged.

Claire knelt beside the cot, ignoring the moans and whimpers all around her. "Betty. It's me, Claire. Can you hear me?"

Betty Logan's eyes opened a fraction. "Water," she moaned through cracked lips.

Claire grabbed a disposable cup from a stand near the tent's upright and filled it with water. She brought the cup and held it to Betty's lips.

More water dribbled from the corner of her mouth than went in, but Betty sighed with relief.

"Where are Matt and Owen?" Claire asked, her lips close to Betty's ear.

Betty's eyes widened. "Claire? Here?"

A lump formed in Claire's throat. The old woman had been so vital. Seeing her in this state was almost unbearable. "Yes. I promised Matt I'd come home."

Betty tried to sit up, her bandaged hands fumbling against the frame of the cot.

Claire eased her back down. "Shh. It's all right. Tell me where Matt and Owen are."

Tears flowed down Betty's seamed cheeks. "Owen, so sick. The worst of us. So little. So little."

Claire's own tears rose and she could hardly breathe. "Is he . . . where is he?"

"Children's," the old woman whispered. "Matt took him to Children's Hospital."

Claire kissed the old woman's forehead gently. "Then that's where we're going." She waved a nearby medic over. "I want her ready to transport."

"Mr. Logan," the nurse said softly. She was a middle-aged Hispanic woman in raspberry-colored scrubs.

Matt was in the waiting room, holding Janice's hand. Dozens of other families: mothers, fathers, siblings, aunts, uncles, cousins, lined the walls. When the nurse came in they all looked up. When she called Matt's name they returned to magazines, whispered conversations, and the occasional game of solitaire. He'd wanted to stay in the ICU with Owen, but the nurse had insisted he wait here. And now she had come for him. The sight of her filled him with dread.

"Is he awake?" Matt asked hopefully.

"No." The nurse's expression was grave. "Dr. Aversano said he doesn't have long left." At Matt's stricken expression she touched his arm. "I'm sorry. I thought . . . you and your wife have should a chance to say good-bye."

Matt didn't correct her perception of Janice. Still holding onto Janice's hand, he followed the nurse up to ICU.

Owen looked like he was made of milk glass. His skin was so pale Matt could see veins in his neck and cheek. Each breath took seconds and grated against Owen's throat. There were flecks of blood on his pillow.

Matt gestured at the top of the ICU enclosure. "May I?"

The nurse, her eyes soft with sympathy, lifted off the plastic cover. "I'll be at the desk." She left Matt alone with his dying son.

Matt leaned over Owen and kissed his forehead. The boy's skin was hot and felt as dry as tissue paper. Tears dripped from Matt's nose, and he wiped angrily at them. He took up his son's hand. "You've got to hang in there, buddy. You've got to fight it. Daddy loves you. Daddy—" His voice choked off. Matt couldn't say anymore. He sat holding Owen's hand, shaking silently. He wouldn't let the last sounds his son heard be his father's tears.

Warm arms wrapped around Matt's shoulders, hugging him. A head nestled on his shoulder. He turned his head and saw not Claire, but a miracle of another sort: Janice.

With his free hand he returned her hug. "I can't do this," he whispered. "I can't say good-bye. I'm a failure. What kind of father can't protect his son?"

Tears fell from Janice's eyes. "You're a great father," she whispered back. "You did everything you could."

"You're my rock," he told her. "You didn't have to help me. I couldn't have made it this far without you." He ruffled her hair.

They sat in silence for a while, listening to Owen's struggling breaths.

The helicopter pilot shook his head when Claire directed the medics to load Matt's mother into the cargo area. "Sorry, ma'am," he shouted. "Greerson's ordered me back to base. This is as far as I can take you."

Claire cupped her hand over her ear. "What?" She climbed up into the cockpit.

"I can't take you to Children's Hospital," the pilot repeated. "Greerson's called me back."

Claire leaned over the pilot until they were nose to nose. "Do you know how far I've come to see my son? Do you know what I've had to endure, how many of my friends have died?"

"I'm really sorry—" He broke off.

Claire pulled the pistol from his side holster and held it in his face. The copilot made a move for his gun and Claire swiveled to face him and relieved him of his weapon. "I don't want to hurt you." She swung the pistol back to cover the pilot. "Either of you. But we *are* going to Children's Hospital and I *am* going to see my son. Do you understand?"

Both pilots nodded, white-faced.

She nodded towards the back of the helicopter where Zhang was settling Mrs. Logan's stretcher into the cargo area. "That Chinaman and I are astronauts; we could fly this helicopter in our sleep. So consider yourself expendable, and act accordingly." She unplugged the handset from the radio and tucked it into her pants pocket. "After I see Owen, Greerson can arrest me." Keeping the gun on the cockpit, she said, "Now fly."

The helicopter lifted off and turned south.

Once they were airborne, Zhang whispered in her ear, "I've never trained on a helicopter."

In a tone too soft to carry to the cockpit, Claire replied: "Neither have I."

Children's Hospital looked remarkably untouched. Only the open windows and the cluster of wheelbarrows and bicycles outside the front door gave any indication that it had been touched by the disaster.

The helicopter touched down on the roof helipad. A team of emergency room doctors and nurses rushed out, gurney at the ready, and unloaded Mrs. Logan. Claire shouted to them what she knew of her wounds. Zhang stepped off the helicopter with the cat.

"Give Greerson my regards," Claire shouted to the pilot

and waved him off. Both guns were stuck in the waistband of her pants. When the EMTs were busy loading Mrs. Logan into the elevator, she handed one to Zhang. "Just in case," she mouthed.

A raspberry-garbed nurse blocked Claire and Zhang from the elevator with an upraised hand. "Generator's running low on fuel. Emergency use only." She pointed to the stairwell. "We walk."

Claire and Zhang, carrying Clarabelle, followed the nurse into the stairwell. It was an anthill of activity: orderlies carrying boxes of supplies, patients in hospital gowns toting IV stands, white-coated doctors shouting orders.

"Where's the ICU?" Claire asked.

"Floor eight, west wing," the nurse said. "Your mother will be in the emergency ward." If she noticed the cat Zhang carried, she made no comment.

Windows were open and battery-operated fans were clipped to counters and gurneys to keep air flowing through the stifling corridors. A boy on crutches hobbled down the hallway, helped by a smaller boy whose chest was bandaged. The shrieking of an inconsolable infant was muffled behind an ICU glass barrier. Not Owen. She would know his cry anywhere, always had.

Up ahead, an impossible sight: Matt carrying a pitcher of water.

Claire broke into a run. She grabbed him around the neck, nearly toppling the pitcher of water. She kissed his face half a dozen times. "Where's Owen?"

Matt steadied the water, and looked at her, dazed. "Claire? Is it really you?" His face was gaunt, with dark purple bruises under his eyes. Several days' worth of beard stubbled his cheeks. He looked as if all hope had been extinguished.

"Owen?" Claire pleaded. Let it not be too late. Please God. Let me see my son.

Matt nodded at the room he'd been about to enter.

The door was propped open to let air flow. Inside were six hospital beds. Claire's eyes skimmed the children: two girls, a toddler, a boy with a broken leg, and—oh, God, so still, in the last bed—Owen.

She flew to his side and clutched his tiny body to her

chest. He was still warm. Tears flowed down her cheeks and dripped off her chin. "Owen, Owen, Owen." The crooning wail became a chant. Don't be dead, she prayed. She cooed the words that she'd soothed him with as an infant: "Mama's here. It's all right, Owen-baby. Mama's here." He felt so light in her arms. Claire felt her heart burst; she'd come too late.

A translucent eyelid fluttered open. "Ma-ma?"

Claire pulled Owen back to look at him. Joy streamed through her, despite Owen's frailty, despite all that had happened. She held her baby boy in her arms. "Yes, baby, Mama's here."

His face was so pale, veins showed through at his bridge of his nose and his temple. "Mama, if you're here . . . am I in heaven?"

Claire crushed him to her chest again and rocked him. "No, sweetie, but I am. I'm so glad to see you." Maternal love, a well that could never run dry, overflowed in Claire and ran down her cheeks. "I love you, Owen. I love you so much. Everything's going to be all right now. I'll never leave you again."

Owen pushed away so he could look at her. "Promise?"

She met his blue eyes with all seriousness. "I promise." Then she waved Zhang over. She took the cat carrier from him and placed it on Owen's bed. "Look who else is here: Clarabelle."

Owen, his face dappled with subcutaneous bruises and balding where his hair had fallen out in patches, broke into a grin like sunlight through clouds. He poked his fingers through the grate in the front of the carrier and Clarabelle rubbed her cheeks against them.

A coughing fit took Owen, and Claire moved the cat to help him sit up and tap his back. She was horrified to see blood fleck his lips when he subsided on the bed. "Mama, what's going to happen now?"

Claire cradled her son's head on her lap and stroked wisps of hair off his brow. "Now that we're together, we'll make it better. You and I and Daddy, and all the other families. We'll make it better together."

Owen sighed, as if that made sense, and closed his eyes.

Claire watched, made sure he was still breathing, and lowered his head to the pillow. She went outside the room, past the children in the beds and the knowing eyes of their parents. In the hallway, the storm she had held off so long overtook her. Claire fell to her knees sobbing. Pressed her forehead against the linoleum floor and bit back a wail.

Cardamom-scented hands pulled her off the floor and into an embrace. "Shush," said a deep voice. "Shush." Zhang rocked Claire as she had rocked Owen.

As she cried into his shoulder, Claire wondered why it wasn't Matt.

When her tears subsided enough for her to draw a shuddering breath, Claire looked up and saw Matt staring at her. He held the hand of a woman with dirty-blond hair braided into twin ponytails. They both wore jeans spattered with mud and looked like they'd been through a war together. And they had.

The woman tried to pull her hand free, but Matt held on. They exchanged a glance, speaking without words. As Claire had been able to do with Matt . . . years ago. "I didn't think you'd make it back," Matt said.

Claire untangled herself from Zhang and wiped her face. "Obviously." She took a step closer to the woman. "You helped Matt save my son?"

The woman nodded. "I'm a nurse. My sister's a neighbor of your mother-in-law. Matt came over in the middle of the night—Owen and his mother were sick—I've been helping him. Owen—your son—needed ICU care, so Matt and I, we—"

Claire held out her hand.

The other woman flinched, then looked down at the proffered handshake. Tentatively, she accepted Claire's grip.

Claire pulled her into a hug. "Thank you for helping Owen." She let go and passed the woman's hand back to Matt. "It's been a long journey. We'll figure out the rest tomorrow."

Claire wiped her face on her sleeve, arranged her hair, and went back into the ward to sit by Owen's bed. She held his pale hand, so delicate it could have been made of pale ashes, and watched her son's chest rise and fall, every breath a victory.

CHAPTER 20

In the three days after Claire arrived at the hospital, Owen continuously gained strength and energy. He was given iodine supplements Claire had brought back from space, but more than that, his mother's return gave Owen the will to live.

Dr. Aversano called it a miracle. Owen continued to lose hair, only golden wisps covering his pink scalp now, but color had come back into his cheeks and he kicked his feet under the hospital blankets and began talking to the little girl in the bed next to him.

"My mommy used to live in the sky," he told her in a breathless ramble. "Then she came back down to live with me."

"She an angel?" the little girl asked. Half her head was swathed in bandages. The left side of her face was unblemished, cornflower-blue eyes above peaches-and-cream skin. "Daddy tells me mama's an angel now." She plucked at her bedsheet. "But she never comes to see me."

In the doorway, holding Owen's breakfast tray, Claire heard the exchange and her heart clenched.

Owen continued in the brutally honest fashion of children. "My mama's not an angel. She's an *astronaut*." The emphasis he placed on the last word clearly indicated his prejudice towards the latter.

Zhang followed her, pushing a cart with trays of food for the other children. The hospital staff was spread so thin that the parents took shifts in the kitchen and helping out the janitorial staff.

Matt's female friend had been absorbed into the nursing staff without a ripple. Claire still didn't know what to make of her. With the clarity of hindsight, Claire realized that her marriage to Matt had been falling apart for years. And really, against the background of the destruction of the United States, what was a little infidelity?

Owen was alive, and getting better. That was all that mattered.

The skin of Zhang's wrists gleamed golden in sunlight streaming in the open window. He dispensed orange juice into paper cups with casual grace. Claire felt guilty she hadn't done more to get him home. Part of her wanted him to stay. He'd been by her side through so much danger and tragedy. He was a comfort. A life-sized good-luck doll.

It was wholly unfair to him. Each day she reveled in seeing Owen grow stronger, he lived not knowing whether his sisters and mother were safe, or even alive, whether his extended family of aunts and cousins had survived the devastation in Shanghai.

From the hallway came a cry of "Wait! You can't—" It was cut off by the clatter of a metal gurney hitting the wall.

Claire crossed the room in three quick strides. She poked her head around the doorjamb.

Two orderlies restrained a mid-forties man in a navy business suit. His pant hems were spattered with mud and one elbow was singed. The man pointed and shouted over his shoulder. "It's her—Claire Logan."

Patients and families camped along the walls turned to look at Claire. A rustling whisper grew.

"You're *that* Claire Logan?" asked the man whose daughter had been talking to Owen.

"All I want is an interview," the man shouted, trying to lunge past the orderly's shoulder. He held up a microphone. Its cord trailed away to a second man, in jeans, with a beard more appropriate to a Harley rider than a radio technician.

"People want to know you're alive. To hear your story," the reporter persisted. "How did you make it down from the space station with no crew return vehicle and no support from Houston?"

"That's enough," the orderly growled. "There are sick people here who need their rest."

"What the people need is *hope*. A hero to believe in," the man shouted over his shoulder as the orderly turned him bodily around and began shoving him towards the stairwell. "Claire! Your words will reach thousands. In days it'll be rebroadcast over the whole country. You were the voice of freedom that told us about the bombs. Everyone wants to know how you survived."

A patient leaning on a crutch opened the stairwell door. The orderly shoved the reporter inside. His assistant, despite his bulk, followed meekly.

"Claire! Give the people your story, something to distract them from the pain and destruction. Come on, Claire!"

Claire looked at the faces that lined the halls: pockmarked with burns from radioactive dust, hollow-eyed from sleeplessness and grief, covered in bandages, dirt, blood, and wisps of hair. Every eye that could open looked at her, every expression curious and hopeful.

Was what she could give them—her story—enough?

Zhang stood behind her, his golden face stoic. The bruises from the beating he'd received from the National Guardsmen were fading to green splotches around his eyes and on his chin.

Then she realized; it wasn't just *her* story.

"Wait!" Claire raised her hand to stop the orderly from closing the stairwell door. "I'll tell you what happened . . ."

There was a collective intake of breath along the corridor. Eyes brightened with anticipation.

Claire put her shoulder around Zhang and drew him forward. "If you interview Commander Zhang as well. He was with me in space. I wouldn't have survived without his help."

*   *   *

Lieutenant Greerson did not look happy. Lines creased his forehead and he glowered at Claire across the doctor's lounge that had been cleared for their meeting. He seemed out of place seated on cracked brown vinyl. In the hospital setting he looked more like college student dressed as a Marine for Halloween than the commander of the southeastern United States. He chewed the end of a pencil so hard Claire was surprised it didn't snap. Greerson removed the pencil and pointed it at Claire. "You had to tell them the Chinaman was a hero?"

Claire remained standing near the door. "I only told the truth."

Greerson waved the pencil through the air, sweeping out territory from the peninsula to the panhandle. "The truth can cause more trouble than a lie. Your story was broadcast coast to coast: Chinese and American astronauts helping each other survive. They picked it up over shortwave in Europe. It may be worldwide by now." He jabbed at Claire. "People are questioning the war. Why we fought the Chinese."

Even though Greerson was ten feet away, Claire recoiled from his violent stab. "Shouldn't they? We've got no oil, just as if we hadn't gone to war—only sooner and at great cost."

Greerson snapped the pencil between his fingers and stood up, casting the broken pieces into the corner.

For a second Claire thought he was going to hit her. She shifted her weight to the balls of her feet, ready to run.

"I admire what you did," he said. "Don't get me wrong." His hands clenched into fists. "But right now people need to believe that all this"—he raised his palms in a gesture that encompassed the overcrowded hospital and the ruined buildings visible outside the window—"happened for a reason. That their suffering is part of the price we paid for freedom. If they think it wasn't necessary, well, it makes it hard to keep the peace." Greerson ran his hands over his close-cropped scalp. "I'm trying to keep the populace safe. I can't do that if they're rioting."

Claire slumped against the wall. She hadn't considered violence would be a consequence of her interview. "What do you want me to do?"

He pulled a folded yellow sheet of paper from his pocket. "I've got a statement I want you to read over the emergency broadcast network."

Claire took the paper and scanned it quickly. "I'll make a plea for peace, but," she retrieved the top half of the pencil from the floor and crossed out a paragraph—"this patriotic stuff has to go. The war was wrong. I won't say otherwise."

Greerson ground his teeth together. "All right."

"Now there's something I need you to do for me," Claire said. "I need transport home for Zhang."

Greerson's eyebrows rose towards his shaved scalp. "All the way to *China*? That's impossible, we can't—"

Claire jabbed a finger at him. "I'll tell you what's impossible. Impossible is being trapped on a space station with a ruptured lifeboat and radiation destroying the electronics all around you. Impossible is building a reentry craft out of spare parts. Impossible is dropping your parachute in the middle of the ocean and somehow making it to shore. I did all that last week. So don't tell me you can't get one man back to Chinese territory."

Greerson grabbed Claire by the shoulders and turned her to look out the window. "The country is in ruins. We're having a hard time getting food out to our own people. We don't have machines or fuel to waste on Zhang."

Fires burned in the parking lot. People huddled around them, the families of patients, or the walking wounded who were treated on an outpatient basis. Beyond, the ruins of Orlando still smoldered.

She saw Greerson's point, and it sickened her. "I promised him that if he helped me, I'd get him home."

"Then I suggest *you* do something about it. Sounds like you do two or three impossible things before breakfast." He let go of Claire and smoothed his jacket. "I'm having a hard enough time holding everything together."

Claire watched a child play fetch with a three-legged dog. Half the girl's hair had been singed off in a fire, and blisters covered her left eye. The dog, a mixture of black Lab and Border collie, bounced after the broken chair leg. The girl's once-crisp school uniform hung in tatters that flapped around her shoulders and knees. She moved listlessly when the dog returned with the bit of wood, throwing it like a mechanical doll acting out a program that no longer mattered.

Beyond her, army trucks covered with camouflage canvas were unloading crates of MREs and oranges, and distributing the food to the people outside.

Greerson stopped at the door and looked back. "You going to read my speech?"

Still watching the girl, Claire responded: "Yes." There was so much wrong in the world. How ever would she make things right?

A hand on Claire's shoulder startled her awake. She'd been dozing in a metal chair next to Owen's bed. It screeched across the floor as she kicked out wildly, defending herself from sharks. "Shh." A soft hand covered her mouth. "It's me, Janice."

Claire shook off the remnants of her nightmare. She'd been floating in the Gulf of Mexico again as rain pelted down, lightning flashing across the sky. "What's wrong— Owen?" Claire stood up and leaned over her son, checking that he still breathed.

"It's all right," Janice whispered. "A helicopter came in. One of the British aid ships pulled a person from the Atlantic. I think it was one of your crew."

Hope leapt in Claire's chest. "Alive?" In another breath: "Anderson?"

"I don't know what her last name is," Janice said. "Will you come see her?"

Claire nodded, a lump in her throat. Anderson's death was a burden she'd carry the rest of her life. He'd been right: In times of scarcity, some lived and others died. She wondered what had become of Hyun-Jin and Mutsuo. Had they survived?

Josephine was in intensive care. She looked frail under the hospital blanket, tubes feeding into her nostrils and an IV pumping fluid into her arm.

Claire knelt beside her.

Josephine's face was covered with a clear salve that gleamed in the low light of the ICU. Her face was sunburnt to the point of blisters, and her nose and forehead were laced with the remnants of peeling skin.

Claire, with the care she would have used with a baby bird, took Josephine's hand in hers.

The young woman's eyes fluttered open.

"Josephine, it's Claire."

Josephine's eyes focused on Claire, and her lips moved, but no sound came out.

"Shh," Claire said, patting her hand. "Don't try to speak. You're dehydrated from your time in the ocean. Everything's all right. We'll talk later."

Josephine's chin quivered. "So much destroyed," she said in a whisper. "In the helicopter, I saw . . . all gone."

Claire kissed her forehead. Josephine was only eight years younger, but right now she seemed as much a child as Owen. "We'll make it better. We'll rebuild."

The British copilot who had brought Josephine in came back to collect the gurney he'd transported her on. He spoke to the nurse who'd come in to check Josephine's IV. "We found her in the Atlantic. Flight suit said NASA. First thing we thought was Claire Logan, but the name tag says 'Josephine Jones.' "

Claire stood up. "*I'm* Claire Logan."

"Beg your pardon," said the copilot. The tag on his flight suit read "Conrad Henly." "I had no idea you were at this hospital. You and she"—he pushed a shoulder towards Josephine—"you were on the space station together?"

"Yes." Claire smiled at Josephine. "She's part of the reason we survived."

The medic wiped his hand against his thigh and held it out to Claire. "Helluva story you broadcast. Me and my mates couldn't believe what was going on when we heard the shortwave. The British government knew nothing, what with the satellites going down and all."

Claire returned his grip. How ironic that the one act of disobedience that would have, under normal conditions, gotten her fired now made her a worldwide celebrity. "Thank you." Inspiration hit. "Your ship, when will you be returning to Britain?"

The medic tugged at his ear. "Soon as we finish dropping off supplies and the Doctors Without Borders staff, I'm afraid. There's too much radioactive dust for a prolonged stay." He looked apologetic at the implied desertion.

"And your captain, is he a fan of my broadcast?"

The medic grinned, happy to be back on safer political ground. "Yes, ma'am. He rebroadcast your latest speech to the crew on our way over. It's a miracle how you and Commander Zhang worked together despite the war. He said it was an example of teamwork we should all aspire to."

Claire circled her arm around the medic's shoulder and drew him aside. "Good. I've got a favor to ask him."

Zhang was pouring apple juice into paper cups and handing them out to the line of children along the hallway corridor. He paused, pitcher in hand, at Claire's approach.

"I've got good news," she said. She grinned in anticipation of his pleasure. "The British aid ship is going to give you a ride back to Europe. From there, they'll help you arrange transport to China."

"Home?" His mouth fell open. "To Shanghai?"

"Yes." Claire clasped his free hand in hers. "Or as close as they can get, considering the danger in traveling to that region. You can be with your family."

Zhang smiled, but it was wan. "Thank you."

"Aren't you happy?" She let go of his hand and stepped back for a better look. "You wanted to find your family. You were as desperate to find them as I was to see Owen."

Zhang put down the pitcher. "Yes, of course. It is a miracle I had not expected. Thank you."

"Then what's wrong?"

Zhang's eyes slid to the line of wounded children waiting for drinks. He handed the pitcher to woman waiting with her son. "Will you?"

The matronly woman nodded and took up the process of dispensing drinks.

Zhang followed Claire away from the crowd. "I am . . ." his dark eyes swam with depths Claire could not fathom. "I am afraid my homecoming will not be as triumphant as yours. My mother is frail, and it has been weeks since the bombs fell."

Claire's heart hurt for him. "You have to go now. The helicopter's waiting."

Zhang nodded. There was no luggage for him to pack. All that he owned, he was currently wearing.

They climbed the steps to the roof. The wind from the helicopter's whirling blades sent grit and dust into their faces. Claire squinted, wondering if it were radioactive.

The British medic Claire had spoken to waved Zhang forward.

Zhang gripped Claire's upper arms. He leaned forward, and for a moment Claire thought he was going to kiss her. Instead, his lips near her ear, he said, "I will never forget you. When I am home, I will tell how you saved me—despite the war. Perhaps our story will make a difference, help heal the rift between our countries. Perhaps one day we will be allies, deploying a whole constellation of solar reflectors."

Claire hugged him. "Be well," she shouted back in his ear.

Zhang climbed into the helicopter and settled himself near the medic. After he strapped in, he looked back at Claire.

She waved good-bye, and he raised a hand in acknowledgment.

Claire stood on the roof, watching the dwindling helicopter. The sky beyond was dark with dust and clouds, But over the Atlantic shore, there was cloud break. A shaft of golden sun hit the waves and turned them cobalt blue.

"In every darkness," she whispered, "there is hope."

Claire climbed down the stairs from the roof, passing nurses and patients with their families. Everyone, hospital staff or no, worked together to clean the hospital, dispense food, and tend to the sick.

The motherly woman was still dispensing apple juice as Claire passed. Her son helped her, passing each cup to a child with a smile. More often than not, the recipient grinned in return.

"Mama, Mama!" Owen's voice cut through the hallway.

Claire whipped her head around in panic.

He clung to the doorway of his hospital room. As she watched, Owen let go of the door frame and took three tottering steps.

Claire's eyes filled with tears, as they had when he'd taken his first steps. She swept him into her arms. "Oh, baby," she crooned. "I'm so proud."

A smattering of applause erupted from the drink line.

Owen's grin lit his face from ear to ear. "Tomorrow I'm going to run all the way down the hall."

From the open window came the sound of hammering and the chiming of a bicycle's bell. The post-oil era had begun. Beyond the dark clouds outside was the deployed solar reflector, just waiting for a signal to punch through the ionizing radiation and turn it on. Free energy to help repair the damaged Earth.

Claire hugged Owen to her chest. "I bet you will, sweetie. I bet you will."

Turn the page
for a preview of

The Last Mortal Man,

the first installment in
Syne Mitchell's new
Deathless series.

11 April 2246

The Montana sky was a lacework of contrails; thousands of drones carried packages and passengers to destinations all over the globe. The only clear blue was a pocket over Watershed Valley. The no-fly-zone was an eddy in the turbid river of commerce.

But even that concession wasn't enough. Particles of nanotechnology and synthetic biology blew in on the wind, fell from the sky in rain, and rode in on the wheels of hay trucks. The world was polluted with the stuff.

Jack Sterling sneezed, sending Liza, his bay mare, into a quick sidestep. The Targhee sheep streaming by startled and plunged in a new direction. Dakota, his border collie, darted left to redirect the sheep, nipping and circling to regroup them and push them towards the corral.

Jack tapped his noseplug inhaler to clear his breathing. He'd have to shower well tonight, or he'd wake up covered in hives.

Each year it was harder to keep his land pure. Last November a lightning strike downed a drone over the eastern pasture. A mist of nanology rained down over hundreds of organic, nonmodified sheep, ruining the sanctity of their heirloom genetics, and spoiling the meat for the halal and gourmet-food markets. The whole flock had to be put down.

More worrisome were the buttes to the south of the ranch. The towering blocks of granite carved by glaciers had stood unassailable for eons. Now nanology ate an ant's warren into the stone, turning hawks' haven into trendy housing and shopping malls. The gray cliffs writhed with animated advertisements that blotted out the stars at night.

Jack wondered how long he could survive against the relentless current of progress.

Dakota gave a sharp bark, startling Jack back to the task at hand. He kicked Liza into motion and followed the flock down. The sheep flowed like water over rocks and around trees.

Like an extension of his hand, Dakota worked the other side, keeping the flock tightly grouped and headed into the corral. A torrent of bleating sheep burst through the gate, complaining and dodging one another's hooves. One went down in a slick of mud and scrabbled up as her fellows cascaded around her.

It was April, shearing season, and a whole cohort of Watershed Valley Mennonites had turned out to help.

When the last wooly body was through, Liam, Jack's head shepherd, banged the gate shut.

Dakota danced on her hind legs, barking delightedly.

Jack lowered himself from Liza's saddle and looped the reins around a crossbeam of the corral. He bent and scritched Dakota's ruff. "Good girl."

The barn was a flurry of activity. Men in denim overalls formed an orderly assembly line, catching sheep and frog-marching them to the shearers. True to their religious beliefs, the Watershed Valley Mennonites, like the Amish sect of Anabaptists, used only seventeenth-century machines. The shearers pumped hand-powered scissors with brisk efficiency. Two little boys rotated extra sets of the tools in and out. When a shearer called out, "Blade!" one would run in with a newly sharpened set and take the old away to a whetstone.

No matter how many times Jack had seen sheep shorn, it always amazed him. The shearers flipped the sheep this way and that, controlling them into sheep-balls with the pressure of their knees and elbows. The fleece peeled away like the skin of an orange, dark with dirt on the outside, creamy white inside.

Women, dark skirts tucked into their belts, dashed in to grab the fleece for sorting and cleaning. One group pulled off the waste and beat the wool with sticks to flush out hay and dirt, while others heated water over an open fire to wash the wool.

Older men applied styptic powder to nicks and scrapes, trimmed hooves, and checked for disease.

Over the course of a day's hard labor, two hundred and sixty enormous dirt-stained sheep would be converted into a flock of pink, slender creatures and an enormous mass of drying white wool.

Jack waded along the edge of the flock and helped Liam catch the next sheep.

They worked side by side for hours, never speaking more than was necessary. It had taken Jack years to get used to the quiet reserve of the Mennonites who worked his land. But over time, their peace had infected him. Save for his clothes and the cut of his hair, he could have been one of them.

Sarah, Liam's sister, collected a newly shorn fleece. A dirt-stained apron covered her black dress and a white bonnet barely contained her russet curls.

Her eyes met Jack's over the smelly fleece and she blushed. She darted away, and Jack was left with the impression of creamy skin, freckles, and the scent of hay and manure.

The sheep in the pen suddenly began bucking and rolling their eyes heavenward. Their bleating became panicked. A sound like a thudding heart pounded from the west.

"Cursed be!" shouted a shearer as the sheep he held wrestled free. Red streaked the half-shorn fleece. The man cradled his hand to his chest, blood flowing freely down his arm.

Jack was the first to reach him. There was a deep gouge between the man's forefinger and thumb. Jack tied the man's wound with a clean handkerchief and showed one of the boys where to apply pressure.

Then Jack vaulted over the corral fencing, ready to do battle with the incoming aircraft. It was a well-maintained antique helicopter, kicking up dust as it bobbed towards a landing. It was pre-nanotechnology, combustion-powered by synthetic fossil fuel.

Jack signaled with his arms, waving the craft towards empty pasture.

"I told you—never near the barn!" Jack shouted, though he knew the pilot couldn't hear him over the cries of frightened sheep and the chuffing of the blades.

The helicopter jinked sideways and settled to earth with the grace of a drunken dragonfly.

A slender form stepped out of the cockpit, swathed in a transparent negative-pressure suit that clung to the black flight suit underneath.

For a second, Jack forgot his fear at what an unscheduled visit from one of Lucius Sterling's servants might portend. He scanned the helmet for a glimpse of golden-brown skin.

Alexa DuBois had been Jack's nanny, his childhood playmate, and the subject of teenage fantasies as he grew into manhood.

When his allergy was identified, Jack's mother had cried for weeks. His siblings went round-eyed with fear and guilt. Jack's father left the Sterling family compound in disgrace.

Only Alexa had been the same afterwards, unchanged in her matter-of-fact attitude, a bedrock in his crumbling landscape.

He'd been thirteen when they'd played chess through the glass wall of Jack's clean-room environment, using an antique marble chessboard instead of the animated creatures his siblings enjoyed.

Jack slammed down a white-veined knight in frustration. "I hate being stuck in here. I hate this game. I want to go outside and ride the wind birds with Lute and Sam."

"No sense wanting what you can't have." Alexa's blunt words were softened by her Louisiana drawl. She moved her queen to threaten his rook.

Jack slid his knight up and left, blocking the queen. A pawn protected his knight, and Jack knew from long hours at the board that Alexa never sacrificed her queen. "I hate being a freak."

"You're no freak." Her honey-smooth voice sent a ripple down his belly. "You just have an allergy, is all."

"Yeah, to *nanology*. If I can't be converted, in sixty or seventy years, I'll grow old—I'll die." Even to his own ears, he sounded whiny. "Everyone else gets to live forever, and I'll be *dead*."

Alexa leaned close to the glass separating them, her delicate fingertips touching the reflection of his chin. "One time, everyone died. What you're going through is just human. *We're* the freaks."

Wind from the slowing helicopter blades blew the fabric of the pressure suit against the pilot's obviously male chest, shattering any illusion of Alexa's lithe form.

Of course it wasn't her. Lucius would never let Alexa leave the compound.

The pilot was tall and well-built, like all moderns. Outside this valley, Sarah's freckles or Liam's crooked teeth would have been repaired before conception. Appearance among the converted varied as skin tones and facial characteristics came in and out of vogue, but the flawless symmetry of their features gave them a uniformity Jack found distasteful.

"Never land near the barn!" Jack shouted again. He pointed back to the Mennonite men who waded among the bucking sheep, trying to calm them.

The pilot's eyes flicked left. If he felt any remorse for the panicked sheep or the man holding a wounded hand to his chest, he gave no sign.

"I've orders to bring you to Maui."

In the fourteen years since Jack escaped from the family compound, he'd never been home. There was nothing for him there but a clean-room laboratory and endless blood draws and skin-prick tests.

"Tell my great-cubed-grandfather that if he wants to talk to me, he can put on a clean suit and come here. I'm not going back."

"I'm afraid, Mr. Sterling, that it was not a request." The pilot thrust forward a document sheathed between acrylic plates.

Jack snatched the plastic case and scanned the document. It was a bill of sale for the Watershed Valley property to Mountainside Condominiums, Inc. It hadn't been executed. Not *yet*. A dated DNA blot authenticated the buyer's identification and agreement to purchase. The seller's information was incomplete, listing just the name of the ranch's legal owner, his ancestor: Lucius Sterling.

There it was, proof that his freedom was illusory. Jack suspected the old man was secretly pleased with Jack's daring escape from the safety of his clean-room prison. But it was only an escape into a larger rat's maze—harder puzzles, better cheese, but just as trapped.

Only Lucius's goodwill and vast fortune kept progress at bay. Jack's welfare, and that of the Mennonite community who had accepted him, depended on his magnanimity.

Jack looked at the Mennonites. As a group, they were frozen, as terrified as the sheep by the technological menace among them. Liam knelt next to the bellwether, pinning her still by the neck. His expression was pensive. Sarah stood just inside the shadows of the barn, eyes wide.

As much as he was tempted to try Lucius's patience, Jack couldn't risk their future. He might find another haven; they had nowhere else in the modern world to go.

"Is this a round trip?"

The pilot's stance was painfully erect. "Mr. Sterling does not confide in me."

For an instant, Jack considering punching the man's beautifully constructed face. He wanted to punish someone for what was happening. But there was the contract, and the danger of infection if he ripped the pilot's suit.

Jack crawled into the helicopter. Hand on the door, he looked back at the ranch, taking in everything in case this was the last time he saw it: the Mennonites, composed and tidy, Dakota's worried growling, the bleating, musky sheep, the gray strewn boulders over hard-packed brown earth, the cloudless blue sky, the feel of the wind on his face . . . Sarah.

He sought her out among the shadows of the barn.

Sarah's eyes met his and her grip on the fleece she held tightened until her knuckles went white.

Jack smiled sadly. Over the past year, she'd left him little gifts on his doorstep in the morning: a pair of tiny blue forget-me-nots, a bundle of cookies, a linen handkerchief with his initials woven into the fabric, a perfect red apple. He'd seen her at it through the window, but hadn't said anything. What she wanted was impossible.

Jack had been accepted by the Mennonites as a necessary defense against the modern world, a good man in his own way, but ultimately not one of them. Sarah's father had made that clear to Jack in a man-to-man conversation when they'd repaired a length of fence along the northern pasture. Both men had agreed that the fence, while a hardship for sheep that might wish to stray, was necessary for the safety of all.

The helicopter lifted off, and everything Jack had worked to build over the past fourteen years dwindled away.

There were fences everywhere.

Award-winning, bestselling author
SYNE MITCHELL

THE CHANGELING PLAGUE

In the mid-21st century, all genetic
experimentation has been outlawed.
But when a desperate dying man takes an
illegal gene therapy drug, he unleashes a
worldwide plague that rewrites the DNA of
everyone he encounters.

Syne Mitchell is
"A consummate storyteller.
Her futures are dark and
entrancing...frighteningly plausible."
—Lydia Morehouse

0-451-45910-5

Available wherever books are sold or at
www.penguin.com

Lyda Morehouse

ARCHANGEL PROTOCOL

0-451-45827-3

First came the LINK—an interactive, implanted
computer-transformed society. Then came the angels—
cybernetic manifestations that claimed to be
working God's will.

But former cop Deidre McMannus has had her LINK
implant removed—for a crime she didn't commit.
And she has never believed in angels.
But that will change when a man named
Michael appears at her door.

FALLEN HOST

0-451-45879-6

An A.I. who dreams of Mecca...A Warrior of God facing
temptation...A fallen angel ready to settle things
once and for all...
Three participants engaged in a race for their own personal
truths, linked in ways they can't begin to comprehend—
until the final terrible day of revelation.